PRAISE FOR
the party

"A tense and riveting story about one night gone horribly wrong . . . I was hooked from the opening scene and could not look away until I reached the very last page."

—Megan Miranda, *New York Times* bestselling author of *All the Missing Girls*

"Cleverly constructed and brilliantly paced, *The Party* is a raw telling of a family coming apart at the seams. Robyn Harding weaves a riveting tale that is impossible to put down."

—Bill Clegg, *New York Times* bestselling author of *Did You Ever Have a Family*

"Robyn Harding spins a masterful tale of the disintegration of a seemingly perfect family in the aftermath of a disastrous sweet-sixteen party. Engrossing and unflinching in its portrayal of the dark side of human nature."

—A. J. Banner, #1 bestselling author of *The Twilight Wife*

"Suspenseful and provocative, *The Party* is a story that will keep you reading and keep you thinking long after you've turned the last page. This is one party invitation you don't want to turn down."

—Barbara Taylor Sissel, bestselling author of *Crooked Little Lies*

"Everyone is flawed in this contemporary tale of mothers and daughters. Everyone behaves badly. And the story is a pure delight."

—Lucy Ferriss, author of *A Sister to Honor*

"Fast-paced and tension-filled, *The Party* explodes the myth of the perfect family and is one invitation you can't turn down."

—Rebecca Drake, author of *Only Ever You*

"In this blistering fast read . . . *The Party* is a domestic drama that spins off the rails with hellish consequences. Consider yourself warned."

—Erica Ferencik, author of *The River at Night*

"A sweet sixteen takes a very dark turn in Harding's taut domestic drama, set in smugly bourgeois San Francisco."

—*Entertainment Weekly*

"An innocent sweet-sixteen sleepover goes terribly awry when a wealthy San Francisco couple awakes to find their daughter crying and covered in blood . . . Shades of *The Dinner* and *Big Little Lies*."

—*The New York Post*

"With teenagers worthy of *Mean Girls*, and a healthy dose of suspense, *The Party* reads like a cross between Megan Abbott and Jodi Picoult by way of James Patterson."

—*Booklist*

"The intricate family dynamics that Harding teases out are complex and engaging."

—*Publishers Weekly*

"The domestic drama is done well."

—*Kirkus Reviews*

the party

ROBYN HARDING

SCOUT PRESS
New York London Toronto Sydney New Delhi

Scout Press
An Imprint of Simon & Schuster, Inc.
1230 Avenue of the Americas
New York, NY 10020

This book is a work of fiction. Any references to historical events, real people, or real places are used fictitiously. Other names, characters, places, and events are products of the author's imagination, and any resemblance to actual events or places or persons, living or dead, is entirely coincidental.

First Scout Press trade paperback edition November 2017

SCOUT PRESS and colophon are registered trademarks of Simon & Schuster, Inc.

For information about special discounts for bulk purchases, please contact Simon & Schuster Special Sales at 1-866-506-1949 or business@simonandschuster.com.

The Simon & Schuster Speakers Bureau can bring authors to your live event. For more information or to book an event, contact the Simon & Schuster Speakers Bureau at 1-866-248-3049 or visit our website at www.simonspeakers.com.

Interior design by Davina Mock-Maniscalco

Manufactured in the United States of America

10

The Library of Congress Cataloging-in-Publication Data for the hardcover edition is as follows:

Names: Harding, Robyn, author.
Title: The party : a novel / Robyn Harding.
Description: First Gallery Books hardcover edition. | New York : Gallery Books, 2017.
Identifiers: LCCN 2016043739| ISBN 9781501161247 (hardcover) | ISBN 9781501161308 (softcover) | ISBN 9781501161292 (ebook)
Subjects: LCSH: Upper class families,ÄîFiction. | Family secrets—Fiction. | Teenage girls—Fiction. | Domestic fiction. | BISAC: FICTION / Literary. | FICTION / General.
Classification: LCC PR9199.4.H366 P37 2017 | DDC 813/.6,Äîdc23 LC record available at https://lccn.loc.gov/2016043739

ISBN 978-1-5011-6124-7 (hardcover)
ISBN 978-1-5011-6130-8
ISBN 978-1-5011-6129-2 (ebook)

For Margaret Lilleyman
(1936–2012)
The most voracious reader I have known
and the perfect mother-in-law for a writer.

the party

kim

THAT NIGHT

Kim should have heard it, would *have heard it if she hadn't installed earplugs and taken half an Ambien. The girls were two floors below, but she'd anticipated giggling, music, a few late-night trips to raid the fridge. . . . To ensure a sound sleep, she'd nibbled a bit of the sedative, despite having had two glasses of white wine after dinner. She'd done it plenty of times without incident. She'd always been a light sleeper, and, lately, adequate rest had become imperative for Kim. There were too many hormones wreaking havoc with her humor. And there was far too much tension in her marriage to handle without a good night's sleep.*

"Mom! Dad!" Kim dragged herself up from under the warm, wet blanket of sedation. It was Hannah's voice, tearful, close. . . . Kim opened heavy lids and saw her daughter at the end of the bed. Tall, pretty Hannah wearing a nightie that looked like a football jersey, the number 28 across her chest. It was Hannah's birthday today—sweet

sixteen—she was having a slumber party. So why was she here, in the small hours of the morning? Why was she crying? As Kim struggled for lucidity, she realized something was terribly wrong. Tears streamed down Hannah's face and there was something on her hands . . . something dark and wet, glistening in the faint glow of the LED clock radio . . .

Blood.

kim

THAT DAY

"Should we wake the princess?" The words hovered in the chill morning air, unanswered. Kim leaned her elbows on the custom butcher-block breakfast bar, took a sip of black coffee, and waited. When he finally responded, Jeff's eyes never left his laptop screen.

"It's her birthday. Let her sleep. . . ."

Kim glanced at the digital clock on the Miele gas range: 8:37 A.M., an unreasonable hour to ask a girl to rise on any Saturday, let alone her sixteenth birthday. Sixteen . . . God, where had the time gone? Kim allowed herself a brief moment of nostalgia, her mind slipping back to that dreary March day when Hannah was born. It seemed like yesterday and an eternity at the same time. That pink, squalling creature she had birthed with such effort was now tall, beautiful, undeniably womanly. . . . Kim was different now, too. Her physical transformation was less dramatic (at forty-six, she prided herself on being able to pass for forty, maybe even thirty-nine—thanks to a strict regimen of Pilates, cold-pressed juices, and the judicious use of fillers), but she was not the same naive, hopeful woman she'd been that day. She had grown up, as surely as Hannah had.

Jeff's relentless *tap-tap-tap*ping drew her out of her reverie: Silicon Valley keyboard torture. "Still working on that presentation?" A tinge of annoyance had crept into her tone, but it wasn't like Jeff noticed. He didn't seem to notice anything about his wife lately. Kim could have been doing a naked handstand on the back of a unicorn and Jeff would have kept pecking away at his keyboard like a chicken on Ritalin.

"Yep." He remained focused on his work, as if he was locked in his Palo Alto office on a Tuesday, not drinking coffee in his open-plan kitchen with his spouse on a Saturday morning. Jeff seemed to have forgotten that this was a day traditionally designated for leisure pursuits and family bonding. Not that Kim had any real desire to bond with her husband of eighteen years. After the *incident* last year, she found civility challenging, let alone quality time. But she couldn't help but feel neglected. And she envied her husband's single-minded obsession with providing financial software solutions to corporations, his unblinking belief that his job as VP of global strategy at Fin-Tech Solutions really meant something. In Jeff's mind, the infrastructure of the entire US economy would come crashing down without his constant attention.

"I'm going to do some work, too," she said, rising from the barstool.

The typing paused as Jeff headed for the coffeepot. "More coffee?"

"I'm fine. Call me when Aidan gets up. I'll make him some eggs."

"*If* he gets up. That kid could sleep for days."

"He's thirteen. He's growing."

Half a lukewarm cup of coffee in hand, Kim padded in slippered feet past the sunken living room, its expanse of windows affording spectacular views of the San Francisco Bay. Her office was at the back of the designer home, tucked between the laundry room and the wine cellar, a tidy, compact space allocated for her freelance copywriting job. "It's just to keep my foot in the door," she'd explained when Jeff told her his salary negated the need for her to work. "I might want to go back when the kids are older." At sixteen and thirteen, the kids officially qualified as *older*, and still, Kim made no move to return to her life in advertising. It was a young person's career, custom-designed for twentysomethings who had the freedom to work late, then go for after-work drinks that usually led to dark nightclubs and ultimately, some uninhibited but regrettable sex with a colleague. It was fun while it lasted, but those days were over for Kim. She'd replaced them with a hardworking husband; two tall, academically successful children; and a three-thousand-square-foot, mid-century modern remodeled home on Potrero Hill (the coveted North Slope, with panoramic views that raised property values by about a million bucks). She'd traded that stressful, stimulating, slightly debauched life for one of staid, domestic perfection. Most days, she had no regrets.

She sat in her ergonomic rolling chair and booted up the computer. As the screen magically illuminated, her stomach twisted with a mixture of guilt and excitement. It was phenomenal, this box of technology that allowed her to sit less than twenty feet from her husband, in her robe and slippers, her hair unkempt and face free of makeup, and reach out to Tony on the other side of town. She opened Messenger and typed.

U working?

The juvenile shorthand made her feel young, giddy, like an eighth grader sending a note to a boy she was crushing on.

Pretending. U?

Her heart fluttered at his blatant admission.

Finishing some stuff.

It was a lie. Her "foot in the door" had dwindled to an ongoing contract with San Francisco's third largest outdoor clothing retailer, to provide copy for their biweekly flyer. The two-line descriptions of waterproof jackets and hiking boots consumed roughly seven hours a week, for which she was able to bill fifteen. But she wasn't ready to admit that the sole reason she was in her office on a Saturday morning was to flirt with her designer, Tony. His message popped up on the screen.

What r u doing today?

Hannah's b-day. Sweet 16

Happy b-day Hannah

The sentiment made Kim's stomach twist again. Tony didn't know Hannah, had no place wishing her a happy birthday. She had not invited him into her personal universe, had not introduced him to her husband and kids. Did Tony really expect Kim to give his regards to her daughter, like some friendly fake uncle? It would have been inappropriate . . . and kind of creepy.

Tony and Kim met twice a month, legitimately, and had recently doubled that as their undefined connection grew. The nature of their relationship remained nebulous: there had been nothing lurid or inappropriate in their communications; a benign, teasing sort of flirtation (again, reminiscent of eighth graders) being the most incriminating aspect. When they met in person, physical contact was limited to a brief hug hello followed by a hand on a shoulder, or a playful punch in the arm as they shared a joke. It was a forced casualness, like two platonic pals, two college buddies, a brother and sister. . . . The only thing lewd about their relationship was the way Kim's heart would race when she heard his voice, received his messages, or spoke his name; how her cheeks and groin would burn with pleasant heat.

She could only assume Tony felt the same way, though at times, his actions gave her pause. Like wishing Hannah a happy birthday. In that three-word expression, he was acknowledging that Kim was a mother, a wife, a woman with a fully domesticated life outside of their relationship. She knew Tony had such a life, too, but she didn't like to think about it. She didn't want to know his kids' names (Declan and Ruby). She didn't want to know that his wife (Amanda) was a successful attorney who worked long hours, leaving Tony to pick up the kids from school, drive them to their extracurriculars, and cook dinner most nights—all while juggling his freelance design assignments. Kim preferred to think of Tony as an island.

Another message arrived from him.

Having a party?

A few girls for pizza and cake

Pizza and cake--LOL

???

They're 16. They'll sneak booze or boys in

This annoyed Kim. Tony didn't know Hannah. He wasn't qualified to lump her in with all the wanton sixteen-year-olds he saw in the media, caught taking pills, having babies in bathroom stalls, or drifting over the center line in her mom's station wagon and killing a family in a minivan. Kim took her job as a mother very seriously, and her children were evidence of that. She read parenting books. She attended workshops put on by the PTA. She knew the delicate balance between implementing boundaries and allowing children to spread their wings, between setting expectations and applying too much pressure. And she talked to her kids. She and Hannah had discussed all manner of teenaged transgressions, from cutting and marijuana to eating disorders and ecstasy. They had definitely discussed the dangers of binge drinking. (Fortuitously, her nephew in Oregon had gotten so drunk at a party that he'd pissed himself in front of his friends and had to spend a night in the hospital hooked up to an IV.) Obviously, she'd told Hannah that her sixteenth would be alcohol-free. Hannah had rolled her eyes—"Of course, Mom"—because she didn't drink anyway. Maybe Declan and Ruby would be typical rowdy teens, drinking and smoking and generally rebelling against a workaholic mother and a father who pretended to be designing flyers when he was really messaging with his female copywriter. But Kim's kids wouldn't. She was doing her job right. She typed:

GTG

Her irritation still simmering under the surface, she deleted the conversation and headed back to the kitchen. She found Tony attractive, charming, amusing . . . and his interest in her was flattering, particularly in light of her husband's lack of it. But Tony's comment reminded her that they really didn't know each other. They'd been working together for almost six months, but they'd never had a meaningful conversation about issues or values. They talked about work or they flirted like adolescents. She'd just signed off with *GTG* like some infatuated teenager too lazy to type *Got to go*. What was wrong with her?

When she entered the kitchen, Jeff didn't look up from his screen. "Done already?"

"There wasn't much left to do." She made her way to the coffeemaker. "You left the empty pot on the burner."

"You said you didn't want any more."

"I don't. But that doesn't mean I want the coffeepot to crack. Or the house to burn down."

He looked away from his computer directly at her. "Why are you so crabby?"

"I'm not," she barked, belying her words. "I'm going to take a shower." She headed for the open staircase that led to the master suite.

"Do you need help getting ready for the party?"

She turned back, softening at the offer. It was a rare overture from Jeff, and it reminded her that they were still a team. No matter how far apart they drifted, no matter how much he had hurt her, they were stuck in this family together. She looked at his sandy hair, mussed from sleep, at his stubbly face, still boyish despite his forty-eight years. Deep inside, Kim harbored a tiny kernel of hope that what they once had was salvageable. She suddenly regretted the ten minutes she'd spent secluded in her office with another man's messages.

"I promised Hannah I'd get her a flourless chocolate cake from that bakery on Cesar Chavez. We could walk there? I think the sun's trying to come out."

"Except I'm going for a swim and a run with Graham."

Her jaw clenched. "Forget it then."

His words followed her ascension up the stairs. "What? The triathlon's in August!"

BY 10:40 A.M., Kim's Audi wagon was chock-full of trans fat–free snack foods, diet sodas, veggie platters, and three bunches of fresh tulips in Hannah's favorite color, purple. Nestled in her Gucci purse was the rectangular box housing the tennis bracelet she and Jeff had decided to buy for their daughter. It had cost over five grand, but it was the girl's sixteenth, after all. And in their affluent world, the bar was high. Hannah had at least one friend who'd been given a car for her birthday. Of course, this friend's father had run off with his dental hygienist, so a fair amount of guilt factored into the purchase. Kim felt a diamond-and-white-gold bracelet showed love without being overindulgent.

Her last stop was Tout Sweet, a candy-colored bakeshop adored by Hannah and her friends. Its macarons, marshmallows, and meringues were so popular that locations were popping up across the city, a sugary coup. She had just ordered her daughter's favorite cake when a voice said, "Kim?" She turned and was instantly swept into a hug. "God! How are you?"

It was Lisa, the mother of Hannah's friend Ronni. The women had been close once, when the girls were small and in each other's hip pockets. Maybe they weren't close—they were more *thrown together*, watching their daughters climb on rickety monkey bars, splash in urine-filled wading pools, and bounce in inflatable castles. When Lisa would pick up Ronni from a playdate, Kim would sometimes invite her in for a glass of white wine. Despite their many differences, the women had forged a bond. Lisa was a New Agey single mom who worked sporadically and lived with her only daughter in an apartment on Potrero's South Slope—not in the housing projects, but still, a far less affluent hood than the Sanders inhabited. Kim had wanted to expose her children to diversity; that's why she sent them to a private school with a robust scholarship program. She had set a good example by befriending someone outside her socioeconomic status. Noblesse oblige.

"Lisa . . . It's been ages."

"I know! Now that the girls are so independent, I never get to see you."

Kim scanned Lisa's long, wavy hair and sun-kissed skin. She was only a few years younger than Kim, but Lisa's style was bohemian, hip, almost adolescent. . . . Kim's Tory Burch tunic and ballet flats suddenly seemed matronly in comparison. "You look great."

"I've been surfing. My new guy, Allan, is really into it. He's a chef, so he's really creative and intense. But he's also very physical"—Lisa leaned in, touched Kim's arm—"if you know what I mean. . . ."

Kim did. She raised her eyebrows and forced an impressed smile, but she felt uncomfortable. It was too much, too intimate . . . and also served to highlight that Kim and Jeff hadn't had sex in nearly a year.

"But I'll get down to business in May. I'm starting a Reiki healing and therapeutic-touch course."

"Good," Kim said as convincingly as she could. Lisa had made some smart real estate investments in the past, but was *Reiki healing* really the best skill to acquire in this economy? And was *therapeutic touch* Lisa's plan to put her daughter through college? Though Ronni had never seemed particularly academic. . . .

That's when Kim remembered the main reason her friendship with Lisa had never flourished. Lisa was a flake. A nut. A kook. Kim knew that Lisa had had a difficult life, and she sympathized. But Lisa was just so *out there*. Kim was grounded. Solid. Practical. When their daughters had drifted apart, so had their mothers. But now Ronni was back in Hannah's social circle.

"Ronni's coming to Hannah's party tonight, right?"

"She can't wait. It's so nice that the girls have reconnected."

"It is." Kim was lying. Even when Ronni was little, Kim had found her precocious toward adults and domineering over sweet-natured Hannah: a typical only child of a single parent. Now that Ronni was sixteen, she seemed worldly and jaded, affecting that bored, disdainful attitude so popular with teenagers these days.

"'Scuse me. . . ." The bakery girl interrupted them. "Do you want writing on the cake?" Coincidentally, the teen reminded Kim of Ronni: thick, dewy foundation; precisely painted-on eyebrows; long, spidery lashes; and pale, glossy lips. These girls were like dolls . . . sexy dolls. It was disturbing.

Kim asked Lisa, "Will the girls think it's babyish if I get 'Happy Sixteenth' on the cake?"

"No, it's cute. They may act too cool for school, but they're still little girls at heart."

Kim smiled and squeezed Lisa's hand. She was a flake but a sweet flake. "It's good to see you. We should have coffee sometime."

"I'd love that."

As Kim strolled back to the car, the cake box weighed heavy in her hands. She suddenly felt fragile, drained of energy, and far older than forty-six. She was glad she'd bumped into Lisa—they were still friends despite the passing years and their many differences—but Kim's life suddenly seemed incredibly mundane. Lisa was training for a new career, she had a new man in her bed, she was *surfing*. . . . Nothing remotely exciting had happened in Kim's orbit since they'd bought the house . . . unless she counted the *incident* last year, which she was not going to. There was excitement and then there was disaster, plain and simple.

She placed the cake box in the hatchback of her car and checked her watch. Hannah would sleep until noon at least; she had some time to kill. She considered going for a facial but she'd had one last week and if she went too often her skin broke out. A mani-pedi was a possibility, but she hadn't brought any flip-flops with her. She paused for just a moment before pulling out her phone and dialing. Her heart hammered in her chest as she listened to it ring.

"Tony Hoyle." His voice, as always, prompted that delicious shiver.

"Hey, it's me."

"Hey, Kim." His voice was professional—overly so. Ruby and Declan were obviously within earshot . . . maybe even his wife. "How's the copy coming along?"

"I'm having a little trouble, actually." She realized she was blushing and sweating, so unaccustomed was she to playing this game. But there was something so wonderfully naughty about it. "I thought maybe we could get together and brainstorm a bit."

"That should work. Where and what time?"

"Umm . . . now. At Farley's."

"Great. I'll bring the files on my laptop and we'll get this sorted out." He hung up.

As Kim pulled away from the parking meter, she allowed herself a gleeful smile. Just like that, she was back in eighth grade.

hannah

THAT DAY

Hannah drifted out of sleep, squinting in the late-morning light that was pushing through her gauzy curtains. It took only the briefest of moments for her consciousness to register the significance of the day. Sixteen . . . *finally*. She rolled over and reached for her phone. Her mom told her not to keep it in her bedroom (Kim had heard about teens who texted all night and never slept a wink!), but thankfully, it was a rule her mom often forgot to enforce. Fourteen texts, all various iterations of the sentiment *HBD!!* Not bad, considering most of her peers were probably still asleep. She checked her social media apps and found even more well-wishes.

Enveloped in the warmth of her luxurious duvet, she took a moment to savor the morning. Her mom usually barged in at some ungodly hour to roust her from her slumber, insisting she needed to get to her studies, her piano, or some inane household chore that didn't really need to be done. This morning, the house was quiet. Her mom must be at Pilates, her dad was working or working out, and her younger brother was undoubtedly plugged into some electronic device and shoveling food into his pimply face. It was a perfect time for reflection, and so she did, in the way that sixteen-year-olds reflect.

Fifteen had been a pretty good year for Hannah, especially the last two months, since Noah. He turned his attention on her and, like flicking a switch or waving a magic wand, he had changed her life. Hannah had been utterly naive to the transformative powers of a popular boy's attentions. She was suddenly cool, admired even. When Noah deemed her worthy of his interest, so did the rest of the student population. And that included Ronni Monroe and Lauren Ross.

The girls were Hannah's age but possessed a sophistication far beyond their years. Lauren in particular was confident, self-assured, and just a little bit mean . . . which everyone knows equates to power in the high school universe. Hannah knew that Lauren liked her only because Noah was hovering around her, but Hannah was sure that she could segue the popular girl's interest into a meaningful friendship. There was a lot to be learned from a girl like Lauren; Hannah was an eager protégé.

Hannah's inclusion in the cool clique wasn't completely out of left field. Ronni Monroe had been Hannah's best friend in elementary school. But in seventh grade, Ronni had outgrown her, probably because Ronni had developed early and attracted the attention of older boys. Hannah was a late bloomer and, prior to Noah, had been virtually invisible to the opposite sex. Ronni also had a mother who let her wear makeup and short shorts to school.

Hannah's own hovering mom seemed determined to thwart her daughter's maturation, banning revealing clothing, eyeliner, rap music, and anything else that might lead to the "hypersexualization" of her daughter. Her mom had seen a documentary on this "epidemic" and talked incessantly about empowerment and self-worth. Just Hannah's luck . . .

Hannah's life hadn't been particularly terrible before Noah—it had just been . . . flat. Her focus had been on school, basketball, practicing the piano . . . basically, doing everything that her parents wanted her to do. And then, about two weeks into her coupledom, Ronni and Lauren had approached her. "Wanna hang?" There was little enthusiasm in the invitation, but Hannah knew enough to be honored. She'd spent two years watching the queen bees stroll through the halls of Hillcrest Academy, bored, jaded, beautiful; Hannah was one of them now.

Her mind floated to her boyfriend, Noah, and lingered on his lazy smile, his blue eyes, the outline of his strong shoulders under his ubiquitous black sweatshirt. Her stomach did that funny little dance and her hand slipped down to her panties. Her fingers crept inside and she scratched. *Vigorously*. Lauren and Ronni insisted she had to shave "down there." Everyone did it—except hippies and religious people. It was cleaner, sexier, and boys loved it—expected it, really. Pubic hair was gross, Hannah agreed. But Jesus, how it itched!

Noah had yet to be introduced to Hannah's hairlessness. Despite the life-altering ramifications of their relationship, they had done little more than kiss up to this point. This was largely due to a lack of opportunity. At Tyler Harris's party, there had been some over-the-clothes fondling, but she knew Noah would be expecting more from her soon. Lauren and Ronni informed her that some guys would be content with petting for a month or two if they *really* liked you, but they'd soon lose interest if you weren't up for at least some oral. And Noah dated Kennedy Weaver last summer and they'd had sex a bajillion times. Any day now, Hannah was going to have to put out.

After another bout of violent scratching, Hannah decided to get up. Before she could reconsider, she threw the pale-yellow duvet off her, her body bracing against the chilled air. Her modern house was stunning, everyone said so, but with its sealed concrete floors, high ceilings, and expanses of glass, it was also freezing. Her feet were literally numb as she scurried toward the double bathroom she shared with her kid brother, Aidan. The haste was necessary. In addition to saving her toes from frostbite, she had a ton to do to get ready for the party.

As the rain showerhead poured over her body, Hannah tried to relax, but there was no denying the importance of this evening to her social status. The most popular girls at Hillcrest would be in attendance, along with two of Hannah's oldest friends. Marta and Caitlin were nice kids, good kids like Hannah, but lately she'd realized that they were kind of immature. Hannah had advised her two pals that they would have to up their game, because tonight was not going to be some childish slumber party. Yesterday, at school, Lauren and Ronni had made their expectations perfectly clear.

They had approached her in the morning as she was putting her books into her locker. "Hey, birthday girl." Lauren had hugged her first. She was so tiny, like a little girl in Hannah's embrace—a little girl with rounded hips, perky breasts, a nipped in waist; a little girl with long honey-colored hair, a glossy pout, and sleepy, sexy eyes.

"It's not until tomorrow."

"Technicality," Ronni said, as she stepped in for a hug. She was a little taller, but still compact, with disproportionately large boobs that stirred covetous feelings in Hannah. Beneath her expertly applied makeup, Ronni had perfect tawny skin and her hair was dark and shiny. Her dad was half Puerto Rican or half Guatemalan or something. He wasn't in the picture, but at least he'd given his daughter some genetic gifts before he disappeared. Around Lauren and Ronni, Hannah always felt huge and dorky. But she also felt special. They had chosen her, after all: the prize puppy, the cutest kitten. Hannah had found the golden ticket; she was going to Hollywood. . . .

Ronni released her, and Hannah caught the envious glance of Sarah Foster as she walked past them. Sarah was tall, lanky, and blond; she wore the right clothes and dated the right boys. Sarah had enjoyed a brief sojourn in Lauren and Ronni's orbit, but something had gone wrong. Rumor had it that Sarah had flirted with a guy Lauren liked, but Hannah didn't trust rumors. A lot of people talked shit about Lauren Ross—small, jealous people who had no chance of ever basking in her heat.

Lauren clocked Sarah's look, too. "Stare much?" she called. Sarah quickened her pace and soon dissolved into the clotted artery of the hallway. Lauren and Ronni exchanged a snicker and Ronni mumbled, "Slut."

Lauren returned her attention to Hannah. "Can't wait for tomorrow night."

"It's gonna be wild," Ronni added.

"Totally," Hannah said, but her stomach twisted with nerves. How could her party be wild when Hannah had the strictest, most vigilant mother in the Bay Area? Her mom had set out the birthday-party decree: no booze, drugs, boys, unsupervised Internet, or R-rated movies. Were PG videos and pizza going to cut it for Lauren and Ronni? Would they giggle and gossip about Hannah's dull, juvenile party? She could almost hear them. "It was like she was turning twelve. Pizza and a Hunger Games movie? Seriously . . . ?"

"We got you a present," Lauren said in a teasing voice.

Ronni added, "For you *and* for Noah."

It had to have something to do with sex . . . A box of condoms? Some kind of sex toy? Flavored lube? Oh God. "What is it?" Hannah asked gamely, but her voice came out strained and tight.

"We'll give it to you tomorrow," Lauren said. "What did Noah get you?"

Hannah's cheeks burned. "I don't know. I haven't seen him yet. And I told him I didn't want anything."

"Can we help you?" Ronni suddenly snapped. It took Hannah a moment to realize the pointed question was directed at Raymond Sun, Hannah's locker neighbor.

Nerdy Raymond stood in the hall, separated from locker seventy-one by Hannah's companions. "I just . . . wanted to get my math book." He sounded nervous, intimidated.

"We'll be done in a sec," Lauren said dismissively. She turned back to Hannah. "What are we drinking tomorrow night?"

Hannah felt a bubble of panic. "I was thinking vodka, maybe? Or do you guys like rum?"

"Vodka has no calories," Ronni said.

"Ummm . . ." Raymond took a tentative step forward. "The bell's about to ring. I have math."

"Chill, loser," Lauren snarled.

"You'll get your fucking books when we finish our conversation," Ronni spat.

Lauren leaned her back against Raymond's locker and addressed the girls. "I don't care what we drink or what we take . . ."

"As long as we get fucked-up," Ronni finished.

"Absolutely." Hannah had grinned her agreement while, out of the corner of her eye, she watched Raymond Sun shake his head and storm off.

Even now, as she tilted her head back to rinse the conditioner from her shoulder-length hair, she felt queasy at the recollection. Was it pity? Or guilt? It's not like that *mathlete* Raymond was her BFF or anything, but they had been hallway neighbors all year. They didn't talk much, but Raymond was always polite, always picked up her lunch bag when she dropped it, once even chasing her pen when it fell and skittered away down the hall. . . . Hannah did not feel a similar sympathy for Sarah Foster, who had also been subjected to the popular girls' derision. Obviously, Sarah had it coming; she had been stupid enough to cross Lauren and Ronni, so she deserved what she got. But Raymond was harmless, an innocent, his only offense possessing the locker adjacent to Hannah's. It was like a pack of wolves attacking a Chihuahua.

But Hannah didn't have time to worry about Raymond Sun's hurt feelings. She shook it off and focused on her mission. She knew what she had to do—Lauren and Ronni's decree was absolute—she just wasn't sure how she would do it. She turned off the shower.

Her hair still slightly damp, Hannah jogged down the open staircase into the silence of the house. "Hello?" Her voice reverberated off the stark walls, the stretch of glass windows, the smooth, polished floors. . . . She moved toward the modern, spacious kitchen. Empty. That's when her younger brother loped into the room, a skateboard under his arm and earbuds stuffed into his ears. "Where are Mom and Dad?" she asked.

"I think Mom went shopping. Dad's running. Or swimming." He reached into the fridge, grabbed a carton of orange juice, and put it to his lips.

"You're a pig."

Aidan gave her a self-satisfied smirk and put the juice back in the fridge. "Tell Mom I went to the skate park." He moved toward the door. Hannah trailed after him.

"You're not going to be here tonight, right?" She did not want Lauren Ross to be exposed to her thirteen-year-old brother. He was childish and annoying and he smelled like a pungent combination of BO, mushrooms, and farts.

"I'm sleeping over at Marcus's."

"Thank God."

"Fuck you."

"Fuck you, too." The siblings reveled in foul language when their mother wasn't within earshot. It was a benign rebellion, but a rebellion nonetheless.

Aidan knelt to tie his skate shoes and Hannah watched him. Could her kid brother help with her predicament? Was she desperate enough to ask him? She took a small breath. . . . "Do people sell weed at the skate park?"

The boy stood, removed his earbuds. "You want me to get you some weed?"

She did, desperately, but she wasn't sure Aidan could be trusted. She took in his shaggy hair, his droopy pants, his poor hygiene . . . all the trappings of badassery, but it was just surface stuff. When she looked into his eyes, she could see his innocence and naiveté. She could see he was still firmly trapped under Mommy's heavy thumb. No way was Aidan cool enough to buy dope from a dealer. And worse, he'd probably rat her out to their parents for even asking.

"Of course not. I was just wondering if you were, like, a stoner now."

"Yeah," he scoffed. "Huge stoner." He reached for the door handle.

"Aren't you even going to wish me a happy birthday?"

"I was going to."

"No, you weren't. You were leaving."

"I'm still here, aren't I?" He turned the handle and muttered as he exited, "Happy birthday, bitch."

"Go to hell!" she screeched, but the door closed on her words.

She was heading back to the kitchen to make a smoothie

when the phone rang. Hannah moved to the dock near the double fridge and picked up the handset. Her mom's number showed in the display bar.

"Happy birthday, sweet sixteen . . ." Her mom's corny term and singsong voice chafed. Of course, Hannah's irritation was probably due to stress and the fact that she hadn't eaten anything yet, but the cliché didn't help.

"Where are you?"

"I'm getting birthday supplies: chips, soda, a birthday cake . . . And a little something special for you, but you can't open it until Daddy gets home."

Chips. Soda. Daddy. The words solidified the fear in the pit of Hannah's stomach. Her birthday party could not destroy her new social standing, could not turn her into a pariah or a laughing stock. She was turning sixteen, for God's sake, and she would not let her parents' denial of this fact ruin her.

"When will you be back?"

"A half hour or so. I'll make you some brunch. Pancakes with chocolate chips?"

Hannah felt an inexplicable lump of emotion form in her throat. Her mom was trying to be nice, but she was treating Hannah like a toddler. It made her feel an almost overwhelming surge of pity for her mother. Kim's life was so dull, so quiet, so . . . over. Not that her mom was old, but what did she have to look forward to? Forty more years of domestic puttering, of writing boring flyers, and a passionless marriage? Her parents' relationship seemed to Hannah a utilitarian coexistence based on an unequal sharing of household and child-rearing duties and a bank account. There was no fondness, no affection, and certainly no passion. Hannah would never accept such a bland existence, would never live vicariously through her children, not realizing that they were pulling away, making their own lives and their own choices. Her mom would never understand the person Hannah was becoming. Kim was losing her, and she didn't even know it.

"Pancakes would be good. Thanks."

Hanging up, Hannah moved purposefully to the booze cupboard above the fridge. Her mom had obviously chosen this location because it was inaccessible to small children. But small children weren't interested in alcohol. Now, at five foot eight, Hannah had both the desire and the reach. She pulled down a bottle of Grey Goose vodka, noting that it was three-quarters full. Her parents rarely had mixed drinks, her mom favoring wine and her dad low-carb, light beer. She bent down to the container cupboard and retrieved a tall, stainless-steel water bottle. Her hands were shaking as she unscrewed the lid and poured over half the vodka into the water bottle. She topped the Grey Goose bottle up with water and replaced it in the cupboard. She hoped her parents wouldn't be making cocktails anytime soon.

Moving with a swiftness borne of fear, she hurried downstairs to the basement rec room. It was cold and slightly damp, but she was fond of this space. Her parents had ripped the house down to the studs, rebuilding it into their sleek, contemporary dream home. But the basement, with its wood paneling and ancient bathroom fixtures, was untouched. Unlike the stark and stylish decor of the rest of their house, the rec room was old-school. A ratty sectional sofa and a dated glass coffee table reminded her of the house they'd lived in when she was little, when her parents were young and seemed to laugh a lot more. And with a large flat-screen and decent speakers, it was a fine place to host her friends tonight. She dove on the tweedy surface of the couch and pushed the water bottle between the cushions. She stepped back and surveyed the hiding spot. It looked fine, but when she flopped back on the sofa, the metal dug into her tailbone. Kneeling, she shoved the bottle under the couch, tucking it into a torn piece of upholstery fabric.

There . . . Her party wasn't going to suck after all.

jeff

THAT DAY

Jeff paced in a circle, his heart hammering in his chest, blood rushing audibly through his veins. He breathed deeply through his nose, feeding oxygen to his traumatized muscles, his overworked heart. In this moment, he was immune to the postcard view of the Golden Gate Bridge, the dark blue of the Pacific, even the endless stream of Crissy Field joggers struggling past. He was conscious of nothing but the pain in his legs, the pressure in his lungs, the mechanics of being alive.

Beside him, Graham crouched, dropping his bearlike head toward his knees. "Jesus Christ . . . Holy fuck."

"That was good." Jeff's breathing was returning to normal. He wiped the sweat from his forehead with the end of his running shirt.

Graham stood, with effort. "Let's get a beer, mate. We deserve it."

"I can't." Jeff's response was automatic, programmed by a year of denying himself the simple pleasure of a beer with friends. "It's my daughter's sixteenth."

"One beer . . ." Graham was from Australia, a culture where you didn't turn down a cold one, no matter whose birthday it was. His wife, Jennie, was American, but she accepted Graham's inherent "blokiness," in fact, seemed to find it adorable. Jennie didn't get pissed off over a training session followed by a couple of drinks. Jennie was cool, relaxed, fun-loving; she was nothing like Kim.

"Can't do it. My little girl's waiting for her birthday gift." He was glad to have a legitimate excuse; otherwise he would have had to make one up.

"Suit yourself, mate. See you tomorrow."

Jeff navigated his Tesla Model S through thick, Saturday-afternoon traffic, a low-grade resentment gnawing at him. It wasn't that he was desperate to have a beer with Graham—he had to limit beer on his triathlon diet, and he spent enough time with Graham at work and on their jogs. But his refusal of his friend's invitation highlighted the fact that Kim had him on a very short leash. On certain occasions, like now, he felt an almost overwhelming urge to strangle her with it.

He knew he shouldn't blame Kim. He'd accepted the terms she'd laid down: the terms to staying married, to keeping his family together. It was only when a friend or colleague suggested something as innocuous as an after-work cocktail or a post-run beer that he felt like a scolded child. And he felt like Kim was his controlling mother instead of his wife.

Easing into a break in Van Ness traffic, he gunned the motor. It was a small burst of aggression, momentarily satisfying, but the bitterness soon returned. He had fucked up—he got that—but it was nearly a year ago. Was he doomed to be punished forever? Grounded for life like a recalcitrant child? He really did want to go home for Hannah's birthday, wanted to be there when she opened the bracelet Kim had picked out for her. He just didn't want to *have* to go home.

It had all started in Vegas (of course, Vegas). It was a conference for software vendors and major clients. Besides keynote speakers, roundtables, and breakout sessions, there were golf tournaments, dinners, drinks, and schmoozing. Jeff had played eighteen holes with a female development exec from Montreal, who may or may not have been flirting with him (he was out of practice; she had a French accent); an overweight colleague from the Chicago office; and the CIO of a large southern university. Naturally, numerous beers were imbibed, but he'd paced himself. When they sat down to dinner, he was still in control.

But somewhere between dinner and 3:00 A.M., tequila joined the party. And when Nathan McIntyre, a twenty-six-year-old wunderkind from their Austin office, suggested they take the party back to his room, things began to spiral. Nathan had a business card for some high-end hookers and he was keen for some Vegas-style debauchery. Jeff had no problem declining the invitation. The thought of partying with a bunch of prostitutes held no allure for him; he was a happily married guy, a dad. And he'd never understood the appeal of paying for it. It seemed desperate and tawdry. Besides his moral convictions, he was way too hammered to get it up, even if he'd wanted to—which he didn't. In fact, he was barely coherent, his vision blurred, his brain fogged. And he was scheduled to speak on global growth strategies at nine thirty the next morning. He needed sleep. With their taunts of "pussy" and "lame ass" in his ears, he stumbled back to his room.

Jeff didn't remember passing out fully clothed on his bed, but he did remember waking up. His head pounded, his mouth tasted burnt and poisonous, and his stomach threatened revolt. It took several seconds for him to realize that the banging was not just in his skull but at his door. He looked at his watch. *Fuck!* It was a quarter to nine. His presentation was in less than an hour and he still needed to shower, gather his notes, and probably throw up.

"Jesus Christ. You look like shit." It was Nathan from Austin, surprisingly fresh despite carrying on long after Jeff had opted out.

"I've got to shower, Nathan." Jeff was abrupt. He didn't have time to socialize. "I'm on at nine thirty."

"I know. I brought you a little pick-me-up. Thought you could use it." He handed Jeff a small vial of clear liquid. Jeff stared at it.

"LSD," Nathan explained, "diluted in overproof vodka and distilled water."

Jeff handed it back. "No, thanks." Jeff had never been into psychedelics, and he wasn't about to start now, at forty-seven years old, right before an important presentation. What the fuck was wrong with this kid?

Nathan sensed his incredulity. "You've never heard of microdosing?"

"No."

"It's big in the industry. Take a few drops of this and you'll be transformed: energetic, focused, insightful . . . and no trace of that hangover."

Jeff had done drugs before, of course he had, but that was in another lifetime. He'd been in his twenties, studying at NYU, partying for thirty straight hours most weekends. He'd smoked pot, tried coke and mushrooms. But he was a different person now, with kids, a career, a marriage . . . all the responsibilities that made drugs unacceptable. Except he was in Vegas . . . and wasn't this city just a throbbing, neon neverland where real life melted away and a man could indulge his inner child—or, in this case, his inner twenty-two-year-old? He didn't have to worry about Kim's judgments or setting an example for the kids. He just had to worry about getting through his sixteen-minute presentation.

"I won't trip?" Jeff asked.

"No chance. At a psycholytic dose, it's like taking Ritalin or Adderall. You'll still be you. Just super-you." He smiled and held out the vial. Jeff took it in his clammy palm and headed for the bathroom.

HE'D KILLED IT! The presentation had been a triumph! Maybe the drugs had skewed his perception of audience response somewhat, but there was no denying that it had been well received. Jeff had been confident, insightful, and in command of the room—with no evidence of a hangover. The vial of LSD nestled in his pants pocket. "Keep it," Nathan said. "You can dose every two or three days . . . Make the most of it. Develop new strategies at work. Learn a language. Write a song . . ."

The vial lasted nearly a month. Jeff rationed it carefully; there would be no more when this was gone. He didn't have drug-buying connections, didn't run in those circles. And he could hardly contact Nathan and ask him to send him some more LSD in the mail. Jeff would just enjoy what he had while he had it—increased clarity, deeper insights, exceptional creativity. One afternoon, he and Graham took a few drops before a run. It was phenomenal! The stamina, the speed, the ability to focus on the physical act of running without the distractions of weakness or pain. It would have been a bit of harmless fun with no ill repercussions . . . if Kim hadn't found the vial.

He looked at the dashboard clock: 4:45. Hannah's friends would descend in a matter of minutes, turning his home into a seething hive of chattering and giggling, a tree full of articulate squirrels. He wouldn't get through this without a beer. Flicking on his indicator, he pulled up in front of a dodgy liquor store—its window crammed with posters and neon signs advertising beer and wine. Plugging a quarter into the meter, Jeff strode down the uneven sidewalk, his mind firmly entrenched in that day last year.

He had tried to lie: it was a vitamin cocktail! But when Kim threatened to sample it, he had to tell her the truth. She was stunned. "What if you'd had a psychotic break? What if the kids had found this?" Her voice was quiet, her eyes glistening with unshed tears. She was sitting on the bed; he was standing in front of her. His work pants were still in her lap, the tiny vial now on the bedside table beside them.

"I can explain." But his account did little to sway her. Kim didn't care that everyone in tech was trying it and that, at such diluted intensity, there was virtually no chance of a bad reaction. She didn't care that it had been a "gift," or that once it was gone, he never planned to do it again. She wasn't content to blame this all on Nathan, who had tried to lure Jeff into partying with hookers—yes, *hookers*—to which he had promptly said no. Kim hadn't been impressed or grateful. On the contrary, she'd fixed him with a look of such withering contempt that he wished he hadn't even mentioned it. All Kim could see was that he'd brought illegal, psychedelic drugs into their home—where their children lived, where she lived. It didn't matter to her that there were only a few drops left (on second thought, this may have made things worse). In her mind, Jeff had broken the law, broken her trust, broken her heart. . . .

They talked most of the night, both of them breaking down in tears on several occasions. Kim wasn't sure she could live with the betrayal. She was blindsided, her entire world suddenly tilted on its axis. She wanted him to leave, but he refused. He attacked her for being a hypocrite. She'd done drugs when she worked at the ad agency—probably more drugs than he ever had. But Kim was resolute that she'd changed, grown up. She put her family first now, above all else. She thought he had, too. He shifted gears and tried to comfort her, tried to tell her that, really, it could have been much worse. It could have been a meth lab in the garage! There could have been dealers involved! And guns! It was a psycholytic dose, barely enough to have an effect! But his "minimizing it," as she called it, just upset her more.

Kim's overreaction was clearly a pretext, the drugs a metaphor for all the other problems in their marriage. She had griped for years about their lack of connection, the "distance" between them, his constant state of distractedness. She resented his *obsession* with his work, though not the work itself, as if that even made sense. Jeff's wife had a vision for their life: beautiful house; nice cars; polite, well-educated children; and a partnership that the neighbors envied, no matter what was going on beneath the surface. Kim should have married a politician.

But Jeff had to put the kids first. He knew from experience that growing up with divorced parents was no picnic, so he had agreed to Kim's conditions. The trust was gone; he'd killed it. She didn't want to treat him like one of the children, but apparently, she would have to. His extracurricular activities would have to be curtailed: straight home after work, no more drinks with the guys or weekend golf tournaments that invariably led to the bar. Business trips presented a problem that they would have to work around. He would check in before going out for dinner in the evening and once he returned at night. She would then call the hotel and ask to be transferred to his room to ensure he was where he said he was. Of course, there was no way she could know if he went out and got "all tripped out" later, but he told her she could call him at any hour of the day or night if she wanted. A year later, the system was still in place. She'd finally stopped rifling through his pockets every night. . . . Or he was pretty sure she'd stopped.

At least he had his triathlon training. Kim grudgingly accepted the time he spent at the pool, on his bike, or on the pavement. It gave him a goal, something to strive toward. It was also a means of escape from the palpable resentment pervading his home. That, and work kept him sane. And the kids. They were worth it.

He was reaching for the greasy handle of the liquor store door when he became aware of a presence to his right. He turned, a little panicked given the dodgy neighborhood. It was a boy, about Hannah's age, with dark eyes and artfully shaved hair. "Hey . . . ," he said, a cheeky grin spreading across his face. Jeff heard distant giggling and glanced over to see two boys with a similar look, lurking at the side of the building. There was a girl with them, too. She was wearing short shorts, her legs a bit too pale and a bit too chubby to successfully pull off the look. But he knew boys that age weren't expecting supermodels. The kid near him blushed and continued. "You look like a cool guy. Would you buy my friends and me some beer?"

Jeff paused for the briefest of moments. Did he look like a cool guy, sweaty and disheveled in his expensive running gear? Driving his cool electric car? *Was* he a cool guy? He used to be pretty cool, back in the day, but things had changed. He had changed—thanks, mostly, to Kim. "Sorry, kid." He said, pulling the door open and cementing his uncool status. He caught a whiff of the kid's words on the air as the door closed behind him. They weren't complimentary.

As he moved toward the beer fridge, he felt a twinge of something . . . like regret. He wanted to be the kind of guy who bought those kids beer. He wanted them to wander off with their six-pack and talk about how great he was, instead of calling him an uptight asshole or whatever the kid had muttered in his wake. Twenty, even ten years ago, he might have been that guy. But he wasn't stupid. He wasn't about to bootleg for a bunch of underage strangers. He knew what could happen.

When he was a teenager, there had been plenty of drinking and partying and general carousing . . . and he'd survived it, even thrived because of it. Mischief and troublemaking built character. When he got together with his friends from school they laughed themselves sick remembering the antics they got up to. Even Kim had a wild side, once upon a time. When they were first dating, they'd spent plenty of nights at crazy parties or in bars. Once, they'd gone to Mexico and Kim had downed tequila shots and danced on the bar in her bra. And then Kim became a mother and it was like flicking a switch. Overnight, Kim became responsible, earnest, doting . . . boring.

He grabbed a six-pack of low-carb, light beer and headed for the counter. He thought about his own kids as he moved. What would they have to look back on when they hit forty? Soccer practice and piano recitals? Debate club and French lessons? Hannah and Aidan were growing up sheltered, overparented, *dull*. . . . His wife was turning them into plastic, perfect Disney Channel kids. What kind of adults would they turn into? God, he shuddered to think.

He placed his piss-weak beer on the counter, a funk of dissatisfaction clinging to him. The clerk, a bland guy in glasses, waved the wand over the UPC code. "That everything?"

Jeff was about to reply yes, when he spotted the display at his right elbow: pink champagne . . . well, sparkling wine. It had a girly label and festive pink foil wrapped around the easy-pop top. It screamed "bachelorette party" or "sweet sixteen"—without actually screaming it and therefore being pulled from the shelves. It was right there, like some sort of sign from above. He grabbed the bottle and plunked it on the counter. "And this," he said.

hannah

THAT NIGHT

Marta and Caitlin were the first to arrive. They bustled in with their cargo of various bags: sleeping, overnight, gift. . . .

"You look beautiful," Caitlin complimented.

Hannah smiled. "Thanks." She had straightened her dark-blond hair and meticulously applied her makeup. She wanted to look mature and sexy, but not so mature and sexy that her mom noticed and made her go wash her face.

"You look like a model," Marta contributed, "so tall and skinny."

Hannah was happy to see her two friends, but their arrival wasn't exactly thrilling. Marta and Caitlin had been coming to her birthday parties since she was eleven. Ronni had attended a few, too, back when they were kids. But Lauren Ross had never been to Hannah's birthday, never even been to her house. Hannah swallowed the fear that the popular girl wouldn't show, but she couldn't deny that her birthday would be ruined without Lauren's attendance.

She led the duo to the kitchen. Caitlin and Marta were comfortable at Hannah's place and her mom liked them. They lived up to Kim's exacting standards: well mannered, academically successful, engaged in school activities. But like Hannah, they were growing up. Marta's parents had taken her back to their native Brazil for Christmas and Marta had met a boy. Marta was pretty, in a stout, swarthy sort of way, but she wasn't the kind of girl the boys at Hillcrest liked. Brazilian boys, apparently, had different taste, because Marta and her new beau had been sexting ever since her return. (Marta had shown Caitlin and Hannah the *dick pic* he'd sent her. Gross. When Hannah *did* go all the way with Noah, she wasn't even going to look at that thing.) Caitlin was still pretty square—it didn't help that she looked about nine, with her curly auburn hair and freckles—but she'd recently admitted to dipping into her mom's medicine cabinet. Hannah prayed they'd be able to up their game for Lauren and Ronni tonight.

The girls loitered while Hannah's parents prepared snack plates for them to take downstairs. Her mom peppered her friends with questions: "How's school?" "Marta, are you still in drama club?" "How's the volleyball team, Caitlin?" And her dad cracked jokes that weren't really funny, but the girls laughed anyway—just to be polite, or maybe because they appreciated the effort. When the doorbell rang again, Hannah knew it had to be Lauren and Ronni. She scurried to answer it, a mixture of relief and excitement making her sweaty.

"Oh my god! You're here!" Crap . . . She sounded like she was in second grade. She had to dial down the enthusiasm. But Lauren and Ronni squealed with delight and hugged her.

Lauren leaned into Hannah. "Tonight is going to be amazing."

"Totally," Ronni echoed.

Hannah felt the butterflies in her stomach activate. She was thankful for the container of vodka tucked under the sofa yet still terrified her parents would discover it. She navigated the girls to the kitchen.

When they entered, Hannah saw her mom's eyes land on the arrivals. Her face relayed blatant disapproval as she took in Ronni's cleavage and thick foundation, Lauren's bare midriff and visible belly-button ring. Kim quickly masked the expression with a phony smile, but not before Hannah caught it.

"Hi, Ronni," Kim said. "I saw your mom today."

"Yeah, she told me."

"It was nice to see her. It's been way too long."

"That's what she said, too."

Kim turned to Lauren. "You must be Lauren."

"Hey . . ." Lauren sounded both bored and uncomfortable at the same time.

Hannah watched the subtle yet unmistakable hardening of her mom's expression. Kim hated Lauren on sight; there was no hiding it. Hannah turned away. It was her birthday and she wasn't going to spend it worrying about what her mom thought of her friends. She was starting to realize that Kim was a really judgmental person. If a girl wore too much makeup, had some body art or a piercing, her mom thought she was trashy. If a kid didn't get straight A's, didn't study three hours a night, or didn't belong to a sports team, she wasn't up to her mom's standards. God forbid a sixteen-year-old wants to have some fun, to create some memories that didn't revolve around sports or academics. Hannah lifted a snack tray. "Let's go downstairs, guys."

Her dad's voice called after them. "You girls go ahead. Your manservant will bring down the pizza." They all laughed, even Lauren. Maybe her dad was kind of funny?

In the musty basement, the girls dumped their gear in a corner and pounced on the sofa. "What did your parents get you for your birthday?" Marta asked.

Hannah held out her wrist for review of the diamond bracelet, and the girls gushed appropriately. She smiled and bit her lip. It was a really cute bracelet.

Lauren said, "What did Noah get you?"

Hannah felt her face flush. "Nothing . . ." Ronni and Lauren exchanged a look that made Hannah feel she should elaborate. "I haven't even seen him today. And I didn't really expect anything. We're still casual."

Ronni said, "I bet he's got something for you."

"Yeah, he's got something for her," Lauren said. "His big dick!"

All the girls burst into laughter, and Hannah forced herself to laugh along, but her cheeks burned with embarrassment.

When the giggles subsided, Marta said, "I got you a present." She moved to her stack of belongings, prompting the others to follow suit.

"You didn't have to," Hannah said as the girls rummaged for their gifts, but she was delighted. Presents from parents were great; they were definitely more likely to be big-ticket, but gifts from friends were guaranteed to be cool, thoughtful, and relevant. When the girls were reassembled, Hannah opened Marta's first. It was a set of floral-scented lotions. "I love them!" She hugged Marta, then turned to Lauren and Ronni.

Ronni hugged the small gift bag to her chest, giggling. "You have to open this one last."

Caitlin handed over a cool pair of earrings that her cousin, an aspiring jewelry designer, had made. Hannah gave her oldest friend a quick hug of thanks. Now it was time for Lauren and Ronni's present. She knew it would be perfect, whatever it was.

Ronni looked toward the door, the gift bag in her hand. "The units aren't going to come down, are they?"

"Not till the pizza gets here. And we'll hear them on the stairs."

Lauren and Ronni exchanged another gleeful look. "Okay," Lauren said, grabbing the bag from Ronni and thrusting it to Hannah. "Open it."

Hannah plunged her hand into the rustling tissue paper, her fingers alighting on something silky. Lauren and Ronni watched with wicked grins as Hannah extracted a slip of sheer, cherry-red fabric.

"It's a thong." Caitlin stated the obvious.

Lauren and Ronni giggled. "There's a matching bra, too," Ronni added.

Hannah pulled out the bra: plunging, red, push-up. It looked like something a supermodel would wear on the runway. Or a stripper on a pole. She feigned enthusiasm. "I love it!"

Lauren leaned back on the sofa. "Noah's going to splooge in his pants when he sees you in that."

Marta and Caitlin gasped, scandalized. Hannah tried to play it cool, but the thought of her and Noah and red lingerie made her whole body prickle.

"Don't let your mom find them," Ronni said. "She'd totally murder you."

"I've got a great hiding place," Hannah lied. "Don't worry."

Upstairs, the doorbell rang: pizza. Soon, a rumble on the stairs and the hot cardboardy scent of pizza announced her parents' descent. Hannah stuffed the lingerie under a sofa cushion just as her dad boomed, "Pizza delivery!" He entered carrying the large square box, trailed by her mom with a stack of plates and napkins. The girls shifted the other snack trays so her parents could set the pizza and accoutrements on the coffee table.

Her dad hovered above them for a moment. "What? No tip?" The girls forced a laugh. He was trying way too hard, and Hannah wanted him to leave.

"You've got everything you need then?" Her mom scanned the room.

"We're good," Hannah said quickly. "Thanks."

"Yeah, thanks . . . ," the other girls murmured.

But her mom wasn't quite ready to depart. "We have a few rules in this house."

"Mom . . . ," Hannah whined. "They've all been here before."

"Lauren hasn't." Her mom looked to Lauren and then included them all. "We won't tolerate any drugs, alcohol, or pornography."

Pornography? God, her mom was so out of touch. As if sixteen-year-old girls sat around looking at dicks as a party activity. She was about to enlighten her mother, but Lauren said, "That's cool," in her bored, nasal voice. Hannah realized she must reserve this tone for adults. Or maybe she always sounded this way but Hannah only noticed it when her mom was listening.

"No smoking, of course," Kim added. "It's a fire hazard in addition to causing cancer."

Was she fucking serious?

"And most important," her dad quipped, "no fun."

Only Caitlin giggled. Her mom studiously ignored the crack.

"When you're under our roof, you're our responsibility," Kim continued. "I expect you to abide by our rules." Hannah felt humiliation burn her cheeks. God, the woman was uptight. Thankfully, her mom turned to leave, but then she paused. "And don't try sneaking any boys in."

"How could we?" Hannah sniped. "There's not even a door down here."

"I just want to be clear."

"You're clear!" It came out pissier than Hannah had intended and she felt a frisson of fear run through her. Kim stared her down for a moment, and Hannah knew what to expect: a lecture on appreciation, on being grateful that her parents were letting her have four friends sleep over, buying them pizza and sodas and cake, and, in return, expecting nothing but a little respect for their rules. She knew the speech was circulating in her mom's head. But she also knew there was a slim ray of hope that she wouldn't humiliate Hannah, in front of her friends, on her sixteenth birthday.

Kim's voice was cool. "Great . . . We'll be upstairs if you need anything." She exited, leaving a subtle guilt trip in her wake. Her dad made a "Heil Hitler" salute to her departing back, but the girls were too on edge to do more than smile.

When they were gone, an awkward silence hung over them. Finally, Ronni reached for her soda. "Fuck."

Lauren reached for a piece of pizza. "Your mom is scary."

"She's not that bad," Hannah tried. "She's all talk."

Caitlin's voice was thin. "If she catches us . . ."

"She won't," Hannah snapped. Caitlin could be such a buzzkill sometimes. Maybe Hannah was outgrowing her oldest friend?

Marta spoke in a hushed voice. "We'd better not do anything until they're asleep. In case they—"

Lauren interrupted with a fierce "Shhhhhhh!"

In the abrupt silence, they heard the feet on the stairs and then Hannah's dad hustled into the room. Hannah looked up and caught his eye: a mischievous sparkle. In his hands, he held the cake box from Tout Sweet. Under his arm, was a paper bag with a bottle inside.

"Unlike some people," he said, as he set down the cake box, "I remember what it's like to be sixteen."

He pulled a bottle of champagne from the bag. It had pink foil around its glass neck and a fuchsia stiletto on the label. Hannah felt a rush of love filling her chest. "Thanks . . . ," she said, her voice hoarse.

"Don't tell your mother," her dad said, handing her the bottle. "And make sure the music's up loud when you pop the top." And with that, he was gone.

kim

THAT NIGHT

Kim should have heard it, *would* have heard it if she hadn't installed earplugs and taken half an Ambien. The girls were two floors below, but she'd anticipated giggling, music, a few late-night trips to raid the fridge. . . . To ensure a sound sleep, she'd nibbled a bit of the sedative, despite having had two glasses of white wine after dinner. She'd done it plenty of times without incident. She'd always been a light sleeper and, lately, adequate rest had become imperative for Kim. There were too many hormones wreaking havoc with her humor. And there was far too much tension in her marriage to handle without a good night's sleep.

"Mom! Dad!" Kim dragged herself up from under the warm, wet blanket of sedation. It was Hannah's voice, tearful, close. . . . Kim opened heavy lids and saw her daughter at the end of the bed. Tall, pretty Hannah wearing a nightie that looked like a football jersey, the number 28 across her chest. It was Hannah's birthday today—sweet sixteen—she was having a slumber party. So why was she here, in the small hours of the morning? Why was she crying? As Kim struggled for lucidity, she realized something was terribly wrong. Tears streamed down Hannah's face and there was something on her hands . . . something dark and wet, glistening in the faint glow of the LED clock radio . . .

Blood.

Kim bolted upright, adrenaline decimating any tranquilizer left in her system.

"What's wrong? Hannah . . . Oh God!"

Jeff was awake now. Unlike his wife, he'd always slept soundly with no pharmaceutical assistance. "What's going on? What's happening?"

"Is that blood? Are you okay?" Kim could feel the panic rising, filling her chest.

Hannah's voice, though choked with tears, sounded calm in comparison. "I'm okay. But you have to help Ronni."

Kim flew down the stairs. Her feet seemed to move effortlessly, floating on a surge of dread, fear, adrenaline. . . . The moment felt surreal and dreamlike. It was the shock. Or the Ambien. But the quiet sobs of her daughter behind her and the heavy thud of her husband's feet in front of her grounded her in the now. She felt thankful that Jeff was there, that he was calm and solid and leading the way.

When they burst into the basement room, the first thing that hit her was the smell: Alcohol. And vomit. Normally, she would have been angry, but relief sagged her shoulders. So that's what this was about. The girls had been drinking; Ronni must have been sick. It was disappointing, of course, but normal for sixteen-year-olds. Tony's prediction flashed in her mind. He'd been right after all. Then she remembered the blood on her child's hands.

"Jesus Christ," Jeff breathed, and Kim snapped to attention. Her stomach plummeted as she caught a glimpse of the crumpled body on the living room floor: Ronni. Jeff rushed toward her, with Hannah on his heels, but Kim hung back, frozen. Just for a moment, she considered hovering near the door, sparing herself the sight of vomit and blood and the inert form of Hannah's friend. She noticed Marta, pale and crying, huddled in a far corner of the couch. Their eyes met for a brief moment, and their mutual desire to flee or dissolve reflected back at each other. But Kim's sense of responsibility was too great, her inherent need to make things better too strong. She was a mother. She moved toward Ronni.

Her view was partially obscured by Jeff, Hannah, and Caitlin, who was crouching on the floor next to Ronni's body. Through them, Kim could make out Ronni's lifeless form: her long, spray-tanned legs splayed like a broken Barbie doll's; a splatter of blood on the pale-pink shorts and tank that she wore as pajamas. "Ronni . . . Ronni, wake up," Jeff was saying with no response. Kim shifted to get a better view of Ronni's face, and that's when she saw it. The glass coffee table was shattered, jagged shards clinging to the frame like the teeth of some giant, prehistoric shark.

Jeff addressed the sniveling girls. "What the hell happened?"

"She got sick," Caitlin said. "She was weak. And dizzy."

"She tripped and fell on the coffee table," Hannah whimpered.

"It broke." Marta added the obvious.

Hannah's voice cracked. "Is she . . . going to be okay?"

Kim noticed a piece of a champagne bottle lying next to Ronni's bloodied hand. Just the foil-wrapped neck, still intact, still festive and girlish and fun. Damn them . . . "How much did she drink?" Kim barked. "What did she take?"

Hannah and Caitlin shared a look, possibly summoning the courage to answer. Jeff surveyed the room and cut them off before they could speak. "Who's missing?"

Kim looked, too, and realized they were down a girl. "Where's Lauren?" she demanded. Marta pointed at the bathroom, too upset to speak.

"She doesn't do blood," Caitlin elaborated.

Ronni emitted a low moan that jarred Jeff into action. "Hannah, go upstairs and get some gauze. Kim call nine-one-one."

The look of terror on her husband's face made her cold, and for the first time, she was aware that she was wearing only a thin nightie. Hannah hurried past her and Caitlin stood, allowing Kim her first glimpse of Ronni's face. It was slack, unconscious, ghostly underneath the smeared makeup. A mask of vomit and blood coated her right cheek; her right hand and arm were sliced, raw, bloodied. . . . Beneath Ronni's eye, a flap of skin dangled, providing a grotesque glimpse of milky-white eyeball bathed in red. Kim felt stomach acid burn her throat.

"Kim!" Jeff snapped. She tore her eyes away and hurried to the phone.

IT WAS DECIDED that Kim and Hannah would ride in the ambulance with Ronni; Jeff would drive the other girls home and explain the night's events to their parents. Normally, the roles would have been reversed. Kim was more articulate, better at explaining the circumstances in diplomatic terms, while Jeff was calm and commanding in a crisis. But Kim knew she shouldn't drive after the wine and sleeping pill. Of course, the shock of Ronni's accident had left her feeling completely alert, but it wasn't a risk she wanted to take. Jeff had only had a couple of light beers with dinner. He was fine.

And so Kim sat in the back of the ambulance beside her daughter, who clutched Ronni's unharmed left hand and cried softly. Ronni's damaged eye was covered with thick gauze, thankfully, but blood was slowly seeping through, staining the sterile white a deep crimson. The injured girl had briefly come to, stammering something about being cold, which the burly male paramedic attributed to shock.

"How much did she have to drink tonight?" he asked Hannah matter-of-factly. Kim took in his cropped dark hair, his ruddy complexion, his robust masculine energy. Really, he was straight out of central casting.

"Umm . . ." Hannah's searching eyes met her mother's, and Kim gave her an encouraging nod. "She had some vodka. And then some rye. Some Jägermeister—I don't know how much—and champagne."

So much alcohol . . . Where did they get it? But Kim maintained her composure, even giving Hannah's knee a supportive squeeze. The girl rewarded her with a grateful smile. The paramedic continued to fuss with Ronni's oxygen mask, checking various digital readouts. "Any drugs?"

Hannah glanced at her mom, then dissolved into tears.

"Answer him," Kim said coolly. She could feel her calm facade slipping. Sneaking a few drinks on your sixteenth birthday was normal, cliché even, but drugs now? Did she even know her daughter? Did she know any of these girls? But a glance at Ronni tempered her outrage. She was intensely grateful that it wasn't Hannah lying bleeding on the gurney. Still . . . she suddenly felt that her years of careful parenting had been for naught.

"I think she took a Xanax." Hannah sobbed. "And maybe some ecstasy." She turned to Kim. "I'm sorry. We were stupid."

"Yes, you were," Kim said, and the magnitude of her failure threatened to overwhelm her. Despite all her devotion and parent education, her daughter had slipped into substance abuse right under Kim's well-informed nose.

"Have you called her parents?" It was the paramedic. Though his attention was fixed on Ronni, Kim realized he was addressing her.

"I-I didn't have a chance . . . ," she stammered. "It happened so fast."

"Call them when we get to the hospital. They need to be with her."

For the first time, Kim started to cry.

LIKE ALL MOTHERS, Kim knew that forgetting her phone meant that one of her children would break his or her arm or the house would catch fire. Even in the terror and chaos of that night, she'd grabbed it off the charger and dropped it in her pocket. (She'd also hurriedly put on a bra and sweater, pulled on a pair of jeans.) Now she paced the sterile hospital hallway, fingering the cold metal casing in her pocket. Of course Lisa had to be called. If it were Hannah lying there covered in bile and blood, her eye dangling out of its socket, Kim would want to be there. And yet, she hesitated.

The thought of delivering the news to her friend made her feel physically sick. This would devastate Lisa. Kim could only imagine being woken from an innocent slumber to the news that her child—Lisa's *only* child—was lying bloodied and broken in a hospital bed. It was too much to bear. But it was more than empathy that made her fingers cold and useless as they tentatively touched the face of her phone. It was fear.

She was scared . . . terrified, actually. It was more than just "shoot the messenger" anxiety. It wasn't that Kim felt culpable, exactly. She had laid down strict rules that the girls had blatantly broken. They'd been sneaky and conniving and deceitful. But still . . . it had happened on her watch, and she knew how Lisa would feel. Any semblance of friendship they'd once had would be destroyed.

A fresh-faced woman, in her early-thirties and wearing a clinical white jacket, was walking toward her: the doctor. Her face was grave. "Are you the mother?"

"No, I'm her mom." Kim pointed at Hannah curled up in a chair in a ratty pair of gray sweats and her dad's sweatshirt. The effects of a night of drinking, panic, and crying were showing themselves on her puffy, makeup-streaked face. "It's her birthday. Ronni was at our house."

The doctor nodded. "Ronni's stable for the moment."

Kim realized this was what she'd been waiting for: reassurance. She could call Lisa now and tell her that Ronni would be okay.

"You need to get the parents down here," the doctor said. "We need to get her into plastics. Someone's got to sign the consent."

"I'll call right now," Kim said, feeling subtly chastised.

"Good," the doctor replied, heading back toward the curtained-off area where Ronni was being assessed. "We'll try our best to save the eye."

Kim heard her daughter's renewed whimpering, but she didn't have time to comfort her. She had to make the call. She couldn't put it off another second.

lisa

THAT NIGHT

Lisa knew, more than most people, that a phone call in the dead of night meant bad news. It had been such a phone call during her first year away at Ithaca College that had announced her parents' death in a boating accident. At nineteen, Lisa had been ill prepared to handle such a shock and had passed out on the spot. When she came to, she found she was even more ill prepared to be an orphan. Despite her recent collegiate independence, she was emotionally immature and far too naive to handle the not insignificant life-insurance settlement bestowed upon her and her sister. That late-night phone call launched a six-year period of self-destructive behavior: drugs, partying, men. . . . The cycle ended only when she found herself pregnant with Ronni. Oh God . . . Ronni.

She threw the blankets off her and jumped out of bed. Allan barely stirred. He'd worked at the restaurant until 11:30 P.M. and then let himself into her apartment and her bed. When Ronni wasn't home, she let Allan sleep over. She liked having him there, even liked being woken in the middle of the night by his soft caresses that turned urgent in his need for her. But his presence provided little comfort in her current state of dread.

With her heart hammering in her chest, she stumbled through the darkened apartment to the phone in the kitchen. The clock on the microwave read 1:47 A.M. For a brief moment, she thought about her Buddhism studies: acceptance of what comes, without question or attachment. . . . Buddhism was not a philosophy for mothers. But the call couldn't be about Ronni. The universe wasn't that cruel. Lisa liked to subscribe to the theory that everyone was allocated a certain amount of suffering. She'd used hers up when her parents died, when she'd gotten herself pregnant by an alcoholic, when she became estranged from her only sister. Ronni would be fine; she had to be.

Of course, since Ronni was at Kim's house, this could be behavior-related. Kim was definitely the type to think that a sneaky viewing of an R-rated movie or smoking a cigarette warranted a middle-of-the-night phone call. And Ronni had been rebellious of late, pushing her boundaries, testing her mother. She'd been wearing too much makeup, copping an attitude, texting constantly with Lauren—Lisa let it slide. It was all part of being sixteen, of feeling around outside the nest before making the jump to midair. Lisa and Ronni were so close that the break was extra difficult, requiring drastic measures to push them apart. Kim had probably caught Ronni with a bottle of beer, or maybe even a joint. And because Hannah was perfect, almost robotic, really, Kim was pushing the panic button. By the time Lisa reached the phone, she was calm enough to answer.

"Lisa, it's Kim."

"Is everything all right?"

There was a pause, probably less than a second but long enough to make Lisa's stomach plunge. Kim said, "Ronni's at CPMC. Pediatric emergency."

"What? Why?"

"It's okay. She's stable."

Stable? Lisa didn't like the ephemeral sound of the word. Panic threatened to paralyze her throat, but she choked out the words, "What happened?"

"They were drinking," Kim continued. "I don't know how they got the alcohol. Someone must have sneaked it in. Ronni fell."

"What do you mean, *fell*?" Lisa's voice had become loud and shrill. "What happened? What's wrong with her?"

She could hear Kim crying softly on the other end of the line. "She took some drugs, too. And . . . she fell . . . through the glass coffee table. She cut herself."

"Oh God."

"She cut her eye."

"Oh God!"

"You need to get down here," Kim sobbed. She seemed to have given up any semblance of calm. "Hurry!"

Lisa hung up and turned to find Allan behind her, naked, bleary, concerned. "What happened?"

Tears streamed down Lisa's face, but her voice sounded surprisingly normal. "You need to take me to the hospital."

THE EFFICIENCY WITH which Lisa and Allan were ushered toward the pediatric OR waiting area was concerning, but it was the sight of Hannah, curled up in a chair like an abandoned kitten, that turned Lisa's guts to liquid. She'd expected Kim's tearful countenance; she'd heard it in her voice on the phone. But Hannah's appearance was shocking, terrifying. . . . This was a girl who'd witnessed carnage—a car accident or a murder. Her ghostly pallor highlighted the black streaks of mascara that she'd unsuccessfully wiped at—or more likely, her mom had wiped at—smearing her face with gray soot. She wore a man's sweatshirt, probably Jeff's, making her neck and wrists look fragile and birdlike as they emerged from the large garment. Lisa looked at Hannah's hands; they were a girl's hands despite Hannah's height and maturity, and they were stained red. Blood . . . her daughter's blood.

Kim hurried up to Lisa, wrapping her in her arms. "She's going to be okay."

Lisa's body froze in response to the hug. She didn't want comforting from the woman who had let this happen to her daughter. "Where's Ronni? Where's the doctor?"

Kim instantly dropped her arms. She looked hurt, embarrassed, awkward. Lisa felt a quick flash of pity for her. Kim tried so hard to be the perfect mom, to do and say all the right things. She'd look on this incident as a personal failing. But Lisa pushed her empathy aside. Nothing mattered now but her child.

"I'll get the doctor." It was Hannah, suddenly come to life despite her inert appearance. She hurried toward the nurses' station. They watched her for a second before Kim turned to Lisa.

"I don't know how this happened. I told them the rules. . . . No drinking, smoking, boys, or drugs. I thought I could trust them."

Lisa wasn't in the mood for Kim's excuses, but Allan said, "They're teenagers. They can be sneaky."

Kim continued. "Hannah's never done anything like this before. I didn't think she drank. I thought I knew her. I thought . . ." Emotion robbed Kim of her voice, and Lisa felt a minor swell of satisfaction. She wanted Kim to hurt, to feel at least an iota of the fear and dread Lisa was experiencing. But how could she? Hannah was here, tearful, traumatized, but basically fine. Not the perfect angel her mother thought she was, but fine.

Allan put a protective arm around Lisa. "The doctor's coming," he said, his lips in her hair.

The doctor, younger than Lisa would have liked but with an authoritative air she appreciated, approached. She had a clipboard and pen held to her chest. "Are you Veronica Monroe's mother?"

"Yes," Lisa answered. "Can I see her? How is she?"

"She's stable." *That word again.* "But I'm concerned about her eye. There are several tears in the retina and damage to the optic nerve."

Lisa tried to form a sentence but found her tongue useless in her mouth. Allan stepped in. "What does that mean?"

"It means she needs surgery if she wants to keep that eye."

"Of course she wants to keep it!" Lisa had regained the power of speech. "She needs it. She's sixteen."

"We'll do what we can. I'm waiting on a consult from an anesthesiologist. Given her state of intoxication, it could be risky to put her under."

"What do you mean risky?" Lisa cried. "You can't operate?"

The doctor suddenly looked anxious to leave. "We'll know more after the consult. I'll leave the permission forms with you." She handed the clipboard and pen to Lisa. "Once you've filled these out, someone will take you to see your daughter."

Lisa stood motionless, staring at the documents in her hand. She felt numb, weighted down, unable to move. "You should sit down," Allan said, steering her toward a bank of chairs. Lisa sat and let him take the clipboard from her hands. "I'll fill these out," he said softly.

"Can I get you something? Coffee?" It was Kim, hovering a few feet away.

Lisa looked up at her. Kim's face was red, puffy, contorted with fear, anxiety, and guilt. Lisa was suddenly filled with an almost overwhelming urge to hit her. But she didn't. "I don't want anything from you," she said.

jeff

THAT NIGHT

Jeff gripped the steering wheel tightly and tried to keep his focus on the road. Beside him sat Caitlin, staring rigidly ahead, while the other two girls—Marta and someone . . . he couldn't remember her name—huddled in the back. One of them was crying softly, and the pungent odor of sick emanated from their vicinity. He felt bad for thinking it, but he really hoped the stench wouldn't permeate the Tesla's interior.

"She'll be all right," he said, as much to fill the silence as to provide comfort. He hoped the girl in the back would stop whimpering. It was driving him nuts.

"We were so fucking stupid," Caitlin said, her voice angry. The profanity seemed entirely appropriate given the circumstances.

"Yeah . . . Well, we've all been there. . . ." Jeff was trying to sound young, relatable, but he was afraid he sounded patronizing.

His words hung in the air for a moment before he continued. "What did you drink?"

Caitlin answered. "Vodka. Rye."

"And champagne . . ." The voice—cold, accusatory—came from the backseat. He looked in the rearview mirror at the two girls leaning against each other. He couldn't tell which one had spoken.

"I brought fucking Xanax," Caitlin continued, the string of f-bombs incongruous with her wholesome, freckled look.

"Shut up, Caitlin," one of the girls in the backseat said.

"What?" Caitlin snapped back. "It doesn't matter now."

"This isn't your fault," Jeff said. "It was an accident." He glanced into the backseat again, but the girls didn't meet his eyes.

"I knew this was a bad idea, but I just . . ." Caitlin paused, decided not to continue.

"Look, you're kids," Jeff said. "You're supposed to make mistakes. Unfortunately, Ronni was hurt. But she'll get through this and you'll all learn from it." No one spoke. He decided to continue. "And, uh—" He cleared his throat. "I'd appreciate it if you didn't mention that I gave you the champagne."

He felt like a creep as soon as he said it, like some pedophile asking his victims to keep quiet. He should have kept his mouth shut. These kids had been drinking hard liquor and taking pills! A few sips of bubbly didn't cause Ronni to fall through the glass table. He listened to the loaded silence. Even the sniveling had stopped. Finally:

"Sure." It was Caitlin. She glanced quickly over her shoulder at the girls in the back, but they stayed mute.

Marta was the first to be dropped off. Jeff walked her to the door and explained the situation to her parents, Ana and Octavio. He may have downplayed Ronni's injuries, but until they knew the extent of them, he could see no reason to alarm everyone. When Octavio expressed his dismay at their covert drinking, Jeff spoke up. "Don't be too hard on her," he said, his eyes resting on Marta snuggled under her mother's protective wing. "I think the shock of all this is punishment enough."

He repeated the process with Caitlin's mom and finally drove the other girl home. Her name was Lauren, he finally recollected. But if he'd met her before tonight, he didn't remember.

"You don't have to take me up," Lauren said when they pulled up to a luxury high-rise apartment complex in SoMa.

"I'd like to explain to your parents," Jeff said. "They'll be worried."

"My dad's not even home. And my stepmom won't care."

"Maybe not . . ." His voice was firm. "But I'd still feel better."

As they rode the elevator up to the twenty-first-floor penthouse, Jeff wished he'd accepted the kid's offer to leave. The ride felt interminably long. Lauren stared at the floor, picking at the sides of her fingernails. She'd thrown up at the sight of Ronni's blood, or Ronni's damaged eye, or just from all the booze and drugs. It was in her hair and on her clothes. The stench threatened to overwhelm him. Finally, thankfully, the elevator dinged to signal they'd arrived.

Lauren had a key and she opened the apartment door. "Do you want me to wake her up?" she asked, pausing in the doorway.

Jeff didn't want her to. The mere thought of explaining the accident again left him exhausted. And while he had at least a passing acquaintance with the other girls' parents, he knew nothing about Lauren's family. Maybe the stepmother really would be indifferent, as the girl said. Or maybe she'd be angry. But he could already hear Kim chastising him if he failed on his mission. It was his job to inform all the parents. And his wife was right. The situation had to be explained. "Yes."

The girl didn't invite him in, so he lingered outside the partially opened door, waiting. The apartment foyer was dark, but Lauren had obviously flicked a light switch somewhere deep in the spacious home. It threw a shaft of light across the gleaming hardwood floor of the entryway, highlighting a teak sideboard adorned with a fancy oriental vase. The whole place screamed expensive. Finally, he heard the rumbling of female voices and the rustling of movement inside. A few moments later, a woman in an embroidered kimono appeared: blond, petite, and young enough to be Lauren's sister.

"I'm Carla. Lauren's stepmom."

Lauren, who had trailed behind her, gave a derisive snort that Carla ignored.

She invited Jeff in and flicked on the light. "What's she done?"

Jeff cleared his throat. "It's not Lauren's fault. . . ." Jeff began, then relayed the night's events.

"Is Ronni okay?" Carla asked, pulling her kimono tighter around her.

"I don't know. . . . I'm heading to the hospital now."

"These girls and their partying. . . ."

"Yeah," Jeff agreed, not bothering to explain that, until tonight, Hannah had never partied. Or, if she had, he and Kim hadn't known about it.

"My husband's out of town. She's supposed to be at her mom's," Carla continued, referencing Lauren, who had disappeared into the depths of the apartment. "She's grounded. For pot. But her mom never follows through."

Jeff pursed his lips, nodded. He didn't know what he was supposed to say.

"We all partied at their age. We all tried things. But Monique refuses to set any boundaries and Darren travels so much. . . ." Monique and Darren had to be Lauren's divorced parents. "I can't do anything. If I say one word, I'm the evil stepmother."

"I should really go."

"Of course. I'll check on Ronni tomorrow. Lisa and I are friendly."

As Jeff rode down the elevator, he breathed a sigh of relief: mission accomplished. Lauren was clearly a troublemaker. Wealthy, divorced parents gave a kid the motive and means to rebel. But all the parents had been perfectly reasonable: concerned but not losing their shit, not pointing fingers or blaming.

Of course, he still had to face Lisa.

THE TESLA'S TIRES squealed on the concrete of the parking garage as Jeff searched for a spot. The lot was packed, and the few available spaces had RESERVED signs on them. He could feel his palms on the wheel getting sweaty. The air in the concrete bunker was heavy and close. If he didn't find a free spot soon, he was going to park in some doctor's space. Fuck 'em.

A "compact car" spot materialized and he jammed the Tesla into it. Thankfully, he was slim enough to squeeze through the narrow space the SUV next to him afforded. He scanned the dank lot for an elevator or a stairwell. Found it. He jogged down the stairs and across the street, into the hospital's main lobby. An elderly volunteer with a bouffant hairdo pointed him toward the pediatric ER. Traversing a labyrinth of hallways, he finally reached the waiting area.

He hurried to the reception desk. "I'm looking for my wife and daughter. They came in with—" He stopped, midsentence. Down the hall to his right, he saw Kim. She was talking to two uniformed police officers. Jesus Christ . . .

"We have very strict rules in our house," she was saying as Jeff approached. Kim paused when she saw him. "This is my husband, Jeff Sanders."

The officers, one male, one female, introduced themselves, but Jeff didn't retain their names. He turned to Kim. "How's Ronni?"

Kim's voice wavered. "She needs surgery on her eye."

"Is Lisa here?"

Kim nodded.

The male officer interrupted. "We're trying to piece together the events of the night."

"Of course," Jeff said. "We specifically told the girls no alcohol or drugs. They must have sneaked it in. I don't know how they got it."

"Do you have liquor in the house?" the female officer asked.

"Some. A little."

"A normal amount, I think," Kim added. "We're social drinkers. Maybe a glass of wine with dinner. But never to excess."

"What about your daughter? Has she been caught drinking before?"

"Never." Kim was emphatic. "That's why we're so shocked. Hannah is an excellent student. She plays basketball and Royal Conservatory piano. This is completely out of character for her."

"You'd be surprised . . . ," the male officer muttered. Kim's eyes narrowed, a look Jeff knew well. She wanted to rip this guy a new one, tell him that her precious daughter was not a boozer, a partier, or a rebel. Hannah had been parented properly. Didn't he hear her? Hannah played *piano* and *basketball*. She was on the *honor roll*.

"*Kids* . . ." Jeff chuckled softly to deflect from his wife's contained ire. "But we had no idea what was going on, so we're obviously not culpable." It was phrased as a statement, but the underlying question was clear.

The female officer responded. "We'll need to come by your house tomorrow. Don't clean up or touch anything at the scene."

"It's procedure," the other officer added. "I don't think you need to be concerned."

"I would hope not," Kim said. God. She sounded like a self-righteous jerk.

"Thank you, officers," Jeff covered. "Feel free to come by anytime."

"We will." And with that, they left.

hannah

THE NEXT DAY

Soft morning light peaked its way through heavy eyelids and Hannah enjoyed a few seconds of normalcy before the events of last night tumbled into her consciousness. Oh God . . . She jumped out of bed without hesitation and threw on some clothes. She'd showered when they got home from the hospital, dried blood and the stink of puke swirling away down the drain. A quick hairbrush and deodorant would have to do today. Before she left her room, she texted Lauren.

OMFG.

The response was instantaneous: Fuuuuuck

Hannah wrote: Going 2 c Ronni. Want to come?

Can't. Grounded. Again.

Lauren seemed to be perpetually grounded, not that it curtailed her social life at all. She was an expert at playing her divorced parents off each other. Hannah almost envied Lauren's situation. She didn't want her parents to split up, necessarily, but it wasn't like they actually liked each other. And kids from broken homes had so much more freedom. And then there was the guilt factor. Lauren's dad was always buying her expensive clothes and jewelry to compensate for his lack of engagement. Hannah's own parents could never be accused of that. Damn.

Her mom and dad were sitting at the breakfast bar, drinking coffee and not speaking. "I need to go to the hospital," Hannah announced. "I need to see Ronni."

Her parents exchanged a quick look before her mom spoke. "I think Ronni's family would appreciate some alone time today."

"She doesn't have a family. She has a *mom*. We should be there to support them."

Her dad cleared his throat. "It's a bit tricky right now. . . ."

"What do you mean *tricky*?"

Her mom took this one. "Ronni was hurt in our house. She was drinking and taking drugs. In our house."

"That's all the more reason we should be there for her!"

Her parents glanced at each other again. Suddenly, they seemed to have become some sort of team. "Why don't you sit down?" her dad said.

"No. I'm going to the hospital."

"Sit!" her mom barked. "You're in no position to be insolent." Hannah rolled her eyes but lowered herself onto a barstool like an obedient puppy. Her mom continued. "We have a lot to talk about . . . starting with your actions last night. You're old enough to know that behaviors have consequences. We'd like to discuss those consequences with you. "

Hannah shot her mother a look of pure, teenaged hatred. "Can you drop the perfect-mom act for, like, five seconds? My best friend is hurt."

Her mom's only response was a wounded look. Hannah had been surly and snappish before—what teenager hadn't? But she'd never gone for the jugular, never dared attack her mom's soft underbelly. Hannah glanced at her dad. She thought she saw a glimmer of something on his face: admiration. He quickly swept it away.

Kim's voice was raw. "Lisa is very upset about Ronni. She's angry. At us."

"The police will be coming by the house this afternoon," her dad added. "They're doing an investigation. To make sure we're not at fault."

"Of course you're not at fault. Why would you be at fault?"

Her mom explained. "Adults can be held responsible for underage drinking in their home."

Oh my god. "But we sneaked the booze in. You didn't know."

"Hopefully, the police will agree with you." Her mom sounded smug, like she was enjoying sharing this news. *You won't be so snotty when your parents are in jail and you and your brother are in some dirty foster home.*

Hannah took a deep breath and stood up. "I understand that I'm going to be grounded. For a long time. Forever. But you have to let me go to the hospital."

"It's not a good idea," her dad said. "Lisa's on the warpath."

"I can handle Lisa," Hannah assured him, concealing her doubts. Ronni's mom was always nice, in her own flaky, hippy-dippy sort of way. But Hannah knew Lisa had a dark past. She remembered snippets of overheard conversations when she and Ronni were little: drugs, an accident, abusive boyfriends. . . . And Lisa really loved Ronni. Kim really loved Hannah, too, she didn't doubt that, but there was something fierce about Lisa's love for her daughter. Maybe because Ronni was all she had.

"She doesn't want us there," her mom said.

"She doesn't want *you guys* there," Hannah retorted. "Besides, this is about Ronni, not Lisa. Ronni will want me there. I know it."

Another shared look between her parents, then her dad caved. "I'll drive her."

"Fine," her mom said. "Aidan will be home soon. I'll stay and explain what happened."

Jeff grabbed his keys off the counter. "We should be back before the police arrive."

THE WARD WAS quiet. Hannah could hear the hum of fluorescent lights and her Adidas shoes squeaking on the waxed floor like nervous chipmunks. The nurse at the counter directed Hannah to Ronni's room: 506, right across the hall. She hesitated for just a moment before pushing the door open.

She hovered in the entryway and took in the view. Ronni lay in the hospital bed, her normally lustrous dark hair flat and matted, her skin pale and waxy. Her right eye was covered by a thick piece of white gauze, its edges yellowed with some sort of antiseptic. The other eye stared blankly ahead, awake but unseeing. God. She looked so broken. Hannah was about to step into the room when Lisa appeared, obscuring her view. "Uh-uh," she said, hustling Hannah back into the hall before Ronni even knew she was there.

"Go home, Hannah." Lisa's voice was commanding over the buzzing lights.

"I just want to see her," Hannah said, perilously close to tears. "To let her know that I'm here for her."

"You should have been there for her last night."

"I tried!"

"Obviously not hard enough."

Lisa's words were a slap in the face, a punch in the gut. Hannah's chin quivered and tears pooled in her eyes. "I didn't want them to— I couldn't. . . ." But she didn't know what to say, didn't know how to say it. She was going to fall apart in front of Lisa. Shit . . .

Ronni's mom looked at her and the hard set of her jaw softened slightly. For the first time, Hannah noticed how rough Lisa looked. She was the young mom, the pretty mom. Ronni's accident had taken a toll. When she spoke, Lisa's voice was gentler. "This is a time for family," she said. "Ronni will call you when she gets home."

But she doesn't have a family! Hannah wanted to say. *She only has you and your boyfriend! She needs her friends!* But Hannah couldn't speak. She turned on her squeaky heel and fled.

She held her tears in check through the hall and down the elevator until she stumbled into the coffee shop located in the lobby. As soon as she saw her dad sitting at a back table with a paper cup of coffee and one of those free newspapers, she lost the battle. Tears cascaded down her cheeks, her chest heaved with sobs.

Her dad stood. "What happened?"

"Lisa wouldn't let m-me see her," she stammered. "She's really mad." She launched herself into his arms, just like when she was little and she'd fallen off the swing or crashed her bike.

Her dad let her cry on his jacket, stroking her hair and softly shushing her. "Don't worry, sweetie. This will all blow over." Hannah felt a little better. She pulled away and nodded: it would blow over; it would all be fine. But just as she allowed herself to feel comforted, her dad checked his watch. "We'd better get home. The police will be coming by soon."

jeff

THE NEXT DAY

"You don't have to be nervous," Jeff said, his eyes on the road. "The cops just want to know what happened. They're not trying to get you into any trouble."

"They're trying to get you and mom into trouble," Hannah muttered from the passenger seat.

Jeff let his breath out through his lips. "They just want to know if we were responsible for what happened. And we obviously weren't." He glanced over at his daughter. She stared straight ahead, not meeting his gaze. He suddenly felt awkward, compelled to fill the silence. "Just tell them that you each sneaked in a small amount of alcohol, and cumulatively, it had a bad effect on Ronni."

"What about the champagne you gave us?"

"I wouldn't mention it."

"What about the other girls? What if one of them mentions it?"

"They won't." He sounded more confident than he felt. He sounded so confident that Hannah swiveled in her seat to face him.

"What did you say to my friends?" Her voice was angry, her pretty face dark and accusing when he looked over at her.

"Nothing . . . I just said that it wasn't worth talking about. It's not like one bottle of sparkling wine between five of you caused Ronni's accident."

Hannah turned away and stared out the side window. "So you want me to lie to the police. . . ."

She was upset and scared and she was taking it out on him. It was perfectly normal for a girl her age. He kept his voice calm. "It's safest just to say that you can't remember who brought what."

"Except you. We remember that you gave us nothing."

She was crossing the line into bitchy. "Tell them what you want then. Lay this all on me," he growled. "Your mom will have a fit. I'll get charged and fined and maybe even go to jail. All because I wanted to do something nice for my daughter."

Hannah didn't respond, but he heard her sniffling. Finally, she mumbled through her tears, "I won't say anything."

His heart twisted in his chest. He'd been too harsh. He was tense and on edge. If only he hadn't bought that fucking champagne. This morning, before his run—just a half hour to help him cope with the stress—he'd gone downstairs to examine the carnage. It was then that he saw it, that piece of clear glass wrapped in pink foil, lying in the detritus like a bullet cartridge. He'd picked it up and gingerly placed it in the pocket of his hoodie. On his run, he'd deposited it in a park trash can about three miles from the house. He felt like a criminal, but better safe than sorry. But where was the rest of the bottle? Where were the other bottles?

He glanced over at Hannah, her forehead still pressed against the passenger window. "It's all going to be fine," he said, patting her leg. "But the police will want to know where you got the drugs."

Hannah looked over at him and spoke in a flat voice. "I can't remember who brought what."

THE OFFICERS ARRIVED shortly after Jeff and Hannah. Surprisingly, they weren't the same ones who had interviewed them at the hospital. These two were both male: a slightly chubby white guy in a uniform and an athletic African American in a sport coat. Jeff tried not to read too much into their dress, but didn't detectives usually wear street clothes? There was no way they'd elevated this incident, was there? The officers introduced themselves as Inspectors Bahar and Davis. *Inspectors*. But wouldn't their differing outfits indicate a difference in rank? He'd have to look up police dress code after they left.

It had tortured Kim not to clean up the blood, glass, and vomit in the basement, but she had dutifully complied. Jeff and his spouse hovered near the door as the policemen surveyed "the scene." The men wandered through the rooms, bending over to peer at the shards of glass on the floor, examining the blood, the puke, but touching nothing. No one took notes, which Jeff found encouraging. Eventually, Davis, the fit cop in street clothes, addressed them. "We need to speak to you and your daughter."

They all sat at one end of the massive, reclaimed-wood dining table, Jeff, Kim, and Hannah facing the two inspectors. Jeff didn't know where Aidan was. Kim had obviously sent him out somewhere to spare him the trauma of his family's interrogation. The policemen covered most of the same ground that their colleagues had the night of the incident. They were thorough but sounded slightly bored: a good sign. As before, Kim was laying it on thick.

"We clearly set the ground rules. No drinking, drugs, porn, or boys." She shot Hannah a look. "We assumed the girls would follow the rules. Hannah's never been in trouble before. She's an excellent student. . . . She plays the piano." Kim seemed to think that anyone who played the piano was beyond reproach. Had she never heard of Jerry Lee Lewis?

Inspector Bahar, in the uniform, turned to Hannah. "How much alcohol was at your party?"

"I don't know. Some vodka. And whiskey. Some champagne."

"Can we see the empty bottles?"

Hannah answered, "We got rid of them."

Thank God . . . But when? And how?

Inspector Davis read Jeff's mind. "How did you get rid of them? And when?"

All eyes were on Hannah now. She looked small and terrified. She stared at her fingers, picking at her chipped nail polish. It was black. Since when did she start wearing black nail polish? He'd have to ask Kim about it. "I put the vodka in a stainless-steel water bottle. It's back in the cupboard, I guess. We put the other bottles in the recycling bin in the alley. Before Ronni fell."

The inspector addressed Kim. "When does your recycling get picked up?"

"Wednesdays."

"So the bottles should still be there?"

"Why do you need the bottles?" Jeff asked. He was going for a casual tone, but his voice sounded tense and high-pitched in his own ears.

"To verify quantities. If we found six empty vodka bottles, we'd suspect your daughter was lying."

Bahar stood up. "I'll go."

Kim jumped up, too. "I'll show you where it is."

The others sat quietly as Kim led the uniformed officer out the back door. Inspector Davis turned to Hannah. "Your mom seems pretty strict."

It was Jeff who answered, "She is."

The inspector allowed himself a smirk before addressing Hannah again. "Is there anything you'd like to tell me while she's not here?"

Hannah shrugged. "No."

"Or without your dad here?"

Jeff half stood. "I can go. . . ." He felt so eager to please this policeman, so eager to prove that he had nothing to hide. It was bordering on pathetic. And probably making him look guilty.

"No," Hannah said, eyes fixed on her nail polish.

"Where did you buy the drugs?"

"I didn't buy them. Someone had them. I don't even know who. . . . Ronni took some, I guess. I didn't see."

Davis leaned back in his chair, his eyes fixed on Hannah. "So you've told us everything?" Hannah nodded. Davis continued, "Because if we find out later that you've kept something from us—"

"I've told you everything!" Hannah blurted. She looked the officer in the eye. "Ronni wanted to get wasted. She had more than the rest of us. She was stupid. We were all stupid. None of us will ever do it again."

Inspector Davis held Hannah's gaze but said nothing. It was probably a police tactic designed to pressure suspects into divulging more information. Any second now, Hannah would throw up her hands and say: "Okay, okay, my dad bought us champagne, too! That's what really tipped Ronni over the edge!"

"I'm glad to hear that," Davis said, but he didn't look glad. He looked disapproving. And suspicious. But that could have been through the lens of Jeff's guilty conscience.

Kim and Inspector Bahar returned. The inspector spoke. "There are no bottles out there."

Jeff responded quickly. "There are quite a few vagrants in the area. You put something worth a couple of cents in the alley and it's gone in a flash."

"It's true," Kim said. "The Terrace and Annex house a lot of low-income people. They've even come into the backyard when we've left a few beer cans outside."

The inspectors shared an unreadable look and Jeff realized

how he and Kim sounded. Snobby. Elitist. He hoped these cops weren't part of the anti-gentrification contingent that resented the influx of tech professionals into formerly working-class neighborhoods. Thankfully, Davis clapped his hands on his knees. "I think we're done here." He stood, signaling the end of the interrogation.

Kim and Jeff trailed them to the door. Hannah scurried upstairs—to text her friends or maybe cry some more. Davis handed Kim a business card. "If you think of anything else that might be relevant . . ."

"Of course."

"Thanks for your cooperation," Bahar said, reaching for the door handle.

Jeff had to say something. He couldn't let them walk out without knowing where he and Kim stood. "So what happens now?" The officers paused. Jeff felt Kim's disapproving glare on him, but he plowed ahead. "Are we in any sort of trouble here? Do we need to get a lawyer?"

Davis spoke. "We've found nothing to date that would deem you criminally responsible or negligent."

"Thank you," Jeff said. He felt, and sounded, vindicated. The officers left, and he closed the door behind them, turning the lock.

He looked at his wife and his own relief reflected back at him. The moment seemed to call for something, some kind of gesture or statement to mark their absolution. He reached out and patted Kim's shoulder. She smiled back at him.

"I'm going for a swim," he said.

kim

FOUR DAYS AFTER

On Wednesday, Kim picked up the phone and called Lisa. She had already made several overtures—sending a seventy-five-dollar bouquet to the hospital (anything over a hundred dollars would have implied culpability), and dropping a batch of home-baked healthy cookies (oatmeal, raisin, and flax seed, sweetened with maple syrup) at the hospital's reception desk. But she needed to talk to Lisa; she needed to explain. Her heart thudded in her chest as Lisa's phone rang in her ear.

"Hi. You've reached Lisa Monroe. Sorry I can't take your call right now. . . ."

Voice mail. Kim was somewhat relieved. It would be easier to deliver her rehearsed speech without interruption. Of course, voice mail could mean that Lisa was still angry and screening her, but she couldn't worry about that now. She had things to say.

"Hey! It's me, Kim." She sounded too breezy, too casual. She lowered her register. "I wanted to check on Ronni. And on you. If there's anything we can do, or anything you need, just call. We're here for you. . . ." She paused, gathered her courage. "Hannah can't wait until Ronni's back at school. She really misses her. This whole thing has been hard on Hannah. On all of us. Of course, it's nothing compared to what you're going through. . . ." Her heart thudded louder as she plunged ahead. "The police were here. They said that what happened was a terrible accident, but we're not responsible. We weren't negligent. I mean, it's not like it was a *party* party. There were only a few girls. We had no way of knowing they were planning to drink. . . ." She trailed off. God, she hoped she didn't sound smug . . . or worse, triumphant. "Anyway, I hope you'll reach out if you need anything. Or just want to talk. About anything. I'm here for you." She hung up.

She was suddenly aware of a pungent odor—dirty sneakers—that announced her son's presence. When things settled down, she'd have a talk with him about personal cleanliness. On second thought, Jeff should handle that conversation. It was a father's job to teach his son to shave, to use deodorant, to buy odor eaters for his smelly shoes. . . . Her son's malodorous aura was just one more example of Jeff's failings as a partner.

"Shouldn't you be leaving for school?"

"I'm riding my skateboard. It only takes five minutes."

"Have you got your lunch?" Kim hustled toward the fridge.

Aidan perched on a barstool. "What's going on with Ronni?" He had been spared the drama of that night, thanks to his sleepover, but Kim had filled him in.

Kim peered into the fridge, keeping her tone light. "I think she's fine, but I haven't been able to get ahold of Lisa."

"Is Lisa mad at you?"

"She has no reason to be." Kim found the lunch containers she'd packed for her son the night before and extracted them.

"Wouldn't *you* be mad if something bad happened to me when I slept over at Marcus's house?"

"That's different." Kim deliberately placed the lunch containers in Aidan's insulated lunch bag.

"Different how?"

Kim closed the lunch bag and faced her son across the breakfast bar. "You are a good kid with no history of risk-taking behavior. Ronni, on the other hand . . ." She trailed off.

"So you blame Ronni?"

"I never said that," she snapped. Why was her thirteen-year-old son grilling her like some criminal? Twisting her words to make her seem like the villain? On the upside, maybe Aidan could have a future as a prosecutor?

Kim lowered her voice, spoke firmly but calmly. "We are not responsible for what happened to Ronni, Aidan. The police cleared us. Lisa may be upset, but when Ronni is better and back at school, she'll come around."

She observed her son taking this in, processing it. A flicker of concern contorted his features, but he seemed somewhat appeased. "I should get going."

Kim handed him his lunch bag and kissed his cheek. "Have a good day."

KIM PACKED UP her laptop in preparation for her meeting with Tony. Normally, she would have fussed with her appearance. She wanted to look good, but not like she was trying to look good. She wanted Tony to think she was low maintenance and naturally pretty. But today, she'd let her hair dry into its myriad of waves and cowlicks and dispensed with the carefully applied, muted makeup. Usually, she felt excited to see him, anticipating the illicit thrill of sitting across from him in a quiet coffee shop, their knees almost touching under the table, their hands fluttering self-consciously between their coffee mugs and keyboards. Typically, these sessions consisted of a modicum of work and a lot of harmless flirting. But today, her heart wasn't in it. As she drove to their meeting place in Bernal Heights, her heart felt heavy and tired, too old and worn for playful banter or innuendo.

When she entered the faux-rustic café and saw him sitting there, sipping his cappuccino and staring at his computer screen, she felt a surprising rush of . . . well, *fondness* was the only word that seemed appropriate. It wasn't strong enough to be love—she had only known the guy five minutes! And given recent events, she couldn't muster any lust. But she knew then that this was more than just a flirtation. There was something real between them, a profound friendship, if nothing else. She could talk to Tony, she could open up and he would listen without judgment. She should have been able to talk to her husband that way, and maybe she could have, if Jeff ever stopped working or working out. Or stretching or showering after working out. Or making a protein smoothie after working out. He never seemed to stop moving.

Tony looked up and smiled, and something twisted in Kim's chest. He stood and held his arms out for a perfunctory hug, their standard greeting, but as she walked into his brief embrace, she felt herself collapse against him. Emotion clogged her throat and her eyes were wet. She wanted to lean against his chest; it was narrower than Jeff's, lean and hairy, she could tell from the opening of his shirt. She wanted to bury her face in that hairy chest and weep.

Tony held her at arm's length. "Hey . . . What's going on?"

"It's fine. I'm fine."

"I got you an Americano misto."

Oh God, he remembered her favorite drink. Maybe she *did* love him. She let him maneuver her to a chair, where she sat and proceeded to spill the events of the past Saturday.

Tony could have said, "I told you so," but he didn't. Instead, he muttered, "Jesus . . . How is the girl?"

"I think Ronni's doing okay, but I don't actually know. Lisa's so angry she won't talk to me. She won't even let Hannah visit Ronni."

"Lisa wants someone to blame. It makes her feel better. But this wasn't your fault."

Kim nodded. "The police cleared us of any wrongdoing. But still . . . I should have checked on them. But I'd had some wine and half an Ambien. I just went to sleep." Her voice was trembling. "I thought it would be okay. . . ."

"You told the girls the rules, and they broke them. That's what teenagers do."

"Not Hannah, though." Kim sniffled. "Hannah's a good girl.

She *was* a good girl. We talked about everything. About drinking and drugs and the problems they cause. I thought she understood . . . I thought I'd done my job. I feel like I failed her."

"You didn't."

Kim let out a sardonic snort. "With a dad like Jeff, what did I expect?"

"You can't put this on him."

"Can't I?" Kim was suddenly filled with an intense anger at her husband. She leaned forward and lowered her voice. "Last year, I found a vial of LSD in his pants."

"Really?"

"It was just a little bit, heavily diluted. He got it from some hipster colleague from Austin. But still . . ."

"Is he a druggie?"

Kim sighed. "I don't think so. He called it microdosing. I looked it up, and it's a thing in the tech world. But I laid down the law. I mean, we all had fun in our twenties, but we're in our forties now. We have kids and responsibilities. We're part of the community. We can't do crap like that anymore."

Tony sipped his coffee. "Amanda would kill me."

"I wanted to kill Jeff."

"She used to work in family law. She saw some stuff. Parents with drug problems, kids abused and neglected . . ."

"That's horrible."

"It was. She couldn't take it after a while, so she became a civil litigator. Less trauma."

"Thankfully, the kids know nothing about Jeff's *indiscretion*. No one does. We dealt with it ourselves. Quietly. But maybe

Hannah inherited Jeff's risk-taking behavior? Maybe she's genetically predisposed to take chances and make bad choices?"

Tony smiled. "But half her genes are yours, and you never take chances or make bad choices."

Kim bit her lip. "Sometimes I do. . . ." Their eyes connected. Three innocuous little words but the intention was clear: Kim was about to make a very bad choice.

Tony moved his hand, ever so slightly, so that his last two fingers rested on top of hers. It was a small gesture, and yet, so intimate. There was a table between them, a room full of people around them, but their four fingers were an electric point of connection. Tony's voice was husky. "Do you want to get out of here?"

"Yes."

"You sure?"

No, she wasn't sure. If she thought about it, for even a moment, she would change her mind. This wasn't Kim. She wasn't reckless or even particularly spontaneous. She lived her life according to a plan, following a code of morals and ethics; she always put her family first. But look where that had gotten her: her marriage was a sham, her daughter was sneaky and deceitful, her son refused to cut his hair and smelled of feet. . . .

Right now, Kim didn't want to think. She wanted to plunge ahead, not knowing where they were going or what they would do when they got there. She wanted to indulge herself in the excitement and possibility of this moment, to forget everything that had happened—with Ronni, with Jeff, with all of it.

"I'm sure," she said.

They moved outside without a word. "We'll take my car," Tony said. Kim liked how he was taking charge. It was manly and sexy. She felt like she would follow him anywhere, do anything he asked. He could take her to some cheap, by-the-hour hotel room, and demand she strip. "Take me in your mouth," he would growl at her, and she would do it. With Jeff, she avoided blow jobs as often as possible. Her jaw clicked awkwardly, and it took him forever to orgasm. But in this scenario, the thought of it was positively thrilling! Of course, she may have been taking a leap from the innocent brushing of their fingers to oral sex in a tawdry hotel. Tony might just be taking her toward the beach for a scenic walk. But she knew it was more than that. She obediently followed him toward his Volkswagen hatchback.

Something made her slow her pace. It wasn't that she recognized the vehicle that was pulling into the parking lot—in this neighborhood, the low-emissions Subaru was almost as ubiquitous as the reusable shopping bags draped over every other arm—but some Spidey sense was telling her to proceed with caution. So she was standing stock-still when the car parked beside her and the door opened.

"Coming?" Tony asked, just as Emily Banyen emerged from the silver vehicle. Jesus, San Francisco was a small town sometimes.

"Emily!" Kim said, a smile plastered across her lips.

"Kim! Hi!" Emily approached and squeezed both Kim's hands. "How are you holding up?"

Emily had obviously heard what had happened to Ronni. She had been the girls' fifth-grade teacher and Hannah and Caitlin's volleyball coach. Hannah and her friends had adored Ms. Banyen.

Kim had been in charge of the fifth-grade gift that year: a world's best teacher T-shirt with Emily's beaming face on the front and the entire class's signatures on the back in indelible ink. Kim hadn't seen Emily since she left teaching to have her baby. God, that baby must be four or five by now.

"Jeanette was delivering a baby on Saturday night when Ronni was brought in," Emily explained. Of course . . . Emily's partner, Jeanette, was an obstetrician at the California Pacific Medical Center. That was why Emily had been able to leave her teaching job so readily. Kim had admired Emily and Jeanette's relationship more than once. Not that she found herself attracted to women (though she'd once felt something stirring between her and a bisexual colleague at the agency one drunken night years ago), but it had to be simpler being married to another woman, didn't it?

"It was pretty scary," Kim said.

"It sounds horrifying."

"Hannah's been really upset. She's so sensitive."

Emily squeezed Kim's arm. "The poor thing. She's a sweet girl. And Ronni is, too."

Emily obviously hadn't seen Ronni in a while. With her cleavage and pancake makeup, *sweet* wasn't the adjective that sprang to Kim's mind. But Kim smiled and nodded.

Emily continued. "When Jeanette told me, I was so upset. I sent Ronni's mom some flowers. How's she doing?"

"I haven't seen her, actually. I sent flowers. And cookies." Kim could feel her face turning red and she was eager to shift the topic of conversation. Her eyes flitted to Tony, still standing beside his car. "This is my colleague, Tony. We work together."

“Hi,” Emily said.

“Emily was Hannah’s fifth-grade teacher.”

Tony nodded. “Hey.”

“Tony’s a designer,” Kim continued. “I’m copywriting now. Freelance. We have a contract with Apex Outerwear. We do their flyers.” Emily’s expression was bemused, mildly perturbed. Had Kim been babbling? Going on about herself? She had. She’d been rude and she would remedy it now. “How’s your little boy?” she asked.

Emily seemed taken aback by the question. “He’s good.”

“They grow up so fast. It seems like only yesterday Hannah was in your class and now she’s”—What was she going to say? Drinking? Taking ecstasy? Finally—“in tenth grade.”

“This is a traumatic experience for the girls to go through at such a tender age.”

“They’ve learned a valuable lesson,” Kim said. “The police have looked into it and we’re not responsible. It was really unfortunate, but it’s time we all moved forward.”

“Kim . . .” Emily said, then paused, flustered. “I’m sorry, but I’m surprised you’re taking this so lightly.”

She sounded like the schoolteacher she was, a schoolteacher expressing her disappointment in the fifth grader who colored both Utah and Arizona orange when shading her map of America.

“I’m not taking it lightly.” Kim’s voice was controlled, but she was clearly affronted. “Jeff and I are very upset. We’re disappointed by Hannah’s behavior and we’re dealing with it. Lisa knows we’re here for her. Frankly, there’s not much more we can do.”

Emily's cheeks flushed. "Oh God . . . You don't know, do you?"

"Know what?"

The schoolteacher took a breath, then rested her hand on Kim's forearm. "Ronni lost her eye last night."

lisa

FIVE DAYS AFTER

Lisa hadn't had a cigarette in sixteen years. Okay, that wasn't entirely true. She'd quit smoking when she found out she was pregnant with Ronni and abstained throughout Ronni's infancy. But when her daughter was a toddler there had been the occasional butt (never in the house, never around the baby). Lisa had allowed herself to slip back into her partying ways for a few months then: some drinking, a little weed, nothing hard. . . . That was when Curtis was still in the picture. She had thought she had some support. She had thought she deserved to have a little fun.

Lisa took another deep drag on the cigarette. She wasn't even sure she was enjoying it, but the nicotine coursing through her system was calming her, or at least numbing her slightly to the trauma of Ronni's surgery. Standing there, in the hospital's designated smoking area, her mind drifted back to Curtis Rey. If only Lisa hadn't let herself get knocked up by such a huge loser,

Ronni's dad would be here right now. Not as Lisa's partner—she had Allan, and in no universe could she envision herself married for the past seventeen years—but as Ronni's father. The girl could have used the support; and Lisa would have appreciated some relief.

Their relationship had fallen apart mere moments after Ronni was born. Curtis had a temper when he drank, which was pretty regularly. Had she been drinking less herself, she would have been more vigilant on the birth control front. The guy had some good qualities of course, primarily his chiseled abs, caramel-colored skin, and drone-like ability to find her clitoris. But she couldn't have a sporadically employed, angry drunk around her baby, no matter how good the sex was. She had kicked him out promptly.

Still, Lisa had envisioned Curtis playing a small supporting role in their child's life. And at first, he'd seemed perfectly capable of looking after his daughter once every couple of weeks. If he couldn't support them financially, at least he could babysit once in a while so Lisa could have some semblance of a social life. If she was honest with herself, those nights out were as much about punishing Curtis as they were about her own enjoyment. It took two people to make a baby. Why was she the only one making sacrifices to raise her?

She'd left Ronni in her father's care on a handful of occasions without incident. When she arrived to pick her daughter up, Curtis would hand over his charge, her hair uncombed, last night's pajamas covered in strained peaches or gooey cookie dried to cement-hardness. Ronni was a mess, but she was fine. Until she wasn't. . . .

It wasn't quite a migraine but a persistent headache that had sent Lisa home early that night. In retrospect, it must have been her maternal instinct, an instinct that had deserted her the night of Hannah's party. But fourteen years ago, a persistent dull ache behind her eyes had kept Lisa from enjoying the nightclub, drinking and flirting alongside her childless friends. She recalled a visiting football team—the Denver Broncos or someone—the place full of rich, good-looking guys with money to spend on drinks and Baggies of cocaine in their pockets. It had the potential to be an amazing night, but somehow, Lisa had known that her daughter needed her. With her friends lined up to do shots with the athletes, Lisa had slipped out to her car.

She could have gone home and had a good night's sleep, but something—mother's intuition—had urged her toward Curtis's. There was an emptiness in her chest (she eventually learned to associate this with the nightclub scene and casual hookups), and she needed to hold her daughter. She needed to take Ronni home, to hear her soft breath as she lay in the crib that was squeezed into the corner of Lisa's single bedroom, to wake up to her baby's cheerful gurgle. She smoked a cigarette as she drove, the window rolled down, cold night air blasting her face. It was the last cigarette she would have, until today.

Lisa looked around at her fellow smokers. Most of them were patients, identifiable by the hideous blue gowns. A few had IVs attached to their arms, one was in a wheelchair. . . . They were probably suffering from emphysema or lung cancer or some other cigarette-related malady, but still, they stood in the chill March air, their bare legs covered in goose bumps, and smoked. She stubbed the cigarette out in a tall, overflowing ashtray and headed inside.

As she traversed the shiny, squeaky hospital hallway, she remembered pulling into Curtis's driveway that night. Her dashboard clock read 1:23 A.M., she remembered the figure so clearly—1, 2, 3. A lamp was burning in the bungalow's living room, the faint glow visible through the bent and tattered blinds. Curtis was undoubtedly lounging on the sofa, playing some violent video game and sucking on a beer. He was harmless when he drank beer; only hard liquor brought out his ugly side. He was a child, really. Lisa had been an idiot to ever get involved with him.

The first sign of trouble was the pounding music she heard as she approached the door. How was Ronni supposed to sleep through that? She knocked, but there was no response. Of course, Curtis couldn't hear her over the thudding bass. She turned the handle and found the door unlocked. She shoved it open and stepped inside.

Curtis was not on the sofa as expected. Instead, a girl, about Lisa's age, with greasy blond hair and blank eyes leaned against the bony shoulder of a guy with a shaved head and a Motörhead T-shirt.

"Where's Curtis?" Lisa screamed over the music. "Where's my baby?"

The two stared at her mutely. Maybe they couldn't hear her over the stereo? Or maybe the drugs they were so obviously on had rendered them incapable of comprehending language. Neither of them looked particularly surprised that a stranger had just burst into the living room. They were numb, completely fucked-up. Lisa glanced at the coffee table and saw tin foil, lighters, a plastic bag containing a white substance, and a half-empty bottle of vodka. Jesus Christ.

Lisa hurried past them to the back bedroom where Ronni always slept. As she moved down the hallway, she heard the muffled screams. It was Ronni crying, crying for help, crying for her mother. . . . Had she cried for Lisa as she crashed through the glass table in Kim Sanders's basement? Had she screamed for her mom as the glass sliced into her hand, her face, her eye? No one would say; no one was talking. But that night, fourteen years ago, she had cried and Lisa had run to save her.

The air in Ronni's makeshift bedroom was close and stuffy. The baby's screams were still muted as Lisa fumbled for the light switch. She flicked it on, bathing the room in the glare of a dusty bare lightbulb. That's when she saw that a heavy blanket had been thrown over Ronni's portable playpen. Someone, the blond girl or her skinny boyfriend, had placed it there to stifle the noise. Lisa whipped it off and saw her baby. She was lying on her back, her face red and covered in tears and snot. Her dark curls were pasted to her forehead, and her onesie was damp with a combination of perspiration, tears, and drool. Ronni flinched as the light shone into her face.

"It's okay, baby." Lisa dove into the playpen and picked up her daughter. She was instantly assaulted by the smell. Ronni's diaper was overflowing, shit coating the back of her pajamas up to the collar. "It's okay . . . ," she whispered, making shushing noises as she wrapped a blanket around the little girl. Ronni's tiny chest was still heaving with sobs, but she was starting to settle. She clung to Lisa, burying her moist face in her mother's neck.

Lisa's hand was covered in shit, but she didn't care. It struck her that, pre-Ronni, this scenario would have been unimaginable. She probably would have chopped her hand off if it had this much poop on it. But motherhood had changed her. It had made her tolerate things like poo and barf and snot and sleeplessness. And it had made her fierce, capable of killing to protect her child. With her baby held tightly in her arms, she stormed toward the front door.

The guy and girl were still on the sofa. The girl's eyes were closed, though she sat upright and didn't seem to be sleeping. Lisa paused. "You can tell Curtis that he'll never see his kid again," she yelled over the music.

The girl's eyes slowly opened. Both of them looked at Lisa dully. Finally, the girl spoke. "Something stinks."

Curtis did see Ronni again. Once. He brought the playpen over to Lisa's and tried to explain. He'd been given tickets to see a band. He thought his friends could look after Ronni for a couple of hours. He thought she'd sleep the whole time. How was he to know she was going to shit herself and scream her head off?

Lisa pushed his chest, shoving him toward the door. "Stay the fuck away from my daughter."

"Fine by me," he growled. He stormed out of the apartment, the door slamming in his wake. Not once did Curtis look back at Ronni, sitting in her high chair with a bowl of macaroni, witnessing the whole exchange. Lisa realized then that Curtis really didn't give a shit, not about Ronni and not about her. Some small kernel of decency had kept him semi-available, had pressed him to accept the occasional babysitting gig, but he didn't love Ronni, not really. There was no one Lisa could count on. She was all Ronni had in the world. And vice versa.

When Lisa reached her daughter's hospital room, her friend Yeva was standing in the hall. "I heard about the infection . . ." Yeva rushed toward her and wrapped her in a warm hug. It was a long, lingering embrace, and Lisa knew that Yeva's eyes were closed, that she was emanating love from her heart and trying to wrap Lisa in it. Yeva was a yoga friend. They hugged friends, acquaintances, and even strangers the way most people hugged only newborn babies or kittens. Full-on. A month ago, Lisa had wanted to be filled with that kind of love, to give hugs like that. It seemed so silly now, all the mindfulness, presence, acceptance. . . . Yoga: the opiate of the West Coast.

Finally, Yeva released her. "How's Ronni doing?"

"She's been sedated. I don't think it's really sunk in."

"She's strong," Yeva said, squeezing Lisa's hand. "She'll overcome this."

"When you were sixteen, how would you have handled losing your eye?" The question came out more pointed than Lisa had intended.

Yeva said, "Ronni is a kind, beautiful spirit. She can still do anything she puts her mind to."

Lisa's voice wavered. "All she ever talked about was becoming a model. So that's out now."

"Why?"

Lisa shot her a look. "Have you seen a model with a glass eye?"

Yeva pressed her lips together but didn't answer. "I brought supplies," she said, digging in the canvas bag under her arm. She extracted a stainless-steel thermos and passed it to Lisa. "Ginger tea with licorice root. It's calming."

Lisa accepted the thermos. "Thanks." But it was going to take more than herbs to calm her. Her daughter was permanently disfigured; she was disabled. . . . Yeva could sugarcoat it all she wanted, but it didn't change the facts.

Yeva was still fishing in the bag. "I brought some teas for Ronni, too. Uplifting blends. Calming blends. And I brought her a book of affirmations." She handed a small hardcover book to Lisa. "If she picks a few that she likes, I'll print them out and we can post them around her hospital room."

Lisa looked at her friend: so sweet, so positive, but, ultimately, so ineffectual. "You're really nice," she said.

Yeva flushed a little. "I want to be here for you."

Of course she did. Good deeds caused a serotonin surge, not to mention karma points. "I know you do. But I think that Ronni and I should be alone for a few days. While she processes all this . . ."

"Okay." Yeva sounded slightly relieved. "Just text me if you need anything else. I could bring you some food. Some green juice? Or hummus wraps?"

"I'm fine, but I'll let you know."

As Lisa walked her friend to the elevator, Yeva continued her upbeat monologue. "This doesn't change who Ronni is. She's an amazing, beautiful soul, and whatever happens on the outside doesn't change that. Tell her that this will only make her stronger.

She may go on to even greater happiness because she was able to overcome this challenge."

They stopped at the elevators and Lisa pushed the button. "Don't worry," she said, giving Yeva's arm a reassuring squeeze. "I know how to take care of my daughter."

hannah

TEN DAYS AFTER

"Oh my god. Did you hear?" It was Lauren, looking airbrushed and photoshopped as she approached Hannah's locker. She was wearing skinny jeans, a low-cut T-shirt with a chambray shirt unbuttoned over top of it. It was a casual outfit, but on Lauren, it looked so stylish, so pulled together. Hannah, in her tights and hoodie, instantly felt frumpy.

"I can't believe it," Hannah responded. "It's so horrible."

"It's un-fucking-believable."

"It was some hospital infection," Hannah said, her throat clogging with emotion. "If they didn't take her eye, she could have died."

Lauren placed her polished fingers on Hannah's arm. "Don't feel bad. This isn't your fault."

Hannah nodded her thanks, but she did feel bad, very bad. Ronni had come to her birthday party and lost her freaking eyeball. How could she feel anything but terrible? But Hannah also knew it wasn't her fault. She'd felt pressured by Lauren and Ronni to raise the bar on the party, to turn it from a simple sleepover into some debauched rave. But, obviously, Hannah could never say that.

"It's so fucked-up," Lauren said. "How do you live without your eye?"

"Lots of people do."

"Not kids our age, though. Do you know a single kid with one eye?"

"No . . . but my mom says Ronni will be able to do everything she did before. And glass eyes look a lot more real now."

A burst of laughter escaped from Lauren's shiny mouth. "Oh my god! I can't even think about a glass eye. It makes me want to hurl."

Hannah giggled, too, but it was a nervous, almost hysterical sound. "It's super gross. But we have to be there for her. We have to support her."

"Totally." Lauren ran her fingers through her long hair and Hannah caught a whiff of expensive shampoo. "Did the police talk to your parents?"

"Yeah. They got the all clear. Have they talked to you?"

"Not yet." The girl fiddled with her gold, double-heart pendant: PLEASE RETURN TO TIFFANY & CO. It was a gift from Lauren's dad . . . for her half birthday or getting a C+ or something. "They've called my dad's place a few times, but he doesn't want me to speak to them."

"Why not?"

"He wants me to talk to his lawyer first."

Hannah's stomach plunged. "Why would you need to talk to a lawyer?"

Lauren shrugged. "I don't know. He doesn't want me to get into any trouble or whatever."

"Why would *you* get in trouble?" Hannah's voice was strained.

"I don't know. . . ." Lauren shrugged again. "You know how dads are."

"Yeah."

"Except your dad—he seems pretty chill."

Hannah thought about her dad and the champagne he had given them. *I was trying to be nice*, he'd said. Trying to be *cool* was more like it. She recalled the night of the party, her dad's silly jokes and snide comments behind her mom's back. . . . At the time, she'd felt an affinity with him. But now, after all that had happened, his behavior was just plain weird.

Lauren was peering past her. "Here come Noah and Adam."

Hannah turned to watch the boys approaching. They were both tall, good-looking, and walked with the confident gait of the popular. Noah smiled directly at Hannah, and she felt her stomach flutter on command. When he reached her, he draped a proprietary arm over her shoulders. Hannah stiffened. Shit. She wanted this to feel natural and comfortable, but Noah's proximity made her so tense. His arm was so heavy. And she could smell the Axe coming from his armpits.

"What's up, ladies?" Adam said.

"We were just talking about Ronni's eye," Lauren said. "Or lack thereof . . ."

Adam laughed and gave Lauren a playful shove. "You're bad."

Noah chuckled, too, then became somber. "Sucks."

"Totally sucks," Adam added.

There was a pause where no one spoke; they just stared at the floor feeling the suckiness of it all. Noah coughed into his free hand. "So . . . no one knows what really happened that night, right?"

Hannah's head jerked up. "Of course not. I mean, I definitely haven't told anyone."

"Me neither. And I won't," Lauren said.

"Good," Adam said. "But what about those other girls?"

"Those fucking nerds won't say anything," Lauren answered quickly. "And Caitlin brought her mom's Xanax, so she's just as guilty."

"They won't tell," Hannah said, but her voice was weak. Marta and Caitlin were good people. They didn't lie. They didn't keep secrets. . . .

"Trust me," Lauren said, "If they rat us out, I'll make them wish they were never born."

A frisson of anxiety ran through Hannah at the threat, but she couldn't blow it, not now. "Me, too," she said.

"What about Ronni?" Noah asked.

"Apparently, she doesn't remember anything," Lauren said.

"Not surprised," Adam snorted.

"Wait . . . How do you know she doesn't remember?" Hannah asked Lauren. "Have you talked to her?"

"My stepmonster talked to her mom. She was trying to be *supportive*." She did air quotes.

Hannah tried to sound casual when she asked, "How's Ronni doing? What did Lisa say about her?"

"Not much," Lauren said, playing with her pendant again. "Just that Ronni's super depressed and shit . . . and she doesn't remember what happened."

"Thank fuck," Adam said.

Noah gave Adam a teasing punch in the shoulder. "Are you going to visit her? You know she wants you to. . . ."

"Right," Adam said, "I'll be her naughty nurse." He did a couple of pelvic thrusts and they all laughed.

"Ronni would be up for it," Noah said. "I saw the Snapchat she sent you before the party."

Adam crossed his arms across his chest, feigning trauma. "She cybermolested me. I feel violated."

"There are some pamphlets about that in Mrs. Pittwell's office," Hannah quipped. Everyone laughed, and Hannah's chest swelled with a feeling of inclusion.

The bell rang to signal their next class. Noah pulled Hannah closer with that heavy arm and planted a good-bye kiss on her cheek. It was a sweet gesture, but his presence made her feel panicky and claustrophobic . . . and she was pretty sure she was allergic to the chemical, woodsy scent of his deodorant.

That's when she saw them: two ninth-grade girls, pretty and popular in their own cohort, but virtually invisible to their elders. Their eyes drifted over Noah covetously, then landed on Hannah. She could see their envy and admiration. They wanted what she had, they wanted to *be her* . . . and Hannah knew she could never go back to being bland, square, overparented Hannah. She would push away her awkwardness, her cedar-fragrance allergy, and her misplaced sense of responsibility for Ronni's accident, and she would embrace who she had become.

"Later, babe," she said as Noah strolled off down the hall.

Lauren and Hannah moved in the opposite direction toward their classes. "Let's hang later," Lauren said.

"I wish," Hannah said, "but I'm so grounded."

"We can skip last class," Lauren suggested. "What have you got?"

"English. With Morrel."

"Tell him you're too upset about Ronni. He'll totally fall for it."

Fall for it? But they *were* upset about Ronni, right? Though Lauren didn't seem remotely troubled by her best friend's accident or her abrupt absence from their lives. Hannah suddenly grasped the tremulous state of A-list friendships. Ronni was out: Hannah was in. It was what she had wanted all along. . . . She pushed the sick feeling from her stomach and smiled. "Good idea."

kim

ELEVEN DAYS AFTER

There was nothing to be done now. Kim had made every overture to appease Lisa: phone calls, flowers, cookies, e-mails. . . . What was next? Skywriting? An apology blimp? Lisa wanted to be angry; she wanted someone to blame. Kim would give her that. She would tolerate Lisa's cold silence, even her slanderous accusations. Kim's friend Debs had relayed Lisa's comments after their Wednesday-morning session at SoulCycle. Debs had a daughter, Morgan, who was Hannah and Ronni's age, but Morgan had left Hillcrest to attend a gifted program at another school (Kim had her doubts about Morgan's qualifications). Debs's son was a year younger than Aidan but they played on the same elite soccer team. The third in their regular spin-class-followed-by-lattes date was Sheila, a children's book illustrator who had a son the same age as the girls. He ran with the tech/nerd clique so he was persona non grata to Hannah and her friends.

"I ran into Lisa outside the bank," Debs had said, picking at her post-workout treat—a cinnamon bun with cream cheese frosting that would require at least five spin classes to burn off. "There was no way I could avoid her, so I asked how Ronni was."

Kim had tried for a blasé tone, but her voice came out strained. "What did she say?"

"She said that Ronni is struggling. She's in pain. She's depressed."

"God, it's so awful," Sheila chimed in. Sheila was something of a bleeding heart.

Debs continued, "We chatted about Ronni's therapy for a bit, and then Lisa said, 'Be thankful Morgan's not friends with perfect little Hannah. She could end up maimed.'"

Kim had winced but remained calm. A terrible tragedy had happened in her home; that much she would admit. But Jeff and Kim were not legally culpable. They were excellent parents. Their daughter was a good kid who had made a poor choice. Could the same really be said about Ronni?

"Ronni's always been a little big for her britches," Debs offered, and even Sheila had to agree. Ronni had always seemed on the precipice of some kind of downfall: teen pregnancy, a drug problem, an eating disorder—what did one expect with the unconventional upbringing she'd had?

"When the girls were little, Lisa and I used to chat over wine," Kim volunteered, sipping her Americano misto. "She didn't give me any *specifics*, but she alluded to all sorts of stuff in her past: drug problems, abusive relationships, an online-shopping addiction. . . . Lisa has so many issues that Ronni was destined to fall through the cracks, the poor thing." Her companions had echoed the sentiment.

But still, the party was a wake-up call for Kim. Despite her parenting manuals, classes, and seminars, somehow, she had dropped the motherhood ball. Her daughter was rebelling against something. Or nothing. Was her drinking simply a rite of passage? Or had Hannah picked up on the tension in her parents' marriage? Had she somehow sensed Kim's flirtation with adultery? When Kim thought about what could have happened had she and Tony not been intercepted by the world's best fifth-grade teacher, she felt nauseated. Kim had to put that relationship, whatever it was, behind her. She would commit to her family with a renewed focus.

Before her eyebrow-threading appointment, she called her sister, Corrine, mother of the drunken, pants-wetting nephew. If anyone would understand Hannah's brush with alcohol it was Corrine. The sisters weren't close, emotionally or geographically. Corrine had stayed in Oregon, a forty-minute drive from their parents' home. She lived in a modest house with her second husband, a policeman. Corrine worked in administration at an old-folks' home; she was into gardening and canning her own beans and writing angry letters to politicians about fracking. Kim had to admire her sister's earnestness, though she didn't quite get it.

"It's perfectly normal to experiment with drugs and alcohol," Kim's older sibling assured her. "It's where you go from here that matters."

"I've been looking into wilderness leadership programs," Kim said. "If we send Hannah away for the summer, she'll develop self-reliance and self-esteem. She needs to realize how much potential she has and that it can't be squandered with these kind of mistakes."

"She might view it as punishment, though. With Jeremy, we dialogued it out. There were a lot of tears and a lot of hugs . . . but his relationship with substances is really healthy now."

Trust Corrine to recommend *hugs* as a solution to teen drinking. A girl had lost her eye! But Corrine didn't know this. Kim wasn't about to admit the gravity of the situation to her free-spirit sister. "I just think that, if Hannah's away for a while, some of these unhealthy friendships will fall away."

"We chose not to blame Jeremy's friends. We wanted him to really look at his own motivations and actions."

"I should run. I have an appointment."

"Me, too. It's zucchini-jam day."

Kim hung up, feeling irritated. Corrine often had this effect on her. Her sister was like an annoying bug that she wanted to swat away—a holier-than-thou mosquito or a sanctimonious wasp. She was always so *content*. Why? Corrine had grown up in the same shitty house, in the same shitty town that Kim had. Like Kim, Corrine had watched their father bounce from one blue-collar job to the next, until he was inevitably fired for sleeping off another hangover or sneaking out early for happy hour. And Corrine had been there when their mother started eating.

It was just a few "treats" at first. Their mom would come home from her clerical job at a construction company with a box of ice cream and a pie. She'd hand the girls a chocolate bar as compensation, then take the desserts to her room and polish them off. By the time Kim had graduated high school, her mom had eaten her way past three hundred pounds. She couldn't attend Kim's graduation—her knees—but Kim didn't want her there. She was embarrassed of her. When diabetes took her mom out at fifty-seven, Kim had experienced the appropriate sense of loss—but it was combined with a shameful feeling of relief.

Kim had vowed she'd have a different kind of life. Her kids would want for nothing and they'd never be ashamed of their home or their parents. She'd worked hard to rise out of the muck, while Corrine seemed utterly complacent to wallow in it. Her sister's life wasn't *that* bad, but it wasn't that great, either. She knew Corrine's husband drank—what cop doesn't, right?—and obviously her son had picked up his stepfather's habit. And yet, Corrine was so happy. Despite her middling existence, she always made Kim feel inferior. It didn't make sense.

The doorbell distracted Kim from her musings. She moved to the door and opened it to a skinny, pierced, twentysomething with scraggly facial hair. "Kim Sanders?"

"Yes?" The kid was too young and dirty to be a colleague of Jeff's. And too old and druggie-looking to be a friend of Hannah's. She hoped.

The kid handed her an envelope. "You've been served."

She stood frozen as he jogged back to his late-nineties jalopy and drove off. When she'd collected herself, she tore open the envelope. "Jesus Christ," she muttered, shutting the door and reaching for the phone. His voice mail picked up after three rings. "Jeff, it's me." Her voice was loud and shrill in the quiet house. She was grateful that the kids weren't home—Aidan was playing soccer, and Hannah was at piano. "Lisa Monroe is suing us! We just got a summons. . . ." She scanned the letter, found the figure she was searching for. "She wants three million in damages. Three million!" Her voice cracked with emotion. She paused, tried to calm herself, but she was almost hoarse when she asked, "Where are you?" Jeff could have been in a meeting, he could have been with a client, but, more likely, he'd skipped out of work to go running. Or swimming. Or for a ride on his goddamned bike. As usual, her husband was sequestering himself in his training, avoiding his obligations, hiding from the people who needed him. . . . "Call me." She hung up.

Before she could talk herself out of it, she dialed the number. As she listened to it ring, she knew it was a bad idea. She should hang up. She should deal with the summons. She should call her friend, Lara, who was a lawyer—family law—but she'd be able to recommend someone to deal with this complaint. Lara would refer her to a shark, someone who would squash this childish and vindictive action in no uncertain terms. And then Kim could go get her eyebrows done. But Kim didn't hang up. And when she heard his voice, she was flooded with comfort and relief.

"Tony Hoyle."

"I need to see you."

THEY SAT IN his car, parked in a lot at Fort Mason. It could get busy here, tourists and locals drawn to the former army post for its galleries, food trucks, and spectacular views. But on a drizzly Wednesday in March, they had all the privacy they could want.

Tony held her hand under the artifice of comfort, but even in her troubled state, she could feel the heat between them. "We don't have that kind of money. Our homeowners' insurance will pay only two hundred grand for personal injury. What is Lisa thinking?"

"I guess she's thinking that she's got medical bills to pay. And her daughter's going to need physical and emotional therapy. It's going to add up."

"It's not going to add up to three million," Kim snapped, pulling her hand from his. "Lisa's angry, and she wants to make someone pay."

Tony calmly reached for her hand again. "You're right. She's being vindictive."

Kim teared up. "We'll have to sell the house . . . the cars . . . everything."

"It won't come to that. Amanda's worked a lot of these cases. They usually go through mediation or arbitration and end up settling."

For once, Kim didn't feel an uncomfortable twinge at the sound of Amanda's name. "Really? We could get a mediator to talk some sense into Lisa and we'll end up paying a lot less?"

"That's usually how it plays out."

"I hope so. We've worked so hard for everything we have." Even as she said it, it felt like a lie. Jeff had worked hard, of course, but since his technology strategy job at Fin-Tech was his raison d'être, it wasn't exactly a sacrifice. And since he used it as a means to avoid intimate connections with his loved ones, it was hardly admirable. Kim had worked, too. After she left the ad agency, she had raised the kids, cooked, decorated the house, organized their social calendar . . . God, it sounded so meaningless.

She was suddenly aware of Tony's thumb rubbing over hers. It felt comforting, private, and somehow, sensual. She looked at him, and their eyes locked. He was already leaning toward her and she knew it was going to happen this time. Despite her earlier resolve, she felt almost powerless to stop it. Kim was going to cross that line, she was going to be unfaithful. It was just kissing, but in some ways, that was worse. It was more romantic and intimate, less base and instinctual than actual intercourse. She had always looked down on people who got caught screwing around on their spouses. Where was their self-control? They were weak and their moral compasses were askew. Kim had always held herself to a higher standard. . . .

But with Tony's mouth hot and wet on hers, the internal dialogue ceased and her higher standard dropped a few feet. She was in the moment, *feeling* not *thinking* for once. It was intense, passionate, exciting . . . and it was almost a relief. Sitting in a car, kissing a strange man was, more than anything, an escape. *Desperate times*, she thought, as her hand slipped down and unbuckled her seat belt, desperate times. . . .

jeff

ELEVEN DAYS AFTER

Jeff watched the digital read out on the treadmill: 166. 167. 168. . . . At what point would his heart explode? He was in great shape, but he was closing in on fifty. And he was running like he was being chased by something big, something with fangs: a grizzly bear or a lion . . . or a money-grubbing bitch trying to profit off an accident.

He'd been leaving a client meeting when he listened to Kim's message. At first, he'd been stunned. He'd thought this whole mess was behind them when the police gave them the all clear. And now fucking Lisa was suing them for money they didn't have. He'd never cared for Lisa. Even when the girls were little, practicing cartwheels on the lawn while Kim and Lisa supervised on rattan chairs with glasses of rosé, he'd thought she was a flake . . . but a harmless flake. Not so harmless now. Kim must be losing her mind. He should have called her back, he knew that, but he'd gone straight to the Bay Club. He needed to run it out.

Then, suddenly, he wasn't running anymore. His ankle turned or his knee gave out, he wasn't even sure which. But he was falling, his feet scrambling across the moving surface like some cartoon fawn trying to ice-skate. It must have looked hilarious—he'd seen enough YouTube videos of people falling off treadmills to know it did—but it wasn't funny. People died this way. Still, even as he went down, he felt like a fucking idiot.

A young woman in a gym uniform hurried up to him. "Are you okay, sir?" Her concern was sincere, but he could tell she was stifling a giggle.

"Fine."

"You're bleeding."

He looked down at his shin. The skin had been rubbed off on the track, leaving his leg a raw, bloody mess.

"It's fine," he snapped. He hobbled toward the changing room, listening for her laughter in his wake. He heard the girl cough, obviously covering up her mirth.

When Jeff had showered and dressed, the leg still smarted, but he wasn't about to limp. He walked out of the gym with confidence and purpose, even as the fabric of his dress pants brushed against his raw flesh. It hurt like hell, but he strode on. Hopefully, no one would recognize him as the clown who bit it on the treadmill.

The girl, tiny and blond, was standing beside his car. He was almost upon her before he recognized her. What was her name again? "Hey, Jeff," she said.

"Hey." Her presence confused and unnerved him. "Uh . . . Hannah's not with me. She's probably at home."

"I wanted to talk to you." She indicated the car. "Can we sit?"

He took a step toward the Tesla and its door handles obediently popped out. It was odd to invite this kid into his car, but it was even odder that she was there to see him. At a loss, he watched her move to the passenger side of the car and get in. He felt a swell of relief; he really didn't want anyone to see them together. He hopped in and shut his door.

"What's going on"—*Lauren*. That was her name. He added it to the end of his question—"Lauren?"

"I hear you're being sued by Ronni's mom."

"How do you know about that?"

"My stepmom. She's sort of friends with Lisa Monroe now."

Jeff let out a breath through his lips. "Yeah. Unfortunately, we are."

"My dad says that the lawyers might want to interview me. Like as a witness."

"Well, we're a long way from that," Jeff said, though he really had no idea if they were.

"It must blow to get sued by your friend."

He had to chuckle. "It does."

A bug was splattered on the passenger side of the front windshield, something large and spindly: a crane fly maybe? Lauren reached out and touched the glass where the bug's guts, yellow and red, smeared the other side of the pane. She scratched at it with her deep purple nails, like she'd be able to scrape the mess off from the inside. Was there something wrong with this kid?

Was she high? Brain-damaged? Jeff waited. What the hell did this girl want?

"What do you want, Lauren?"

She looked up at him then. Her eyes were gray; her lids sparkled; her lashes were caked with navy-blue goop. When Hannah wore that much makeup, Kim sent her back to her room. But Lauren's parents were obviously more lenient.

"I want to know what you want me to say."

"To whom?"

"To the lawyers or whoever—I don't want to get you into any trouble."

His heart softened. She was a good kid underneath the cool facade. "Kim and I have been cleared by the police. We won't be in any trouble. . . ." He gave her hand a friendly pat. "We'll wait until Ronni's mom calms down and talk about this rationally. I'm sure she'll see sense."

Lauren stared at him intently for a beat. There was no denying she was a pretty kid under all that goop. "What if I told them about the champagne you gave us?"

Jeff's jaw clenched. Seriously? Now this *teenager* was trying to shake him down? "What are you getting at?"

"Would you get into trouble? Would you have to pay Ronni's mom tons of money?"

There was something taunting in her tone, and Jeff wasn't going to stand for it. "Do you want money, too?" His voice was menacing, a growl. "How much?" He dug for his wallet still in his pants pocket.

"No!" She pressed his arm to stop him. "I don't want your money."

"Then what the hell do you want?"

She picked up one of his business cards that he'd carelessly tossed into the console of the car, and played with it. "I won't tell anyone about the champagne," she said, looking up at him then. "And I'll make sure the other girls don't say anything, either. . . ."

Was he supposed to be grateful now? He didn't know how to respond, so he gave a slight nod.

Lauren gave him a small smile. "Can we go get some food or something?"

"No. We can't."

She looked down at the business card again, her long hair obscuring her face as she traced his name with her finger. "I just feel really alone right now. My best friend's in the hospital. My dad's away on business. My mom drinks. . . ." When she finally looked up, her eyes were full of tears. "Can we get some ice cream at least?"

He felt his heart twist. He knew this type of girl: conniving, manipulative, and growing up way too fast. But there was something so lonely in her gray eyes that he couldn't help but pity her.

"Ice cream," he said. "And then I'm taking you home."

lisa

FOURTEEN DAYS AFTER

Lisa hovered near the kitchen counter, observing. Ronni was on the sofa, a blanket over her legs, her eyes glued to the TV. Make that her *eye*—Jesus. She was watching Netflix, some show about teenagers and vampires. She appeared engrossed and, if Lisa hadn't known better, perfectly content. Hoisting the plate and bowl that rested on the Formica countertop, Lisa made her move.

"Snack time," she said, heading to the sofa. Ronni didn't respond, so Lisa set the bowl of hummus and side plate of raw veggies on the coffee table. "You have to eat something, hon."

"I'm not hungry," Ronni mumbled.

"You've barely eaten since you got home. You need to get your strength back."

"Why?" For the first time, her daughter looked away from the TV. Lisa still wasn't used to Ronni's gaze: the left eye looked right into her soul but the right eye remained still and unseeing. The doctors had done their best to repair the socket, but part of the bottom lid had been unsalvageable. To compensate, they had pulled the skin tight, creating a thin, nearly translucent web at the corner of her eye. There was something embryonic about it, something not quite right. The eye surgeon had tried to reassure them. "Ocular prostheses have come a long way," he'd said. "She's lucky." But Ronni didn't feel lucky. And when Lisa looked at her beautiful daughter and her discomfiting stare, she didn't feel lucky, either.

Lisa forced a smile. "You need to get back to school. Get back into your old routine."

Ronni turned back to the vampires. "No way. I can't go back there."

"Honey . . ." Lisa grabbed the remote and paused the show. "Of course you can. You need to learn and be with your friends and have a normal life."

"My *friends*?" Ronni said, and her eyes filled. (Lisa had quickly learned that a glass eye still allowed tear flow.) "I don't have any friends anymore."

Lisa thought about Hannah showing up at the hospital the day after the accident. "I just want to see her, to let her know that I'm here for her," Hannah had said. She'd been upset, on the verge of tears. But Lisa couldn't let that friendship stand, not with everything that was going on. She patted her daughter's leg. "Of course you do. . . ."

"I haven't heard from anyone! I've had like one text from Lauren. She's supposed to be my best friend."

"If she was really your best friend, she'd be there for you."

"She says her parents don't want her caught up in all this mess." She wiped at the tears streaming down her face. "So I'm a mess now."

Lisa grabbed Ronni's hand and kissed the tears off it. "It's not you, honey. You're not the mess."

"I'm a freak! And a monster!"

"No, baby. You're a beautiful girl. Lauren's dad's talking about the"—the words were tumbling out before she could stop them—"lawsuit."

Ronni pulled her hand away. "What lawsuit?"

Lisa turned away from her daughter and focused on the clutter on the coffee table: fashion magazines, teacups, used tissues, Ronni's cell phone and iPad. . . . She tidied as she talked. "Hannah's parents should have taken care of you girls. You were in their house, so your safety was their responsibility."

Ronni gasped. "Are you suing them?"

"My insurance didn't cover all your medical costs."

"This wasn't their fault!"

"You said you don't remember anything—how can you be so sure?"

Ronni threw the blanket off her lap and leaned forward. "I remember that we *always* got drunk at sleepovers. We always sneaked booze from our parents or got it from a boot. We always had pot or pills or whatever we could steal from home. This could have happened here. It could have happened anywhere. . . ."

"But it didn't happen here. It happened under Kim and Jeff Sanders's multimillion-dollar roof."

Ronni glared at her. "Everyone will hate me. They'll take Hannah's side. She's popular now. She's going out with Noah Chambers."

"No one will hate you. You're the victim here."

"Don't you remember high school at all?" Ronni's voice was shrill, angry, nearly hysterical. "No one likes a fucking victim!"

"Don't talk like that."

"Then don't do this to me!" Ronni screamed.

"*To* you?" Lisa shrieked. "I'm doing this *for* you!" She loved Ronni more than life, but sometimes her teenaged self-absorption made Lisa want to shake her.

"This isn't about me," Ronni spat. "This is about you." She sat back on the sofa and fixed her mother with half a hateful stare. "You've always been jealous of Kim Sanders."

"I'm not a materialistic person, Ronni. You know that. I don't conform to traditional standards of happiness." She sounded like one of the speakers at her mindfulness retreat. Had Lisa really drunk the Kool-Aid? Or was she trying to convince her daughter that her motivations were pure?

"Give me a break," Ronni scoffed. "You'd love to have Kim Sanders's perfect house, her perfect marriage, her perfect family. . . ."

"They're not that perfect," Lisa retorted. "Trust me. I know some things."

"They're a lot better than this"—Ronni gestured around her—"this shitty apartment. Your stupid boyfriend. Me and you."

Her daughter was hurting, she was lashing out, she didn't really mean it. . . . Still, Lisa felt her face crumple. She had stayed strong, angry, and defiant through this whole nightmare and now, sitting among the clutter of her daughter's convalescence, a teenaged vampire frozen on the television screen, she was going to lose it. "I love you more than anything," she managed to croak through the emotion clogging her throat. "I wouldn't change anything about you or me or our life."

Ronni stared at her, one eye full of hate, the other blank and blind. "I would," she said calmly. "I'd change everything." She turned away from her tearful mother, and hit the play button on the remote.

kim

SEVENTEEN DAYS AFTER

Kim sat across a tiny round table from Dr. Ana Pinto. The Eighteenth Street café was Italian, the tiny table matching the tiny cups of espresso they were drinking. It was quaint, but it meant she and Ana were awkwardly close, their elbows almost touching as they drank their strong, bitter drinks. Kim liked Ana, admired her even. Ana was a pediatric oncologist who had emigrated from Brazil fifteen years ago. "I wanted Marta to have a better life," she'd stated. "So we left." Ana had put her only child before her career, her extended family, and her friendships. It was the same choice Kim would have made, that's why she respected Ana . . . that, and for saving all those kids with cancer.

"It's still hard to believe that Ronni was so seriously injured," Kim said, endeavoring to bring her cup to her mouth without jostling Ana's elbow.

Ana replied, in perfect but accented English, "It's a tragedy."

"A terrible accident." Kim sipped her coffee, swallowed. "And Lisa's reaction has made it all so much worse. . . . You heard she's suing us?"

"I did."

"It's natural to want someone to blame, but Jeff and I are not at fault. The police cleared us. . . . But I guess Lisa wants her pound of flesh."

Ana pursed her lips and gave a slight nod, not overt agreement with Kim's statement, but it was enough for Kim to forge ahead.

"We've had to hire a lawyer. She says we need to gather some witnesses—just for discovery, she's sure we won't have to go to trial." Kim took a breath. "We were hoping we could count on Marta."

"To be a witness?"

"She's known our family for years. She knows we're not negligent—we're not partyers. . . . And I'm sure she told you that I was very clear about our house rules."

"Yes . . ." Kim waited for it. "But . . ." There it was. "I asked Marta if you and Jeff checked on them that night. She said you didn't."

"They're sixteen, not four!" Kim's voice was too sharp, too defensive. She softened. "We thought we could trust them. Hannah and Marta and Caitlin have always been such good girls . . . but Ronni and Lauren are different."

"So this is Ronni's fault?"

"I'm not laying blame here," Kim retorted. "Lisa's the one doing that. I'm just saying that Ronni has a history of rebellious behavior. It's no wonder— She has no relationship with her father. And Lisa's had more than a few boyfriends. . . ."

There was a glimmer of interest in Ana's eye. Kim continued, forcing a sympathetic tone. "Lisa's had a hard life: abusive relationships, drugs, drinking. . . . I know she loves her daughter, I know she tries her best, but . . . she has a lot of issues."

Ana's expression was inscrutable. "I don't think Lisa's issues are relevant to this situation, are they?"

"They go to character, don't they? Kim spluttered. "And . . . who knows if Lisa has fallen back into bad habits? Maybe Ronni has seen things she shouldn't have? She might have access to substances. . . ."

Ana checked her watch. "I should go."

Kim spoke quickly. "Can we count on Marta's support?"

Ana's accented voice was cold and clipped. "If Marta is called as a witness, she'll tell the truth." She stood. "Thank you for the coffee, Kim." She strode out of the café.

KIM FELT SLIGHTLY sick as she flew down the 101. The meeting with Ana had not gone as she'd hoped. The woman acted like Kim had offered Marta a bribe—a new laptop or a spa day—in exchange for her testimony. Kim only wanted Marta to tell the truth. And the truth was that Kim and Jeff weren't culpable. All Kim had wanted from the meeting was for Ana to pat her hand and tell her it was going to be okay, that she understood. This could have happened in Ana's home, or any home. Kim and Jeff were good parents. Ana was a pediatrician for Christ's sake. Where was her empathy?

But Kim couldn't dwell on this now as she exited the freeway onto Oyster Point Boulevard. Her hands on the wheel were sweaty, her stomach churning with anticipation and anxiety. She was on her way to meet Tony. He had rented them a room in a secluded inn near the marina. They had planned it that afternoon in his car when they'd first kissed. It had been so intense, so passionate that they'd nearly had sex right there in the backseat of his Volkswagen. But Kim couldn't risk it. What if they'd been caught? Kim would be branded a public fornicator *as well* as a neglectful parent.

"We can't," Kim had whispered, pulling on Tony's hair to lift his head from its location between her breasts.

"Why not?" He kissed her neck, his breath hard and hot in her ear.

"Not here," she said. "It's too risky."

"That's what makes it so hot," he mumbled, his hand finding its way between her legs. Her body wanted to rock against the pressure of his fingers, to build friction and find release, but her mind prevailed. They were in a public park, in broad daylight, for God's sake.

"Stop. Please . . ." But he didn't. He could feel her body responding, feel how close she was. "We're married. We're parents," she managed to say. "We have to be discreet."

This got through to him and he pulled away. He looked at her, his eyes glazed, his chest heaving. He appeared confused and disoriented. Then he ran his fingers through his hair and let a word slip through his lips. "Fuck . . ."

Kim was flattered. He wanted her so much it seemed almost

painful for him. It was hard for Kim, too. She wanted to be with Tony, to share that incredible intimacy with him. He had been a comfort and an escape during this nightmare. She felt a gratitude and fondness toward him that was surely bordering on love. And so, she and Tony had hatched their plan.

KIM SPOTTED THE sign—MARINA SIDE INN—and pulled her car into the parking lot. It was quaint (despite its proximity to the airport), and not at all indicative of the debauchery that was about to take place inside in the middle of the afternoon. She grabbed her purse and hurried toward room 108—a cottage. Tony had texted her the number so she wouldn't have to go to the front desk. As she walked across the hot pavement, she felt queasy. She wasn't sure if it was from excitement or guilt.

She had thought that Ronni's accident, followed so closely by Lisa's litigation, might have brought her and Jeff closer together. They were both being wrongfully accused, both being blamed. It would be normal for them to unite in the face of adversity, to support and comfort each other. But it seemed Jeff had pulled even further away—swimming, cycling, and running harder, faster, longer. . . . How far could you run before you dropped dead? He'd been drinking, too, she was sure of it. That Aussie friend of his was always pressuring him to go out for beers. Jeff came home later and later, heading straight for the shower and chewing gum like a guilty teenager. Like Hannah.

The cottage was a few steps away, and she took a deep breath. There was no backing out now. She reached out and knocked, her heart thudding in her chest. But when Tony opened the door, she instantly relaxed. His presence had that effect on her. "You made it," he said, stepping back to usher her inside.

"Traffic," she said, moving into the tiny bungalow. The charm of the exterior hadn't quite translated inside. A plethora of throw rugs, doilies, and tchotchkes attempted to mask the cheap linoleum floors and chipped Formica countertops. "Cute place." But it sounded insincere.

Tony chuckled. "It'll do," he said, moving toward her and kissing her. So this is how it would work: no jokes about the octogenarian interior decorator, no awkward chitchat about the lost art of crochet, just straight down to business. Tony's kisses were already passionate and urgent, his hands were already roaming her body. "Let's go," he mumbled, leading her toward a bedroom that she correctly predicted would be full of frills.

He lay Kim down on the floral bedspread and went to work on her, unbuttoning her blouse and unclasping her bra. He took her nipple in his mouth and it felt good, she was aroused, but Kim couldn't stop thinking about the bedspread. They should pull it back and have sex on the sheets. Hotel sheets were regularly washed but not the bedspreads. Had Tony never seen a TV exposé on hotel cleanliness? Had he never seen the blue light revealing the buckets of semen deposited on the typical hotel counterpane? Tony seemed more focused on adding to the collection than worrying about hygiene.

Tony pulled off his own shirt, revealing his narrow, hairy chest. Kim felt a mild surge of lust at his nakedness and the look of hunger in his dark eyes. She just needed to focus on the matter at hand. He unceremoniously yanked up her skirt and dove between her legs. She closed her eyes and tried to go with it. But it was then, with her lover's head snuffling around in her crotch, that Kim felt a powerful surge of guilt, remorse, and shame sweep over her. No, it was more than that; it was self-loathing. What was she doing here? A girl had been maimed in her home and her response was to cheat on her husband? She could lose her savings, her home, her reputation . . . and now she was risking her marriage. Ana's judgmental expression replayed in Kim's mind. The woman had looked at Kim like she was dirt. She propped herself up on her elbows. "Stop."

But Tony didn't. Maybe he hadn't heard her. Maybe he didn't think she meant it. Suddenly, the pressure of his face between her thighs made her feel disproportionately angry. She wanted to hit him, to kick him hard in the face. She shoved his head away. "I said STOP!" She scrambled away from him on the bed, yanking her skirt down as she did. "This was a mistake."

"You just need to relax," Tony said. "I brought some wine. Let's have a drink."

"I don't want a drink. I want to go home."

Tony gave a mirthless laugh. "Are you kidding me?"

"I'm sorry . . . but with everything going on, I'm just not into it."

"You're *just not into it*?" He shook his head in disbelief. "I paid three hundred bucks for this room. In cash."

Kim was already getting up. Where had she left her shoes? "I'd be happy to reimburse you."

"You'd be happy to *reimburse me*?" Was he going to repeat everything she said like some angry parrot? She felt Tony's eyes on her as she searched the room, but he said nothing. Finally, he spoke: "You fucking tease."

Kim turned toward him and saw his face curled into a mask of hatred.

"You've been leading me on for months." He angrily pulled on his shirt. "I have a wife. I have a family. I was willing to jeopardize everything for you."

Kim suddenly felt like dissolving into tears of self-pity. "So was I . . . but it was a bad idea."

"I'll say it was a bad fucking idea."

"It's just . . . with the accident and the lawsuit . . ." Her voice cracked.

"Poor Kim," he said, his voice mocking. "Some kids got wasted at your house. They fucked up, like kids do. But all you care about is your reputation. And your bank account."

"A girl lost her eye." Tears streamed down Kim's cheeks. "Her mother is suing us. We could lose everything."

Tony's expression was pure disgust, like the fact that he'd ever considered her a sexual being turned his stomach. And it felt apt. She would have looked at her own reflection the same way. She was selfish and superficial, disloyal and adulterous: a contemporary Madame Bovary.

"Good luck dealing with all your shit," Tony said, stalking from the room. Kim heard him grab his car keys off the table and the door bang closed behind him. She fell on the semen-stained bedspread and wept.

jeff

EIGHTEEN DAYS AFTER

Jeff was sleeping, fitfully, when he heard it. The ding was muffled by his jeans—he'd left his phone in his pants pocket after the pool—but still, it woke him. Usually, he turned his ringer off before bed, but he'd been so exhausted after his swim that he must have forgotten. He was sleeping in the spare room—Kim said his *breathing* disturbed her—so he wouldn't wake her . . . although, since Lisa's complaint against them, his wife had been on a strict evening diet of white wine and sleeping pills. Neither his breathing nor the muted alert would have roused her.

He crawled out of bed and stumbled toward his pants balled up on the bedroom floor. The clock radio on the nightstand gleamed 2:17 A.M. Who the hell could be texting him at this hour? It had to be Graham. His friend had been known to tie one on and then suggest Jeff join him at whatever Aussie bar he was frequenting. Jeff always texted back his excuses: I'm sleeping. . . . I have an early meeting. . . . I already had a few beers with dinner, so I can't drive. . . . Jeff never admitted he wasn't *allowed* to go out.

The number on the screen was unfamiliar, but the message instantly provided clarity.

It's Lauren I need help

Jesus Christ. How did the girl get his number? She must have found it on Hannah's phone. And why would she ask him, of all people, for help? But only a monster could ignore a missive like that. He texted back:

What's wrong?

Through typos and grammatical errors, Jeff was able to discern that Lauren was drunk or high (fucked up, she'd texted), and at a party at some guy's apartment. She'd gone with her older sister, but her sister had ditched her when Lauren went to the bathroom. Now she was alone, and wasted, and she didn't know how to get home.

Did she seriously expect Jeff to get out of bed in the middle of the night and rescue her? Call your dad, Jeff insisted. But Lauren said she couldn't. Her dad would merder her. He'd send her away to a school for delinkwents.

Call your mom

Lauren informed him that her mom was undoubtedly passed out drunk by this time of night. But there had to be someone else: her stepmom, an aunt, a cousin, a friend with a car? It didn't make sense for Jeff to be rescuing this girl. He barely knew her. There was something wrong about it . . . and downright creepy. Lauren was getting angry now:

Fuck you then

I'll go out to the street and wait for someone to offer me a ride

Shit . . . Jeff had no choice.

He slipped out to his car and headed to the address Lauren had texted. It was in the Tenderloin: no place for a kid at night . . . or in the day, for that matter. She was on the sidewalk, waiting for him. She looked older, twenty at least, in her short, tight dress, high heels, and big hair. She looked like a prostitute; she fit right in. Thank God he had come when he did.

Lauren piled into the passenger seat and Jeff saw that her makeup was smudged from crying.

"Are you okay?"

"I don't want to talk about it," she said, slamming the door behind her. She turned away from him, pressing her forehead against the cool side window.

Jeff pulled the car onto the quiet street. Lauren didn't provide a destination, so he headed toward her dad's high-rise. It was only a couple of weeks ago when he had delivered her there, crying, sniveling, covered in vomit. . . . And now, she was in his car again, and she was crying again. He glanced over at her to make sure she wasn't going to vomit again. But she was whimpering softly, her face turned away from him.

"Don't take me to my dad's," she said, apparently recognizing the route. "Take me to my mom's. In Noe Valley."

Without a word, Jeff made a right. Lauren continued to snivel as they traveled, but Jeff didn't press her for any details. He didn't want any—he just wanted to get the girl home and out of his car. It felt inappropriate to be driving through this seedy neighborhood with a sixteen-year-old girl who was not his daughter at nearly three in the morning. It felt illegal. He checked his rearview for cop cars.

Finally, he pulled up in front of a brightly painted but run-down Victorian conversion. He put the car in park but consciously left the motor running. "Are you going to be okay?"

Lauren turned her tearful face toward him for the first time. "No one cares if I'm okay or not."

"That's not true," he said, though maybe it was. Her father was absent, her mother a drunk, her stepmom clearly didn't like her, and her sister had just left her at some strange guy's apartment. He came up with, "Hannah cares about you."

"Hannah doesn't know the real me. No one does. If they did, they'd hate me."

"No, they wouldn't."

"*I* hate me." She was crying harder now, sobs shaking her narrow bare shoulders. The girl was drunk and messy and melodramatic, but Jeff felt sorry for her. Anyone would have: she may have been fucked-up and dressed like a hooker, but she was just a girl and her pain was real. He glanced around to make sure there were no witnesses, then he put his arm around her.

Lauren seemed to take this as an invitation to launch herself into an embrace. It was too close, too intimate, too familiar . . . but she was bawling her head off, her tears dampening his sweatshirt. He could hardly push her away in that state. Who knew what she might do? Run off into the night? Fling herself in front of a passing car? He patted her back paternally. "It's okay," he said. "It's going to be okay."

Finally, she regained the ability to speak. "Thanks for coming to get me," she murmured, into his shirt. "For caring about me when no one else does."

"You know that's not true," he said, and kissed the top of her head. Even as his lips were brushing her hair, he regretted the fatherly gesture. It was automatic, instinctual, but totally inappropriate. This girl was not his daughter, not his niece, not a family friend. . . . He pulled away, quickly forcing Lauren to sit up. She looked at him, confused for a moment, and then a smile curled her lips. She was staring at him with such blatant adoration that it sent a chill through him. There was something else hidden in her smile . . . desire. Oh God.

"You need to get to bed," he said, reaching across to open the door for her.

Lauren obediently got out, then turned and peered back in at him. "Talk to you soon, Jeff." She closed the car door and tottered, in her heels, down the path toward her building.

"No!" Jeff called into the vacuum of the car. "We won't talk, Lauren! We can't!" But she didn't turn back. She didn't hear him . . . or didn't want to hear him. He waited until she was safely inside her building and then he drove toward home. It was over. He had delivered the girl without incident. But the tight knot of dread in his bowels told him this wasn't the end.

hannah

THIRTY DAYS AFTER

"Ronni's back." It was Marta, flanked by Caitlin as usual, who hurried to Hannah's locker with the news. Hannah's throat tightened. She knew Ronni would return to school eventually but had hoped she'd stay away for a couple of months at least. Ronni's presence could upset the delicate social order that had been established since she left. Hannah was on top now, but it was still new and her position was precarious. Ronni could walk back in and topple Hannah from her perch. They had all witnessed Lauren's fickle side when she had dropped Ronni as damaged goods. It could cut both ways.

And then there was the lawsuit. Lisa Monroe was obviously furious with Hannah's parents. She blamed them for Ronni's accident and wanted them to pay her three million dollars! Kim and Jeff didn't have that kind of money—her mom reiterated this point in phone calls with their lawyer and hushed bickering with

Hannah's dad. How did Ronni feel about everything? Did she hate Hannah now? Blame *her* for the accident? Or did Ronni think her mom was being a "vindictive bitch" as Hannah's dad said when he thought Hannah was out of earshot?

Hannah closed her locker and pressed her math books to her chest in an effort to appear ambivalent. "Where is she?"

"I saw her from a distance in the counseling suite," Marta said. "She was with Mrs. Pittwell. Her eye . . . it looks kind of scary."

"So you didn't talk to her?" Hannah asked.

"No. I came straight here."

"I don't know how to act around her," Caitlin said. "It just feels so weird."

"She's still the same Ronni," Hannah said with a confidence she didn't feel. For all she knew, this experience had transformed Ronni into someone completely different.

Marta said, "I know . . . but it's sort of awkward. Like, I don't want to stare at her eye or anything."

"Yeah," Caitlin said. "I don't want to make her uncomfortable."

"You wouldn't," Hannah said, "Ronni really likes you guys." The words sounded insincere, but they weren't a lie exactly. Ronni had never said she *disliked* Marta and Caitlin—they just weren't really on her radar. Hannah stepped into the flow of students heading to class, and Marta and Caitlin fell into step beside her.

"I was hoping you could do me a favor," Hannah ventured, as they moved through the halls.

Marta sounded suspicious, "What favor?"

"Umm . . . maybe talk to Ronni and see how she's feeling? About the party? About me?"

Caitlin stopped walking and exchanged a look with Marta. "We don't really want to get involved."

"It's just a simple question," Hannah retorted. "It's no big deal."

She watched another furtive look between Caitlin and Marta. Marta spoke in a low voice. "Lauren told us to stay out of it."

"Stay out of *what*?" The stream of students headed to class was thinning, an indication that the second bell was about to ring, but Hannah stood her ground.

"Everything," Caitlin said in a quiet but resolute voice. "She said to forget that night ever happened. . . ."

"Or we'll be *fucking sorry*," Marta added, a touch indignantly.

"She didn't mean it," Hannah scoffed. She had been standing right there when Lauren assured Noah and Adam that the other girls wouldn't talk. Still, Marta and Caitlin were making it sound so *ominous*, like Lauren had threatened to kneecap them if they breathed a word. Hannah tried for a lighter tone. "Lauren just doesn't want anyone to get into trouble."

There was another look exchanged between Marta and Caitlin, then Marta said, "We're not going to say anything. About where the booze came from. About any of it."

"If anyone asks us, we'll say we don't remember anything about that night," Caitlin seconded.

"Which is true, basically," Marta elaborated. "We were all wasted. It's normal to forget."

"I know. I barely remember anything," Hannah said. "From the alcohol. And the shock . . ."

The second bell rang. "We should go," Caitlin said, and they all moved toward their classes. "Get Lauren to talk to Ronni," she suggested.

"She's Ronni's best friend," Marta echoed, "she'll know if she's pissed at you or whatever."

Hannah could feel the cohesion between her two friends, and as a result, her own exclusion. The girls had obviously discussed it and decided they didn't want anything to do with Ronni or Lauren or Hannah. Hannah had worked so hard to foster a relationship with Lauren, but suddenly, she felt nostalgic for the familiar, comfortable fold of her friendship with these two. It had been so simple and pure and easy . . . but the party had changed everything. Marta and Caitlin could put it all behind them; they could just walk away. Hannah couldn't.

"You're right," Hannah said breezily. "I'll ask Lauren at lunch." The girls branched off and headed to social studies. Hannah walked alone to math class.

HANNAH WAS STILL in class when her phone buzzed. After a first-day lecture about a zero-tolerance policy on texting in class, her math teacher had seemingly lost interest and most students texted freely under the guise of using the calculator app. Hannah peeked at her phone under the desk. It was Lauren.

We need to talk

K

Meet me in the tech wing after class

K

When she was finally released from the monotony of geometry, Hannah hurried to meet Lauren. She was terrified of bumping into Ronni along the way. What if Ronni screamed at her? Lashed out at her physically even? Or broke down in tears? But Hannah managed to find Lauren, leaning on the vending machine, without incident.

"Thank fuck," Lauren said, grabbing Hannah's arm. "Let's get out of here."

"What's going on?"

"Outside." She tugged Hannah toward the nearest exit.

They walked swiftly across the playing field, heading toward the school fence. Hannah tried not to glance back at the school, but she worried about missing her science class. There was a unit test next week and she could use the review. But based on Lauren's agitation, this was more important.

Finally, when they had exited the school grounds and were walking along the sidewalk, Lauren spoke over passing traffic. "Principal Edwards called me into her office."

"What for?" Hannah called over the hum of tires on pavement.

"She wanted to talk to me about fucking Ronni."

Fucking Ronni? Hannah wasn't sure if the expletive meant that Lauren was angry at Ronni, or just angry at the principal for wanting to discuss her situation.

"Edwards said that Ronni needs support and love and all that shit. Ronni's really fragile and she needs her best friend. I didn't want to say it to Edwards, but I'm totally on your side in this."

"My *side*?"

Lauren stopped walking and faced her. "Ronni and her mom are trying to ruin your family."

"Ronni's not. I mean, she might not even know about the lawsuit."

"Please . . ." Lauren rolled her eyes. "Ronni and her mom are like BFFs. They're totally weird and codependent. That's what happens when you're an only and you don't have a dad."

"I guess. . . ."

They walked again. "I told Edwards, I'm not even that close to Ronni anymore and she can't make me babysit her."

"What did Edwards say?"

"She was all, like, disappointed in me. . . . Whatevs. She can't force us to be friends with Ronni. I mean, you and I are super close now. It would be kind of a downer to have the one-eyed freak hanging around like a third wheel."

Hannah gave a weak smile of agreement but her head was reeling. She had been afraid that Ronni might replace her in Lauren's affections, but she hadn't expected this: that they would turn on Ronni, that she would become an outcast, the enemy. Wasn't Ronni the real victim here? Wasn't she the one who was really suffering? Was this all because of Lisa's lawsuit?

Lauren said, "Did you know Ronni Snapchatted her tits to Adam?"

"No. When?"

"Like, a week before your birthday. I kind of liked Adam then, and she just went after him. What a whore."

"Totally."

"Still . . . I have to talk to her," Lauren continued. "To make sure she won't say anything. I already made sure Marta and Caitlin won't rat us—or your dad—out."

"Yeah."

"How's he holding up?" Lauren asked breezily. "Your dad?"

It was a weird question. Hannah glanced over at her friend, but Lauren looked completely blasé. "Fine. He runs and swims a lot. It's good for stress."

"I used to do yoga at the Bay Club. I saw him working out there a lot. He's really fit. For his age."

Ewwww. "I guess. It's my mom I worry about."

"I wouldn't worry about her," Lauren said.

"She's really upset about the lawsuit and everything. . . . She and Lisa Monroe used to be friends."

"My mom says your mom is more worried about her *precious reputation* than anything else," Lauren relayed. "And my stepbitch says this all could have been avoided if your parents had offered to pay Ronni's hospital bills, or given her some money for college or something. Just as a way of saying sorry. She says your parents brought this on themselves."

Hannah felt hot anger rise up in her chest, into her throat, and color her face red. The depth of her rage surprised her. She'd never felt protective of her parents before—she'd never had to. And she had idolized Lauren for so long . . . but right now, she wanted to slap the girl's perfectly made-up face. She wanted to pull her shiny hair and kick her in her J Brand–clad shins. How fucking dare Lauren and her dysfunctional parents judge Hannah's family? How fucking dare they? Hannah stopped walking. She could feel her cheeks burning, her eyes filling with angry tears. She couldn't lose it, she just couldn't.

"I'm not really cool with your family talking shit about my family," she said, her voice trembling.

Lauren stopped and gave Hannah an appraising stare. She took in the anger contorting Hannah's features, the red complexion, and the tears shining in Hannah's eyes. "Chill out," the popular girl said. "You know my mom is a fucking mess. She's on all these antidepressants and she drinks wine, like, all day. And my stepmom is a nosy, do-gooder bitch. It's not like I care what they think. I was just saying. . . ."

"Cool," Hannah croaked, terrified that she was about to burst into tears.

Lauren's lips twitched and it looked like she was going to laugh. Hannah was mortified. She'd overreacted, freaked out, nearly bawled like some weak little baby. . . . Her shame made her face burn hotter. Don't cry, don't cry, don't cry . . .

"Do you want to go back to school?" Lauren asked.

Hannah heard the challenge in her friend's tone and realized this was a pivotal moment. Hannah's answer would define her in Lauren's eyes, and it would cement her future. She took a deep breath.

"Fuck no. . . . Do you have any weed?"

lisa

THIRTY-FIVE DAYS AFTER

Lisa wrapped her hands around the large cup—a bowl really—of steaming ginger rooibos tea. She was seated across from Carla Ross, Lauren's stepmom, who was sipping from her own bowl: herbal lemongrass. Lisa had only met Carla perfunctorily before today. A couple of months ago, she had picked Ronni up at Carla's luxurious, South of Market apartment where she lived with Lauren's father, Darren. Usually, Ronni took transit home, but that night she'd stayed late, supposedly working on a science project. When Lisa picked up her daughter, she'd decided to introduce herself to Lauren's parents . . . and check out the luxury penthouse.

Lauren despised her stepmom, but that wasn't a reflection on Carla's character. Ronni had taken an instant dislike to more than a few of Lisa's lovers. (This instant contempt was, in fact, preferable to the rare occasions when Ronni had grown fond of and become attached to a man her mom had been seeing.) For several years,

Lisa had avoided introducing her boyfriends to her daughter—until Allan. The two were amicable, but Lisa kept them in separate orbits as much as possible.

Carla had called Lisa right after the accident to express her concern for Ronni. Then, a few days ago, she'd sent an e-mail:

> Hi Lisa,
>
> I wanted to check on Ronni. I hear she's back at school and I hope she's doing well. I'm really upset that Lauren isn't being a better friend to her through all of this. My husband says to stay out of it, that I don't know everything that's going on, and I don't. But I do know that real friends should stand by each other through good and bad times. I'm sorry that Lauren's mom never taught her that. If you ever want to have tea and talk, I'm here.
>
> Carla xo

It surprised Lisa how much she wanted to have this conversation about Lauren. Lisa's parenting style had always been noninterference. She didn't want to decide who Ronni's friends were, control what Ronni did for fun, or supervise how she spent every waking minute. Unlike some control-freak mothers she could name, Lisa wasn't going to dictate who her daughter became. Of course, Lisa had met Lauren on several occasions. She seemed polite enough, with a touch of attitude. The same could have been said for Lisa's own child, before the accident. So if Ronni had chosen Lauren for a best friend, then Lisa would respect her daughter's opinion. But it now appeared that Ronni could have used some guidance in that department.

"Ronni's first week back at school was really hard," Lisa said, removing her hands from the mug and gripping the handle. It was an understatement. Ronni had begged not to go, sobbing and clutching at her mother like a frightened toddler. "It'll be fine," Lisa had assuaged her. But it wasn't fine. When Ronni returned from her first day at Hillcrest, she'd gone into her lilac bedroom and slammed the door. Lisa heard banging and thumping, drawers opening and closing, objects being thrown around the room. She'd hurried to see the source of the commotion.

"You can get rid of all this crap," Ronni cried, indicating a pile of designer clothes, stylish jewelry, and expensive makeup in the middle of her bedroom floor. "I don't need any of it."

"What are you talking about?"

"No one looks at me anymore!" she screamed. "Or when they do, they whisper, or snicker, or look away really fast. Even my so-called friends are hiding from me because I'm so fucking ugly!"

"You're not ugly! Don't say that!" But Lisa's words were drowned out by Ronni's sobs as she dropped to the floor, tearing at her clothes, smashing makeup cases, destroying treasured necklaces and earrings.

Lisa took a sip of her nearly flavorless tea. "She feels abandoned. And isolated."

"That makes me so sad," Carla said, her eyes shiny with emotion under her impeccable makeup. How old was she? Thirty? Thirty-five at the most? How old was Lauren's father? Probably in his fifties . . . Carla had trophy wife written all over her, but she could still be a caring soul.

Carla continued, "My husband is a good man, but his work is his life. He travels all the time. He's not the hands-on parent that

Lauren needs. And her mom is so bitter and angry. I shouldn't say anything, but she drinks. . . ."

Lisa shook her head, sympathetic.

"Lauren's hated me since the day we met," Carla continued, her chin crinkling with the emotion of her words. "Her mom poisoned her against me. Darren and I met when he was still married. Nothing really happened, but there were feelings there."

"I understand," Lisa said, because she did. There had been some married men in her past. Sometimes there was a connection that went beyond all impediments. She wouldn't judge.

"I've tried to bond with her," Carla continued, "but she seems so cold and heartless. Then her dad comes home and she turns on the charm."

"Divorce is hard on kids," Lisa offered, bringing her cup to her lips, but it felt like an excuse. Lauren's cruelty toward Ronni bordered on sociopathic. Obviously, Lisa wasn't qualified to make a diagnosis, but she had once dated a complete and utter asshole whom her friend Hilary had tagged a sociopath. Lisa had researched the term and it seemed to fit Lauren to a tee. The girl was charming, she was a leader, and she obviously had a total lack of empathy. Lisa's maternal protectiveness could be coloring her judgment, but the diagnosis fit.

"Half of all kids today come from broken homes," Carla said. "I think she just needs boundaries. Her mom will ground her for doing drugs, but then she never follows through. Darren's not home enough to punish her, and if I try to set any limits, I'm the Wicked Witch of the West."

"Being a stepparent is a tough job."

Carla was on the verge of tears now. "I love Darren; I love our life together. But honestly, if I'd known his daughter was going to be so hateful, I'm not sure I would have married him."

"I'm sorry."

"Darren doesn't want any more children. He says he's too old. I agreed when we first got married, but that's when I thought I'd be a part of Lauren's life. I didn't think she would hate me so much."

Lisa suddenly saw this meeting for what it really was: a counseling session for a distraught stepmom. Carla wasn't an ally who was going to make Lauren see what a shitty friend she was being to Ronni. Carla just wanted Lisa to affirm that Lauren was a cruel little bitch and that all the discord in their stepparent-stepchild relationship was the girl's fault. Lisa looked at Carla: her flawless makeup, her manicured nails, her yoga-toned body, and her pretty hazel eyes filled with tears. The poor thing. Carla had chosen to marry a wealthy older man and she hadn't factored in all the baggage that came with him.

Lisa could have easily said the words Carla wanted to hear, could have given her the sympathy she so clearly coveted. But Lisa didn't have the energy to support someone else right now. Her focus was on helping Ronni. Only Ronni. She changed the subject. "Has anyone talked to Lauren about Ronni? About how alone she feels?"

"I've tried, I really have, but she doesn't listen to me. I doubt her mom has," Carla snorted. "Monique is completely useless as a mother. . . . Darren thinks Lauren should stay away from Ronni until you settle your lawsuit." She took a sip of tea. "How's that going?"

Lisa leaned back in her chair. "The Sanderses have refused to accept any responsibility, but I'm not backing down."

"Darren thinks you should settle. He says that the police found the Sanderses not criminally responsible, so you don't have a leg to stand on."

Lisa felt affronted. Darren knew nothing about what happened that night. And, frankly, he should spend less time judging people and more time parenting his nasty daughter. But she pasted on a patient smile. "We have our examination for discovery on Monday. When the Sanderses see the case we have against them, they'll come to the table. There's a lot more going on beneath Jeff and Kim's perfect facade than people realize."

Carla cocked her head. "Really? They seem pretty squeaky clean."

Lisa reached for her mug but noticed her hands were shaking. She folded them in her lap. "Well . . . they're not."

"Jeff Sanders is such a health nut. He does triathlons, doesn't he? He's quite attractive. Kim, too . . . in her conservative way."

Lisa gave an ambiguous nod. Kim was classically pretty, well preserved, always put together . . . but she had no warmth, no sex appeal that Lisa could see. And Jeff was fit and boyish, but when she'd met him, all those years ago, she'd picked up his subtle air of condescension. Jeff was a privileged pretty boy with no depth, no character, no complexity. . . .

"They may look like the perfect couple," Lisa said, "but there's a lot of shit going on in that multimillion-dollar house."

Carla leaned forward conspiratorially. "Like what?"

Lisa wasn't about to jeopardize her legal position by disclosing dirt to a virtual stranger. "I really can't talk about it," she said, "but if this goes to trial, you'll know more than you ever wanted to about the Sanderses."

The younger woman looked positively gleeful at the prospect. "Do you think there'll be a trial? Darren says these cases usually get settled through mediation."

Darren says, Darren says, Darren says . . .

"I'm not interested in mediation," Lisa said. "The Sanderses are used to getting what they want. They're used to everything being easy and working out for them. But they're going to take responsibility for what they did to my daughter."

The intensity of Lisa's words seemed to make Carla uncomfortable. "I hope it works out," she said, eyes darting to her watch.

There was an awkward silence that neither of the women knew how to fill, so Lisa said, "I should go. I don't like leaving Ronni alone for too long."

"Right," Carla said with obvious relief. She slid her chair back. "I'll try to talk to Lauren, but she won't listen."

Lisa managed a smile as she stood. "Probably not. But thanks for trying."

jeff

THIRTY-SEVEN DAYS AFTER

The conference room table was made of some pale hardwood polished to a gleaming sheen. Jeff could see Kim's reflection in it as she sat stiffly beside him. He couldn't quite make out her expression but he didn't need to see it to know that it was grim, tense, and hostile. Next to Kim sat their plain, competent attorney, Candace Sugarman. Across the table sat the enemy, looking young and waiflike in her bohemian clothes. Despite her fragile appearance, there was something fierce in Lisa's eyes—either rage or hatred, Jeff wasn't sure. Lisa was flanked by her attorney, Paul Wilcox, a pudgy thirty-five-year-old man in an expensive suit.

At the end of the table, impossibly young and perfect and pretty, was Lauren Ross. Beside her sat her mother, Monique. Perhaps it was the elder woman's haggard appearance juxtaposed with her daughter's youth that made Lauren appear so ethereal. Jeff knew what Kim would think: Lauren was too made up, too overtly sexual for her age, like some pedophile's fantasy. And Kim was right. But there was no denying that the girl was beautiful. Every time Jeff looked at her, which was rarely, he felt sick to his stomach.

"I know I could have done a written witness statement, but I just felt like I had to be here. . . ."

Of course she did. Lauren wouldn't miss a chance to insert herself into this mess.

"Thank you, Lauren." It was Candace's practiced voice. "Now, tell us what happened that night."

Lauren glanced at Jeff and then over to Lisa before addressing the attorney. "It was the same as any sleepover: we all stole a bit of booze from home, a few pills from our medicine cabinets, and then we got wasted."

Kim made some noise at the back of her throat and Lauren's mom rolled her eyes and shook her head. But Candace was encouraging. "You're doing great, Lauren. How much alcohol did each girl bring?"

"I don't recall."

"Do you recall who brought what substances to Hannah's birthday party?"

"Not really . . ."

"Not really, or no?" Candace pressed. Jeff's eyes were fixed on the table. He didn't dare look at Lauren, and he hoped she was smart enough not to look at him.

"No," Lauren said. "I just remember that everyone brought something, so we can't really blame one person."

"Thank you," Candace said, "I know this wasn't easy for you."

"It was the right thing to do."

Monique, Lauren's mother, pushed her chair back. "Are we done here?" Her voice was raspy; she was clearly a smoker.

Candace looked to the other lawyer, Paul, who nodded assent. "Yes, thank you."

Lauren and her mother moved toward the door, and Jeff felt his shoulders collapse with relief. He hadn't even realized that his traps were in a vise until Lauren got up to leave. The tension was understandable. If anyone in that room knew what had been going on between him and the girl, he'd be crucified.

They were almost gone when Lauren turned back. "I just have to say one thing. . . ." Jeff felt his stomach drop, but Lauren's gaze was fixed on Lisa. "I think what you're doing to Jeff and Kim is really bad. It's not their fault that Ronni lost her eye. She wanted to get wasted, we all did. . . ." Monique gripped her daughter's upper arm and tried to hustle her out the door, but Lauren wasn't finished. "This lawsuit is making it harder for Ronni at school. No one wants to hang out with her because of all the crap going on around her. I think you should drop the lawsuit and focus on your daughter getting better."

Lisa stood. "You don't care about Ronni," she said, her voice dripping with contempt. "You've barely talked to her since the accident."

"That's because of all this." Lauren indicated the room. "My dad said to stay out of it."

Monique snorted. "So that's why you manipulated me into bringing you here."

Lauren said, "I just want this all to be over for everyone. For Ronni . . ."

Lisa leaned forward, placed both hands on the table. "Don't pretend you care about Ronni, you phony, superficial little bitch."

"Hey! Fuck you!" Monique said, revealing unexpected maternal protectiveness. Jeff glanced over at the court reporter, a blank-faced woman who was transcribing the proceedings. She appeared to be transcribing this comment, too.

Candace stood, tried to regain order. "Please, everyone just calm down. Lauren and Monique, we appreciate your time, but we need to get back on task."

"Get out of here, Lauren," Lisa spat. "Go home and do your hair."

That's when Lauren looked at Jeff. Their eyes locked for the briefest of moments and a chill ran through him. Lauren's expression was almost pleading. *I tried*, her eyes said, *I did this for you*. Surely, everyone in the room could sense their connection. It had to be obvious what had transpired between them; that Lauren was far more than just a friend of his daughter's. . . .

If only he could go back in time to that day when Lauren showed up at the gym. He should have sent her away. Her threat to tell the police about the champagne was bluster and he could have shut her down. But instead, he'd taken her for ice cream, like an idiot. And then her late-night call for help had come in, and like some stupid, obedient Saint Bernard, he had gone to her rescue. It was the wrong choice, he knew it then and he knew it now. Still, when Jeff dropped Lauren off at her mom's apartment that night, he'd hoped it was over. It wasn't.

The texts were innocuous at first:

So board. What's new

Did you suck at science as much as I do

I hate school. Wish we could go for lunch.

He'd barely responded, at most a one-word answer, more often: in a meeting. But, it wasn't enough to discourage her.

And then it had come: A *nude.* He'd heard Hannah and her friends use the term when a boy from their school was expelled for sharing one of his ex-girlfriend. Jeff had been alone in his office, thank Christ, when the image popped up on his phone, the expanse of flesh instantly catching his eye. It was Lauren, naked, or maybe she was wearing a G-string—he hadn't looked closely. Her expression was provocative, pouty, an adolescent porn star. As soon as he registered what and who it was, he had deleted it, his hands shaky and his forehead sweaty. He wiped his phone immediately. It was a work cell; he could be fired for this. Kim could divorce him. He could go to jail! What the hell was this stupid little tart thinking? He could have strangled her.

But he was angry at himself, too, angry that he had opened the door to this sick flirtation. It was *his* fault that Lauren thought that her photo would be appreciated. And he was even angrier at the physical response he'd had to the stimulus of naked, teenaged flesh. Mentally, he was repulsed—like he'd been sent a photo of a mutilated corpse—but he couldn't deny the arousal he'd felt when he'd looked, ever so briefly, at the naked image. It made him sick to his stomach.

Somehow, no one in the office seemed to read the history between him and the girl about to exit the conference room. Monique grabbed her daughter's arm, rather roughly, and hustled her out the door. Lisa let out a bitter, sardonic laugh, and Kim shook her head. Candace was already pushing papers across the table to Paul. "We have three other witness statements that corroborate Lauren's testimony."

So Lauren had made good on her promise. Somehow, she'd convinced the other girls to lie about the champagne, to perjure themselves under oath rather than face Lauren's wrath. How powerful was this girl? What was she capable of? Of course, it was possible that Marta and Caitlin didn't remember him gifting Hannah that bottle of bubbly, but he knew it was wishful thinking. . . .

It was Paul's turn to attack now—or to *examine for discovery*. He set his sights on Kim first. "Do you drink, Mrs. Sanders?"

"Socially," Kim said, though Candace had instructed them to answer yes or no whenever possible.

Paul looked up from his papers. "So never alone?"

"Sometimes I'll have a glass of wine when I'm making dinner, before my husband gets home."

"Did you drink wine the night that Veronica Monroe was injured in your home?"

"Yes."

"One glass of wine? Two? Three?"

Jeff remembered Kim pouring a large second glass after they'd taken the pizza down to the girls. She was upset about their daughter's "attitude." "Ronni and Lauren are bad influences," she'd griped. "Hannah never talked to me that way before they entered her universe. She's trying to impress them."

Kim looked Paul in the eye and calmly said, "I don't remember." She was good at this.

"Do you take any prescription or recreational drugs?"

"No."

"No? Not even sleeping pills?"

"Sometimes I take half an Ambien to help me sleep."

"Did you take half an Ambien the night Veronica Monroe was injured in your basement?"

Kim hesitated and Jeff was sure she'd say she didn't remember. But how could she not? She took half an Ambien practically every night. She was always "wound up" she said, about something trivial, like the tile guy taking too long on their new backsplash, or Aidan not getting enough playing time on his soccer team, or it was Tanya's turn to host book club but she was fobbing it off on Beth. But Kim finally said, "I believe I did."

Paul interlaced his pudgy fingers. "So you had one, maybe two, maybe three glasses of wine and a sleeping pill the night of Ronni's accident."

Kim's composure faltered. "I'm not sure. Probably one glass of wine and half a sleeping pill—I only ever take half. . . ."

Jeff glanced at Lisa and saw the smallest of smiles curl her lips. He felt a surge of anger course through him. She was enjoying this.

Paul turned his attentions to Jeff. "Mr. Sanders . . . are you a drug user?"

"No."

"So you've never used illegal drugs? And may I remind you that you're under oath."

"When I was younger, I smoked some pot and stuff."

"And stuff? Can you elaborate?"

He could feel his face getting hot. "I think I did mushrooms. Maybe tried cocaine. It was a long time ago."

"So when was the last time you used illegal drugs?"

Kim didn't flinch, she didn't move at all, but he could sense her muscles tensing to granite beside him. "I have no idea," he said.

"Have you used LSD within the last year?"

Jeff maintained his outward composure while his stomach plummeted. What the fuck was going on here? Did this lawyer know about that one tiny indiscretion? It had nothing to do with what happened to Ronni. It was completely irrelevant. Why wasn't Candace objecting?

His voice remained steady, "I don't recall."

"So if we were to ask your colleague . . ." Paul looked at a piece of paper in front of him, found the name he was looking for, "Nathan McIntyre, from your Austin branch. Would he corroborate what you're telling us? That you have not used LSD in the past year?"

How did Paul know about Nathan McIntyre and his little vial of magic? Jeff felt the weight of Kim's eyes on him and he met her gaze. He'd expected anger and accusation, but he saw only fear. And then he knew. Kim must have told Lisa about the LSD. This was *Kim's* fault. He looked to Candace for help, but she was jotting notes on a pad like she'd just remembered to add toothpaste to her grocery list. Jeff took a breath and prepared to speak.

"Lisa, please!" Kim blurted. "We'll pay all Ronni's medical

bills. We'll pay for counseling and set up a college fund for her. Just be reasonable."

Candace looked up from her grocery list. "Kim, calm down."

"I am calm!" Kim shrieked, sounding anything but. "We're friends, Lisa. Why won't you settle?"

"My daughter is blind, Kim!"

"She's not *blind*. Give me a break!"

"What would you do if *perfect* Hannah lost her eye? How would your disfigured daughter fit into your perfect little life?"

Kim was crying now. "I would love her and help her. . . . I wouldn't point fingers and lay blame!"

Lisa laughed. "You'd lose your mind, Kim! You'd burn this city down to make someone pay for hurting her!"

The volume of their discourse was attracting attention beyond the glass walls. Jeff noticed people milling about outside, peering in at the melee. He saw the concern on their faces and watched a woman dial on her cell phone. Security was being called.

Paul said, "I suggest a recess," but Kim was standing now. She stabbed a finger toward Lisa.

"You're jealous because we have money and a home and a traditional family. You always have been."

Lisa rose. "You're a sad, bored housewife, Kim. Why would I be jealous?"

The lawyers were on their feet now, so Jeff rose, too. He put his hands on his wife's shoulders, but she shrugged him off. "All we want to do is help you and help Ronni, but you insist on trying to destroy us!"

"You did that all on your own with your wine and your sleeping pills," Lisa hurled back.

"We're not paying you three million dollars!" Kim screamed, marching toward the door. "If you won't negotiate with us, we'll go to trial! And you'll get nothing!"

Kim stormed out of the room just as an elderly, slightly fearful security guard arrived.

kim

THIRTY-SEVEN DAYS AFTER

Jeff drove them home from the examination for discovery, his jaw set, his knuckles white on the steering wheel. They were racing up Market, going too fast in the ubiquitous traffic and uncharacteristic spring fog. Normally, Kim would have asked her husband to slow down, complained that he was being reckless, but she said nothing. The speed felt freeing somehow, almost comforting. If Jeff lost control and careened into an oncoming bus, at least all this shit would be over.

"Why did you tell Lisa about the LSD?" Jeff said, his voice quiet with suppressed rage.

"I didn't tell her," Kim snapped back. "I haven't talked to Lisa about anything in years!"

"Well, you must have told someone. . . ."

"Why would I?" she cried. "I was humiliated!"

Jeff snorted, like being humiliated about your husband's use of psychedelics was a character flaw. "Slow down," Kim demanded, regaining perspective. She did not want to die in a fiery crash just because she was being sued and having her reputation destroyed. Jeff let his foot off the accelerator ever so slightly.

"Who did *you* tell, Jeff? Were you bragging to your friends about getting high behind my back?"

"Fuck you. I didn't tell anyone."

"Fuck you! Neither did I!" They traveled in indignant silence until they pulled into their attached garage. It was only then that Kim realized her outrage was unjustified. She *had* told someone about the LSD. Despite her shame, she had told Tony. What had he done . . . ?

Jeff was too upset to go back to the office, so he took his road bike out (of course). The kids wouldn't be home for a couple of hours, at least, and Kim knew she had to make the most of the empty house. She hurried to her office and dug out the legal file she'd started the day she received the summons from Lisa's attorney. There, on that official document, was the name of Lisa's law firm: Lazar, Neville, and Stenton. Kim hurried to her computer and pulled up their website.

As expected, the site was professional and user-friendly. Lisa wasn't going to hire some mini-mall solicitor to ruin Kim and Jeff. "Meet Our Team," one of the tabs invited, so Kim clicked. As she scrolled through the professional photographs of stiff-looking attorneys, she couldn't quite believe that Tony would betray her this way. Of course he was angry; he felt she'd used him and led him on, but would he really do something so cruel? So unethical? Did he hate her that much? And then her questions were answered.

There, in the senior associates section Kim saw her: civil litigator Amanda Hoyle.

Tony's wife was polished and attractive, with dark hair and arched eyebrows. If it weren't for the length of her face, giving her a somewhat horsey appearance, she could have been a TV lawyer. Amanda looked intelligent and confident, an image validated by her résumé: Pepperdine University School of Law, bar admissions in Northern and Central California, various awards and distinctions. Would this accomplished woman really sink so low as to feed gossip she got from her husband to Lisa's fat lawyer? And what exactly did Tony say to his wife? "You know that civil suit your firm is handling, where the girl lost her eye? I was messing around with the defendant and she mentioned that her husband used LSD last year." Of course, he'd spin it so he appeared totally innocent. "The defendant in that case where the girl lost her eye . . . she's the copywriter for Apex Outerwear. She's been really unreliable lately, so I asked her what was up. She told me about the lawsuit. And she admitted that her husband took LSD last year."

Suddenly, Kim was overcome with fury. She picked up the manila file full of legal papers and threw it across the room. "Fuck!" she screamed, as the papers escaped the folder and wafted to the floor like wounded birds. She swiped the desk organizer off the desk, sending pens, pencils, and paper clips clattering across the concrete floor. Kim was angry at Tony, but she was even more angry at herself. How could she have shared Jeff's indiscretions with a stranger? How could she have thought that Tony could be her confidant? When she thought how she had kissed him and touched him, how she had thought she might have loved him . . . Jesus, he wasn't even her type! So skinny and hairy and artsy-fartsy. He designed flyers, for Christ's sake! Jeff was vice president of global strategy at a multimillion-dollar tech company!

Tony was clearly emasculated by his attorney wife, so he was trying to screw around on her to make himself feel like more of a man. But when Kim rejected him, he attacked her like the puny, pitiful flyer designer he was. Kim reached for the phone, then hung it up. No, this was not happening on the phone. She needed to see Tony's face when he admitted what he had done to her. She needed him to see how his petty vendetta over blue balls had damaged her life, her family. She opened her filing cabinet and withdrew one of Tony's invoices. His address was printed prominently on the top.

Kim hurried to the kitchen and grabbed her car keys from the bowl full of glass pebbles. She halted near the door and checked the mirror that hung there for last-minute touch-ups. As angry as she was, she still wanted to look good. She still wanted Tony to want her so she could laugh in his face. Luckily, rage seemed to suit her. Her cheeks were flushed and her hair was sexily disheveled. Maybe Kim should lose it more often? With the way her life was spinning out of control, it was a definite possibility.

TONY'S HOME WAS one of three suites in a reclaimed Victorian on Russian Hill. Kim pressed the buzzer for A AND T HOYLE. She knew Tony would answer. Amanda would be at work, and the kids would be at school, followed by one of their numerous extracurricular activities that Tony often moaned about. After a few seconds, she heard Tony's upbeat voice through the speaker. "Hello?"

"It's Kim. I need to talk to you."

There was a long pause and then, "I have nothing to say to you."

"I'm not leaving here until you let me in."

Click. The bastard had hung up. She pressed the button again. And again. She would buzz until Tony opened the door. Or lost his mind. Eventually, his voice came through the speaker. "Calm down, Kim."

"I'll calm the fuck down when you talk to me like a man!" she screamed into the tiny speaker. "You can't hide from me, you cowardly fuck! I'll buzz all your neighbors until someone lets me in and then I'll—" *BZZZZZT.* It was the door unlocking.

Kim marched up the stairs to the Hoyles' second-floor suite, her heart thudding in her chest from exertion and rage. The door swung open before she'd reached the landing and Tony appeared. He looked rumpled and handsome. A few weeks ago, she would have been ready to jump his bones. The thought made her ill. "Get inside," he growled, and she knew she would have found his gruff tone erotic in their previous iteration.

She crossed the threshold into Tony's abode. Despite her anger, she had to admire the refurbished apartment. Walls had been removed to open up the late-nineteenth-century space. Gleaming hardwood floors, an embossed tin ceiling, and elaborate cornices were indicative of the era, but modern furnishings and contemporary art pieces made the home current. The place had been decorated by a couple who knew art and design. Kim refocused herself. "How could you?"

"How could I what?"

"You told Amanda that Jeff used LSD."

Tony gave an incredulous laugh. "What?"

"Lisa's hired your wife's law firm. We just had an examination for discovery and they knew about Jeff's drugs. You're the only person I told."

"Jeff must have told someone."

"He didn't!" Kim screamed. "That incident nearly destroyed us! Why would he tell someone?"

"I don't know. . . ." Tony ran his hands through his hair. He seemed at a loss for words. Finally, he said, "What do you want from me?"

"I just want to know . . . do you really hate me that much?"

"I don't hate you," he muttered, his eyes on some of his kids' sporting equipment stacked in a corner.

"You must. You're helping your wife's firm destroy me. Jeff and I could lose everything."

Tony looked at her then. "I don't hate you. I feel sorry for you."

Kim snorted. "Why?"

"You're so unhappy. And you won't even admit it to yourself."

"*I'm* unhappy?" she barked. "If your life's so perfect, why did you try to have an affair with me?"

"My life's not perfect!" Tony yelled. "I've got plenty of fucking problems! My marriage is hanging by a thread. My career is a fucking joke. But at least I'm aware of it. . . ."

"I'm extremely aware that my life is a disaster," Kim said. "And thanks to you, it's about to get a hell of a lot worse!"

"I just tried to be there for you, Kim. You're the one who made it sexual."

Kim felt a surge of humiliation. "That's a fucking lie! I'm not even attracted to you!"

"Really?" He grabbed her shoulders and kissed her hard on the mouth. His tongue pushed between her lips, pressing against her clenched teeth. She wanted to fight him, but her body was responding. She felt her jaw release and open up to his probing tongue, her back arched toward him as his hands gripped her ass. He was right: she was attracted to him. But only for a moment.

She pulled away and slapped him, hard, across the face. They stared at each other, chests heaving, both of them in shock. Kim had never hit anyone in her life, and it appeared that Tony had never been hit. Kim found her voice. "You make me sick."

There was a metallic noise, a key fumbling in a lock, and Kim and Tony turned toward the door. It opened to reveal a heavyset Mexican woman, probably Kim's age, trailed by two, sandy-haired kids: Ruby and Declan. The woman stopped short, clearly sensing that she had walked in on something intense. No one spoke for a moment, then Tony said, "Hey, guys," in a hoarse voice.

Kim was still breathing hard and her head was swimming, but she had to pull herself together. She couldn't let these children know that, mere moments ago, she was kissing and slapping their father. She addressed Tony in a professional voice. "Thanks for the information on Apex. I'll forward it on to them." The nanny and her charges cleared the way as Kim hurried out the door.

hannah

THIRTY-SEVEN DAYS AFTER

Ronni had been back at school for a week, but Hannah had yet to run into her. Phoebe Winslow, who was a Christian, so she was really nice to everyone, had been supporting Ronni and updated Hannah on her revised schedule. According to Phoebe, Ronni only came to school for half days and spent most of them talking with Mrs. Pittwell, the counselor, about her feelings. She spent the rest of her limited time going over the lessons she missed with a resource teacher. Phoebe said that Ronni was having a hard time and had already missed a couple of days. It was wrong to be relieved, but Hannah was. The less chance there was of running into Ronni, the better. Hannah spent every school day on edge, waiting to round a corner and find her old friend, disfigured, depressed, and probably ready to stab Hannah in the neck with a pencil. It didn't help that this morning Hannah's parents had gone to their lawyer's office to face off against Ronni's mom. There was no way that had gone well.

So Hannah nearly jumped out of her skin when she closed her locker to find a female face mere inches from hers. But this face had two eyes with crow's-feet, and an unflattering haircut. "Mrs. Pittwell," Hannah said, trying to compose herself, "you scared me."

"Can we talk, Hannah?"

"I have English."

"I'll talk to Mr. Morrel. . . ."

Hannah obediently followed the older woman through the crowded halls to her office. As she trailed behind Mrs. Pittwell, she passed Noah and Ryan, another kid from his circle. Their expressions said it all: *Shit*. Hannah gave them a casual nod: *Don't worry. I got this.* But she didn't have it. She was terrified. The counselor had no reason to talk to her except about Ronni. And she knew it wouldn't be good.

When they were enclosed in Mrs. Pittwell's windowless office, she got to the point. "Ronni's not doing well."

"There's a lawsuit," Hannah said, her eyes spontaneously filling with tears. "Her mom is suing us." Her voice cracked, and she silently berated her lack of control. Why couldn't she be more like Lauren and tell this "do-gooder bitch" to leave her out of it? She wasn't even Ronni's best friend! Why was Mrs. Pittwell singling her out? But she couldn't say any of that. If she spoke, she'd dissolve into sobs.

"I know about the lawsuit, hon. . . . But I think there's an opportunity for you to be the most mature person in this whole situation. What do you think?"

Hannah shrugged. She didn't know what being the most mature person entailed, but she was pretty sure she wasn't up for the job.

"I know your parents are upset. And Ronni's mom is, too. But Ronni just wants things to go back to normal. She needs her friends, Hannah."

Hannah stared through her tears at a framed photo on the desk: two boys, around eight and ten, with haircuts much like Mrs. Pittwell's. Her sons, obviously . . . poor kids. "It's just really awkward," Hannah croaked.

"But you can be the bigger person here. You can reach out to Ronni and be there for her. You can rise above the anger and blame, and you can show your parents and Ronni's mom what true friendship looks like."

"Ronni's not mad at me?"

"She's not mad at you. . . ." Mrs. Pittwell leaned forward in her chair. "She misses you."

That's when Hannah broke down. "But . . . Lauren said . . ." She was sobbing so hard she could barely get the words out. She was relieved when the counselor cut her off.

"Lauren is dealing with her own issues. She's not supporting Ronni because she doesn't have the strength of character. But you do, Hannah. You can stand up to these other kids. You can stand up to your parents."

But Hannah didn't want to be the girl with *strength of character*. She wanted to be the cool girl, the popular girl, the girl with the hot boyfriend. The counselor was asking her to throw all that away just so Ronni wouldn't be lonely. How could Mrs. Pittwell be trained to work with teenagers and be so clueless?

Mrs. Pittwell slid a box of tissues across her desk. Hannah took one and blew her nose loudly. "I can't go to English," Hannah said, "I'm too upset."

"Go home early. I'll explain it all to Mr. Morrel."

Hannah jumped up, eager to get out of there, but the counselor wasn't quite finished. "Just promise me one thing."

"What?"

"That you'll think about being a friend to Ronni. If you turn away from her, you'll look back on this one day and be filled with regret."

"Fine," Hannah snapped. She'd had enough of this guilt trip. And she wanted to get her coat from her locker and leave the school before classes let out and the hallways filled again. She looked terrible when she cried. "I'll think about it."

THE HOUSE WAS eerily quiet when Hannah entered. She checked her watch and realized it was only 2:40; school didn't end until three. Her brother wouldn't be home yet, which was a relief, but her mom would be there. Her mom was *always* there after school: to ask how their days had been and how much homework they had; to make sure they ate a nutritious snack before she drove them to soccer or basketball or piano. Except no one answered when Hannah called "Mom?" into the cavernous house. Hannah peered into her mom's office: empty. The small space was usually orderly, but papers were strewn across the floor from a manila folder that now rested against the far wall, and pens and paper clips were scattered across the floor. The mess looked like the result of some temper tantrum, but Hannah knew that couldn't be the case. Her mom didn't lose her temper, although a lot had changed since the party. She headed to the kitchen breathing a small sigh of relief. She was alone.

Hannah grabbed a cup and filled it with chocolate chips. "They're for *baking.* Besides, you need protein at the end of the day." That's what her mom would have said, but her mom wasn't there. Hannah moved to her room, closed the door, and opened her laptop. Some mindless comedic YouTube viewing was in order, the sillier the better. She needed a distraction from the meeting with Mrs. Pittwell. She was searching through various cat videos, when Skype alerted her to a call. It was Noah. She clicked to accept and his handsome face filled her computer screen. "Hey. Watcha doing?"

"Chilling. Snacking." Hannah was getting a lot more comfortable with her boyfriend since she was grounded and hence, never allowed to spend time alone with him. "Are you home already?"

"Got out of gym early. What did Mrs. Pittwell want?"

"She wanted to talk about Ronni."

"What about Ronni?"

"She wants me to be *there for her*. Give me a break." Even as the words came out of her mouth, Hannah felt guilty for saying them. She sounded so heartless. . . . She sounded like Lauren.

Noah said, "I don't know why Ronni came back. She should have changed schools."

"I guess. . . ."

"If she says anything about that night, we're all fucked."

"She won't," Hannah assured him. "Ronni doesn't remember anything."

Noah was drinking a Coke and he took a swig from the can. "Memories can come back," he said. "It would be better for everyone if Ronni was gone."

"Gone where?"

"A different school. A different town. Who cares?"

He was right. It would have been easier if Ronni had never returned. But she had, and they would have to accept it. "Yeah . . . but there's nothing we can do about it."

"I think there is. . . ." He was smirking.

Hannah's stomach churned, but she kept her cool. "What are you up to?" Her tone was teasing and conspiratorial, concealing the anxiety she was feeling.

"Adam's got some ideas. He's a sick fuck."

"He has no mercy." She laughed and ate a handful of chocolate chips. She was getting so good at playing the role of the popular girl: cool, narcissistic, callous. . . . The only problem was, her insides were twisting into knots of wrong.

There was a noise from downstairs. "I just heard my mom come in," she said. "Gotta go." Before Noah could answer, she clicked and he disappeared.

Hannah wiped any trace of chocolate from her lips in case her mom came upstairs, but she didn't. After a few minutes, Hannah headed to the kitchen, where she found her mom pouring a glass of wine.

"Hey."

"Hey." Kim took a drink of wine.

"I don't want to go to piano today."

"Fine."

"What's wrong?"

"Nothing's wrong. Why?"

"You never let me miss piano. And you're drinking wine and it's not even three."

"We had our examination for discovery today," Kim said. "It was tense." She took a big drink of wine: *a gulp*. Then she looked at her watch. "Why are you home so early?"

"Mrs. Pittwell, the counselor, said I could go early. I was upset after she talked to me."

Kim set down her wine. "What did she talk to you about?"

Hannah felt the emotion rise in her chest. "About Ronni . . . She's not doing very well. She's depressed and sad and she feels like everyone has deserted her."

Her mom drank more wine. "I'm sorry to hear that." But she didn't sound sorry. She sounded distracted.

Hannah moved closer, until she was across from her mom. She rested her hands on the smooth wooden countertop. "Mrs. Pittwell knows that there's stuff going on between you and Lisa, but she said that I should rise above it. She said that I should be there for Ronni."

"What do you think?"

"I don't know. . . ." Hannah felt emotion clog her throat again. "I feel bad for her."

Kim sighed and looked at her daughter. Her mom usually looked pretty and put together and younger than her age. Today, she looked worn-out and Hannah saw the wrinkles on her forehead and around her mouth. Had the wrinkles appeared in the last weeks, or had Hannah just never noticed them before?

"It's a real mess right now, Hannah. I'm sorry Ronni is struggling, but I think you should keep your distance."

Hannah bit her bottom lip and nodded. She had always considered her mom a good person. She was a little superficial, a little snobby, but deep down her mom had a good heart. Kim had taught her children to be grateful for all they had, and to give back to those less fortunate. Every Thanksgiving, the family volunteered at a soup kitchen. At Christmas, they filled shoe boxes with gifts for kids in Africa. But this was different. Lisa was attacking them, threatening their luxurious home, their expensive cars, their affluent existence. . . . Apparently, Ronni didn't deserve their charity.

"Got it," Hannah said, and headed back to her room. It was what she had wanted: the all clear to disown Ronni, not risking her tenuous social status with a pity friendship. But the irritating buzz of her conscience kept the events at the party replaying in her mind. She had said she couldn't remember, but she did. Despite all the alcohol she'd imbibed, Hannah remembered it all. And she couldn't stop feeling like shit.

hannah

THAT NIGHT

"This is boring," Lauren said, nibbling a rubbery carrot stick. The five girls were splayed on the couches and on the floor, picking at room-temperature pizza and listening to Drake. There had been some dancing, some gossiping, some giggling as they'd indulged in the sparkling wine and various libations they'd smuggled in, but now the alcohol was gone, leaving a lethargic malaise in its wake.

"We could watch a movie," Marta suggested lamely.

Ronni groaned, like Marta had suggested making mud pies.

Hannah's worst fears were manifesting: her party was sucking. It was dull and juvenile and after it, Lauren would deem Hannah unworthy to bask in the glow of her popularity. Hannah felt distressed and panicky, but more than anything, she felt angry at her parents . . . well, at her mom. Kim's hard-ass rules were the reason this party resembled all the birthdays that had come before it. The woman simply refused to accept that her daughter was growing up! Hannah knew cool parents who let kids drink and smoke dope in their homes: "They're going to do it anyway, I'd rather they do it under my roof." But not Kim Sanders. She could never be accused of being cool.

"I brought some of my mom's Xanax," Caitlin said. *Hannah gave her a grateful smile—the girl was trying—but Ronni and Lauren remained unimpressed. Ronni was busy licking salt off chips and then depositing the soggy remains on a napkin. She barely acknowledged the offer.*

"I know what this party needs," Lauren said with a wicked smile. *"Some testosterone."*

"Totally," Ronni seconded.

"Yeah," Hannah agreed weakly, but other than inviting her corny dad to join them, she wasn't sure how to add the hormone to their gathering.

But Lauren clearly had a plan. She was already moving toward the small basement window and inspecting its size. It was small, but discreet entry was still possible. She turned to Hannah and smiled. "Text Noah."

Of course Hannah complied. How could she not? Her heart pounded as she waited for his response. If he turned her down, her party would be a failure; if he accepted, she risked being grounded for life. She had never disobeyed so many of her parents' rules before: booze, drugs, boys. . . . All they needed was some cigarettes and porn and it would be a home run. And what would Noah expect from Hannah tonight? She was inviting him to sneak into her unsupervised basement, where they would drink and dance and take drugs. . . . What else would he want? His text arrived and her stomach churned.

Be there in twenty

As the other girls tidied the room, Hannah tiptoed to the main floor in her stocking feet and disabled the alarm. (Both Hannah and Aidan had memorized the code. The alarm was finicky and prone to be set off by wind or sudden cold snaps.) Padding silently through the house, she felt like a burglar. But a burglar wouldn't have been this nervous. Her heart was pounding so hard she was afraid her parents would hear it from the floor above.

When she returned, Ronni had added to the guest list. "Adam's coming, too," she said gleefully.

Lauren pulled Hannah aside. "Ronni's so hot for Adam, but he's not into her. He wants me."

"Really?" Hannah whispered, thrilled to be Lauren's confidante. "Do you like him?"

"Fuck no," Lauren said. "He's so immature. And his eyes are weird. They're too close together or something."

Hannah nodded her agreement, though she had never noticed Adam's weird eyes.

"Ronni can have him," Lauren said. "I can do better."

In that moment, Hannah felt there was a real chance she could replace Ronni in Lauren's affections. She looked over at Ronni then and saw the insecurities shining through her perfect makeup and fashionable outfit. Ronni's sophistication was clearly a facade, not like Lauren's. Lauren was the real deal; Ronni was no cooler than Hannah.

"Let's put on our pajamas," Ronni suggested.

"Slumber party. Every guy's wet dream," Lauren said. The girls scurried to their overnight bags and extracted their sleepwear. Hannah had bought a new nightie for the occasion and she put it on. It

had sporty stripes on the sleeves and the number 28 emblazoned across its chest. She had thought it would look cute and sexy, like she was wearing Noah's football jersey. But now, she realized it would only be cute and sexy if it was *Noah's jersey and not some knockoff she'd picked up at Macy's. When she saw Ronni in her pink short shorts and tank, and Lauren in a satin slip, she felt dowdy and infantile in her knee-length, boxy garb. Thankfully, Caitlin was wearing full-length dad pajamas and Marta was in a shin-length gown.*

There was a soft tap on the glass: the boys had arrived. The girls watched and whispered excitedly as the guys squeezed their large male bodies through the small basement window. When they were in, Noah handed Hannah a bottle of Jägermeister. "Happy birthday." He gave her that sexy, intimate grin, and Hannah knew she'd made the right decision. She was only going to turn sixteen once; she had to make it count.

"Let's get wasted," Ronni said, and Lauren echoed the sentiment by grabbing the bottle from Hannah and taking a big drink. As they passed the sweet, strong liquor between them, Hannah felt no guilt, no regrets. Even if her mom came down right now and lost her shit, she couldn't take away the thrill of this moment. Even if Kim called the other kids' parents and grounded Hannah for the rest of her life, she would have this memory.

"Let's get this party started," Adam said, withdrawing two tabs of ecstasy from his pocket. He put one on his tongue and held out the other. "Who wants?" He was staring at Lauren when he said it, but Ronni stepped up, more than eager to let him place the pill on her outstretched tongue.

Caitlin pulled a piece of tissue from her pocket and revealed three oval pills. "Xanax, anyone?" she said, sounding pleased with herself. "If we break them in half, there's almost enough."

Marta did the math. "Someone has to miss out."

"I'm cool," Hannah said, hoping she sounded generous and not like she was afraid to take Xanax, which she totally was.

"But it's your birthday," Noah said. "You should have one."

"They just put me to sleep," she said, then turned coy. "I don't want to pass out on you."

"Don't," he said.

They played music at low volume and danced. Ronni was all over Adam, grinding up against him in her sexy little outfit. He may have liked Lauren, but he was no match for Ronni's aggression and soon, they were making out. Maybe the ecstasy had kicked in; maybe Ronni was just putting on a show, but she was dancing for Adam, pulling her top down, touching herself, touching him. . . . She had the champagne bottle and she was drinking from it, stroking it, rubbing it against her crotch. It was explicit, pornographic even. Lauren leaned into Hannah's ear. "What a slut." Hannah felt warm inside.

The alcohol circulated. Adam had brought a small bottle of whiskey to supplement the birthday Jäger. Hannah never turned down a mouthful—she wanted to lose her inhibitions. So when Noah led her to the sofa, she was relaxed and ready.

They made out for a while; she wasn't sure how long. His hands were in her hair and on her breasts and between her thighs. She felt practically naked in her flimsy nightie, but she went with it, she didn't chicken out. The other kids were only a few feet away, giggling and dancing, so she knew it wasn't going to get too heavy. She wanted to show Noah that she was into it, that she wasn't afraid.

She heard someone retch, and then Adam said, "Fuck me!"

There was more heaving. "Jesus, Ronni . . ." It was Lauren's annoyed voice.

"Go to the bathroom," someone, either Marta or Caitlin, said.

Hannah was tempted to pull away, but Noah was still kissing her, completely oblivious to the fact that Ronni was puking a few feet from them. This happened with ecstasy, Hannah knew. It was one of the reasons she didn't want to try it. She pushed away the sound and the smell. She didn't want to be distracted by the mess her friend was making. They could clean it up after; it was no big deal. Hannah didn't want to be uptight about stuff like that; she didn't want to be like her mom.

And then it came: a crash and a scream. Hannah pulled away from Noah and stood up. She saw Ronni lying there on top of the broken coffee table, bits of glass all around her. The champagne bottle she'd been holding had broken neatly in half—the neck, with its pink foil scarf, still clutched in Ronni's hand. Hannah must have been in shock because she laughed; it just seemed so surreal. And Ronni seemed okay. She dropped the broken bottle, half sat up and said, "Fuck . . ."

Hannah hurried to her and grabbed her hand. "Get up," she said, still giggling. She must have been hysterical. It was all so much: the drinks, the drugs, the boys, the puke . . . and now the broken table. She'd have to make up some really creative excuse to explain it to her mom and dad. Her hand in Ronni's slipped and that's when she noticed the blood. Ronni noticed it, too. Ronni looked, with bewildered detachment, at the gash in her forearm, the source of the blood that coated her arm and hand. The champagne bottle had made a deep, diagonal slice across the soft flesh of her inner arm. Ronni looked up and her eyes met Hannah's. Oh Jesus, her eye . . .

Under the mask of puke and blood, Ronni's face went pale, and her body went limp. She collapsed back into the pile of glass, unconscious. "Oh fuck." It was a male voice, Noah or Adam.

"Oh my god! Someone get help!" Marta cried.

"I can't . . . ," Lauren said, and rushed toward the bathroom.

"Go get your parents!" Caitlin shrieked.

Hannah hurried toward the door, but Noah's voice stopped her. "Hannah, wait!" she turned back. "We need to get the fuck out of here." Hannah saw that Adam was already hoisting himself through the window. Noah, holding the empty liquor bottles, was on his heels. Her boyfriend looked back at her, at Marta and Caitlin, too. "We were never here," he said firmly.

lisa

FORTY-FIVE DAYS AFTER

The vegan café was bright, kitschy but virtually empty. It was two in the afternoon, so the lunch rush was over . . . if there had been a lunch rush. Lisa knew the challenge of making delicious food without animal by-products. She had been a strict vegan for almost six months, back when she had time to care about things like that. . . . Now, she accepted that the world was a brutal place, and swapping almond milk for cow's milk was not going to improve it.

Yeva and Darcy were seated beside and opposite her, enjoying their kale and tahini salads. Lisa had a roasted yam dish that was quite delicious, but she wasn't very hungry. Her companions were talking about cleansing: a favorite topic among their cohort.

Darcy said, "For me, dairy was the devil. Once I gave it up, my skin just brightened and cleared so much."

"Your skin is beautiful," Yeva said.

“Mmmm . . .” Lisa murmured her agreement. Darcy was not particularly beautiful, but she radiated good health.

“When I eat dairy, the whites of my eyes have a grayish hue,” Yeva said.

“That could also be from sugar,” Darcy countered. “Do they have a yellowish tinge?”

“Not really . . . Sugar gives me dark circles, though.”

“I know!” Darcy cried. “I had one bite of cake at my brother’s wedding—one bite—and I broke out in pimples all over here. . . .” She indicated her chin.

Lisa forked a yam and put it in her mouth. She could have chimed in: she had done the same cleanses, had eliminated every evil food at one time or another, but it all seemed so indulgent now. As she chewed and pretended to listen to Yeva’s account of a single glass of wine giving her a yeast infection, she felt eyes upon her.

The woman was tall, angular, and unfamiliar . . . but she was the right age to be a Hillcrest mom. She was seated at a corner table with a man—her husband, probably—it didn’t appear to be a business meeting, given the woman’s yoga pants and hoodie. Her blue eyes kept darting over toward Lisa. When their gazes connected, the woman spoke softly to her companion and stood. Lisa hurriedly swallowed her yam as the tall woman approached.

“Sorry to interrupt . . .”

Yeva stopped talking about candida midsentence.

The woman said, “Hi, Lisa . . . my name’s Karen. You probably don’t recognize me, but my kids go to Hillcrest. I’ve seen you at school events—a play or a volleyball game or something.”

“Right,” Lisa said, though she couldn’t recall ever seeing this tall stranger. Ronni had never been in a play, never played volleyball or any other sport. Her daughter wasn't really a *joiner.*

"I just wanted to offer my support. . . . You and Ronni have been through so much."

"Thank you."

"My kids don't really know Ronni, but I told them that they should be kind when they see her. And if they witness any of the bullying behavior, I told them to go to a teacher."

"*Bullying behavior?*" Lisa asked in a choked voice. She knew Ronni had felt isolated and ostracized, but she'd never complained of overt bullying.

"I don't know any of the specifics. . . ." Karen clearly felt awkward. "If I did, I would have called the principal. My kids just said that there are some kids who are saying things . . . at school and online . . . mean things. "

"Ronni never told me. . . ." Lisa felt Yeva's supportive hand land on top of hers.

"Maybe you should talk to her counselor?" Karen said, flustered. "I could have gotten it wrong—my kids aren't the most reliable sources."

"I will," Lisa said, roasted yams turning to lead in her stomach. "Thank you for coming over."

"If there's anything I can do . . . I'm friends with Ana Pinto, Marta's mom. She can send you my details."

Marta. She was at the party that night. Her mom, Ana, had sent Lisa a note. . . . She couldn't remember what it said, but the woman was a doctor. It was monogrammed on her stationery.

Yeva spoke for her. "Thank you, Karen. That's kind of you."

"Thanks," Lisa managed, as Karen backed away toward her table.

Darcy's hand reached across and joined the supportive hand pile. "You okay?"

Lisa nodded. "I'm going to go."

"We'll come with you," Yeva offered, as Lisa pulled her hand away and stood.

"No, stay. Ronni and I need to talk. Alone . . ."

Darcy was on her feet. "Let me buy her a vegan raspberry scone. They're amazing."

THE WHITE BAKERY bag crinkled as Lisa let herself into the apartment building. She hoped the vegan scone wasn't dry. Ronni didn't have much of an appetite lately and would be easily turned off. Lisa rode the elevator to their fourth-floor apartment, so lost in thought that when the elevator stopped on the third floor (someone must have called it and then changed their mind), Lisa got off and walked to the end of the hall before realizing her mistake. She and the scone took the stairs up.

It was quiet in the apartment, but Lisa knew Ronni was there. She almost never left anymore, except on those days when Lisa could cajole her into attending school. Her reluctance made sense now. . . . Ronni had the entire apartment to herself this afternoon, but she was closeted in her lilac bedroom, as usual, with the door tightly closed. Her personal space was a shrine to what had been: pictures of her and her friends covered bulletin boards, filled frames, hung from a makeshift clothesline draped along one wall.

Concert tickets, postcards, and music posters papered the rest of the space, a tribute to her former passions.

But Ronni didn't listen to music these days: too emotive. She would undoubtedly be watching Netflix—teen millionaires, teen vampires, teen detectives—and wishing she were someone else, someone with money, fangs, or sleuthing skills. Lisa moved toward the room, holding the scone in both hands like an inadequate gift for royalty.

Usually, Lisa knocked—she had always respected her daughter's privacy and she still did—but she was distracted today, reliving her tense meeting with Karen, so she pushed open the door with no announcement. Ronni was sitting cross-legged on her bed, her back to the door, with her laptop in front of her. Lisa had full view of the screen as she moved into the room. It wasn't Netflix but Facebook; Lisa recognized the blue bar across the top. Ronni was looking at a large picture of a cartoon character: it was green with a round body, skinny appendages, and a big friendly smile. Lisa vaguely recognized the creature from the Pixar movies that Ronni had watched as a kid, and she felt amused and comforted that Ronni was revisiting her childhood memories. But why was Ronni's name printed across the bottom of the image? And then she saw it: the creature had one eye.

At that very moment, Ronni sensed her mother's presence and slammed the laptop closed.

"What is that?" Lisa's voice was quiet, her throat constricted with dread.

"Nothing," Ronni snapped, but her face was flushed and her eyes were full of tears.

"Let me see it."

"No."

"Give me the laptop, Ronni."

Her daughter's voice was desperate. "Just forget it. It's nothing."

Lisa lunged for the device, and Ronni yanked it out of reach. Lisa had never been physical with her daughter, but she needed to see that webpage. She was filled with such urgency, such panic, that she shouldered Ronni roughly out of the way and grabbed the laptop. "Ow! God!" But Lisa ignored her daughter's feigned injuries and opened the computer.

It was just as she feared, and Lisa felt bile rise in her stomach. "Who did this? Who made this profile page of you?"

"I don't know."

"You must have some idea."

"I don't!" Ronni screamed. "It could be anyone! Everyone at school thinks I'm a monster! Look at all the comments."

Lisa scanned them, but they were too painful, too cruel. "This is cyberbullying. I'm calling the principal."

"No!" Ronni shrieked. "You'll make it worse."

"Then I'll call Facebook."

Ronni let out a high-pitched snort of laughter. "Oh my god." She covered her face as hysterical giggles shook her shoulders. "You're unbelievable," she spluttered, throwing herself face-first onto the bed. Within moments, the laughter had segued into anguished, wrenching sobs. Lisa set the laptop on the floor and leaned over her only child, shielding her with her body, stroking her hair and murmuring, "Who is doing this to you? Why . . . ?"

Eventually, Ronni composed herself and sat up. "I can't go back to that school."

"There are only a few months left in the school year. It's too late to change now."

"I can go to the public school down the street. They have to take me because I'm in the district."

"That school is full of gangs and drug dealers," Lisa said. "That's why I sent you to Hillcrest in the first place."

"Hillcrest is full of snobs and assholes!" Ronni was starting to cry again.

Lisa took her daughter's hand and held it to her chest. "Listen to me," she said firmly. Ronni took a deep, shuddering inhale and pressed her lips together, forcing her sobs back down into her chest. "You are strong, Ronni. You have already been through more than people like Lauren Ross or Hannah Sanders will ever go through. You're better than they are. You're a survivor."

Ronni managed an affirmative shrug and nod.

"What bullies want is a reaction. If you don't give it to them, they'll lose interest. And you're not going to let them scare you out of a good school. You're going to walk in there with your head held high and you're going to finish out the year. And next year, you can go to the best private school in the city, not just one that offers scholarships. And you'll have the best education money can buy and you'll have an amazing life. You'll show them all."

Ronni met her mom's eyes and held them for a moment. "Is that why we're suing Hannah's parents?"

We. Ronni and Lisa were a team again, them against the world. "Yes," Lisa said. "You deserve the best, baby, you always did."

hannah

FORTY-SIX DAYS AFTER

Hannah paused at the back door of the school. The lunch bell had rung, and students moved to their eating spots like salmon swimming instinctively upstream to spawn. Now that Hannah was seeing Noah, her spawning place was a covered area behind the school with a concrete ledge perfect for perching and eating. Noah, Adam, and Lauren would be there already; the boys would be eating, but Lauren wouldn't. Sometimes Lauren would nibble on some almonds or pick at a muffin, but for the most part, she drank vitaminwater. Hannah hadn't been particularly hungry lately, either. Her mom still packed her a nutritious, homemade lunch most days, but it often ended up in the trash.

Before she became part of her current clique, Hannah had eaten in the cafeteria with Marta and Caitlin. It was loud and chaotic and smelled like beef stew—not an appetizing environment by any means, but back then, Hannah had no problem devouring her chicken salad with halved grapes. Back then, she had watched, covetously, as Lauren and Ronni wandered past her table, expensive colored water in hand, to meet the hot boys outside. They had seemed so much older, so jaded and worldly that Hannah couldn't imagine being a part of their scene. But now, she was.

As Hannah reached for the door handle, it jerked open from the other side. Suddenly, Sarah Foster was standing in the doorway just inches away. The pretty blonde looked startled, her eyes darting around in search of Hannah's posse. When Sarah found no sign of Lauren Ross, her face relaxed.

Hannah stepped aside. "Go ahead . . ." She ushered Sarah into the school. The stylish girl breezed past her without a word, her perfume—something adult and expensive—wafting behind her. Hannah was about to exit, when Sarah's voice stopped her.

"You know she's going to turn on you, right?"

"What?"

"Lauren. She turns on everyone. It's only a matter of time." She brushed her silky hair away from her face. "You're pathetic if you think you're any different."

Hannah scrambled for a comeback, the right words to defend herself, to defend her friend, but all that came out of her mouth was "Whatever . . ." She hustled herself outside.

The sky was blue and the sun was shining, warming Hannah's face as she crossed the asphalt courtyard. Sarah Foster was clearly jealous. She had disparaged Lauren because she wanted to be in with her, in with *them*. If Sarah could have traded places with Hannah, she would have done so in a heartbeat. So it was ridiculous, the nostalgia Hannah was feeling for the noisy, smelly cafeteria. Her life had been mundane then, she reminded herself. Marta and Caitlin were fine, they were comfortable, but they didn't challenge or excite her, not like Noah and Adam and Lauren did. Maybe what she was really craving was the simplicity of that time—before the party, before the accident, before the lawsuit.

As predicted, her three friends were in the designated spot. Noah and Lauren sat on the ledge while Adam stood in front of them. He was holding his brand-new iPhone out for them and Noah and Lauren were peering at the tiny screen. All three of them were laughing. Hannah walked up to them but said nothing.

Noah noted Hannah's presence immediately and stood. "Have you seen this?" he asked, nodding his head toward the phone as he slipped his arm around her.

"So fucking funny," Lauren said. Her voice was slightly slurred and her eyes were glassy. She was probably stoned—on pot or Ativan. Lauren's mom had taken her to see a doctor after the *trauma* of Hannah's birthday party. "I laid it on thick and I got like sixty Ativan and a refillable prescription," she'd bragged.

Adam passed the phone to Hannah. "Ronni's new profile page," he said, stating the obvious. Hannah looked at the cartoon character, its bright smile, its one huge eye, at Ronni's name plastered beneath it. She knew she was supposed to laugh, but she couldn't. She felt nauseated, a huge lump rising up from her stomach. "Who did this?" she managed to say.

"Don't know," Noah said, with a wry smile at Adam.

"Some genius," Adam said, taking the phone from her. "Check out the comments." He passed the phone to Lauren, who read them in her sleepy, slurry voice.

"'She was a stuck-up bitch when she had two eyes. . . . Will she be half a stuck-up bitch now?'" The boys chuckled. Lauren continued. "'Being a drunken slut is all fun and games until . . .'"

Noah and Adam joined in for the chorus, "'Someone loses an eye.'" They all dissolved into laughter. After a few seconds, Lauren composed herself to keep reading. "'Why are you guys picking on Fetty Wap?'"

"Awesome!" The three of them convulsed again. Hannah forced a noise out of her throat and hoped it resembled a chuckle.

Lauren read, "'This page is cruel and whoever made it should be ashamed of themselves.'"

"Let me guess," Adam said, "Someone from the God squad."

Lauren peered at the tiny name. "Yep. Phoebe Winslow."

"Do-gooder bitch," Noah snorted.

"Ronni didn't even like Phoebe," Lauren said. "But now that Ronni's a freak, Phoebe's her BFF."

"Phoebe will report the page," Noah said. "She probably already has."

Adam said, "That's okay. I'm sure Ronni has had a chance to see it."

"Yeah . . ." Noah added, "as long as she got the message."

"Oh, she got it," Lauren said smugly.

Hannah was gripped with an urgent need to remove herself. "I'm going to get a drink from the caf," she said tightly, stepping away from Noah's side. "Anyone want anything?"

Lauren's glassy gaze fell on her then and a shiver ran through Hannah. Lauren could see that Hannah agreed with Phoebe Winslow: the Facebook page was sick and cruel and not funny.

Lauren could see that Hannah was a Goody Two-shoes, a *suck-up*, and she didn't belong with the cool crowd, didn't deserve a hot boyfriend like Noah. Lauren knew Hannah was a fraud, a wannabe, and she was going to call her out now. Hannah braced herself; it was over. . . .

But Lauren's eyes drifted back to the phone and she mumbled, "I'm good."

"Me, too," Adam echoed.

Noah reached for Hannah's fingers. "You okay?"

It was a caring and intimate gesture. A month ago, Hannah would have melted at Noah's words, at his touch. But today, she felt nothing. "Just thirsty." She gave him a fake smile and pulled her hand from his. She walked back to the school, feeling his eyes on her back.

Inside, she didn't go to the cafeteria. She walked, on autopilot, toward her locker. Hannah didn't know what she would do when she arrived there: remove books, then put books back in, search her backpack for a highlighter or a hair elastic that wasn't there . . . anything to fill her time, to keep her away from Lauren and Adam and Noah—and to keep her from thinking about that Facebook page.

She turned the corner and approached her locker. At the far end of the hall was a gaggle of girls speaking in hushed, alarmed voices, but Hannah paid them no attention. She moved, like a drone, toward her destination. She wanted the bell to ring; she wanted lunch to be over so she could immerse herself in French verbs and forget about the social aspect of high school. At her locker, sweaty, slippery fingers fumbled with the lock. Had they been sweaty and slippery when Noah had taken her hand? To her surprise, she didn't care.

"Hey, Hannah."

Hannah looked up. It was Phoebe Winslow, flanked by several of her friends from the "God squad": Nat, Eliza, and Thea. The group was like a pamphlet on diversity: Eliza was Asian and gender fluid; Nat was overweight; Thea was petite, cute, and black; and Phoebe was tall, gawky, and outspoken. The crew had common traits, too: they all belonged to a number of school clubs, contributed enthusiastically to in-class discussions, were adored by their teachers and dismissed by their peers.

"Hey," Hannah said.

"Did you see it?" Eliza asked.

"Yeah, I saw it."

"Ronni's devastated," Phoebe said. She sounded kind of proprietary, like, all of a sudden, she was an insider in the whole Ronni saga.

"So she saw it?" Hannah asked.

"This morning." It was Thea this time. "She came in and saw it and she ran out."

Hannah was confused. "Who showed it to her?"

"No one *showed* her," chubby Nat said, her tone rather bitchy for someone so unpopular. "It's *her* locker."

"Wait . . . you're not talking about the Facebook page?"

Phoebe sighed. "Ronni saw that, too. Yesterday. But then her locker . . . It was the last straw."

Hannah felt a now familiar feeling in her stomach: a toxic combo of guilt, remorse, and dread. She croaked, "What did they do?"

Phoebe led the way to the east wing offshoot hallway that housed Ronni's locker. Of course Hannah knew where Ronni's locker was: she'd met her there often in the last few months. But even before Hannah's inclusion in Ronni's universe, she had been aware of the location. Hannah would pass by on her way to class and she and Ronni would exchange a wave. Even when Ronni was popular and Hannah wasn't, they couldn't forget the childhood connection they'd shared: all those years at the playground or the midway, baking cupcakes or building Play-Doh landscapes while their moms stood by, so different but still friends, couldn't be forgotten.

There were several kids standing in a semicircle around the rectangular metal box that contained Ronni's school supplies, gym clothes, and probably some makeup, gum, and tampons. Someone had set three orange pylons on the floor around it—the custodian, most likely—to keep onlookers away as he prepared to clean up the assault. Hannah stopped a few feet behind Phoebe and her friends and read the word that ran vertically down the locker:

C

Y

C

L

O

P

S

The spray paint was red. It had trickled down in places and was drying, thick and still tacky, like blood. Like the blood that had come from Ronni's eye that night. No one who had seen Ronni lying there bleeding and hurting could have written this. But who else would have done it? And why? Adam, Noah, and Lauren wanted to send Ronni a message, to make sure she kept quiet about that night, but would they really be this brutal?

"Horrible," Nat said, and the other Godsters murmured their agreement. Hannah felt a ragged sob shudder through her chest. She turned away from the carnage and headed toward the bathroom.

"Hannah!" Phoebe called after her, but Hannah didn't want her Christian comfort. It wasn't real. Phoebe *had* to be nice to everyone because she didn't want to burn in hell. Hannah didn't believe in hell, but if she had, she'd have been pretty worried right about now.

As she hurried down the deserted main hallway, Hannah could feel her composure slipping. Her cheeks burned, her chin quivered, and tears pooled in her eyes, clouding her vision. There were no witnesses here—everyone was entrenched in their lunch cliques in the cafeteria, or lounging on the beanbag cushions set up in the foyer, or out in the sunshine perched on various benches or ledges—so she let the emotions come. Tears slid down her cheeks and her face contorted with the anguish that was inside her. People were horrible. Her boyfriend, her best friend, her own mother . . .

A sob was rising in her chest and she quickened her step. She was almost at the refuge of the girls' restroom, when Noah appeared around the corner. "Hey." His handsome face was concerned. "What's wrong?"

Hannah hesitated. She should blame a failed test, or a text fight with her mom, or her period . . . but the words tumbled out. "I just saw Ronni's locker."

"Oh . . ." Noah said, gaze drifting to the floor. And that's when she saw it: the tiniest hint of amusement dancing in his eyes before he turned somber. "Harsh."

"Who did it?"

"I don't know."

"Really?" she scoffed. "Maybe Adam knows then? Or Lauren?" The tears and anguish were morphing into something new inside her: anger. Unfortunately, her fury was manifesting in an ugly lack of facial control and increased tear flow. Noah was going to be repulsed.

"Chill, Hannah," he said.

She was sobbing now. "What you're d-doing . . . to Ronni . . . is sick!" She was horrified by her loss of composure but she couldn't stop now. "It-it's mean . . . and it's wrong!"

"Calm the fuck down." Noah's eyes skipped past her down the hallway. He was worried her outburst would alert the principal or a teacher. "I was in shop class when Ronni's locker got spray-painted. Ask Mr. Kiewitz."

Hannah took a calming breath and was almost able to get the next sentence out without blubbering. "How do you know when it got spray-painted?"

"I'm assuming it happened before lunch, when everyone was in class."

“What about the Facebook page?” Hannah said, surprised by her confrontational tone. “Were you in shop class when that got made, too?”

Noah looked down at her with hard eyes, then his lips twisted into a cruel smirk. “People told me not to go out with you. They said you were a lame little virgin. A spoiled little goody-goody. I guess they were right.”

“M-maybe I’m just a good person? Maybe I don’t think being cruel to someone is funny?”

“If you want to be friends with the Cyclops, be my guest.” He took a step toward her and she feared he was going to grab her arm, or shove her up against the wall, or spit in her face . . . but he didn’t. “If you tell anyone we were there that night, we’ll take you down,” he growled. “Just like we’re taking Ronni down.”

All Hannah’s bravado dissipated then. “I’d never say anything. I promise.”

Noah looked past her. A group of teachers had emerged from the staff room and were headed their way. “You’d better not.” He turned and left her.

jeff

FORTY-SIX DAYS AFTER

Jeff and Kim walked down the gradual decline of stone steps from Candace Sugarman's law office in the Financial District. Jeff held his wife's arm as Kim cried softly behind her dark glasses. To the suits passing by, he looked like a caring supportive husband, a perfect gentleman, but he was having a hard time garnering sympathy for the woman beside him. And her incessant sniveling was testing his nerves.

They reached his Tesla without exchanging a word. Jeff opened the passenger door and let Kim, still whimpering like she'd lost a beloved pet, into the leather interior. He got in on the other side, his weight on the seat automatically starting the motor. He was about to drive when Kim's hand on his arm stopped him.

"What do we do now?"

Jeff looked at his wife, at her large, square Chanel sunglasses despite the overcast day, at her trim blazer and slim black slacks.

She was an attractive woman for her age, for any age, but he looked at her like a painting or a photograph: visually appealing with nothing behind it. He remembered how he had loved her once, how he'd wanted her and ravished her . . . but that was a different Kim. Maybe, it was a different Jeff, too.

"Lisa turned us down," he said. "We need to strategize another offer, one that she has to accept."

"Or we go to trial."

"You heard Candace. It's a bad idea. It will be expensive and hard on the kids."

"But she said we could win."

"*Could* win. We could also lose."

Kim blew her nose loudly into a tissue. "I can't believe Lisa's being so vile."

"Money brings out the worst in people."

Kim snorted. "Lisa acts so spiritual and Zen with all her yoga and her *healing work*, but she's nothing but a greedy, vindictive cunt."

"Whoa . . ."

Kim dissolved into embarrassed giggles. "Oh my god . . . did I really just say that?" Jeff couldn't help but smile. For a moment, she reminded him of the old Kim, the one who swore and cracked jokes and laughed. "God, I am losing it," she finished.

"You and me both."

Kim checked her watch. "I have to make cookies for Aidan's soccer game, but I don't want to go home yet." She dabbed at her eyes with the clean end of the snotty tissue she'd blown into. "I don't want be alone in the house, thinking about all this."

Jeff watched her for a few seconds. "Want to go for a walk somewhere?"

THEY DROVE TO Baker Beach and joined the Coastal Trail. It was an easy hike, a walk really, with incredible views of the crashing water, distant sailboats, the Golden Gate Bridge, and Marin Headlands across the bay. It was a path they'd walked before, when the kids were preteens, when they still did things as a family. When had that stopped? When Jeff's career ramped up? When they moved into the new house? When Kim decided that the kids' learning to play sports and instruments and express themselves creatively was more important than family time?

"I miss this," Kim said, taking in the view as they strolled next to each other.

"It's beautiful."

She turned her face toward him. "I meant *this*. Me and you, spending time together."

"Really?" Jeff scoffed.

Kim snapped back. "You're the one who works ten hours a day and then works out for two or three more."

Because I'm avoiding you! he wanted to yell. *Because you're cold and bitter and you treat me like a bratty six-year-old!* But he said nothing, clenching his teeth together instead. He could feel Kim's eyes on him.

"I'm sorry," she said. "I don't want us to fight. I want us to be a team."

"We are a team," he muttered. He felt Kim's hand reach for his and hold it as they walked. It was warm and dry and surprisingly comforting. An older couple was heading their way, striding along with Nordic hiking poles. They nodded hello, and Jeff realized how he and his wife must look: like a couple so in love that they took a scenic walk together, in the middle of the day, on a Wednesday. The older pair would never have guessed that Jeff and Kim were there because a former friend was suing them and had just refused their offer of half a million dollars.

Kim pointed to a branch in the path. "Let's head down to the beach." They dropped hands to traverse the trail down to the water, but as soon as the terrain leveled out, Kim slipped her hand into Jeff's again. It was April and still cool, so there were no sunbathers—naked or otherwise—and they had the beach to themselves. "This is nice," Kim said. "You could almost forget all the crap that's going on in our lives right now."

"Almost."

Kim turned to face him. She slipped her hands under his jacket and wrapped them around his waist. It was the most intimate touch they had shared in months. "It's cold," she said, by way of an excuse, as she snuggled into him. Jeff's hands instinctively wrapped around her. Kim's face was pressed against his neck and he felt himself soften toward her. So much anger, so much resentment . . . but maybe there was still something there, something more than just history.

"I feel like, if we stick together, we can do anything." Her words were muffled by his jacket collar.

"Yeah," he said, noncommittal. He felt her lips on his neck, a hesitant kiss at first. When he didn't push her away, her mouth became more urgent and passionate.

"Kim . . ."

Her mouth was hot and wet as it gnawed on his neck. Her hands groped his ass, between his thighs, clutching his crotch. "Let's go behind those rocks," Kim whispered, her voice loud and desperate in his ear. "No one will see us."

Jeff was aroused—it had been so long since Kim had touched him this way, in any way, really—but something felt wrong. Since when was Kim willing to do it in a public place, to risk humiliation, even arrest? Even the old Kim, wild Kim, wasn't an exhibitionist. There was something too desperate, too forced in her suggestion. And Jeff had recently decided to shut himself down as a sexual being. The sexts from Lauren had prompted a physical response in him that made him feel ill. He was not going to let himself be turned on by a sixteen-year-old girl, no matter how dead his sex life was. He would exercise and work and take care of his family: he didn't need sex. He grabbed Kim's wrists and held them. "This isn't a good idea."

"I just want to be close to you. I want to be with you, like we used to be."

"Sex on a public beach isn't going to solve years of problems."

Kim took a step back. "You're right. I'm sorry. We probably need therapy. And lots of it. But for now"—she moved closer to him—"we need to come together. We need to go to trial and beat Lisa. Together."

"We can't go to trial."

"Don't worry about the drugs. It was one tiny indiscretion. It was ages ago. . . ."

"You didn't act like it was a tiny indiscretion."

Kim took a ragged breath and her eyes were liquid. "I'm sorry. I held you to an impossible standard last year. I know no one's perfect."

"Except you." His tone was critical: *perfect* was not a compliment.

"I'm not," she said. "I almost made a huge mistake." She reached for his hand and held it. He knew something was coming, something big, but he waited and watched her struggle to find the words. "I almost had an affair."

It didn't surprise him. What surprised him was how little he cared. "Almost?"

"I couldn't go through with it. I knew it was wrong. . . ." Her eyes welled up as she continued. "We've been so distant for so long, Jeff. You're so involved in your job, and I've been so involved with the kids and the house. I started flirting with a guy I was working with. He's not my type—I don't even like him—it was just . . . a distraction. It was just attention."

"But you didn't go through with it."

"No. I couldn't."

"Because it was wrong. . . . Not because it would hurt me, not because you loved me, but because it was wrong."

She dropped his hand. "I learned a lot, Jeff. About making mistakes and holding people to unrealistic standards. I was too hard on you; I know that now. You've screwed up, I've screwed up. We're imperfect human beings. But what we've done is nothing compared to the skeletons in Lisa's closet."

"Lisa's background has nothing to do with the case against us."

"And neither does the fact that you did LSD last year. They won't even be able to use that in court."

"Why not?"

She looked down at the sand. "The guy I was almost with . . . I was upset and I told him. About the LSD." She looked up, something like dread in her eyes. "His wife is a lawyer at the firm Lisa hired. The guy . . . he must have told his wife and then she must have told Lisa's lawyer."

"Christ, Kim."

"So that makes your drug use inadmissible. . . . I'll have to confirm with Candace, but I'm pretty sure it does." She clutched his hand desperately. Her cheeks were red and she looked really pretty. "I'm not going to roll over and let Lisa ruin us. I'm not going to let her destroy the life we've built over an accident that was not our fault."

"We can't go to trial, Kim."

"I just told you we can! We can win!"

I went for ice cream with Lauren Ross. And then I sneaked out in the middle of the night to pick her up from a party. I sat with her, in my car, and I held her while she cried. And then she started texting me. . . . I barely answered her, but she just kept texting. And then she sent me some nude photos. . . . I didn't look at them, I deleted them right away. I wiped my phone and blocked her number, but the kid is crazy! She's delusional! And if they call her to the stand, I don't know what she'll say!

But he couldn't tell his wife that; he couldn't tell anyone that. It sounded so fucked-up, so perverted . . . so stupid. Instead, he said, "I gave the girls a bottle of champagne that night."

"Why?" Kim whispered, her face registering anger, distress, fear. . . . God, if she only knew how much worse it was.

"I wanted Hannah to have a good time, for once, without all your rules and conditions. It was her sixteenth birthday for Christ's sake. Every kid wants to have a drink on their sixteenth."

Kim said nothing but he could see the wheels turning in her head. What did this mean for them? For Lisa's lawsuit? For their chances at trial? She looked up at him. "I remember it now. There was a piece of the bottle near Ronni's hand— What did you do with it?"

"I took it on a run and threw it in a trash can miles from the house."

"You disposed of evidence."

"It seemed prudent," he retorted.

Kim opened her mouth to speak, then seemed to realize her righteous indignation would be way out of line. She pressed her lips together and gave a slight nod of acquiescence. Jeff decided to hammer in the last nail.

"After the accident, when I drove the other girls home . . . I told them not to tell anyone about the champagne. I told them to keep it a secret or I'd get into trouble."

"Jesus Christ, Jeff."

"The cops and lawyers don't seem to know about it, so I guess they kept it quiet."

Kim's voice was shaking. "Did you threaten them? What did you say to them?"

"Is that really what you think of me? That I'd threaten a bunch of teenaged girls?" He turned away and started walking down the beach.

Kim trailed behind him. "They've been questioned under oath! They perjured themselves! They lied for you! Why?"

Because Lauren Ross is my guardian angel. Because she did whatever mean, popular girls do to sweet, less-popular girls to make sure they stay quiet.

But instead, he whirled on her. "I don't know why. Maybe they realize that a bottle of champagne between five of them didn't cause Ronni's accident. Or, maybe they just don't remember."

"Give me a fucking break."

"You always think the worst of me!"

A black dog, probably a Labrador-shepherd cross judging by its broad face and shaggy coat, came out of nowhere and ran toward them, barking angrily. Kim froze and instinctively stepped behind Jeff. The dog stopped, about ten feet away, but continued to bark.

"It's okay, buddy," Jeff said. "We won't hurt you."

Kim's voice was tense and irritated. "Where is its owner?"

On cue, a sixtyish woman in a knitted sweater came into view. "She's okay!" she called out. "All bark and no bite." She called to the dog, "Come here, Rosie. Good girl."

As Rosie turned back to her master, Jeff said, "Beautiful dog."

Kim's words overlapped his: "She should be on a leash."

Silently, they headed back toward the trail.

kim

FORTY-SIX DAYS AFTER

Kim stared into the metal bowl of the KitchenAid mixer and watched the butter and brown sugar cream together. She was lost in thought, her mind still on the beach, listening to her husband's confession. Jeff had lied to her, lied to the police, lied to the lawyers. . . . He had removed evidence from the scene, asked children to lie for him, asked his own daughter to perjure herself. He had given alcohol to minors, brought LSD into their home. . . . What else was Jeff capable of?

Something jolted Kim back to the present and she flicked off the mixer. She had overcreamed the butter and sugar and now it was a wet, greasy paste. The cookies would be flat and leaden, but she was pretty sure Aidan's soccer team wasn't too discerning. Most parents brought a box of granola bars when it was their turn to provide snacks, so there would be no complaints. A soggy frozen banana laid dripping and thawing in a bowl. Kim oozed it from its blackened skin, then proceeded to mash it with a fork, harder than was necessary.

Oddly, Kim didn't feel angry at Jeff. Perhaps she'd grown accustomed to him letting her down. Or maybe her expectations were so low that nothing he did could raise her ire. Or maybe, she was just angry at herself. She didn't go in for Lisa's New Agey crap, but Kim believed that everyone created their own life. She, alone, was responsible for the way her husband treated her, her kids, her sister, her friends, everyone . . . so it was Kim who had built a family that lied to her, that disobeyed her and kept secrets from her.

What really stung was the fact that Jeff and Hannah were in cahoots together. They were a deceitful little team, keeping Kim in the dark. She could imagine how that evening had played out, could almost hear the exchange as Jeff gave Hannah the champagne.

Don't tell Mom. You know what she's *like.*

Hannah would have laughed. *She'd totally freak out.* Then she'd thank Jeff for being the cool parent, and all her sneaky little friends would agree.

It wasn't that Kim was jealous, exactly, but she had hoped for a different relationship with both her husband and her daughter. She couldn't fault Hannah for her deceit; she was just a kid after all. But Kim had wanted an open, honest marriage, one where Jeff talked to her, colluded with her on issues like providing champagne to underage girls. "Just this once? Just a glass each?" Given the opportunity, Kim might have said yes. She might have said, *Let me call all their parents and if they're okay with it, so am I.* Then there would be no question of their liability. But instead, Jeff and Hannah had sneaked around behind Kim's back, laughed at Kim's naiveté. She added chocolate chips to the mixing bowl—someone had been eating them despite the label she had affixed: FOR BAKING. DO NOT EAT. At least she still had a chance with Aidan.

She had just taken the last tray of cookies out of the oven, when she heard a key in the lock and Hannah let herself into the house. "Hey, you," Kim said cheerily.

"Hey." Hannah marched directly to the stairs, headed for her room.

"I made power cookies," Kim called. "They're for Aidan's soccer team, but I'll leave a plate for you."

Hannah didn't pause. "I'm not hungry."

"What's wrong?"

"Nothing."

Kim hurried to the foot of the staircase and spoke to her daughter's departing back. "Stop!" Kim wasn't entirely sure that Hannah would listen. A few months ago, she would have had no doubts, but Hannah was a different kid these days. But the girl halted and turned to face her mother. Kim had been about to launch into a stern lecture about being polite toward those who offer you fresh-baked cookies, but Hannah's expression stopped her. Her sweet, youthful face was pale, her features contorted with anger, or grief, or both.

"What happened, Hannah?"

"Oh, not much," Hannah said, aggressively sarcastic. "My boyfriend dumped me."

"What?" *Hannah had a boyfriend*? Kim had no idea. God, their relationship was even worse than she'd thought.

"Yeah. He broke up with me because I don't want to join in in bullying Ronni."

"Kids are bullying Ronni? Why?"

"Like you care." Hannah turned and stomped up the stairs.

"Of course I care!" Kim cried, hurrying up after her. By the time Kim reached Hannah's room, the girl had thrown herself onto her soft-yellow bed and covered her head with a pillow. "Why are kids bullying Ronni?"

Hannah kept her face buried. "I don't know. I guess because she was pretty and popular, and now she's not."

"I'm sure she's still pretty. . . ."

Hannah sat up then. "Everyone says her eye looks scary. Her eye socket is like deformed."

"That's unkind, Hannah."

"No, it's not! It's the truth! You're the one who's unkind!" She was screaming now. "Everyone's being horrible to Ronni. They're saying cruel and nasty things. Even her friends have turned on her. I want to be there for Ronni, but I'm not allowed!"

"I didn't say you weren't *allowed*. . . ." Kim's voice was tremulous. "It's just . . . very complicated with Lisa's lawsuit."

"That stupid lawsuit again."

"Lisa's trying to ruin us, Hannah."

"And everyone at school is trying to ruin Ronni! But all you care about is money."

"I care about this family!"

"No, you don't! You and Dad hate each other!"

"We don't hate each other. Being married is just hard sometimes." But it sounded unconvincing, even to Kim's ears.

Hannah climbed off the bed and moved toward her mom. "You care about the house, and the cars, and the *stuff*!" She was in Kim's face now, screaming. "You don't care about me! You don't care about Ronni! You don't care about what's right!"

Kim instinctively stepped back in the face of her daughter's rage. She wasn't afraid of Hannah, but the girl was so angry, so incensed, that Kim felt helpless. She struggled to find the right words, but no parenting manual had ever addressed the complicated scenario they now found themselves in. And what had all those carefully chosen parental platitudes gotten her? A child who lied, a child who kept secrets, a child who did not respect her mother.

"You know where I stand," Kim managed, her voice hoarse.

Hannah looked at her mom with such overt contempt that it felt like a physical blow. The girl started to say something, something ugly, something horrible, something that would damage their relationship forever, but she stopped herself. Instead, Hannah burst out laughing.

Kim stood, for several awkward seconds, until her daughter got some sort of grip on her hysteria. She glanced at Hannah's bedside clock. "I've got to take Aidan to soccer. I'll pick up some dinner on the way home." For some reason, this set Hannah off again. She threw herself onto her bed, giggling uncontrollably. Kim left, her daughter's inane laughter getting quieter as she hurried away.

HILLCREST MIDDLE SCHOOL was conveniently adjacent to Hillcrest High School; Aidan would move to the larger school next year for ninth grade. Her son was waiting in the parking lot, as arranged. He barreled into the passenger seat in his soccer uniform, displaying a surprising lack of coordination for a gold-level soccer star.

"Hey, hon." Kim smiled at her boy. "No one else needed a ride to the game?"

"Nah. Connor's mom has a van and Coach Patrick took four kids." He was already rifling in the backseat. "Do you have snacks?"

"The power cookies are for the team. But there's a turkey wrap and a container with apples and almonds for you."

As Aidan dug in the insulated bag for his sustenance, Kim eased her Audi onto the road. She treasured these moments alone with her youngest, when he wasn't distracted by screens or friends. She liked to think Aidan valued this time, too—otherwise he could have squeezed into Connor's mom's van or hitched a ride with the coach.

"How was school today?"

"Decent," he said, removing the whole-wheat wrap and taking a huge bite.

"Anything exciting?"

"Nope."

They drove without talking for a few minutes. Kim listened to her son chewing and the radio edit of a rap song where every third word went silent to hide the *fuck*s and *bitch*es and *ho*s. Why did they bother cleaning up songs like that? There were basically no lyrics left. Kim turned down the radio, cleared her throat. "Have you seen Ronni Monroe since . . . the accident?"

"Just once."

Kim wasn't sure how to ask the question without sounding insensitive. But this was a teenaged boy: they personified insensitivity. "How does she look?"

Aidan turned toward his mom, and the vexation on his face revealed how Kim had misjudged him. "Not very good. Her eye . . . it's not right."

"It's a glass eye, so it won't move with the other eye. It's just like Uncle Doug, Aunt Corrine's first husband. He had a lazy eye."

"It's not like that. Ronni's eyelid is kind of stretched across, and you can see too much of the white part of her eye. It's freaky."

Kim took a deep breath. "Hannah says the other kids are being unkind to Ronni."

Aidan shrugged solemnly and bit his wrap. "I heard something about that."

"What did you hear?"

"Some kids made a Facebook page. It had Ronni's name with a picture of Mike Wazowski."

"Who's Mike Wazowski?"

"The monster from *Monsters, Inc*. The little green guy with one eye."

"Jesus Christ . . ." Kim knew human nature could be ugly, and teenaged human nature was the ugliest of all. People loved it when the pretty, popular, and privileged were toppled from their roost. But Ronni was maimed. She had lost an eye. Were her peers savage enough to be delighting in her misfortune? Kim's hands trembled on the steering wheel.

Aidan, the most sensitive member of the family, sensed his mom's distress. "I'm sure someone's reported it by now," he said to console her. "It's probably been taken down."

They were nearing the soccer field. Kim's questions would go unanswered if she didn't ask them now. "Why do you think the kids are being so mean to Ronni?"

"I don't know . . . maybe because of Lauren Ross. She's like this power b—," He stopped himself before he uttered the word *bitch* in front of his mother. "Lauren's really popular, and people are kind of scared of her."

"So Lauren's leading this vendetta against Ronni? I thought they were friends?"

"Lauren doesn't like her anymore or something. I don't know. . . ." Aidan stared out the passenger window, clearly uncomfortable with the subject. "Ask Hannah. They're *her* friends."

Kim pulled into the parking lot next to the soccer field. "It's hard for Hannah to talk about it. I think she feels caught in the middle."

"Yeah," her son mumbled, already opening the door before the car had come to a full stop.

"Careful, you," she admonished gently. "The rest of the team just got here. There's no rush." But Aidan was already jogging toward his teammates, shoving the last vestiges of his wrap into his mouth.

Kim took her time following. The boys would warm up for a good twenty minutes before the game started. Gathering the plastic container of power cookies and the water bottle Aidan had left in the front cup holder, she strolled toward the team bench. She dropped the water bottle near Aidan's running shoes and set the cookies in the designated spot near the coach's folding chair. When Aidan was younger, moms were allowed to present the snacks at halftime, but at this age and skill level, parents were considered a distraction. Kim missed the appreciative smiles, the occasional "Thanks, Mrs. Sanders," but she understood.

She stood on the sideline and watched her lanky son grapevine across the field with the other boys. "Pick it up!" the coach barked. He was about Kim's age, a stocky guy in a cap who oozed aggression. The boys tried to obey him but they were just kids growing into their man-size bodies. Kim didn't like the coach. He was too harsh, too competitive, but Jeff said that's what it took to win the city championship. Aidan didn't seem to mind, so Kim shook it off.

Her eyes followed one of the smaller boys. He was quicker and more dexterous than Aidan and the taller kids, moving with the easy coordination of the compact. It took Kim a moment to realize it was James, her friend Debs's son. Scanning the handful of parents on the sidelines, she spotted her spin-class partner. Kim hadn't been to SoulCycle in weeks. Since Lisa filed her lawsuit, Kim had struggled to make it to her twice-weekly Pilates sessions. She moved down the field toward her friend.

Debs was with a couple of women who Kim didn't know, but the taller of the two was familiar. The woman was obviously a soccer mom, and Kim was pretty sure she'd seen her at the school, too—some parents' night or at a school play. The other woman, the stranger, looked up and spotted Kim. She muttered something to her group, and Kim felt the perceptible shift in body language. She took in Debs's rigid posture, the way her back was purposefully angled away from Kim. It became clear: Debs knew Kim was there, and she was avoiding her.

Kim wanted to turn and scurry back to her car, but she was practically on top of them now. It would have been too obvious, too awkward. . . . Her eyes darted around for another escape route, perhaps a friendly face in the crowd that could divert her attention, but there was no one. Debs turned around and feigned surprise. "Kim. Hey . . ." There was a hint of warmth, just enough for Kim to hope she'd read the situation wrong.

"I wanted to come say hi," Kim responded. "It's been ages."

"Mmm, it has." She'd imagined the warmth. "Do you know my friends Jane and Karen? This is Kim."

My *friends* Jane and Karen. The lack of identifier before Kim's name stung, because she and Debs *were* friends, weren't they? At least they had been. Maybe they weren't deep confidantes, but they had gone for coffee, and they had shared gossip and anecdotes about marriage and raising teenagers. That's what friends did. What they didn't do was ignore each other just because one of them was involved in something unpleasant. But perhaps Kim was being too sensitive. Damn hormones . . .

Kim turned toward Debs's friends. "Hi," she said cheerfully. Jane and Karen gave Kim cool, almost dismissive nods. Who were these women, and why were they being so bitchy? She tried to ignore the elevation of her heart rate: fight or flight. She politely asked, "Do you have boys on the team?"

"My son's number eight," Jane offered.

Karen, the familiar, angular one said, "Mine's number twenty-two."

"Mine's number five," Kim offered. "The tall, awkward one."

Nothing. Not a comment about the typical thirteen-year-old lack of dexterity, or sons growing taller than their moms, or any of the usual parental banter. Just icy silence. "I've got to send some work e-mails," Kim said lamely. "Debs, good to see you." To the others: "Nice to meet you both."

"Actually, we've met before," Karen said, eyes narrowed, tone truculent. "At the Literacy Foundation's fund-raiser in January. I was with my friend Ana Pinto."

Shit. Ana Pinto, Marta's mom . . . Kim's mind skipped back to the Italian coffee shop where Ana had turned Kim's simple request for support into an admission of guilt, a plot to take down Lisa, a lack of empathy for Ronni. The pieces fell into place then. Ana had poisoned this Karen person against Kim, and in turn, Karen was spewing Ana's story to the others in the mom network. She could see it in their eyes, in the judgmental set of their chins and the tense distance they kept between them and her. Kim was guilty. Despite the police clearance, these women had made up their minds.

There were so many things Kim could have said to defend herself, but their resolve was evident. They wanted to blame her; they wanted to hate her. . . . She could see how much they were enjoying it. Their schadenfreude was palpable.

"I remember," she managed to say. "How is Ana?"

"She's fine. . . . Trying to support Marta with all she's been through. It was very traumatic for her."

"For everyone," Kim said softly. "It's a tragedy."

"It sure is," Debs added smugly. The other women made affirmative snorting noises and turned their eyes toward the field.

Without a word, Kim turned and headed for her car. Tears were already obscuring her vision, but she would not hurry, she would not give those bitches the satisfaction of knowing they had broken her. A whistle blew on the field and Kim glanced over through the scrim of her tears. The coach was calling the boys in for a last-minute pep talk. Aidan was jogging across the field, all his attention focused on the impending game. He didn't notice his mother, shunned and holding back tears, on the sideline. He had probably forgotten she was even there.

Kim got into the driver's seat and slammed the door behind her. In the stuffy warmth of the Audi wagon, she let her composure go. Tears poured down her cheeks and ragged sobs shuddered through her chest. She felt so alone, so ostracized, so *bullied*. Bullied like Ronni. Oh God, Ronni . . . Kim thought about the website, about the ugliness and cruelty of adolescents. There was only one thing as mean as teenagers: soccer moms. She cried even harder.

They would sweeten their offer to Lisa. They would make sure Ronni never wanted for anything. Her life would actually be better now than it was before the accident. Ronni may have lost her eye, but she would gain financial independence. She wouldn't have to rely on a mother who surfed all day and thought Reiki healing was a legitimate career choice. Jeff and Kim would ensure Ronni had the financial support to create her own future. The girl just had to survive high school. . . .

Kim dug in her purse for a tissue and felt the familiar rectangle of her phone. She withdrew it with a handful of crumpled Kleenexes and dropped it in her lap. As she blew her nose, Hannah's earlier words replayed in her mind: "I want to be there for Ronni, but I'm not allowed!" Not *allowed*? The girl was sixteen, for Christ's sake! She hadn't asked permission to drink alcohol or to have a secret boyfriend, but somehow, she needed permission to support a friend?

Kim wiped the greasy touch screen on her pants, then tapped to compose a text to her daughter.

I'm sorry about before. Do what you think is right.

She took a breath and hit send.

jeff

FIFTY-TWO DAYS AFTER

"Did you read the RFP I sent?" Graham was standing in Jeff's office doorway, filling it with his Australian bulk. "I need your notes ASAP."

Jeff looked up from his computer screen. "I'm about halfway through," he lied. He had meant to read the document last night, but lately, he was so damned tired. "I'll finish it tonight and get you notes for the morning."

"Thanks." Graham hovered for a beat. "How are things going at home?"

"Fine. Good." Jeff gave Graham a dismissive smile and returned his focus to the e-mail he'd been composing. He didn't want to get into it with Graham, or with anyone. Jeff wanted to keep his mind on work, and on his training.

But Graham never could take a hint. He entered Jeff's roomy office and pulled up a guest chair. "What's going on with the lawsuit?"

Jeff swiveled his chair to face his colleague. "We made a generous offer to settle and she refused," he grouched. "That's what's going on with the lawsuit."

Graham leaned back and stretched his long legs. "So what comes next? Will you make her a better offer?" Graham wasn't thick, but he seemed to lack a certain emotional intelligence that other people had. Like how other people would have realized this was a touchy subject. Maybe it was an Aussie thing.

"I don't know," Jeff said. "Kim wants to go to trial."

"You can't do that, mate. A trial would be brutal."

"I know. But Kim's pissed. She wants to take down Lisa. She wants to prove we're not guilty."

"That would be awful for the kids. Don't put them through that."

"I know."

Graham crossed a leg over his knee, getting comfortable. "So what's she like? The bitch who's after you . . ."

"I always thought she was a New Age, hippy-dippy weirdo."

"She can't be that enlightened if she's trying to fuck you and Kim in the ass."

"I don't know if Lisa's trying to 'fuck us in the ass,' exactly," Jeff explained. "Kim thinks the lawsuit is some personal vendetta. But Lisa's daughter lost her eye. She probably feels like some monetary compensation will ease the pain."

"My dad's best mate only had one eye. It didn't seem to hold him back any."

"But Ronni's just a kid. Kids are cruel . . . and it's different for girls. They're already so insecure about their looks. I can't imagine how Hannah would deal with being disfigured."

Graham winced at the word. "Have you seen it? The eye?"

"No . . . but Aidan said it's pretty nasty."

"Poor girl." Graham uncrossed his legs. "If I were you, I'd write the mother a big fat check. I'd sell a car, divest some stocks, whatever it takes to make it go away."

"Kim thinks if we give Lisa a big payout, we're admitting that we're at fault."

"No, you're not. The police cleared you."

"So if we did go to trial, we'd have a chance."

"Don't do it. I'm serious. My brother got sued back in Oz—the lawyers were ruthless. I mean, who knows what shit could come out at trial?"

Jeff looked at his hulking friend and his eyes narrowed. "Why do you care so much?"

"I don't. . . . But you'll feel a lot better if you compensate Lisa and Ronni for their pain and suffering." Graham checked his watch and stood. "And the sooner you do, the sooner you can get back to what's important. Like my RFP." He sauntered out of Jeff's office.

Jeff chuckled and turned back to his work, but the brief disruption had made it hard to focus. His mind returned to Ronni and Lisa and the lawsuit. Graham had a point. The best way to get Lisa to leave them alone was to throw money at her. He could sell his boat. It just sat there in the marina costing him dough for most of the year. He'd add that money to the pot and sweeten Lisa's deal. Kim would have to go along, now that she knew about the champagne, now that she knew he'd asked the girls to cover for him. Maybe she was already on board? It was hard to know, since they'd basically stopped talking to each other.

His phone rang. It was the new receptionist, Tara. She'd been with them for only a month, but she seemed to be working out okay. The job wasn't exactly challenging. He picked up the receiver and Tara's voice came through the phone. "Your daughter's here."

Hannah was there? She should be in school. And it would take her at least an hour to get to Palo Alto via transit. Something must be wrong. . . . He stood up, smashing his thighs into the top of his desk, shaking his computer, his coffee cup, and his pen holder in his haste. "I'll be right out."

When Jeff entered the lobby, he didn't see his daughter. The waiting area was empty but for a petite young woman in a skirt and heels, her head bent over a magazine. He turned to Tara. "Uh . . . you said my daughter was here?" Maybe Tara had summoned the wrong person? Maybe she wasn't working out as well as he'd thought.

"She's right there," Tara said, clearly bemused.

The young woman in the waiting area looked up from her magazine. Her long hair swept back to reveal her face. She wasn't a woman; she was a girl. Fuck.

"Hi, Daddy."

Jeff's heart was hammering in his chest as Lauren stood and smiled. She was in a fitted skirt, a short top that grazed its waistband, and sky-high heels. Her makeup was dark and impeccable. She looked twenty-one at least. He reminded himself that she wasn't; she was sixteen.

"Hi."

He had to get her out of here. Jeff rushed toward her and grabbed her arm. Pulling her toward the office doors, he whispered, "What the fuck are you doing here?"

"I needed to see you," Lauren said.

"You can't just show up here," he growled, pushing open the glass doors and leading her through them. As they hurried toward the elevator, Jeff was sure Tara was watching them. He knew it didn't look right. And even if the new receptionist bought that Lauren was his daughter, there were plenty of people on staff who had met Hannah. He stabbed the elevator down button multiple times.

Mercifully, the elevator was empty when it arrived. He pressed the button for the parking garage and prayed no one would get on. He remembered the last time they were in an elevator together, riding up to Lauren's dad's apartment after the accident. He remembered the tense silence and the smell of vomit. She'd been a stranger to him then. It seemed like months ago and minutes ago.

"I tried to text you but you blocked me," Lauren said. She stood in the back corner of the elevator, leaning against the walls. For the first time, he noticed her glassy eyes and unsteady balance. The girl was fucked-up on something. Great.

Instinctively, he took her to his car. As they peeled out of the underground parking garage, he had no idea where they were going, but a moving target was harder to shoot. When they were on the open road, she said, "Where are you taking me?"

"I'm taking you home."

“No fucking way. I’m not going home.”

“I’ll take you back to school then.”

She laughed. “Yeah? Are you going to take my hand and drag me inside? That wouldn’t look weird at all.”

She had him there. “What the fuck do you want from me, Lauren?” He hadn’t meant to yell, but he did. The girl didn’t respond. Jeff tore his eyes away from the road and looked over at her. She was crying quietly.

“I love you. . . .”

Jesus Christ. He couldn’t deal with a delusional, wasted teenager and drive his car at the same time. He still hadn’t used the Tesla’s autopilot function (despite his affinity for technology, he still felt his brain and reflexes were superior), and now was definitely not the time to start. He took a right and steered the car down a commercial side street. Traffic was sparse in this area, but still, he hunched down in his seat. When he deemed them a safe distance from his office, he pulled into a Staples. He stopped in a deserted corner of its massive parking lot and turned off the car.

Jeff faced forward, staring through the windshield at the depressing expanse of gray retail park. Someone had abandoned a shopping cart within his frame of view, and a white plastic bag had attached itself to the wheels. A small breeze caught the bag, tugging at it and twisting it, but it was hopelessly stuck there. Jeff kept his eyes forward and spoke slowly. “What the fuck are you talking about, Lauren?”

“I love you,” she sniveled.

“You don’t love me. You don’t even know me.”

She placed her hand on his knee. "We have a connection, you know we do. Don't try and pretend we don't."

Jeff looked down at her hand, small, pretty . . . a child's hand. He turned and looked at her then. "We don't have a connection. You're a kid. You're my daughter's friend. You're nothing to me." He tossed the hand off his leg like it was a piece of burning garbage.

He may as well have slapped her. She covered her face with her hands and cried into them. He knew he was being harsh and he didn't enjoy it, but pitying her was what had gotten him into this mess. Damn that fucking ice cream. . . . Damn that fucking ride home. . . .

"I should just kill myself," she mumbled through tears and fingers.

It was a cry for attention, yet another manipulation, but Jeff felt a twinge of something. "Don't say that." She was just a screwed-up kid. That night in his car, she'd told him that no one loved her, no one cared about her. He didn't want to push her over the edge. He pulled a tissue out of his pants pocket and handed it to her. "Here"—she took it—"pull yourself together."

Lauren dabbed at her eyes and then blew her nose loudly. She flipped down the visor and peered into the embedded mirror. Her makeup must have been waterproof—shellac—but she ran her fingers under her eyes anyway. Then she flipped up the visor and settled back into her seat. She suddenly seemed extremely composed.

"Did you like the pictures I sent you?"

He felt a surge of anger. The little bitch was playing him. "No,

I didn't," he said firmly. "They made me feel uncomfortable. And sick."

"You're lying. . . ." He looked over at her. She was smiling, trying to look coy and sexy. She looked ridiculous.

"I'm being completely honest with you, Lauren. I don't find you attractive. I don't have feelings for you. I just want you to leave me the fuck alone."

The waterworks started again, but he wasn't falling for it. He started the car. "I'm taking you home."

"I'll tell about the champagne!"

"Go ahead. You've been deposed. If you change your story now, you'll be charged with perjury."

"I'll tell your wife then!"

Jeff spoke in a measured voice. "My wife knows. You've got nothing on me anymore. You can't blackmail me or manipulate me. It's over." He put the car in drive.

"I've got your texts."

The texts. Fuck. He looked over at Lauren. Her face was wet with tears, but she was smiling, a smug, self-satisfied smile. He turned the car off again. "I never said anything incriminating. . . ." But his throat constricted and his voice came out high, almost feminine, belying his fear.

"Still . . . I think Hannah would be pretty upset to find out you sent me, like, thirty texts."

"No, I didn't!"

"Thirty-two actually. I counted them. And if I told her how you came to get me that night and how you held me and kissed me. . . ."

"I didn't—" But he stopped himself, remembering the paternal peck on the crown he'd given her when she was wasted, sobbing about how no one knew her, no one cared about her. Hardly a *kiss*, but still . . . totally inappropriate. He looked at the child in his passenger seat. Through her tears and runny nose, she was smirking.

A rage welled up inside of him like he'd never felt before. He wanted to grab this girl by the neck; he wanted to smash her head into the dashboard. He wanted to make her disappear from his life, forever, and there was only one way to do that. Jeff had never hit anyone, had never even been in a fight, but he owned *The Sopranos* boxed set and he'd watched it all the way through, twice. He could do it. He could choke the life out of this little bitch. He'd enjoy it, too, seeing the fear in her eyes, the realization that she'd fucked with the wrong guy. When she was dead, he'd drive out to the forest and bury her sixteen-year-old corpse deep, deep in the ground. No one would ever find her. And no one would miss her. Lauren had said so herself.

But Jeff was not Paulie Walnuts. "What do you want, Lauren?"

"I just want you in my life," Lauren said, suddenly sweet and pleading. "I want to be able to talk to you and text with you. You're the only person who really understands me."

Jeff almost laughed out loud, but he held it in, creating a coughing/snorting sound in the back of his throat. He spoke gently. "You need help, Lauren. A therapist or a psychiatrist."

"No, I don't. I just need you." Her hand crept back to his lap. He removed it gently.

"You can't have me."

“Then I guess I have no choice.” She smiled and he felt a chill run through him: this girl was a psychopath.

Jeff’s eyes moved to the small purse resting between her knees. He could snatch it and grab her phone and smash it on the asphalt. He could take the SIM card and destroy it, throw it in the ocean. But Lauren seemed to read his mind. She tucked the bag farther up her thighs, under her butt. He couldn’t get it now without molesting her. Lauren smiled at him, victorious, and Jeff felt the fight drain from his body. He’d been worn down and beaten by a teenaged girl.

“I’ll unblock you,” he said. “I’ll be there for you.”

Lauren beamed, a little girl getting a pony for Christmas, then she leaned over and pressed her lips to his cheek. She held them there, longer than she should have. He could smell her shampoo and some fruity lip gloss, and Jeff didn’t want to feel what he was feeling. It was perverted and wrong and he wanted to push her off him. But he couldn’t. Finally, she sat back in her seat and smiled.

“Okay. You can drive me home now.”

lisa

SIXTY DAYS AFTER

Lisa perused the document, her eyes flitting over the confounding legalese. Her lower back was hurting from the hard, modern client chair she'd been offered by her lawyer, Paul. He sat on the other side of his pristine desk in leather ergonomically designed comfort. He watched her wade through the paper, his stubby fingers tented in front of his Cheshire smile.

"Eight hundred and fifty thousand is an incredible offer," Paul said. "They're definitely motivated to settle this."

A low whistle emanated from Lisa's boyfriend, Allan, seated beside her in a matching modern chair. "That's serious money," he said. She'd invited him along for moral support, in case things didn't go well. Based on his wide grin and raised eyebrows, he thought things were going extremely well.

Lisa spoke directly to Paul. "That's not even half of what I asked for."

Paul folded his hands on the desk. "The three million was never realistic," he explained. "The Sanderses aren't that rich. It was tactical. To show them we mean business. . . ." He leaned back in his chair, triumphant. "I think they got the message."

"I'll say." Allan gave her another grin, another eyebrow lift. She shouldn't have brought him.

Lisa slid the papers back toward Paul. "I've had to put my career plans on hold to take care of Ronni. Once I've paid the hospital bills, the physical and mental therapists, school tuition . . . there won't be much left."

"Have you worked out a budget for all that?" Paul asked, sharing a conspiratorial glance with Allan. "I think there should be a significant amount left."

Lisa turned to look at her boyfriend, his tall, lithe frame spilling out of the uncomfortable chair. Despite the awkwardness of his pose, he was smiling like he'd just won the lottery. He caught her withering look and rearranged his features. "It's almost a million bucks, Lis."

"My daughter has lost all her friends. She's depressed, she's being bullied . . . and people stare at her like she's some sort of monster every time she leaves the apartment." Lisa turned to Paul now. "Ronni may never recover from this. She may never lead a fully functional life. It's my job to take care of her."

Paul said, "Jeff and Kim Sanders don't have three million liquid."

"No, but they can get it. They have fancy cars, a fancy house; I think Jeff has a boat. . . ."

Allan looked over at her. "You want them to sell their *house*?" He sounded so stunned, so appalled, like asking Jeff and Kim to downsize a little was akin to torching their grass hut while they slept.

"If that's what it takes to take care of Ronni, then I guess I do," she snapped.

Paul said, "There are several alternative dispute resolutions available to us: mediation, arbitration, neutral evaluation, a settlement conference. . . . No one wants this to go to trial."

"I'm happy to go to trial," Lisa retorted. "Jeff and Kim are the ones afraid of a trial. They don't want to expose all their dirty little secrets."

Paul pressed his lips together for a moment. "Everyone has aspects of their life they'd rather weren't dragged into the open."

"I don't. I mean, nothing that's relevant to what happened to Ronni that night."

"Lawyers have a way of twisting things to make them relevant," Paul admitted.

Allan made some worried noise that Lisa ignored. "Jeff and Kim have never accepted responsibility for what happened. They've never apologized to Ronni. . . . They think they can buy their way out of this, but I won't let them."

Paul picked up the papers "All right. I'll call Candace Sugarman. I'll tell her where you stand."

"Three million." Lisa stood, preparing to leave. "Or we go to trial."

ALLAN WAS QUIET as they walked back to his truck. They'd parked on a side street, a few blocks away, giving them ample time to stroll in tense silence. Finally, Lisa addressed the palpable hostility. "What's wrong?"

"Nothing."

She considered letting it go. Being a hard-ass was not her true nature and she found it taxing. But Allan was clearly upset, and she didn't want to fall out with him right now. He was her only support system in this mess—unless you counted Yeva and the yoga crew who thought Lisa could breathe her way out the other side. She didn't have the energy to fight Kim and Jeff, and her boyfriend, too. She touched his arm. "You're upset. Talk to me."

Allan stopped walking and turned to her. "Eight hundred and fifty grand is not enough money for you?"

"It's not for me. It's for Ronni."

"You act like Ronni will never have a job, never go to school, never be anything but the victim of this fucking accident."

Lisa was getting riled, but she maintained her composure. "I hope Ronni will go on to have a happy and productive life. I hope this will be nothing but a bad memory one day—but what if it's not? What if she'll never be the same Ronni she was? That's the eventuality I have to deal with."

"But you got a bunch of money when your parents died. You said it was the worst thing that could have happened to you."

"That was different. I was alone! I had no one to guide me! Ronni will have me. We'll invest the money so that she can start a business one day, or travel, or whatever she wants to do when she's older. I'm not going to let her blow it on drugs and partying."

Allan was quiet, and Lisa could see him absorbing her viewpoint. "So this isn't about trying to ruin Kim and Jeff?"

"I want them to hurt," Lisa said, her voice cold, dispassionate. "I want them to feel at least a little of the pain Ronni is feeling. But no . . . it's not about ruining them. It's about my daughter."

Allan was softening, she could see it in his shoulders, in his downcast eyes. "When we met, you said your life goal was compassion. For everything and everyone . . ."

"When we met, I was high on pot brownies."

Allan couldn't help but chuckle. "That was a great vegan potluck."

"Remember the red lentil dal? So good."

Still laughing, he wrapped his arms around her and kissed her hair. "Sorry if I'm not being supportive. It's just that . . . eight fifty seems like a lot of money to me."

"It is a lot of money. . . . But it's not enough to guarantee Ronni's future."

"You're right. Not in this economy."

"And it's a drop in the bucket to Jeff Sanders. I mean, Kim doesn't even work. She could skip a spin class and get a job." Anger had crept into her voice, and she felt Allan's arms loosen around her. She took a step back and looked at him.

"I'm not a horrible person, Allan. I'm a mother. If you had a child—a child who had been hurt badly—you'd know how I feel. But you don't."

His expression was unreadable. Lisa didn't know if she had hurt, offended, or finally gotten through to him. But he moved forward, reached out for her . . . "You're right. I don't know what you're going through."

Lisa melted into him. She was strong and independent, she'd

had to be, but she couldn't deny how nice it was to have someone in her corner. Allan was a good guy. And his strong, lean body was so comforting, his large hands stroking her back so tender and loving. . . . She felt like she might cry.

"Want to go back to my place for a bit?" he said.

That's when she noticed it: the pressure on her thigh. Allan was aroused. She'd thought he was holding her to be caring and supportive, but he was turned on. She felt oddly repulsed. She pulled away from him. "I should get home."

"It's been so long, babe."

"I know, but I won't be able to relax with Ronni home alone."

"She'll be fine for half an hour."

Lisa looked at Allan and saw the desire in his eyes. The first months of their relationship had been so sexual, so exciting and intense, but since the accident, things had shifted. Lisa hadn't felt amorous, in fact, sex had become distasteful. She only wanted to be comforted, to be held . . . and Allan had obliged. He had stood by her—he had more than stood by her, he had been her rock—through the whole mess. She owed him the romp of his life.

Lisa smiled and bit her lip. "I'll give you twenty minutes."

hannah

SIXTY DAYS AFTER

Hannah stood on the sidewalk across from Ronni's apartment building, summoning the courage to cross the street. She was skipping her morning classes—foods and English—but she knew she'd have Mrs. Pittwell's blessing. The counselor could explain to Hannah's teachers that she had gone on a mission of mercy, a task far more important than discussing *Atticus Finch, morality personified*, or baking banana muffins. Even Hannah's mom seemed to have had a change of heart regarding Hannah and Ronni's friendship. Or at least that's what Hannah presumed from her mom's cryptic text: Do what you think is right. . . . Was Kim finally willing to loosen the reins and let her eldest explore independent thought? Hannah was going with that.

Hannah had psyched herself up to take on Lisa Monroe this morning. Hannah would ring the buzzer, and if Lisa answered, Hannah would give her the practiced pitch: *Ronni needs my sup-*

port. My mom is willing to let me be there for my friend. You should, too. Hannah had been about to cross the street, had steeled herself to confront an angry adult, when a battered truck pulled up out front. Moments later, Lisa, looking young and pretty but really serious, had emerged from the building. Without a glance in Hannah's direction, Lisa got in and drove off with the guy—her boyfriend, probably.

So why was Hannah still standing there, almost an hour later? As she stood rooted to the spot, she realized it was Ronni she was afraid of, not Ronni's anger or blame, but her eye. Ronni had been back at school for a month, but Hannah still hadn't seen it. She had seen the back of Ronni's glossy, dark-brown head from a distance, but with Hillcrest's population of two thousand students and Ronni's drastically reduced class schedule, their paths hadn't crossed. The school had a special program for kids with learning disabilities, or issues at home, or now, kids who had lost their eye at a sweet sixteen party. . . . The "specials," Adam called them. Even before the accident, Ronni hadn't been very academic. She was more interested in fashion and beauty, interests Hannah had assumed Ronni would segue into a career. Well . . . maybe not now.

But Ronni's eye couldn't be as bad as everyone said. The kids talked about her like she was a monster, a grotesque aberration, a Cyclops. . . . A lump formed in Hannah's throat: pity and sadness. She forced herself to cross the street.

Hannah punched the code into the keypad and listened to the phone ring in Ronni's apartment. There was no answer, but Ronni had to be there. She wasn't at school, she wasn't with her mom, and it's not like she had any friends to hang out with anymore. Hannah hit the pound key to reset and tried again. Finally, a small, flat voice came through the speaker. "Hello . . ."

"Ronni, it's Hannah. Can I come up?"

Silence. It lasted so long that Hannah thought the call had disconnected, but finally Ronni said, "Are you alone?"

"Yes . . . it's just me, Ronni. Let me come up. . . . Please." There was another pause, then the door buzzed loudly. Hannah jerked it open and hurried into the lobby.

In the tiny elevator, she steeled herself for the encounter. She would not react to Ronni's altered appearance, even if it was as bad as she'd heard. Because Ronni was more than just her injury. Hannah would treat her like she was the old Ronni, the girl she had known since childhood, like she was *normal* . . . because she was still Ronni, she was still normal, even if everyone else had forgotten that.

To her credit, Hannah didn't flinch when Ronni opened the door. Ronni had parted her dark hair differently, in an effort to hide the damage, but it was still evident. It wasn't the sightless eye that was disturbing; it was the area around it. The lower lid was gone, or mostly gone, and the skin on the side was pulled tight. The impression was frightening but vaguely cartoonish—like the eye was about to pop out of its socket over a nasty surprise.

"Hey . . ." Ronni muttered.

"I wanted to see you," Hannah said, eyes fixed on the tip of her friend's nose. "Can I come in for a bit?"

"My mom will be home soon."

Hannah suddenly felt completely terrified at the thought of Lisa's arrival, but she couldn't back out now. "I won't stay long."

Ronni stepped back to let Hannah enter. As she did, Ronni looked down at the floor, allowing her long hair to obscure the right side of her face. Hannah noted how pretty her friend was, how she still wore impeccable makeup, and had clearly straightened her hair. This effort contrasted with Ronni's baggy gray sweatpants, flannel shirt, and fuzzy slippers.

"Do you want to sit?" Ronni indicated the sofa. There was a blanket and a pillow on it, like she'd just woken from a nap. Maybe that was why Ronni seemed drowsy, lackadaisical, almost sedated. . . .

"'Kay . . ." The girls sat on the couch, knees angled toward each other. Ronni was half on the blanket, half on the pillow; she hadn't bothered to remove them. "I haven't seen you at school," Hannah said.

"I don't go much anymore."

"Lucky . . ." As soon as she said it, Hannah realized it was a stupid remark. She tried to cover. "School sucks right now."

"Yeah?" There was a glimmer of interest.

"I broke up with Noah."

"Really?"

"Yeah . . . Or maybe he broke up with me. Anyway, it's over. And he hates me. He gives me dirty looks every time he sees me. And Adam and those guys are worse. They always sneer or whisper or laugh at me."

"I wonder what that's like?" The deadpan delivery did nothing to undercut the sarcasm.

"Sorry."

Ronni said, "What about Lauren?"

"I haven't really talked to her. . . ." Since the breakup with Noah, Hannah had seen Lauren only once, from a distance. The popular girl had been down the hall, near Adam's locker, with some other guys. They were all talking and snickering, probably at someone's expense, probably at Hannah's. But maybe she was just being paranoid? Hannah hated to admit it, but she clung to the hope that Lauren might still deem Hannah worthy without Noah's affections, that Lauren might side with her, eventually snubbing the boys and dissing them for their poor treatment of her friend. It was completely unrealistic—she knew that. And she kind of hated herself for wanting it.

"Lauren doesn't come to school much lately," Hannah said. "And when she does, she seems pretty high."

"I haven't heard from her," Ronni said, tipping forward so her hair covered her face again.

Hannah knew enough to change the subject. "What have you been doing?"

"Netflix . . . Going to therapy . . . Painting."

"I didn't know you painted."

"Mrs. Pittwell is making me go in the art show," Ronni said, brushing the hair off her face before remembering and hiding behind her bangs again.

"I'm going to be in it, too," Hannah said. "I did some black-and-white photos in photography class."

"Mrs. Pittwell says it's a good way for me to integrate back into the school." She yawned. "Like I want to . . ."

“Yeah.”

“I’ll be going to a better private school next year anyway,” Ronni said, “after—” She caught herself and stopped.

After your mom sues my parents for three million dollars? But Hannah wasn’t going to go there. She was a bigger person than that; she was the biggest person in this whole mess.

“Can I see your painting?”

Ronni hesitated, then shrugged. “I guess.” She stood and shuffled toward her room, her slippers scuffling along the hardwood floor like she didn’t have the energy to lift her feet. Hannah followed in her wake.

While the rest of the apartment was fairly tidy, Ronni’s room was a mess: dirty clothes, coffee mugs, and magazines littered surfaces already cluttered with open makeup containers, hair products, and jewelry. Photos of Ronni’s former life still plastered the walls, but a few had fallen from their stations and lay forgotten on the floor. The double bed, unmade, took up most of the space, but in the center of the room, propped on a kitchen chair in lieu of an easel, was the painting.

The deep canvas was about a foot by a foot. The background was painted a dark color, almost black but not black, a combination of gray and brown perhaps. Moving toward the center, the colors lightened, oranges, yellows, greens, until the fulcrum, where a luminous burst of turquoise splattered across the canvas. Hannah knew nothing about abstract art, but the painting was oddly haunting.

“It’s great.”

“It’s what I see out of my right eye.”

See?

Ronni turned to Hannah. For the first time, she didn't bother to camouflage her eye with her hair. "People think that blind people are in the dark, but that's not true. . . . Not for me anyway. When I close my other eye, I see all these colors and bursts and clouds."

"Sounds cool."

"It's not." Ronni turned back to face the painting. "It's bright. And noisy. I can't sleep. I can't even think. . . ."

Hannah stared at the painting. The color was too flat, the technique too rudimentary to convey light, and yet, somehow it did. Somehow, Hannah felt like she was inside Ronni's head, seeing what Ronni saw.

"I'm sorry," Hannah said softly, emotion clogging her throat. She turned toward Ronni, but Ronni kept staring at the canvas. Hannah pushed on anyway. "I'm sorry about what happened to you at my house. I'm sorry my parents didn't check on us before you fell. I wish I never had a birthday party."

Ronni's gazed remained fixed. "It's not your fault. We would have gotten wasted anywhere. I told my mom that. But she won't stop."

"My parents have lots of money. They should help you."

Ronni turned toward her, damaged eye exposed again. "They've offered to help, but my mom says it's not enough. She wants to 'set me up for the future,' 'cause, you know, now that I'm a hideous monster, I'll never go to college, never get a job, never get married. . . ."

"That's not true," Hannah said. "You're not hideous." But tears were filling her eyes as if to belie her words.

"It is true," Ronni said blandly. "Didn't you see my Facebook page? Read the comments—I'm disgusting. I'm a freak. I deserve this because I was such a stuck-up bitch. . . . Maybe they're right. I wasn't that nice."

"*They're* disgusting, not you!" Hannah's voice was quivering and she felt perilously close to tears. She hadn't come here to fall apart, but she could feel herself slipping closer to the edge. "I'm not friends with any of the popular kids anymore. I hate them. They're horrible and they're mean and they're bullies. They think they're so cool, but they're stupid. They're all going to grow up to be losers and drug addicts and assholes. And you and I can go on with our lives and we'll never have to see any of them again."

"But I'll still look like this." Ronni looked down then, her hair forming its usual mask. "I was used to people staring at me because I was pretty and hot. And now they stare at me because I'm damaged and ugly."

"Looks aren't everything." God, she sounded like her mom.

Ronni met Hannah's gaze squarely. "I'm not smart like you are, Hannah. I'm not good at school or sports or anything really. But I was pretty and popular, so I had that. . . . Not anymore."

"You're a good artist," Hannah tried, indicating the painting.

Ronni shrugged. "Yeah . . . I could probably get ten, maybe fifteen bucks for it."

It took Hannah a second to realize Ronni was joking. She went with it. "I'd push for twenty. . . ." Thankfully, Ronni giggled. It was so good to hear her friend's laugh, to feel her spirit lift, just a little, that Hannah spontaneously hugged her. Ronni was unresponsive in the embrace—she'd never been affectionate or demonstrative—but eventually, Hannah felt the girl's arms tighten around her, and her body relax toward her. She felt the shudder as Ronni let go and cried in Hannah's arms.

Ronni's sobs, though soft, must have obscured the sound of Lisa's entry. But suddenly, there she was, standing in the doorway. "No," the woman said, moving into the room, a gust of hostile energy preceding her.

Instinctively, the girls stepped apart. "Mom—" Ronni started, but Lisa interjected.

"This is not happening."

Hannah was momentarily confused. Maybe Lisa thought there was something illicit in the girls' embrace, but she knew Lisa was open-minded and gay-friendly. And yet, her disapproval of the situation was blatant. It had to be about Hannah. Lisa quickly confirmed it.

"You can't be here, Hannah. You can't be Ronni's friend right now."

Hannah had rehearsed her line about their parents supporting the friendship, but the tension was muddying her mind. How did it go again? Her voice was tremulous. "My mom is willing to let us be friends even though—"

"Don't talk to me about your mother," Lisa spat. "She doesn't care about Ronni."

"Mom! Stop!" Ronni cried. "Hannah's literally the only friend who has come to see me. Don't chase her away."

"That's not true," Lisa said. "Those other girls came by. . . . Phoebe and the other two . . ."

"They're not my friends! They're just, like, good Christians who visit people who are having a hard time."

Hannah tried again. "The lawsuit has nothing to do with me and Ronni. Why can't we be friends?"

"Because you can't," Lisa snapped, grabbing Hannah's arm rather roughly. "Time to go."

"Ouch!" Hannah snatched her arm away. It wasn't painful, exactly, but Lisa's aggressiveness was frightening.

"Jesus, Mom, you're hurting her."

"She's not hurt," Lisa spat. "*She's* perfectly fine." Lisa looked at Hannah with such open contempt, that Hannah truly felt Lisa was capable of harming her. Tears sprang to Hannah's eyes and she knew she had to flee. She had to get away from Lisa, from her rage and hatred, or she was going to fall apart. Hannah pushed her way past Lisa, out of the bedroom, and ran toward the front door.

"Don't go!" Ronni cried behind her, but Hannah couldn't stop. She was almost at the door when she heard Ronni turn on Lisa. "Mom! What the fuck?"

"This is for your own good," Lisa said, then something like, "She is not your friend. Don't let her fool you."

Hannah stepped into the stuffy stillness of the hallway and closed the door behind her. As she hurried down the hall, she could still hear mother and daughter yelling at each other. Mercifully, she couldn't make out what they were saying.

kim

SIXTY-TWO DAYS AFTER

Kim sat in the small, nondescript boardroom at Apex Outerwear, a polystyrene cup of water in front of her. She found it odd, the use of a foam cup, in a business that was all about appreciating nature and the outdoors. A reusable glass would have been more environmentally sustainable and on brand. She hated the thought of that cup sitting in a landfill for hundreds of years. And as she took a sip, she hated the way it felt on her teeth.

Her client, Neil, entered. "Sorry to keep you waiting," he said, taking a seat across the utilitarian table from her. Neil also seemed incongruous with Apex Outerwear's brand. He was an incredibly stylish, rather effeminate man who seemed infinitely more suited to sipping fine wine and watching opera than snowshoeing through the wilderness to pitch a waterproof tent.

"Thanks for coming in," Neil said. He seemed to have forgotten that Kim had actually requested the meeting. She had put it off as long as possible, but it was time to discuss finding a new designer. Obviously, she and Tony could no longer work together. They had delivered the last flyer on time and on budget; though Kim had submitted her copy to Tony a couple of days late. With all the crap going on in her life, she deserved a little leeway. And in a passive-aggressive way, she had wanted Tony to stress and panic. In the end, they'd pulled it together. But Tony had to be replaced.

She had considered contacting him as a professional courtesy; she'd gone so far as to compose an e-mail before deciding it was redundant and deleting it. Tony was a jerk, but he wasn't stupid. He had to know Kim would be finding someone new. And he had plenty of other projects to keep him busy.

"Good of you to see me," Kim said. "I know how busy you are."

"It's insane," Neil said. "So I hope you don't mind if I get straight to the point."

The *point*?

"We're going to take the monthly flyer in another direction. We want to focus more on social media and our online presence."

"I can adapt to that," Kim said confidently. At best, Kim had a cursory knowledge of social media platforms. She'd created a Facebook profile and an Instagram account—neither of which she looked at—to keep her kids on their toes, but she wasn't exactly a Luddite. And she was an intelligent woman. She could learn Internet marketing; it wasn't neurosurgery.

"We think this is a logical time for us to find another writer . . . someone more tuned in to the eighteen-to-thirty-four market."

"I'm tuned in to that market," Kim lied, her voice shrill and tinged with desperation. "I've got a lot of millennials in my life." But she didn't. Her nephew in Oregon qualified, though their relationship had dwindled to an annual Christmas card with twenty bucks inside—twenty bucks because she had no idea what to buy someone that age. Damn.

Neil sighed and looked down at the table. "I'm sorry, Kim. But we're not going to renew your contract. We'll give you a month's notice and write you a good reference, but . . ."

There was something loaded in that *but*. This wasn't about tapping into millennial buying patterns; there was something deeper at play here. She felt anger well up inside her. "What's really going on here, Neil?"

"As I said, it's time we updated our approach. It's not personal. . . ."

"Have you talked to Tony Hoyle?"

Guilt flitted across Neil's almost feline features. "We've always loved Tony's design work. He came to us with a proposal. We liked what he had to say."

"He was my subcontractor. The relationship started with me."

"You were on a month-to-month contract, Kim. Tony brought us an exciting young writer who had innovative ideas on platform management. It's time to step up our game."

Kim leaned back in her chair. "This is ageism."

"It's not." Neil leaned back, too, mirroring Kim's body language. "Tony said you're having some legal troubles. He said you were having trouble getting your copy in on time."

"Once. And I was only two days late."

Neil pursed his lips for a moment before addressing her in a purposefully gentle voice. "It sounds like, perhaps, you should focus on your family and your lawsuit for now. I'm sure you'll be able to pick up more work when your personal life settles down."

He knew. He knew everything: Ronni's eye, the lawsuit, Jeff's drug use, Kim and Tony's brush with adultery. . . . Tony had shared every sordid detail with their client in order to steal the account. The evidence was in Neil's eyes, full of pity, disgust, judgment. . . .

Her cheeks burned with humiliation as she stood. "I'm sorry you feel that way," she said, voice quivering. "I've always been a consummate professional."

Neil stood, too. "And my reference letter will reflect that."

Kim moved toward the boardroom door, her body vibrating with rage and shame. Neil didn't follow, didn't offer to walk her out, but his relief at getting rid of her was palpable. He couldn't wait for the dismissal to be over so he could forge ahead with his new, hipster flyer team. Well, it was not going to be quite that neat and tidy.

She paused in the doorway and turned toward him. "I didn't want to say anything but . . . Tony's being investigated for child pornography."

"What?"

"You heard me." She walked out.

IT SHOULDN'T HAVE upset her so much. She didn't need the job—Jeff had made that abundantly clear since the day she'd signed the contract—but she *wanted* the job. That flyer was the only thing Kim had that was hers alone. It was her foot in the door, her semi-creative outlet. It was the only fucking thing that kept her from becoming the cliché of the overbearing stay-at-home mom with no life outside her children. "I work part-time," she would say, and watch the impressed expressions on people's faces, see them marvel at her ability to juggle a job and hands-on parenting. As she drove toward Hillcrest, her chest felt heavy with the weight of longing and regret.

She had to pull herself together. It was her children's art show this afternoon and she could hardly show up tearful and pitiful. Kim now knew that she was gossip fodder; she knew there would be eyes on her, judging her and watching for some slipup. There was no way she would give those jerks the satisfaction of seeing her sniveling over the loss of her blurb-writing job. And while part of her wanted to go home, crawl into bed, and cry for two hours straight, Kim would not let her kids down. Aidan was displaying an etching he'd made in eighth-grade metal work (a promising handful had been selected for inclusion in the upper-school art show), and Hannah was showing some photographs. Kim was still a devoted, if unemployed, mother.

The school-wide art show was set up in the main entryway and flowed down several offshoot hallways. With nearly a thousand art students displaying their masterpieces, the building had transformed into a rather manic, makeshift art gallery. Kim strolled past long tables hosting collages and sculptures, past easels bearing self-portraits and animal sketches, stopping to admire the more talented and smiling appreciatively at the attempts of the less. Most of the parents wandering the displays were strangers to her. Despite sitting on the PTA, organizing the annual holiday cookie bash, and contributing to the teacher appreciation lunch, Kim knew only a handful of attendees. Most parents regarded high school as a time to back off after the endless demands of an elementary education. After seven years of driving on field trips, aiding in craft days, baking for fund-raisers, it was tempting. . . . But Kim knew better. Teenagers needed engaged parents more than ever.

Still, Kim noted a few sideways glances at her, a modicum of whispering. At any moment she could stumble upon Debs and her overtly hostile crew. Kim texted both her children:

Where are you?

She knew they were there, somewhere, probably giggling with friends, devouring the "edible art" that the foods class set up every year. They weren't worried about their mother feeling vulnerable, judged about what happened in her home. They faced it every day. Kim moved through the works of art, searching for the metal etchings and photographs.

Turning down a hallway, she found herself immersed in the abstract oil paintings. Despite the simplistic brushwork, the obvious lack of skill or care in most cases, the bright colors drew her in. Kim had always had a *thing* for painting. She could picture her future self, hair gone gracefully gray, painting in the backyard studio she would build for herself. She'd wear Jeff's old work shirts and drink mugs of tea, dabbing paint with precise abandon. She wouldn't sell her canvasses but give them as meaningful, heartfelt gifts. They'd become heirlooms, of a sort, passed down from her kids to theirs and on and on. . . . When she had time, she would take a class. *When she had time . . . Damn you, Tony.*

She was standing, staring at an interesting piece—a dark background gradually becoming bright, almost luminous in the center—when she heard it.

"Want to buy it?"

The voice was instantly recognizable; the intonation more than the resonance. It wasn't tinged with judgment, like Debs's or Karen's, it was full of blatant loathing: Lisa.

Kim hadn't prepared herself for this encounter. She'd steeled herself for sidelong glances and critical whispers, but not for a full-blown confrontation with her nemesis. Hannah said Ronni barely went to school anymore. And even in the best of times, Lisa wasn't one to attend school functions. Why was she here? Kim looked at the painting again. In the bottom right corner, scrawled in blue paint, an *R*.

She turned toward Lisa and saw the hatred she'd heard. "That's what she sees now," Lisa said, with a twisted smile. "Out of her blind eye. Pretty, isn't it?"

"Lisa, I—"

"The painting's yours if you want it, Kim. We're asking three million. Oh, wait . . . you don't have that kind of money."

"I don't."

"Right. You might have to go without a spa treatment. Or sell one of your luxury cars." She gasped. "You might even have to get a *job*."

Kim felt anger well up inside of her. She wanted to fire back, *You're one to talk, you aspiring Reiki healer!* But she held her tongue. She couldn't attack Lisa, couldn't even defend herself. Kim knew no one would take her side in this battle. "We want to help Ronni," she said calmly, though her voice wavered. "We want her to have everything she needs."

"She needs her eye," Lisa spat. "Can you get that back for her?"

"I w-wish I could. . . ." A crowd was forming, a few ninth graders elbowing one another and snickering, a handful of concerned parents looking on. "But I can't."

"And you had the nerve to send Hannah over to our apartment. Was it a reconnaissance mission?"

"I didn't send her!" Kim said. "If she went, she went as a true friend."

"Yeah right!" A mirthless laugh. "Ronni's been through hell since Hannah's party," Lisa said, her voice getting louder. "She's been bullied. She's been dumped by her supposed friends. She's fallen way behind in school. In a way, her eye is the least of her problems."

"I'm sorry," Kim said softly, her gaze flitting over the bystanders. There was the woman from the soccer game, the friend of Debs's and Karen's. What was her name? Jane. Jane looked almost amused, evidently enjoying the show. There was Caitlin . . . And Maddie, from Hannah's basketball team. They were whispering furiously, one eye on the confrontation, one eye scanning the halls for someone: Hannah? Ronni? The other faces were strangers, some shocked, some bemused, some uncomfortable.

But Lisa didn't seem to notice. Or if she did, she didn't care. "It's all about your fancy house and your fancy cars and your fancy lifestyle. You don't give a shit about my daughter's well-being."

"That's not true."

"It is true! Or you would have checked on them, Kim! You

would have searched their bags for alcohol and drugs. You pretend you're such a diligent parent—"

"I am diligent," Kim said, her heart hammering in her chest, in her throat, in her ears. . . . She gulped some air before continuing. "I laid out the rules. The kids broke them."

"Because they're fucking kids!" The f-bomb elicited a few giggles and whispers from the peanut gallery. "That's what kids do. Maybe if you weren't on pills and wine, you'd have thought about what a bunch of unsupervised, sixteen-year-old girls could get up to at a sweet sixteen party."

Kim heard the snickering, heard someone say: "Maybe we should get Principal Edwards?" They'd become a sideshow. A laughingstock. Two naughty children who needed separating by an authority figure. The weight on Kim's chest was heavier now, the pressure making it hard to breathe. Lisa's angry face was obscured by shimmering spots of light.

"I have to go."

Kim took a step to leave, but she was light-headed. Her feet felt numb, her hands, too. She was afraid she might fall; she needed something to hold on to. Still, Lisa's voice followed her.

"That's right. Run back to your mansion, Kim!"

It's hardly a mansion, Kim wanted to say. It was a fairly modest home that they had made impressive with a challenging and time-consuming renovation. But Lisa wouldn't listen, no one would.

"Go back and tell your banker how you can't afford to buy Ronni's painting! How you can't afford to pay for ruining Ronni's life!"

"Mom, stop. . . ." The voice was soft and flat, but firm. It had to be Ronni. She was the real victim in this whole mess, but here she was, stepping in, taking control, rescuing Kim from her mother's ire. . . . Kim turned back to thank the girl, to give her a grateful smile at least, but Ronni was obscured by Lisa's toned form. Kim was having trouble focusing, but she smiled in the girl's direction.

"What are you smiling at?" Lisa hissed. "Is this all a fucking joke to you?"

"Mom, Jesus!"

Ronni stepped into view then, and for the first time, Kim saw the damage. The girl's hair attempted to camouflage the wounded eye, but it was not up to the task. The whiteness of the eyeball glared through the veil of her bangs, giving her a grotesque, horror-movie aspect. In this day and age, was that really the best the plastic surgeons could do for her? Kim and Jeff would pay for another surgery. A better surgeon! They would make Ronni look better, look normal again. She'd been such a pretty girl. . . .

And then, everything was going dark. Kim's hands and feet were tingling and the weight on her chest was restricting her breathing. She heard a voice say, "Are you okay?" Not Lisa's voice this time, but someone concerned and caring. But she wasn't okay. She was having a heart attack. She was dying, right here, at the school art show, in front of students and parents and teachers. The kids would never forgive her for this. Kim felt an acute sense of embarrassment as she crumpled to the floor.

hannah

SIXTY-FIVE DAYS AFTER

Like school didn't suck enough, now Hannah's mom had gone and had some kind of *conniption* in front of half her classmates. . . . Of course, Hannah felt sorry for her mom; Hannah knew firsthand how menacing and scary Lisa Monroe could be. But when Lisa had come at Hannah, she hadn't collapsed on the floor, a quivering, apoplectic mess. "Marcus saw the whole thing," her brother had said in a rare moment of sibling commiseration. "He actually thought Mom was *dying*." It was so fucking humiliating.

Someone, a concerned parent or a teacher, had called 9-1-1. Two paramedics had rushed into the school to attend to Hannah's prostrate mother. As a crowd of Hannah's peers looked on, the paramedics checked Kim's blood pressure, her heart rate, asked her to lift both arms, had shone a little flashlight in her eyes. . . . After their thorough assessment, it was determined that Kim had had a panic attack. A fucking panic attack! If it was epilepsy or some kind of stroke, people would at least feel sorry for them.

Hannah desperately wanted to transfer schools, but changing this far into the term would have been "academically disastrous," as Mrs. Pittwell put it. "You could end up having to repeat tenth grade." The last thing Hannah wanted was to make this hellish experience even *longer*. But she knew that, at the right school, tenth grade could be salvaged. She'd heard of kids who were failing school—there was a girl with an eating disorder who'd missed three months, a boy with a daily pot habit who skipped the majority of his classes—who ended up passing with the right educational support. Their parents had shelled out for an elite private school to provide a delicate balance of structure and coddling that got them back on track and through the grade. It seemed you got what you paid for when it came to education. Hillcrest was fine if you were smart, had a traditional learning style, and no drama going on in your life . . . but as soon as the shit hit the fan, it was sink or swim.

Hannah had considered asking her parents about switching to a different school, but the timing was all wrong. With Lisa's lawsuit, they were worried about money. She knew they weren't going to flush the Hillcrest tuition down the toilet and shell out for another school, just to please their disobedient daughter. And there was already so much tension in the house; Hannah was afraid her request might cause another meltdown. She'd overheard her parents talking (yelling) in the kitchen.

"Lisa's bullying us," her mom had cried. "She's so angry that she's not rational."

"I could say the same about you," her father shot back.

"What's that supposed to mean?"

"You're willing to go to trial to hurt Lisa, even though you know what it would do to us all! I'd be dragged through the mud! The kids would be humiliated!"

"Maybe you should have thought about that before you gave liquor to children! Before you asked them to cover for you!"

"And they did cover for me!" her dad yelled. "We could pay Lisa off and this would all go away, but you're so fucking vindictive!"

The admission stirred something uncomfortable in the pit of Hannah's stomach. Why were her friends willing to lie, to *perjure themselves*, to cover for her dad? She thought of Lauren threatening Marta and Caitlin to keep quiet about the events of that night. Hannah had thought Lauren was protecting herself, protecting Noah and Adam, but was she covering for Hannah's dad, too? If she was, why? She couldn't ponder it—*wouldn't* ponder it.

Hannah wouldn't devote any more energy to her fucked-up parents; she had bigger problems to deal with, like surviving the gulag that was high school. A quick look at her phone confirmed that there were still seven minutes left in math class. Ironically, class time had become a refuge of sorts, where she could disappear into the lessons or into her thoughts, without stressing about social politics. Once, she'd waited anxiously for the bell signaling the end of classes; now, the trill filled her with trepidation. Lunchtime was the worst. Abject terror—that's what Hannah felt when entering the cafeteria alone, knowing that no one wanted her to eat with them, no one wanted to talk to her. . . . Marta and Caitlin may have grudgingly let her sit at their table, but she had been a shitty friend to them. They *had* to resent her for thinking she'd outgrown them; they must be enjoying her comeuppance. And then there was Noah and his friends, who blatantly loathed her. And Lauren, who remained a wild card. Hannah was like a prisoner released from solitary into gen pop. She ate lunch alone near her locker, watching her back.

But Hannah had a new strategy. She had made the decision last night as she lay in her darkened room listening to the unintelligible bickering of her parents. She was an outcast now, a pariah; she had to accept that fact and find her people . . . or her person. She already knew someone who was ostracized, pitied, and mocked. She would find Ronni and, together, they would bravely enter the lunchroom, sit at a prominent table, and eat their sandwiches. (Well . . . Ronni would probably just drink vitaminwater but she may have added midday food to her routine since the accident.) If this were a movie or an after-school special, the other kids would be moved by their bravery, touched by the resilience of a friendship that had survived so much . . . but those kinds of kids didn't exist in real life.

The bell rang and her classmates sprang from their seats and hurtled toward the door. Hannah moved slower but she felt less apprehensive than she had in ages as she navigated the crowded hallways to the counseling suite. It was 11:00 A.M., so Ronni had probably just arrived at school. She would undoubtedly be in Mrs. Pittwell's office, likely being counseled about the *seizure* Kim had had at her feet. Hannah could use some counseling over the matter herself.

Tentatively, Hannah knocked on the counselor's closed door. It was possible Mrs. Pittwell was with another student—there had to be other kids with problems at the school—but odds were none were as critical as Ronni's. When the door swung open a crack, Hannah saw that her supposition was correct. Behind Mrs. Pittwell's boxy frame, Hannah caught a glimpse of shiny dark hair.

"Hannah . . ." the counselor addressed her. "Did you want to talk?" There was concern in her tone . . . and pity. Mrs. Pittwell had obviously been made aware of Kim Sanders's art show meltdown.

"I actually wanted to talk to Ronni," Hannah said. "I'll come back later." She turned to go, but the counselor stopped her with a hand on the arm.

"Come in . . ."

Hannah moved into the stuffy office. Ronni was occupying the only chair, but Mrs. Pittwell offered Hannah her swiveling, padded model. The counselor stood, looming over them like a judge on the bench . . . or God. She smiled benevolently down at Hannah. "Did you want to talk to Ronni about what happened at the art show?"

"Umm . . . not really." She glanced at Ronni. "I'm sorry and everything, but"—she turned back to the woman standing over her—"Ronni already knows my mom is kind of . . . *wound up* right now."

Ronni actually smirked. "Not as wound up as my mom is."

Hannah chuckled. "I'd say it's a tie."

Mrs. Pittwell laughed, too. She seemed positively thrilled by this glimpse of humor.

Hannah spoke to Ronni. “I came here to ask if you wanted to eat lunch today. In the cafeteria . . .”

Something like fear, or dread, or physical pain passed over Ronni’s features. The counselor saw it, too. “I think that’s a great idea,” Mrs. Pittwell seconded.

Ronni’s eyes—eye—darted from Hannah to the counselor. “I usually just hang out in here at lunch.”

Mrs. Pittwell didn’t miss a beat. “I’ve got a dentist appointment at twelve fifteen. I’ll have to lock my office while I’m away.”

Hannah couldn’t tell if the woman was lying to facilitate the lunch date or not, but she could see Ronni weighing her options. “Sure . . . ,” she finally said, though her voice was weak.

Mission accomplished. “Cool . . . I’ve got social studies now, but I’ll meet you in there at noon.” Hannah stood and shared a conspiratorial—or was it triumphant?—look with Mrs. Pittwell. Then she left the closet-like space.

The second bell rang while Hannah was in the hall, but she didn’t rush to class. Since Ronni’s accident, Hannah had experienced a perspective shift. Despite the values her mother had tried to instill in her, getting straight A’s wasn’t *actually* the most important thing in the world. Survival, that’s what mattered. Getting through the gauntlet of tenth grade with your self-esteem intact was what counted. Hannah wasn’t about to fail any of her classes—she wasn’t even close—but so what if she did? The world would not stop spinning. If she showed up late, or not at all, life would still go on. It was an epiphany.

She headed into the bathroom and moved directly into a stall. As she peed, she let herself feel just a little bit pleased with her accomplishment. Last night, she had set a goal to find a lunch partner, and today, she had brought it to fruition. Of course, things could still go horribly wrong: Ronni might not show; they might be laughed at, or even pelted with sandwiches. . . . But things might go absolutely right, as well. She and Ronni might regain acceptance; they might sidle back into the mainstream, not cool or popular, but accepted. That's all Hannah wanted now.

Then she heard it: retching. She had thought she was alone, but a few stalls down, someone was barfing. Bulimia was not exactly in vogue at the school, but it wasn't unheard of, either. Or a student could have been drinking. It was morning, but it had been known to happen. Hannah flushed and hurried to the sinks. She wanted to get out of there before the smell hit.

She was hurriedly wiping her hands on a paper towel when the stall door opened and Lauren Ross emerged. Despite the audible evidence to the contrary, the girl seemed in perfect health. Hannah feared it might be her turn to rush into a stall and void her stomach. This was the first time she had been alone with Lauren since her ugly split with Noah. She was terrified.

Lauren, however, seemed unfazed. "Hey," she muttered as she headed to the sink.

"You okay?" Hannah asked.

Lauren bent over and splashed water into her mouth. When she righted herself, she was blasé. "Fine." Despite the unflattering fluorescent lights and her recent sickness, Lauren looked as perfect and polished as always. She moved to the paper towel dispenser right next to Hannah. Hannah caught the waft of alcohol as Lauren dried her hands. That explained it. . . .

Lauren tossed her balled-up towel toward the garbage can, but it landed on the floor. The girl made no move to pick it up but turned toward Hannah and gave her a glassy smile. Hannah's heart was pounding. This was the pivotal moment that would determine the fate of their friendship. Hannah had decided to embrace her outsider status, had decided to join Ronni as a social leper, but if Lauren threw her a lifeline, she would grab it and haul herself back up the ladder of popularity, she knew she would.

Lauren said, "I heard your mom saw Ronni's eye and had a breakdown."

"Kinda . . ."

Their eyes met, and Lauren smiled. "Ronni is pretty fucking scary."

As enamored as she still was with Lauren, Hannah could not overtly betray Ronni, not now. "It doesn't look that bad, actually. You get used to it."

Lauren shuddered to convey that she would never get used to it. Then she said, "Is your mom okay?"

Hannah was warmed by the concern. "She's fine. She's just been under a lot of stress."

"I heard she was like seizuring all over the floor. *So* embarrassing." There was no empathy in Lauren's tone and her lips twitched with amusement. The girl was enjoying this. She wasn't interested in reviving their friendship; she was only engaging Hannah to mock her.

Anger filled Hannah's chest, constricted her throat, and colored her cheeks. Lauren was cruel and stupid, and Hannah hated her. But she hated herself more. She had stood there, waiting to see if Lauren would accept her back into her circle. Had Lauren deemed her worthy, Hannah would have jumped at the chance. Was she really that weak, needy, pathetic . . . ? Self-loathing consumed her and made her reckless.

"I'm glad you find this all so funny."

Lauren had the basic decency to act affronted. "I actually feel bad for you guys—you and Ronni have no friends left. Your mom is losing her shit. . . ." Her face turned mean and ugly. "And your poor daddy is caught up in the whole mess."

That sick feeling gurgled in Hannah's stomach. "Don't talk about my dad."

"Why not? Jeff and I are friends."

"You're not *friends*."

"I protected him. I made sure no one told the police or the lawyers about the champagne he gave us." Lauren smiled coyly. "And things just grew from there. . . ."

"He's practically fifty! You're disgusting!"

"Jeff doesn't think I'm disgusting—he thinks I'm hot. And sexy."

"Fuck you!" Hannah was shaking now. She wanted to hit this girl, to punch her in her pretty, perfect, drunk face. What would happen if she did? She'd only recently come to terms with being late for class; fighting in the school bathroom was another story.

"You can't blame him, Hannah. Your mom's a lunatic . . . and you're so *childish*. He had to turn to someone for comfort."

Hannah's voice was quivering with rage. "You're a liar."

"I'm not." Lauren dug her smartphone out of her back pocket. "And I've got the texts to prove it."

Hannah's hand balled into a fist. She didn't know how to throw a punch; she and her brother had had the requisite shoving and wrestling matches, but they'd never actually struck each other. Kim would have grounded them for life! But Hannah was going to have to learn fast.

Lauren was scrolling through her phone. "Here are his texts. . . ." She looked up at Hannah and bit her lip. "Want to see your dad's dick pic?"

Hannah's fist glanced awkwardly off the side of Lauren's jaw. If the girl's face hurt half as much as Hannah's hand did, the punch had had the desired effect. The scream Lauren emitted verified her pain, or maybe just her shock. The phone flew from Lauren's grasp and skittered across the linoleum into one of the empty bathroom stalls.

"You fucking cunt!" Lauren shouted at the top of her lungs. "You hit me!"

The volume was bound to bring teachers or a vice principal running to intervene. But despite Hannah's throbbing hand and pounding heart, she felt vindicated. She smiled at the red welt on Lauren's cheek. "You deserved it."

Lauren suddenly realized her phone had been knocked from her grasp. "If you broke my phone, I'll fucking kill you." The injured girl hadn't seen where it landed, but Hannah had. As Lauren scanned the floor for the device, Hannah rushed directly to it in the bathroom stall. She picked up Lauren's phone and held it above the toilet. If Lauren was to be believed, the gadget held incriminating texts, sexy messages, even a photo of her father's penis. . . . But Lauren couldn't be believed. Hannah's dad would never, ever do that. But just in case . . . she dropped the phone into the toilet and flushed. The school commode was commercial grade, built for heavy and frequent use; it swallowed the phone like it was just another deposit of shit.

The next thing Hannah felt was her hair being yanked from behind. "You fucking bitch!" Lauren shrieked, near hysteria. "You're going to buy me a new phone!" She threw Hannah to the floor and kicked her in the ribs.

"What the hell is going on in here?" It was Vice Principal Wong, petite but intimidating.

"She punched me in the face!" Lauren cried. "She flushed my phone!"

The vice principal looked at Hannah, and Hannah registered the woman's surprise. Hannah Sanders was not the kind of kid who engaged in bathroom catfights, who flushed expensive property down the toilet. . . . Then she saw something like realization soften Ms. Wong's features. Hannah had been through a lot lately and she was cracking under the pressure. They would go light on her . . . Hannah hoped.

"Both of you, in my office," VP Wong barked.

As Hannah followed the petite authoritarian down the hall, she pondered her fate. Expulsion? Probably overkill. But suspension was definitely in the cards, for both her and Lauren. High school protocols didn't factor in who threw the first punch or who was provoked when doling out punishment. Kim was going to lose her mind when she got the call. Neither Hannah nor Aidan had ever received a disciplinary call home.

But when Hannah glanced over at Lauren and saw the welt rising along her jawline, she knew it was all worth it. Whatever happened to her now, she had done the right thing. It wasn't until they reached the office doorway that Hannah realized: she was going to stand up Ronni for lunch today.

jeff

SIXTY-FIVE DAYS AFTER

Jeff marched into the house and crashed right into the wall of tension pervading the space. Kim had called him at the office and insisted he come home immediately. She wouldn't tell him why, just that no one was hurt, but it was *serious*. "I've got meetings," he'd tried, but his wife had been adamant. If this was something like finding porn sites in Aidan's browser history, or texts full of swearing on Hannah's phone, he would lose it. But Kim had gained some perspective since Ronni's accident.

The energy in the house was dark and heavy, and Jeff knew this wasn't just Kim overreacting. He found his wife and daughter in the kitchen. Kim stood near the center island nursing a glass of white wine (it was barely two in the afternoon—not a good sign). Hannah perched on a barstool, her nose red, her eyes glassy, and her general demeanor one of emotional exhaustion. Something bad had happened.

"Your daughter's been suspended for *fighting*," Kim blurted, taking a gulp of wine.

"What?" Jeff looked at Hannah, who was staring blankly at the butcher-block countertop.

"I just got back from the vice principal's office," Kim elaborated. "Your darling girl punched Lauren Ross in the face."

Jesus Christ. Hannah had attacked Lauren? Why? He knew he couldn't ask. He looked at Hannah again, sitting still and quiet. "I thought you two were friends."

She looked up at him then, a hint of a bitter smile. "Nope."

Kim drank more wine. "And you'll pay for her phone, missy. You can get a job. Or you can babysit . . ."

Jeff addressed Hannah. "You broke her phone?"

"She flushed it down the toilet!" Kim offered.

Hannah lifted her gaze to meet Jeff's and he saw it: anger, disgust, betrayal. . . . His daughter knew. Whether she knew the truth or some twisted lie that Lauren had told her, Hannah knew. She had destroyed the phone to protect her father; she had destroyed texts that could incriminate him. Still . . . he had to ask. "Why?" His voice was hoarse.

Hannah looked at him for a tense, loaded moment. With a handful of words, she could destroy his life, end his marriage, and change their father-daughter relationship forever . . . but Hannah just shrugged. "Seemed like the right thing to do."

"The *right* thing to do?" Kim shrieked. "Who are you? What is wrong with you?"

Hannah stood. "Leave me alone." She strolled toward her room.

"Don't you walk away from me!" Kim screamed after her, but it was clear the girl was done listening.

"Let her go," Jeff said.

"She beat a girl up! She destroyed her personal property! So we should just give her a time-out?" Kim was pouring more wine.

"This has been hard on her."

"Hard on *her*?" Kim let out a harsh laugh, drank her wine. "It's been hard on all of us, but you don't see us beating the shit out of people and destroying their electronics."

She was getting drunk now and becoming irrational. Jeff wasn't in the mood. "I'm going back to work."

His wife's angry words followed him to the door. "Excellent parenting, Jeff! It's no wonder Hannah's acting like a fucking hooligan!"

BUT JEFF DIDN'T go back to work. He went to a hole-in-the-wall bar near Chinatown and ordered a Scotch. He'd been doing this lately—sneaking out for an afternoon drink or two—not getting drunk but taking off the edge. When he'd first visited a bar, he'd been surprised to find a lively culture of day drinkers, not the sad, lonely alcoholics he'd expected. Who were these guys (they were 80 percent male) and what afforded them the means, flexibility, and desire to go for several pints in the middle of the afternoon? Shift workers, maybe . . . Or sailors . . . ?

Jeff sat alone at the rough-hewn wooden bar. He wasn't there to mingle or make friends—that was considered exceedingly creepy in the day-drinking scene—he was there to relax, to numb himself to the shit going on in his life. The Scotch burned pleasantly in his belly and the knots of tension in his shoulders were loosening, but he couldn't stop thinking about Hannah. And Lauren Ross. He didn't want to think about Lauren anymore, but she was stuck in his head like a fly in his mind's web.

The evidence of Jeff's *relationship* with Lauren had been destroyed. When Hannah flushed Lauren's phone down the toilet, she had erased the texts, the nude photos, any proof that Jeff and Lauren had ever been in contact with each other. There was a chance that Lauren had backed up her data, but Jeff knew she hadn't. The girl probably didn't know how, for one. And he'd pressed Hannah to back up her devices and she'd blown him off. Teenagers didn't want to leave a paper trail; that's why Snapchat was invented. And restoring contacts was as simple as a Facebook post: *new phone, send digits*. So Jeff and Kim could go to trial now. Jeff could shoulder the blame of giving the girls a bottle of champagne if Lauren decided to turn on him. It wasn't even a glass each! Kim could nail Lisa to the wall, could make sure she and Ronni got nothing. His wife would be thrilled.

But what had Lauren told Hannah to make her destroy the phone? When Hannah drowned the device, she had erased the confirmation that things between Jeff and Lauren were basically innocent. The texts clearly illustrated the unrequited crush of a young girl on an older man. Jeff had never laid a finger on her; he wasn't some pedo creep! And now . . . he couldn't prove it.

He needed to see Lauren. He wasn't exactly sure why, but the yearning was visceral. As he downed the rest of his Scotch and ordered another, his motives became even more fuzzy, but no less urgent. He had to see the girl . . . to ask her what the hell had happened in the school bathroom. And for some fucked-up reason, he needed to know that she was okay. Lauren didn't deserve his pity, he knew that, but the kid was weak and alone and confused. Hannah had positive self-esteem. Hannah had parents who loved her. Lauren Ross was a mess and she had no one.

Of course, Jeff had no way to contact her now. Their only link had been destroyed when Hannah killed that phone. He could look for Lauren at her mom's run-down apartment or visit her dad's expensive high-rise, but that would be weird, crossing the line. But lines had been crossed already, hadn't they? Not *the* line . . . but lines. His kiss on the top of her head, her lingering kiss on his cheek, the texts, the photos, the confidences . . . So it wouldn't be completely insane for him to search her out, ask her what she had told Hannah, make sure she was okay—not completely insane, just a little. His mind was reeling and he couldn't think straight. He drank more Scotch.

His phone in his jacket pocket buzzed; work or Kim. He debated not checking it, but he had rushed out of the office with little warning and he had projects that demanded his attention. Alternatively, things could have devolved into a melee at home. Kim and Hannah had been at each other's throats for weeks now. . . . He dug the phone from his pocket and checked the text.

Text me if you want to talk about what happened

A chill ran through him. It was her. She'd always gone on about their *connection*, a line he'd dismissed as teenaged romanticism. But maybe she was right. He'd been thinking about her, worrying about her, wondering how to contact her, and *ding!* She had reached out to him, just like that. But if she still had his number, did that mean she'd backed up her data after all? Did she still have his texts?

You lost your phone but you still have my number?

You left a business card in your car

I kept it

So that's how Lauren had gotten his contact info in the first place, how she'd found his office . . . Another thought flitted through his cloudy mind. The girl's phone had been destroyed less than four hours ago and it had already been replaced. *A fistfight in the school bathroom? You get a brand-new phone!* Darren and Monique Ross should be nominated for parents of the year! Jesus. The girl didn't have a chance. She was so pretty, so lost and confused. . . .

He took another drink and realized what he wanted to do. The Scotch was probably clouding his judgment, but fuck it. He was going to follow his instincts for once. Kim would have murdered him if she knew what he was planning, but fuck Kim. She didn't really care what he did, she only cared how it looked. Fuck appearances. Fuck being a pillar of the community, never pissing anyone off, never rocking the boat. Look where that had gotten them.

He texted back.

I need to see you.

Nothing for a few moments and then . . .

Are you mad

He didn't hesitate with his response.

No. Not at all. Where are you?

Apple store Union Square

I'll pick you up.

Another slight hesitation . . .

kk

SHE SAT IN his passenger seat, all lip gloss and mascara and dewy soft skin. If her face bore any evidence of the fight, she'd covered it expertly with makeup. "Where are we going?" Lauren was smiling, she was thrilled to be with him. It was wrong, but it felt kind of nice. He hadn't had that effect on anyone in years.

He smiled back at her. "It's a surprise. Something I've been wanting to do for a long time."

She bit her lip. "Will I like it?" She was flirting again, egging him on. There was no way this was wrong.

He didn't want to answer. She wouldn't like it, not at first anyway. . . . He changed the subject. "What did you say to Hannah?"

"Nothing." She stared out the front window. Her voice was defensive, whiny, sixteen. "We were talking about Kim's breakdown and I asked how you were holding up. She kind of freaked."

"You must have said something else."

"I said that we were *friends*. That's it." She touched his knee. "I'd never get you in any kind of trouble."

He looked over at her, smiled. "Promise?" Who was flirting now?

She loved it; she ate it up. "I promise." She beamed back at him.

He stepped on the gas and the car accelerated with a thrust. Lauren made some kind of squeak of excitement, thrilled at the car's surge of power. But Jeff had to be careful. He wasn't *drunk*, but he might blow just over the legal limit. He couldn't afford to get pulled over, not now. If anything made him pause, even for a second, he would lose his nerve.

"Tell me where we're going," Lauren begged. Her hand was still resting awkwardly on his thigh.

He tossed her a grin. "You'll see. . . ."

She gave him an excited smile. "Can't wait."

BUT HER TUNE changed when they were alone in the elevator. "I don't want to," she whimpered softly.

"It's too late. It's happening." Jeff glanced at their reflection in the mirrored walls: a fit middle-aged man and a girl that could have been his daughter, could have been his lover, could have been his captive. . . . Jeff held Lauren's wrist behind her back, away from the round, unblinking eye of the camera that stared down at them. If someone got on, he'd have to let her go, but for now, he held her roughly, tightly. She could have screamed, scratched, bit, fought him, but for some reason, she didn't.

"Please, Jeff . . . Don't make me do this."

"It's for your own good," he growled, eyes fixed on the flashing numbers above the door: 12, 13, 14. . . .

"I thought we were friends," she tried. "I thought you cared about me."

I was never your friend, he wanted to say, *I never cared about you. . . .* But that would have been a lie. He felt something for this mess of a girl, something soft and tender, fierce and protective. Why else would he be willing to risk all he was about to risk?

"That's why I'm doing this," he said, as the elevator lurched to a stop. The doors opened on the twenty-third floor. Lauren turned to face him, her pretty gray eyes full of fear, full of tears. "Come on," he said softly. "It'll be okay."

THE LOBBY WAS elegant, expensive, modern . . . appropriate for a near billion-dollar biotech company. Jeff had googled "Darren Ross" and "San Francisco," and learned he was CEO of a big pharma company that made drugs for ADHD and OCD, among others. A fortyish, blond receptionist with matte red lips and precise eyeliner, sat behind a pale wood desk, staring at her computer screen.

"Where's your dad's office?" Jeff asked Lauren quietly.

"I don't know." She could have been lying, stalling . . . but it was entirely possible that she had never been invited to her father's workplace. The two weren't close, obviously. And while Jeff considered himself a pretty hands-on dad, even Hannah and Aidan had only visited Jeff's office once, maybe twice. The receptionist glanced over blankly, making it clear that she didn't recognize Lauren as her boss's daughter.

His hand on Lauren's elbow, Jeff hustled her to the reception desk. "We're here to see Darren Ross," Jeff said, his voice authoritative. "This is his daughter, Lauren. I'm . . ." Fuck. What was he?

And how did he put it so as not to raise alarm bells? "Her principal."

Lauren looked over at him: liar, but the receptionist (obviously hired to match the decor) didn't pick up on it. "He's in an investor meeting right now. He can't be disturbed."

"This is extremely important," Jeff said. "I suggest you interrupt him."

The receptionist looked at Lauren's tearful, trembling countenance and reconsidered. She stood, and without a backward glance, moved down the hall behind her.

"Come on," Jeff whispered, gripping Lauren's elbow and trailing behind the blond woman. He didn't trust this perfectly coiffed femme-bot to convey the urgency of his message. Lauren let herself be led, though she dragged her feet.

The boardroom had glass walls exposing five suits surrounding a massive table. Darren Ross was at the bow; Jeff could tell it was him. He was smaller than Jeff would have expected: short, compact, with tanned skin hinting at beach holidays or perhaps ski trips, and gray, almost white hair that did nothing to negate his virile, youthful affect. Lauren had inherited his eyes, his jawline, maybe his lips (some features were hard to translate from middle-aged father to teenaged daughter); there was no doubting their biological connection.

Jeff's supposition was confirmed when the receptionist walked directly to the man at the table's head and leaned to whisper in his ear. From their vantage point in the hall, Jeff watched Darren Ross take in the news, then look at an expensive watch on his wrist. He said something to the gatekeeper, something like: I'll be out in twenty minutes—get them a cup of coffee. Fuck that. Fuck him. He'd put his daughter on the backburner for long enough. Without a word, Jeff grabbed Lauren and pulled her into the room.

"You can't come in here!" The receptionist said, trying, belatedly, to do her job.

Darren Ross stood and addressed his clients: three men and a woman. "I'm sorry about the interruption. My daughter's principal needs to speak to me. . . ." He turned to Jeff. "Let's take this in my office." Despite the tolerant smile pasted on his face, there was something threatening in his tone. It filled Jeff with an almost overwhelming anger. He was going to knock this prick down.

"I'm not Lauren's principal," Jeff said, his voice full of contempt. "You'd know that if you participated in her life at all. . . ."

The female client stood. "We should go."

The others made to follow suit, but Jeff addressed them. "Please. Stay. This won't take long."

The clients looked to Darren Ross for guidance, but his eyes were fixed on Jeff. He probably thought Jeff was some lunatic about to pull a gun, or blow himself up, maybe light himself on fire. . . . Darren didn't look frightened just . . . coiled for action. The clients exchanged awkward glances but settled back in their seats.

He spoke directly to Darren. "I'm Jeff Sanders, Hannah's dad. She's one of Lauren's friends."

The name seemed to register with Darren. "The lawsuit . . ." he muttered.

"Lauren and Hannah got into a fight at school today. I'm sure the principal called you."

"They would have called my ex-wife," Darren said coolly. "I'm working."

Jeff gave a mirthless laugh. He was actually going to enjoy hurting this cold prick. "Your daughter has been texting me. Sending me naked pictures of herself. Asking me to meet her. Telling me she loves me . . ."

"You're disgusting," Darren Ross growled.

"No, I'm not," Jeff retorted. "Lucky for you. Lucky for your daughter."

He became aware of Lauren sniveling at his side; he'd almost forgotten she was there. "Daddy . . ." She said plaintively, but her father's expression was stony. "Please don't hate me." Jeff realized that Darren's insult had encompassed Lauren as well. He suddenly felt that fierce, misplaced protectiveness.

"Lauren's not disgusting," Jeff spat at the small man. "She's sixteen. She's confused and alone and messed-up. She needs love and guidance and her father's attention." Jeff's voice was getting louder, angrier.

"You need to leave," Darren Ross said, cool, calm, dismissive. But Jeff was just getting started.

"Your ex-wife's not a parent. She's a drunk, bitter, pill-popping disaster. And you're never there for Lauren. You're always working or traveling. You expect your bimbo of a wife to do the parenting, but she doesn't have a clue!"

Darren suddenly snapped. "*You're* judging me? A kid lost her fucking eye at your house."

Jeff had never wanted to hit someone so much in his entire life. And he could take this leprechaun out with one punch. It would feel so good, so fucking rewarding. But Darren Ross would charge him with assault. Lisa would have more ammunition against them. Kim would murder Jeff. . . .

Jeff wouldn't touch him, but Darren didn't know that. Jeff took a menacing step forward. "Fuck you, you piece of shit," he growled.

Lauren clung to Jeff's arm. "Don't hurt my dad, Jeff. Please!" It sounded inappropriate. The way she was hanging off his arm was too familiar, too proprietary. The clients were muttering among themselves now, gathering papers, digging out cell phones, preparing to leave or call for help.

Darren Ross paled under his tan. He made a move toward a phone on the credenza. "I'm calling security."

"Don't bother, I'm leaving." Jeff strode to the door, then paused. He turned back toward the CEO and spoke, his voice softer, almost plaintive. "Parent your daughter," he said. "Pay attention to her . . . before it's too late." Then he left, practically jogging through the lobby, back to the elevator.

It wasn't until he was safely ensconced in his car, creeping through downtown traffic, that he felt his blood pressure return to normal. He felt something else, too, a weight off his conscience, a lightening of his spirit. He wasn't drunk—the adrenaline of the confrontation had taken care of that—he was . . . relieved. It was over. He actually laughed out loud at the prospect.

He spoke to his car. "Dial. Home."

The car obeyed and he listened to the ring. It would be echoing in his spacious, modern house, bouncing off clean white walls and stylish, uncomfortable furniture. The only clutter in the place was emotional: tension, stress, regrets. . . . After a few moments, Kim answered, "Hello." Her voice was cool and angry. She was obviously still pissed that he'd walked out on her this afternoon. Little did she know, he was about to make her fucking day.

"Let's go to trial," he said into the phone. "Let's prove this wasn't our fucking fault."

hannah

SIXTY-EIGHT DAYS AFTER

Hannah's clock radio blared an overplayed Adele song (was there any other kind?) to wake her up. She rolled over and stopped the auditory assault. The red LED numbers glowed in the early-morning light: 7:15 A.M. She had nowhere to go, nothing to do, but her mom had insisted she get up at her usual time. Hannah's suspension from school "was not a goddamn holiday," and she wasn't going to "laze around in bed like she was on a fucking vacation." Hannah remembered when her mom didn't swear. It wasn't all that long ago.

She dragged herself into a seated position and rubbed at her eyes. Any minute now, her mom would storm in to make sure she hadn't hit the snooze button. God knows Hannah didn't deserve ten extra minutes of slumber after what she'd done! Hannah listened for the angry footsteps on the stairs. This was the third day of her punishment, and her mom showed no signs of easing up. The woman had a gift for staying pissed.

Hannah heard nothing, but she had to be prepared for a sneak attack. She got up and found her slippers, placed neatly at the end of the bed. Day one: *Clean up your filthy room! It's no wonder your life is going off the rails, living in this pigsty!* Kim Sanders seriously believed that clutter could cause juvenile delinquency.

She was putting on her plush, mauve robe when she became aware of a presence outside her door. Her mom was about to burst into the room and lay out the day's schedule of chores, homework, and any other penance she could drum up. Hannah was ready: awake, alert, and suitably dour given the cause of her day off school.

There was a soft rap at the door—Kim did not announce her entrance these days—followed by, "Can I come in?" It was her dad. Though Hannah didn't respond, the door opened a crack and Jeff poked his head inside. "Hey." He stepped into the room. "Can we talk?"

Hannah belted her robe and fixed him with an icy stare. She wanted to say no; she wanted to tell him to leave her alone, to go for a bike ride and ignore her, like he usually did . . . but something had to be wrong. Her dad was never home at 7:15 A.M. Early-morning training sessions were his favorite.

"What's going on?"

He moved over to the bed and straightened the butter-colored duvet. Then he sat and patted a space beside him. "Come sit."

"I'll stand," she retorted. She wanted to keep her distance. She didn't want her dad trying to hold her hand, or stroke her hair, or comfort her in any way. He disgusted her.

Jeff nodded and took a deep breath. "I need to talk to you about Lauren Ross. . . ."

A bubble of revulsion churned in her stomach. Hannah wanted to storm out of the room; she wanted to slap her dad across the face; she wanted to crawl into his lap and cry. . . . She did none of those; she just stood there.

Her dad continued, "I don't know what Lauren told you about me . . . about me and her . . . but Lauren is a very troubled girl."

Hannah gave him a *duh* look but remained mute.

"I need you to know the truth, Hannah. There was never anything going on between Lauren and me."

Lauren and me. Could she cover her ears and sing? But her dad just kept talking.

"Lauren came to the gym one day and I gave her a ride home. I shouldn't have done it, but I felt sorry for her. Then she started texting me. I wanted her to stop, but she wouldn't. Somehow, she got it into her head that there was something between us . . . something *romantic*. . . ."

Oh God. It was getting worse.

"She sent me photos." Hannah knew what was coming. She kept her eyes on the floor, but she could hear the strain in her dad's voice. "*Nude* photos . . . I didn't look at them. I deleted them right away. And I blocked her number. But then she showed up at my office. She was trying to blackmail me over the champagne, telling me she'd turn you against me. I—" His voice broke.

Oh Jesus, please don't let her dad be crying.

Jeff coughed loudly into his fist, which seemed to compose him, thank God. "I was afraid of Lauren . . . afraid of what she might do, what she might say, to you, to your mom, to the lawyers. . . ."

Hannah looked up at him and spoke in a weak voice. "Did you send her any pictures?"

Her dad jumped up. "Absolutely not! God, Hannah, I would never!" He rushed toward her and reached for her hand. She let him take it. "Lauren is a sad and lonely and confused kid. Her parents are useless. She drinks and takes drugs. She lies and manipulates. . . . I'm sorry you ever got involved with her."

Hannah's lower lip trembled. "Me, too."

Her dad wrapped her in a hug then, and the emotions she'd been holding in check broke free. She cried into his sports coat, blubbering like she was a little girl again, while he stroked her hair. There had been a marked lack of physical contact in her family of late, everyone too angry, too resentful, and too secretive to offer up comfort.

"Does Mom know about all this?" she sniveled into her dad's chest. Hannah believed everything her dad had told her, but Kim was a tougher customer.

"She knows everything. No more secrets. We need to be honest now."

Now?

Her dad released her, held her elbows. "Get dressed and come downstairs. Your mom and I have to tell you something."

HANNAH AND HER dad sat on the low sofa in the living room, drinking cups of coffee and waiting for Aidan to leave for school. Kim stood at the door with him. His backpack was on, his skateboard under his arm, but he was not going easily.

"What's going on? Why isn't dad going to work?"

"He is going," her mom said calmly. "We just need to talk to Hannah for a few minutes."

"About what?"

"Nothing that concerns you right now."

"Aren't I a part of this family?"

"Of course you are," Kim responded. "And I promise you'll know everything . . . when the time is right."

"You always treat me like a goddamn baby," he grumbled, storming out the front door.

"Language!"

It was bad timing for Kim to bring out the swear jar, but her mom was right about one thing: Aidan was way too young to take in all the mess going on around them. Hannah, at sixteen, was infinitely more equipped to handle the harsh truth of their circumstances. Aidan's life still revolved around soccer and skateboarding and whether he could convince Mom to let him go on Accutane for his zits. Lucky . . .

Kim joined them on the sofa. She set her mug on a coaster

and turned to Hannah. "Your dad and I have made a decision about Lisa Monroe's lawsuit."

Jeff placed his coffee next to his wife's. "We're going to go to trial to prove that Ronni's accident wasn't our fault."

"Okay . . ."

"That doesn't mean we're not upset about what happened to her at your party," her mom added, looking suitably concerned. "We are. And we want to help Ronni with anything she might need."

"Of course," Jeff said. "But we feel—and our lawyer feels—that what Lisa Monroe is asking for is not commensurate with Ronni's injuries. It's punitive."

"I'm in tenth grade," Hannah sniped. "I didn't go to law school."

Jeff and Kim exchanged an amused look before Jeff elucidated. "Lisa is really angry. She wants someone to blame, she wants to hurt us—that's why she's asking for so much money."

"We've offered her quite a lot of money already," her mom contributed, "but she turned it down."

"She's trying to ruin us, financially," her dad said. "But we're going to protect you and your brother. We're going to protect our home and the life we've built."

"Okay . . ." Hannah nodded. It all sounded perfectly reasonable. But she knew from TV that lawsuits were never perfectly reasonable.

Her dad cleared his throat. "Some things could come out at trial . . . things that could be embarrassing."

Hannah's eyes narrowed. "Like what?"

Her parents exchanged another look. There had been more

"looks" exchanged between them in the past five minutes than there had been in the past six months.

Kim said, "This stuff with Lauren could come out. She might take the stand. She might lie. . . ."

If Lauren Ross stood up in court, in front of lawyers and judges and whoever else, and said that Jeff Sanders had sent her a dick pic, Hannah would spontaneously combust. She felt her chin wobble.

"She won't lie," Jeff said quickly. "Her dad knows everything now. He's on top of it. He won't even let her take the stand."

Hannah wanted to believe him, but she still felt sick. Her parents didn't know how cruel Lauren was; they didn't know what she was capable of.

Kim continued, "Lisa's lawyers might mention that I drink a little wine most evenings."

A *little* wine? *Most* evenings?

"And that I occasionally take sleeping pills."

Her dad said, "Lisa's lawyers will attack us in any way they can. They'll dig up stuff that's not even relevant."

"Like what?"

"I don't know," Jeff said, but Hannah got the feeling he did know. "Stuff like . . . I train a lot, that I've gotten a few speeding tickets, that we tried drugs in the past. . . ."

"When we were in college," Kim added quickly. "The lawyers will try to damage our character in any way they can."

"They want to make it seem like we're irresponsible parents."

"But you're not." It was just the truth, but it made both her parents smile.

Kim said, "Whatever they say in court, we will discuss as a family."

"We're going to be open and honest with you and Aidan," Jeff seconded.

"Okay . . ." Hannah wanted to leave. She wanted to take a long, hot shower and wash away the filth of all this contention. "Anything else?"

Another quick look flashed between the adults, then her dad smiled at her. "I think that's it. We're meeting with our lawyer this morning. We'll know more after that."

Hannah got up and headed to the kitchen with her coffee cup, but she paused on the boundary between the two rooms. "When I go back to school next week . . . I want to hang out with Ronni."

Her mother's lips tightened. Her dad looked at the floor and shifted in his seat. Kim spoke first. "That's your decision, and we will respect that."

Jeff added, "But when Lisa finds out we're going to trial, she might feel differently."

"We'll see . . . ," Hannah said, and continued on her way.

AFTER HER SHOWER, Hannah felt better. She had vigorously scrubbed herself with a loofah, washing away Lauren's lies, the secrets her parents had kept from her and from each other. Her mom and dad were gone when she went downstairs, off to their lawyer's office to discuss their vindication. Hannah should practice the piano, or do math review, or even some squats and planks, but she wasn't going to squander a couple of hours of freedom. She found her tablet and opened Netflix.

She was halfway through an episode of *Breaking Bad* when the doorbell startled her out of Walter White's seedy world. Her first thought was that she'd been caught slacking off, but her parents wouldn't ring the bell. She hurried to the door and opened it to reveal Caitlin.

"Hey . . ." Hannah was confused by the ginger girl's presence.

"Mr. Morrel gave me a homework packet for you," Caitlin explained, thrusting a plastic folder of papers into Hannah's hands. "I said I'd drop it off during my spare."

"Thanks." Caitlin hovered on the doorstep. She had straightened her red hair, which made her look older, like she'd suddenly grown up while Hannah had been distracted by Lauren and Ronni and Noah. Caitlin didn't seem in a hurry to leave, so Hannah asked, "Do you want to come in?"

"Just for a second . . ."

Hannah led the way into the quiet house. Caitlin had been there so many times, but she looked around her like it was her first visit. "Your parents home?" she asked.

"Nope. Thank God."

They settled on the sofa. After Caitlin declined Hannah's offer of tea or banana bread, she said, "Your mom must have been pretty mad that you got suspended."

"You know my mom . . . she's pretty chill," Hannah joked.

Caitlin giggled. "So what the fuck happened with you and Lauren?"

The homework delivery was just a pretext; Caitlin wanted the scoop. Hannah could hardly blame her. If it had been Caitlin who punched Lauren in the girls' bathroom, Hannah would have been desperate for details.

Hannah shrugged. "She was being a fucking bitch and . . . I just lost it."

"Wow," Caitlin said, clearly impressed. "When we heard, we were just like 'Go Hannah!' I mean, we're sorry you got suspended, but . . . Lauren is so fucking mean and horrible, but everyone is too scared of her to do anything about it. . . . Even Sarah Foster is afraid of her. But not you."

Hannah pressed her lips together and tried not to smile. She didn't want to look smug, but she was pleased.

Caitlin leaned forward. "So . . . what did she say to make you *that* mad?"

Hannah was enjoying her friend's adulation, but she couldn't tell her what Lauren had said. There was no way she was going to articulate Lauren's sick obsession with her dad. "Just more mean shit about Ronni and stuff . . . I don't really remember."

Caitlin flopped back on the sofa. "I saw Ronni . . . Mrs. Pittwell asked me to take some homework to her. Somehow, I've become the homework delivery girl."

"How's she doing?"

"Not great . . . But she was pretty impressed that you beat up Lauren Ross."

"I didn't *beat her up*," Hannah said, smiling again. "Wait . . . why did you have to take homework to Ronni?"

"She hasn't been at school for a while . . . ever since what happened in the cafeteria."

"What happened?"

Caitlin's freckled face darkened. "Ronni went in to get some food and some kids started chanting 'Cyclops' at her."

"Jesus . . ."

"I know, such assholes. Her eye's not even that bad, once you get used to it."

That must have been the day Hannah had invited Ronni for lunch, the day Hannah had stood her up. . . . She felt sick.

But Caitlin wasn't finished. "Ronni's trying to stay off social media—there's so much mean shit about her on there—and she's been getting some horrible texts."

"Who from?"

"Unknown number . . . But we all know who's behind it."

Hannah nodded. They did: Adam, Noah, Lauren . . .

"Ronni just wants to leave Hillcrest, but her mom and the school are making her finish the year." Caitlin brightened a little. "She'll start over next year. At a better school."

"Unless my parents win this lawsuit," Hannah muttered, almost to herself.

"What?"

"My mom and dad don't want to pay Lisa so much money, because they didn't do anything wrong."

"I guess . . ."

Caitlin's ambiguous response made Hannah feel surprisingly defensive. "They told us no drinking or drugs. They told us no boys, but we invited them anyway. This could have happened at anyone's house . . . even at your house."

"Maybe, but . . ."

"But what?"

Caitlin opened her mouth to say something but stopped. "Nothing . . . I have to go." She stood. "I'm supposed to be doing my online math."

Hannah followed her friend to the door, where they hovered for a moment. "Thanks for the homework," Hannah said, her voice hoarse.

"No problem." Caitlin reached for the door handle, but Hannah's hand shot out, touched her wrist. She couldn't let Caitlin leave, not yet. There were things she needed to say . . . if only she could get the words past the emotion clogging her throat.

"I know I was a shitty friend to you guys. . . ."

"It's okay," Caitlin said, making another attempt to leave, but Hannah pressed her hand on the door.

"I thought I was too cool for you when I was dating Noah and hanging out with Lauren, but I was just so fucking stupid. . . ."

"Yeah . . ."

"I wish I could go back in time, be like we were. . . . I'd never even look at Noah. I'd never even talk to Lauren fucking Ross."

"But you can't."

"I know . . . but I hope, maybe, you guys can forgive me one day?" It sounded pleading, desperate, and pathetic. Caitlin should laugh in her face, tell her she got what she deserved. But Caitlin wasn't mean like that.

"I'll talk to Marta," she said. "We're not mad . . . not anymore. You've been through enough."

Hannah felt like bursting into tears, but that would be beyond lame. How could she have dropped such a kind, understanding friend for a bitch like Lauren?

"I don't know if we can ever go back to how we were before," Caitlin said, a little less kind and understanding. "And Marta's mom says she can't come over here anymore. She got into it with your mom or something . . . so that's kind of awkward."

"We don't have to be like we were," Hannah said. "I get that. But maybe we could eat lunch sometimes? Maybe with Ronni, when she comes back?"

Caitlin gave her a small smile that Hannah took as encouraging. "I'll see what Marta thinks." Hannah let her leave then. She stood on the porch and watched Caitlin's straight red hair swing as she walked down the front steps.

jeff

SIXTY-EIGHT DAYS AFTER

It was official: they were going to trial. Candace had been frank about their chances: sixty-forty in Jeff and Kim's favor. She had also been frank about the ugliness, the toxicity they would be forced to endure. Paul Wilcox might look like a hairless panda bear, but he could be brutal in court. Jeff didn't doubt it after the way that Teletubby had gone after him at the hearing for discovery. Candace also advised them that Paul had some ruthless investigators at his disposal. Still . . . Jeff felt a sense of calm as he cruised through mercifully light, late-morning traffic. There was no more dirty laundry to be aired: he'd told Candace about the bottle of sparkling wine he'd given the girls and she wasn't overly concerned; she'd confirmed that Jeff's LSD use was "fruit of the poisonous tree," since Paul had learned of it through inappropriate channels; and Kim's wine and sedative use was commonplace and didn't constitute neglect. A trial might be hard, it might get nasty, but it was the right thing to do. Kim, seated in the passenger seat, felt the same way. At least he thought that was what she was twittering on about.

"I actually feel relieved. . . . I mean, at least we'll get the chance to stand up for ourselves." Kim paused, clearly waiting for Jeff's affirmation. He made an *mm-hmm* sound that served the purpose. "When Lisa realizes we mean business, I wouldn't be surprised if she backs out. She'll see that eight fifty was an incredibly generous offer. Of course, she's not going to get that now."

He glanced over at his wife and saw her smile: smug, self-satisfied, almost triumphant. . . . Kim was confident they were going to win before they'd even started. Jeff was confident, too, but he was smart enough to know that no trial was a sure thing. Judges could be biased. Jury members could be swayed. Kim seemed positively jubilant, and it was way too soon.

"It's almost noon," Kim said, glancing at her Cartier watch. Her hand reached over and touched his forearm. "Want to grab some lunch? It feels like we should mark the occasion in some way . . . maybe oysters at the little place by the water?"

He was right. She was trying to turn their declaration of battle into a celebration. "I have to get back to work," he lied. "I've got a meeting. I'll drop you back at the house."

Kim didn't speak, but her body language said it all. She sank into the leather seat, getting smaller, shrinking into herself. He had hurt her and he felt bad . . . but not bad enough to drink wine, clink glasses, and eat oysters with her.

"Let's go out for dinner this weekend . . . take the kids for pasta," he said cheerily. "We haven't been to Flour and Water in forever."

Kim nodded and gave him a small smile. Hopefully, she was appeased.

He let his wife out in the driveway and, without going inside, drove the 101 straight to the office. There was no pressing meeting, but he and Graham had talked about going for a run during their lunch break. Kim always resented his training, that's why he'd made up the story about a meeting. His spouse viewed his exercise regimen as an excuse to be away from her, away from home, away from the kids. Kim didn't understand that he needed it more now than ever. There was nothing like a run to get the endorphins going, increase serotonin production, lower stress . . . maybe there was a drug that could do the same job, but obviously that wasn't an option.

Graham was loitering outside his office when he arrived. "Where have you been? I thought we were going for a run."

"We are. Let me get changed."

There was a six-mile route that ran from the office, along the edge of the Stanford campus and back. Six miles was nothing to Jeff, but Graham struggled with it. In fact, they'd just reached the edge of the stunning Spanish-inspired Greenleaf Lab when Graham requested a break.

"Sorry, mate. Too much beer last night."

"Too many hangovers at work can be career limiting."

"Says the guy who showed up at noon and then went for a run." Graham stretched his calf. "Where were you this morning, anyway?"

"Lawyer's office. We're going to trial."

Graham abruptly stopped stretching. "Are you fucking serious?"

"Kim and I thought a lot about it, and we've decided to stand up for ourselves. We feel good about it."

Graham wiped his sweaty face with the end of his shirt. "You can't do this."

"We can and we are. . . . Lisa's being punitive and vindictive. Our lawyer agrees."

Graham stared up at the sky for a moment, like he'd just noticed clouds for the first time. Then Jeff realized the man was shaking his head, almost chuckling with incredulity. "No fucking way," he muttered to the birds.

"Uh . . . yes way."

Graham looked at his colleague. "There's something you need to know, Jeff . . . about the LSD."

Fuck.

"My wife knows about it."

"You said she didn't."

"Because I thought you were fucking smart enough to keep this out of court!" Graham's face was red, not just from the exertion. He was angry. And scared. Oh shit . . .

The big man paced as he continued. "Jennie knew I was on something when I came home that day. So I told her we'd taken some LSD. I didn't think she'd freak out—she's not an uptight twat like Kim."

"Watch it, asshole."

Graham continued to move back and forth like a caged bear.

"But Jennie freaked out . . . Taking psychedelics in the middle of the day made her think I was some crazed drug friend."

"Right. Okay . . ." Jeff said over the hammering in his chest. "But obviously she's not going to volunteer this information."

"It gets worse." Graham stopped pacing. "Jennie needed to get away after she found out. She said she needed space to 'process it.' She went to a fucking *mindfulness* retreat . . . yoga, meditation, lots of juice . . . I don't fucking get it."

"And?"

"She made a new friend there . . . Lisa Monroe."

Jeff could hear the blood pounding in his ears and his chest tightened. Was this a heart attack? A panic attack? Maybe he wasn't in as good of shape as he thought? But Graham just kept talking, like Jeff wasn't about to collapse into a quivering pile of jelly right in front of him.

"Jennie told Lisa everything—Lisa's dealt with druggie boyfriends in the past, so she was Jennie's confidante, her sounding board. Lisa was all too happy to listen to every gory fucking detail."

"Jesus Christ, Graham. Why didn't you tell me this?"

"Because I thought you'd take care of it, asshole! I thought you'd make it right!"

"We are making it right. It was an accident! It could have happened anywhere!"

Graham resumed his pointless walking. "Jennie will be subpoenaed. . . . She'll have to testify that you and I took LSD together. She'll be humiliated."

"Let me talk to my lawyer," Jeff said, keeping his voice calm and steady. "Maybe we can prevent her from taking the stand."

"We'll both get fired. I've read the company drug policy. It's black-and-white."

Fuck . . . fuck, fuck, fuck . . . But Jeff didn't say this out loud.

Graham stopped walking and loomed over his friend. "If you go to trial, I'm fucked. I'll lose my job, my reputation. . . . I could lose my wife!"

"You won't. I'll deal with it."

Graham bore down on him. "You had your chance to deal with it, Jeff! You could have made this all go away! But you and Kim care more about your fucking bank account than a girl's eye!"

Blind rage took over, and Jeff was lunging at Graham before he had time to think. If he *had* thought, Jeff would have ascertained that Graham had at least thirty pounds on him, six inches of reach, and a decade of brawling his way through Aussie rules football games, leaving Jeff with virtually no chance of victory. But still, Jeff threw his slight body against the side of beef that had so incensed him.

Unfortunately for Jeff, the side of beef was angry, too. Jeff's shoulder had just made contact with Graham's ribs when the bigger man shoved him violently away, then hauled back and punched Jeff neatly in the face. There was a crack—knuckles connecting with the bridge of Jeff's nose—and the force threw him backward, but there was no pain (that would come later). Jeff must have been in shock, for even as the blood began to seep from his nose, dripping steadily on the pavement like a leaky udder, one thought kept running through his mind: *Kim's going to kill me.*

"How many more lives are you and Kim going to ruin, huh?"

Graham spat. "How many more innocent people have to pay for your fucking mistakes?"

"Fuck you," Jeff muttered, blood dripping into his mouth, making him cough and splutter. He could feel Graham's eyes on him, assessing his hunched over, bleeding form. The big Aussie was going to finish him off with a knee to the stomach, an elbow to the back, a boot to the face. Jeff braced for it; in fact, he'd almost welcome the distraction from his nose, which was beginning to pound with pain. But no blow came.

"You're pathetic," Graham grunted. Then a ball of spit and phlegm landed at Jeff's feet. As Graham walked away, Jeff watched the loogy mingle with the nose blood pooled on the sidewalk. The mixture of bodily fluids meandered its way, languidly, across the pavement.

lisa

SIXTY-NINE DAYS AFTER

The sun snaked its way through the heavy curtains, bringing with it evidence of the bustle of midmorning playing out beyond this masculine bedroom. It served to dampen the romantic mood Allan had worked hard to create—candlelight, soft music, satin sheets—not that Lisa was in an amorous mood today . . . or any other day when they convened at Allan's one-bedroom apartment to make love. This had become a ritual, an attempt to normalize their romantic relationship while Ronni was at school. Usually, Lisa was willing to put in a performance to appease her partner; it seemed a small price to pay for the support and comfort he'd provided her through this ordeal. But today, Ronni was at home, in bed, and Lisa found herself unable or unwilling to make the effort. As Allan's hands roamed her body, her mind stayed firmly on her child's dilemma.

"Ronni's refusing to go back to school," she said, shifting Allan's hand from her lower belly to the less erogenous zone of her hip. "But if she misses much more, she'll have to repeat the year."

"What about online courses?" Allan murmured, his hand drifting down her thigh.

"I don't want Ronni shut away in our apartment like some freak. High school's about more than courses. It's about learning to socialize and work with other people. She deserves the full experience."

"Of course she does," Allan said into her neck. Lisa subtly shifted away from him. She hoped he'd get the hint that she wasn't in the mood for sex right now. But the fact that she had dutifully crawled into bed naked with him may have been contradicting that message.

"I told her she has to go back Monday. She can't hide from those disgusting little fuckers any longer."

"Whoa, Lisa . . ." Allan looked at her like she'd just spewed a stream of racial slurs. "They're just kids."

"They're bullies," Lisa retorted, shifting farther away from him. His naked body rubbing against her was suddenly repulsive. "I told you what they did to Ronni in the cafeteria."

"That was horrible," Allan said, reaching for her arm. "But kids are stupid. They don't realize how cruel they're being."

Lisa had a sudden urge to punch him, but instead, she threw the sheet off her and got out of bed. She was shaking as she stepped into her underpants, her stomach twisting into knots of turmoil. It was as if Lisa had been in the cafeteria that day . . . but it was worse. She *hadn't* been there, hadn't been able to protect her daughter. She had one job. . . .

She could picture the scene vividly in her mind's eye. Ronni bravely entering the lunchroom alone. A friend had promised to meet her there (probably one of the religious girls who had recently taken a shine to her), so Ronni had scanned the room for a companion. The girl must have been running late, so Ronni had gone to the lunch counter and grabbed some food—veggies and hummus, the girl lived on the stuff—and found an inconspicuous table at the back. She had nibbled at a carrot stick, keeping one eye (the seeing eye, obviously) trained on the door.

Then it started. A spoon was banged on a table and a boy began to chant: "Cy-clops, Cy-clops, Cy-clops . . ." Ronni wouldn't say who it was, but Lisa would have guessed Noah Chambers or that Adam kid. They had been her daughter's friends, but, like Lauren Ross, had turned on her since the accident. Why? What defect in their personalities, what deficiency in their parenting had made them so heartless? So cruel? But it wasn't just them. . . . Another boy joined the chant, then a few girls, until there was a rousing chorus. "Cy-clops. Cy-clops. Cy-clops." It wasn't everyone in the lunchroom, but enough of them. Ronni had stood and fled. She hadn't been back to school since.

"Don't go," Allan pleaded as Lisa zipped up her jeans.

"I just . . . I can't right now, okay?"

"We don't have to have sex." He reached toward her. "You're upset. Let me hold you."

She looked at him lying there: naked, vulnerable, younger than her by five years, but by decades emotionally. He didn't get it. How could he? "Ronni will be up soon. I need to be there."

"Okay." Allan threw his legs out of the bed and stood. "I'll come with you."

"No, go surfing or something," Lisa said, struggling into her bra. "I've got a busy day. I'm meeting Paul this afternoon. He thinks we should have a jury trial—it's more complicated and more expensive, but with the emotional stakes in this case, he thinks it's the way to go."

Allan was putting on his robe. "Are you up for that?"

"The jury will have to look at Ronni every day in court, at what Jeff and Kim did to her. We can't lose."

"And you're willing to put Ronni through that?"

"It's a means to an end. Ronni understands that." Lisa pulled her shirt over her head, slipped her arms into the sleeves. "We both just want it all to be over. . . ." She almost smiled when she said, "I'm kind of looking forward to seeing Kim's face when all their personal shit comes out."

Allan clearly didn't share her anticipation. "What about our personal shit? I smoke pot pretty regularly. Could they use that against you?"

"It's just pot. And you're not really that big a part of my life." She saw him wince, so she backtracked. "I mean *Ronni's* life. You're important to me, but you don't live with us. You don't sleep over. . . . Besides, Jeff Sanders took LSD!"

"Trials can get ugly."

"Yeah, they can. But in the end, we'll win. And Ronni will get what she deserves."

Allan moved toward the bathroom. "I'll have a quick shower. I don't have to be at the restaurant until four, so I can come with you."

Lisa could hear him peeing. She called over the volume, "It's okay. I don't need you there."

The stream finished and Allan poked his head out the door. He still had his dick in his hands, she could tell. "Then I'll hang out with Ronni while you're out."

For some reason, this intimacy galled her. How had she let Allan get so close to her that he could talk about her daughter while he was "shaking the drips"? She had let her guard down and Allan had sneaked into her inner sanctum. Lisa had let herself be distracted by his kindness, his tight ass and muscular pecs. . . . It was supposed to be Lisa and Ronni against the world, and she had let herself be sidetracked by sex. She had to focus now. This trial would be the fight of her life.

"Really, it's fine," she called. "Go for a surf."

"It's okay!" He disappeared, and she heard the shower turn on. She knew what she had to do. She hurried into the bathroom.

He was about to step into the glass stall when she said, "I don't think I can do this right now."

Allan paused. "Do what?"

"This . . . Us . . . I don't think it's working."

He turned off the faucet and faced her, stark naked, completely comfortable. "What are you talking about?"

"You've been great, Allan. You're very sweet but . . . it's not a good time for me to be with someone."

"I *want* to be here. For you and for Ronni."

"I know you do. But . . ." She had to hurt him; it was the only way. "You're a distraction that I don't have time for."

Her words stung and she saw him flinch. Then his jaw tensed. "A distraction from your hate and your anger?"

"You're a distraction from my daughter . . . and what she needs."

"What she needs is love and support and understanding. Not lawsuits and rage and acrimony."

Fuck him and his sanctimony. "Thanks, Deepak Chopra." Lisa stormed out of the bathroom. She wasn't about to listen to Allan's two-cent psychoanalysis, more New Age bullshit about love and forgiveness. Lisa had cut Yeva and Co. out of her life because of it. She was going to have to do the same with Allan. It was time to leave. Where had she left her purse? Her keys?

Allan trailed behind her, following her through the cramped apartment like a puppy . . . a naked puppy. "Why are you so afraid to let anything good into your life?"

Lisa turned on him. "I'm not! I'm about to let three million bucks into my life."

He shook his head. "You don't even realize how horrible that sounds."

"Horrible? My daughter is blind! She's disfigured!"

"She's not blind, Lisa! She can still see! And she's not *disfigured*. Maybe she's not perfect, like she was, but she looks fine. I mean, it's not like she had acid thrown in her face or something."

"Oh my god . . ."

He tried to save himself, but it was too late. "I'm not minimizing what Ronni's been through. It's terrible. And traumatic. But I don't think this war with the Sanderses is helping things." He reached for her but she stepped away from his grasp. "You're so angry, babe. You're so focused on making them pay. You should be thinking of Ronni and helping her heal."

Lisa stared at this man, this naked stranger standing before her. How could she have thought he was her ally? How could she have leaned on him for support? He didn't understand what it was like for her and Ronni. She spotted her purse on the end of the sofa and snatched it up.

"Go to hell, Allan." She hurried to the door.

AS SHE DROVE back to her apartment, Lisa's anger slowed to a simmer. In fact, it seemed to be morphing into a compelling urge to burst into tears. She knew the adage "the truth hurts," but that wasn't the case here. Allan made it sound like Lisa was hell-bent on a vindictive mission to the detriment of her only child. Not true, not true at all. She simply wanted the Sanderses to take responsibility for what happened under their roof that night, and make sure that Ronni was compensated for her pain and suffering. When the trial was over, when the money was in the bank, then they would focus on healing. Together. Without the distraction of a sexy but sanctimonious chef who thought he was the second coming of Dr. Wayne Dyer.

Her favorite coffee shop appeared on her right and she spontaneously steered into the small parking lot. She didn't want to bring anger and negative emotions into the home, didn't want to infect Ronni with them. She needed to stall. She went inside and ordered two lattes and a "morning power muffin" for Ronni. It was heavy and leaden, chock-full of seeds and dates and flax. It would be good for her. By the time Lisa was back behind the wheel, she was beginning to feel almost level.

The apartment was quiet when she walked in; Ronni must be sleeping late . . . extremely late. Lisa would have checked her watch, but her hands were full of lattes and a quarter-pound muffin. As she set them on the small dining table, she noticed the half-empty mug of tea, still warm, on the table. Ronni was up after all. . . .

She called into the quiet. "Hi, hon! I brought you a muffin and a latte!"

No response.

Lisa walked down the hall and peeked in Ronni's bedroom. The bed was empty but for the open laptop perched on the tangle of covers. She had to be in the bathroom. Lisa went to the door and listened for the shower. Silence. She knocked. "Ronni?" Nothing.

Her heart was beginning to pound with unsubstantiated fear. Where was her daughter? She walked into her own room, marginally larger and tidier than her daughter's. Of course she wasn't there, why would she be?

"Ronni?" Lisa called, louder this time as she moved back to the kitchen. She scanned cluttered counters and the fridge magnets for a note but found none. A glance at the door confirmed the presence of Ronni's shoes. She was here; she had to be. Her heart hammering in her ears now, she ran back to the bathroom and tried the door. It was locked.

Panic took over. "Ronni! Ronni!" she screamed, rattling the door handle. "Answer me, goddammit!" She threw her slight body at the flimsy door. It gave a little under her weight, but she wouldn't be able to knock it off its hinges. She beat it, pounded it, kicked it, screaming until her throat hurt. "Ronni! Please! Answer me!"

A bobby pin. When she was a kid, she would pick the lock on her sister's door with a bobby pin. She sprinted into her daughter's room and combed through the clutter on her dresser: hair bands, nail polish, earrings, and there, next to a sticky bottle of some kind of hair product, were four bobby pins. She ran back and inserted one into the lock. She jiggled, felt the cheap locking mechanism release.

There was a moment before she opened the door, when she pleaded with God, the universe, the higher power, whatever . . . *Don't let this be.* But she already knew. As she opened the door and felt it stop, a weight blocking its path, she knew. She slipped through the gap in the door and saw her. Ronni lay crumpled on the linoleum, in her pink robe, inert, pale, so pale. . . . Lisa dropped to her knees and grabbed for her baby, pulling the limp form into her arms, pressing it to her chest. There was blood on Ronni's mouth and her chin, splattered onto the fleece of her robe. "What did you do?" Lisa screamed at her lifeless form. "What did you do?" Then a bubble of blood appeared on her daughter's lips, then another. Breath. Ronni was alive. She set her daughter down and ran to the phone.

kim

SEVENTY DAYS AFTER

When Candace Sugarman arrived at Kim's door on a Saturday morning, Kim knew it must be serious. Now that Jeff's LSD use was admissible, their odds of winning had obviously changed. Kim had made Jeff call Candace immediately, made him admit that his so-called *friend* had ratted him out to his yoga-loving wife who, in turn, had snitched to Lisa Monroe. And that wasn't to mention the current state of her husband's face. What judge or jury was going to side with a man with two black eyes and a swollen nose? Candace must be here to tell them they were going to lose the case now. They should pay up before their dirty laundry was aired in open court.

"Would you like coffee?" Kim asked, leading the attorney into the quiet kitchen area. Hannah was studying in her room (Kim had just been about to sneak upstairs to ensure she wasn't watching Netflix on the laptop she deemed necessary to view Khan

Academy); Aidan was at soccer practice; and Jeff was on a forty-kilometer bike ride in preparation for the August triathlon (despite everything going on in their lives, her husband remained dedicated to his training regimen).

"I'm fine," Candace said, climbing onto a breakfast barstool. For the first time, Kim noticed the lawyer's wan countenance and shaky demeanor. Candace was one of those plain, almost masculine women who exuded competence, confidence, and composure . . . but not right now. Right now, she looked like she might cry.

"What's wrong?" Kim asked, her voice tight.

Candace's unadorned eyes were liquid. "Maybe you should sit down, Kim."

Blood pounded in Kim's ears. "Just tell me."

"Ronni Monroe attempted suicide yesterday."

Kim sagged against the counter. "Jesus Christ . . ."

"She . . . drank drain cleaner," Candace said, her voice hoarse.

"No."

"Her mother found her in the bathroom. They rushed her to the hospital. She's alive but it's touch and go. Her esophagus is badly burned."

Spots were swimming in front of Kim's eyes. Her forehead was sweaty and her knees wobbled. She was going to faint. Candace, competent as always, was right: Kim should have sat down. The lawyer sensed Kim's imminent collapse and moved toward her. "Come sit . . ." Candace helped Kim to the barstool she'd just vacated.

But even seated, Kim couldn't think, couldn't form words,

couldn't accept this. It was like some sick, dark horror movie, a nightmare. . . . Kim didn't live in a world where a teenager lost her eye and then was bullied so mercilessly that she drank poison. This was not the life she had meticulously built for herself and her family. This was some kind of cruel, fucked-up alternate universe. She became aware of Candace's hand patting hers, trying, in her mechanical way, to provide comfort to her client. Kim appreciated it, no matter how ineffective.

Finally, Kim found her voice. "What does this mean?" The words came out without any forethought, spilling from her mouth like a reflex, a phonic tic. She wasn't even sure what she was asking, but this vague, ambiguous question seemed the only logical utterance.

Not surprisingly, Candace responded in legal terms. "It changes things, Kim, I'm not going to lie to you. It will demonstrate the defense's case of extreme emotional distress. A jury's going to want you to compensate for Ronni's pain and suffering."

Kim nodded. For the first time, she realized she was crying, tears pouring silently down her cheeks.

"On the other hand," Candace continued, "Lisa may be more likely to settle now. I can't imagine she'll want to subject Ronni to any more trauma . . . Or herself, if Ronni doesn't . . . *pull through*."

The voice, little more than a tremulous whisper, came from the hallway. "What?"

"Hannah . . ." Kim managed to stand, though her legs were still weak. "Come here, sweetheart."

Kim held her arms out to her daughter, but the girl didn't budge. "What's going on?" Hannah was directing the question to

Candace, but the attorney looked, with panicked eyes, to Kim. Candace didn't have children and they seemed to frighten her.

"Ronni's . . . in the hospital," Kim said. "Come sit, Hannah."

"What happened to Ronni?"

Kim's every instinct was to protect her daughter, to shield her from this ugliness, but she knew she couldn't. "Ronni attempted suicide."

The sound that burst from her daughter's chest was primal, almost animal. Hannah dropped into a crouch and sobbed, her forehead resting on her knees. Kim rushed to her, bent down, and wrapped her in a hug, but the girl shrugged her off. Kim didn't force it. She accepted that her daughter needed space. Hannah cried for a few more moments before raising her head. "How?"

"It doesn't matter how."

"It does to me."

Kim swallowed, but her voice still sounded clogged when she whispered, "She drank drain cleaner."

"Oh my god!" Hannah wept into her hands.

"She's getting the best care possible," Kim said, tentatively reaching out to stroke Hannah's soft hair. The girl let her, which Kim took as a positive sign. "Ronni is young and strong. She has a good chance of pulling through."

Hannah yanked her silky head away from her mother's touch. "A good chance? You mean she might die?"

Kim looked to Candace; the woman had brought the news of Hannah's crisis, after all. But the lawyer shot back a terrified look, like she'd rather be bathing with electric eels than standing there, in Kim's kitchen, dealing with this. Kim couldn't blame her. How did one tell a sixteen-year-old that her friend could die? But Kim had to. . . . "She might."

Hannah stood to her full height, a few inches taller than her mother. Her features were harsh and twisted when she said, "And yet, you two were in here talking about the trial." She was still crying, but her voice was angry.

"No . . . I just said—"

"I heard what you said," Hannah spat. "You drove Ronni to drink fucking drain cleaner, and all you care about is whether you still have a chance to win your fucking case!"

"Don't talk like that." It was Kim's automatic response to the f-bomb, though the curses were the least concerning of the content. "You can't blame this on us."

"Yes, I can." The girl looked at Candace then. "How can you live with yourselves?"

Candace looked terrified, like she was facing down a grizzly bear, not a blubbering teenaged girl. "I should go," she mumbled, reaching for her utilitarian purse that sat on a barstool.

"No, I'll go," Hannah snapped. "You stay. You two can plot how you're going to finish Ronni and Lisa off for good."

"Hannah!" Kim cried, but the girl was already running to the door. Kim took off after her at a sprint, the lawyer following in her wake. "Don't go! Honey! We need to talk this through."

Hannah was stepping into her UGG boots. "I have nothing to say to you."

"You shouldn't be alone right now," Kim tried. "You've had a shock. You need love and support."

Hannah's boots were on, her hand on the door handle. She

turned to her mother and almost growled through her tears. "Leave . . . me . . . the fuck alone." She yanked open the door and ran out.

Kim followed her onto the porch in her stocking feet, "Hannah!" she called after her daughter's fleeing form. "Come back!" For once, Kim didn't care if she attracted the neighbors' attention, if they wondered what the hell was going on over there, or what kind of parent she was. She just wanted her daughter to come home.

"Let her go," Candace said, behind her. "Hannah needs to process all this." Kim whirled around to face her. This spinster was suddenly a parenting expert now? But the lawyer was composed in the face of adult anger. She calmly continued, "Hannah knows what Ronni's been going through at school and online. . . . Give her some time. She'll realize this isn't your fault."

It actually made sense.

"I have to get back to the office." Candace moved past her to the front steps. When you've had a chance to talk to Jeff, call me. We'll talk about how to proceed."

Kim nodded. "He won't be home for a couple of hours. . . ." Her voice cracked. She suddenly realized how utterly alone she was. A sob filled her chest. Oh God. She was going to come apart. Candace, sensing Kim's impending collapse, gave her a consoling pat on the shoulder and hurried away.

But Kim didn't come apart, not completely. She allowed herself a loud, ugly crying jag that echoed through the empty house, her wails bouncing off the smooth concrete floors and skittering over the gleaming countertops. She pounded silk throw pillows, let snot and tears drip onto Italian-woven upholstery and smear the imported alpaca blanket. And then she got up, washed her face, reapplied her makeup, and headed to her car.

If anyone asked where she was going, she would say she was looking for Hannah. Not that she would find her daughter by driving the streets of San Francisco. The girl would be holed up somewhere, with or without friends, cursing her greedy, money-grubbing parents. But who would ask where Kim was going, anyway? Not Jeff. He was still racing down some windy stretch of highway on his bike, high on an endorphin rush. By now, he might be lounging in the hot tub at the Bay Club, his aching muscles an excuse to stay away from home a little longer. Aidan would be finishing soccer soon, but then he was going to play video games at Marcus's house. Kim had friends, women who might text to check in, expressing concern but keeping her at arm's length. No . . . no one cared where Kim was going.

Half an hour later, she pulled up across the street from the vintage home and turned off her car. It was a conspicuous spot, but Kim didn't care. It was the perfect vantage point to watch people coming and going from the reclaimed triplex. And she couldn't risk missing him coming. Or going. Kim felt an almost primeval urge to see Tony—though she didn't exactly know why.

Her feelings toward him were mixed, of course. He had stolen the Apex account out from under her, taking with it her income and identity. When she rejected him, he had called her a fucking tease, mocked her, and pitied her. But she couldn't forget the comfort he'd offered in the aftermath of the party, when he'd bought her coffee, listened without judgment, and then sucked her face off in his car, which was an excellent distraction. Maybe that was what she really missed? His desire for her, his lust . . . Was she there for some *hate sex*? She had heard the term before but never understood it, until now.

She had plenty of time to contemplate her presence as she sat in the car for half an hour, then forty-five minutes, and then an hour and ten minutes. . . . That's when Tony appeared, hiking up the street toward his home, carrying two canvas grocery bags. He was alone, thank God, and Kim felt her heart flutter to life in her chest. She watched him . . . the familiar thin frame, the loose gait, the narrow shoulders hunched against the weight of his cargo. Observation reaffirmed that Tony was not her physical type, but there was something languid, serpentine, and sexy about the way he moved. Had she noticed it before? Or forgotten? Tony was getting closer to his building now, almost to the edge of the lot, and soon, he would disappear inside. Kim had moments to decide: Why had she come here? What did she want from him? But she was reaching for the door handle before her mind had formulated an answer.

"Tony!" she called, standing behind her open car door. But he didn't stop walking, didn't turn toward her. Then Kim noticed the white wire traveling from his ears to his pocket: he was plugged in. She slammed the car door and jogged toward him.

"Tony!" She was a few feet behind him now. "Tony!"

He heard, or sensed, Kim's proximity and he whirled around. When he saw her, the look on his face was one of dread—no, it was worse than dread—it was *fear*. Kim felt her pitter-pattering heart sink like a stone in a bucket. Tony was afraid of her. He thought she was crazy . . . a stalker . . . a psychopath. She should never have come.

Tony ripped the buds from his ears. "Kim . . . what the hell are you doing here?" His voice was both angry and scared, like he was annoyed that Kim had showed up to murder him in front of his neighbors.

"I'm not here to cause any trouble," she said, which sounded just like something a stalker would say before she stabbed the object of her obsession to death, "but I had to see you."

Tony glanced toward his front door: Assessing a run for it? Worried his wife, kids, or nanny might emerge? Both were plausible . . . He looked back to Kim. "Is this about Apex? Because that was all on the up and up."

"It's not about Apex."

"I didn't exactly appreciate you telling them I had a child-porn addiction."

"I'm sorry. . . . That was wrong."

"Yeah, it was. . . . What do you want, Kim?"

Her presence on Tony's doorstep suddenly seemed completely ludicrous. "I . . . came to apologize," she said finally. "I recently learned that you didn't tell your wife about Jeff's LSD use."

"Of course I didn't," he snapped. "I told you that."

"I'm sorry that I didn't believe you then . . . but I know the truth now."

He shifted his grocery bags on his shoulders. "Fine. Apology accepted." He was desperate to leave; she could see his body yearning to escape, his eyes darting, longingly, at his front door. But she couldn't walk away from him, not yet.

"There's something else. . . . It's about Ronni."

"Who?"

Kim couldn't speak, as the depth of her stupidity threatened to overwhelm her. Tony didn't care about her or what she was going through. He barely remembered the party, the accident, or the lawsuit. She had created a fantasy world where Tony was her solace, her comfort, her sounding board. . . . She was such a fool. "Nothing." Her voice was hoarse as she turned to go. "Forget it."

She was walking away but Tony's voice followed her. "Amanda and I are working on our relationship. I'd appreciate it if you didn't come here again."

Kim didn't stop. "Don't worry, I won't." She was sincere, but for some reason, her voice came out snarky and angry. Without a look back, she got into her car and turned on the ignition. She had one more stop before she could go home.

jeff

SEVENTY DAYS AFTER

As soon as he entered the house, Jeff knew something was wrong. . . . Or *wronger* . . . Or *more wrong* . . . There had been a tangible feeling of unease in the house for months—since Ronni's accident, since Lisa's lawsuit, since Kim's flirtation with adultery, since Jeff's flirtation with acid . . . but something heavy and dark was permeating the air, dragging him down from his post-bike-ride high, decimating his post-hot-tub Zen. . . . What now?

Kim and Aidan were huddled together on the sofa, the boy's head resting on his mother's shoulder. Aidan was thirteen, a highly undemonstrative age, and yet there he was, curled up next to his mom like a baby lamb. It was alarming.

"What's going on?"

Kim didn't answer right away. She kissed her son's shaggy head. "Go upstairs, hon. Dad and I need to talk." The boy obeyed, walking by his father without a glance, his eyes downcast and morose.

His son's demeanor sent Jeff's heart hammering in his chest. "What the hell happened? Where's Hannah?"

"She's upstairs. She's okay." Kim patted the sofa beside her. "Come, sit."

Jeff hurried to the couch. "Are my parents okay? Is it my sister?"

"They're fine. It's Ronni Monroe."

Of course it was. He should have known.

"She tried to kill herself."

"Jesus Christ!" Jeff's body convulsed with the shock. "What happened? Is she going to be okay?"

"She drank drain cleaner," Kim stated. "It's touch and go."

"God, no . . ." Jeff dropped his head into his hands. He realized he was going to cry . . . it had been awhile, but there was no stopping the tears now. He tried to hide it—male instinct—but his shoulders shook as the repressed sobs racked his body. Kim's hand landed on his back and rested there, gentle and calm, so weirdly calm.

"I'm sorry," he spluttered, trying to compose himself, but he couldn't, not yet. It was so horrible and disturbing and such a fucking mess. How did they get here? Where did they go so wrong? He turned toward his wife, sitting stoically, patiently beside him. For the first time in a long time, he wanted Kim to take him in her arms, wrap him up in her love, and hold him till the crying stopped.

Instead, Kim reached over and plucked a tissue from the box on the coffee table. She handed it to Jeff, who took it obediently and blew his nose.

"You okay?" Kim said, her voice still oddly placid.

Jeff nodded and shrugged at the same time: sort of.

"I saw a Realtor today, Jeff. I want to sell the house."

"No, you don't. You love this house."

"The Realtor said we'll easily get two point six million in this market. If we sell the boat and some stocks, we can give Lisa three million."

"That's a bit extreme, Kim."

"Drinking Drano is extreme." She motioned around her at the expansive space. "This is just a building."

"A building that we live in and love. A building that we poured our hearts into redoing."

"I don't love it here anymore."

Jeff blew his nose again. Kim was right: it had been ages since he'd appreciated the house they had slaved over for almost two years, bickering, resenting each other, but working on a common goal, side by side. He remembered how excited they'd been when it was finished, how proud they were to inhabit such a lavish home. . . . They used to throw dinner parties, invite friends from out of town, host family celebrations. . . . But now, they just lived there.

"Where would we go?" he said resignedly. Selling the house still felt rash, but he didn't have the energy to fight Kim, Lisa, Graham . . . basically everyone in his life.

"I don't want to disrupt the kids by moving away from the school. We won't be able to get back into the housing market in the city," Kim said, "but we could buy a condo."

Jeff shook his head. "We have a house full of stuff. It won't fit into a condo."

"It will fit into two condos."

It took a beat to sink in. Jeff looked at his wife, her eerily calm demeanor, her quiet resolve, and he knew. It was over. He felt anger swell up inside of him. "Are you serious? Hannah's best friend just tried to kill herself and you're asking me for a divorce?"

"Not right now," Kim said. "I don't want to upset the kids even more. But going forward, I think it's the right thing to do."

"Jesus Christ . . ." He felt like he was going to cry again. They had been miserable for so long, Jeff had considered leaving a thousand times, but his wife's words were so resolute and so final. . . . It made his heart ache.

Kim reached for his hand. "I want to love you, Jeff. And I want you to love me . . . but we just don't anymore."

"I do," he croaked through the lump in his throat. And it was true . . . in this moment, anyway. Despite years of antipathy at worst, apathy at best, he suddenly realized there were feelings there, buried under all the anger and bitterness.

"We care for each other, but we don't love each other, not like we should. I'm tired of pretending. I'm tired of worrying about what everyone else thinks. I just want to give Lisa her money so she can take care of Ronni. . . . I just want to stop fighting."

He nodded, relating to the feeling. But ending a marriage should not be done on a whim. His wife was being reactive, she hadn't thought this through. "This will change your lifestyle, Kim. A lot." It wasn't intended as a threat, but it sounded like one. Still . . . Kim had to be warned. If they sold up and gave all their profits to Lisa, their lives would have to change drastically. He couldn't afford two mortgages on his salary, not without Kim contributing. "You'll end up in a tiny apartment. No more Pilates, salon visits, shopping, lunches . . ."

For the first time, Kim's composure faltered. "I don't care," she snapped, getting up off the couch. "All I care about is giving Lisa her money." She stalked off, disappearing somewhere into the bowels of their house.

Jeff stayed where he was, collecting his thoughts. His wife was in shock; she wasn't being logical. When Ronni got better . . . or, God forbid didn't get better, they would have a rational conversation about their future. Sure, Jeff and Kim were unhappy, but plenty of married people were unhappy. That didn't mean they had to destroy the life they'd built together. And Kim couldn't just walk away from him. She had nowhere to go! She didn't even have a job! This wasn't the end of their marriage, it was just . . . a turning point.

He got up, went to the fridge and grabbed a beer. Even Kim couldn't begrudge him a drink on a day like today. As the bitter liquid poured down his throat, he resolved to fight for his marriage. . . . But why? Was it automatic? Expected? He didn't know. He drained the bottle and reached into the fridge for another. Returning to the couch, he sat alone in the dimly lit living room, sipping his beer. As the alcohol fogged his thoughts, his analysis of his marriage, his life, became even more convoluted. Jeff didn't know what he was fighting for—and he didn't know why. . . . He just knew he wasn't ready to let it all go.

hannah

SIX MONTHS AND FOUR DAYS AFTER

Hannah sat in English class and stared out the window. It was the third week of junior year, but it still felt new . . . strange, and different, like she'd changed schools but she hadn't. Her teacher, Ms. Chan, was assigning homework, and Hannah knew she should pay attention, but her focus remained on the damp parking lot outside the window . . . and on Lauren Ross's car.

It was a MINI Cooper, not the luxury model Hannah would have expected Mr. Ross to buy for his daughter. But maybe the smaller, cheaper car was punishment for Lauren driving Ronni to drink drain cleaner? Hannah wasn't making light of the incident, but the way all the parents had reacted was pretty comical. Hannah's parents had decided to blow up her life; Lauren got new wheels.

Lauren didn't go to Hillcrest anymore, her parents determining that the school was to blame for their daughter becoming the anti-Christ. They transferred her to an all-girls religious school where they wore demure uniforms and prayed every morning. Darren and Monique Ross must have hoped Lauren would find new, pious friends with charitable life goals, like building an orphanage in India, or teaching refugees to speak English. But if Lauren had friends at her new school, she didn't spend much time with them. Almost every day, Lauren returned to the Hillcrest parking lot, sat in her compact car, and waited.

Hannah tore her eyes from the soft grayness outside back to the harsh fluorescence of the classroom. Ms. Chan was writing their *Hamlet* assignment on the whiteboard, her marker tapping along the shiny surface like a manic woodpecker. Hannah dutifully copied the words into her notebook, but her mind remained fixed on the occupant of the car outside.

The change in social order since last year was absolute. Lauren and Ronni were gone, Sarah Foster was on top. The stylish Sarah had long been poised for a takeover: she was pretty enough, cool enough, and ruthless enough. The only question that remained was which of her sycophantic friends would become her number two. Sarah was the new Lauren, no question; the jury was still out on the new Ronni.

Hannah's gaze drifted from her paper to Noah Chambers, sitting across the room, third desk from the front. Last year, Hannah would have been thrilled to have a class with Noah. She would have struggled to maintain a decent grade, distracted by his proximity, his woodsy scent, his square jaw, and broad shoulders. . . . Last year, he had been her boyfriend . . . for a few months at least. It seemed like a daydream, a blip, like it never really happened.

Was it normal to have such intense feelings for someone one day and feel basically nothing for them the next? She should ask her parents.

In a way, Noah's transformation was the most remarkable. Last year, he'd been cool and cocky, roaming the school with his popular, arrogant posse. This year, he was sullen and withdrawn, traversing the halls with a scowl, keeping to himself, except for Manny Torres, a bookish kid Noah knew from elementary school. Apparently, Noah's parents had come down hard on him after the Ronni incident. (Despite their former relationship, Hannah knew nothing of Noah's family life. They'd never really gotten beyond talking about music and parties and their mutual love of ramen.) But Noah's parents had determined he'd been running with a bad crowd and they were concerned about his character. No one knew how they enforced it, but their son had turned himself into a studious loner at his parents' request.

As if on cue, Noah's former best friend appeared outside the window, walking, with forced casualness, toward the MINI. Adam must have skipped last period, or just walked out of class early. The kid was untouchable. He was the reason for Lauren's presence in the school parking lot practically every day. They'd been dating since the summer, brought together by Ronni's trauma and its subsequent fallout. Had Lauren liked Adam all along? Was that why she had turned on Ronni? No one would ever know . . . except Lauren.

Hannah's lips curled with distaste as she watched the boy cross the parking lot. He emanated cruelty, arrogance, misogyny . . . he was a perfect fit for that bitch Lauren. If Adam had followed his girlfriend to some religious school, Hannah's junior year might have been tolerable. But Adam had stayed at Hillcrest. He was always there to sneer when Hannah walked past, to whisper cruel comments to his friends, to remind her of the ugliness of last year. . . .

Everyone knew that Adam had started the cyberbullying campaign against Ronni. There were various rumors as to why he was never punished, the most plausible being that he'd convinced an eager-to-please Chinese exchange student to set up the social media pages and administer most of the assaults. The student had left the country and with him went the evidence. Adam got off scot-free. Of course, some elite cybercrime unit could have pulled proof off of a server somewhere, but apparently, elite cybercrime units had bigger fish to fry. And it wasn't like the student body was going to point fingers at Adam; they'd all seen what he was capable of.

Adam was climbing into the passenger seat now, closing the door behind him. Through the windshield, Hannah could just see him leaning toward Lauren Ross. The girl's hands wrapped around his neck and they kissed. And kissed. Adam's eyes must have miraculously grown farther apart, because Lauren seemed really into him. The car windows were starting to fog up and Hannah turned away, mildly sickened. The two were a match made in hell.

The bell rang to end class, to end the week, and to end her stay with her dad. Every Friday, Hannah and her brother changed homes, shuttling between her dad's spacious but virtually empty condo in Presidio Heights and her mom's modest two-bedroom and den apartment in the Upper Haight. Hannah gathered her books and shuffled toward her locker. She felt tired, exhausted at the thought of relocating her life, yet again. Her mom said they'd get used to it, but they'd already had a couple months' practice and the process still left Hannah feeling drained. She'd probably be off at college before she got comfortable with the arrangement.

At her locker, she collected her homework for the weekend. After her brief flirtation with popularity, Hannah was focused on school again. It wasn't like she had a choice. Her social life had slowed to a trickle, and this was an important year if she wanted to get into a good college, which she did. Her backpack was nearly bursting with textbooks as she closed her locker door. Thankfully, her dad had offered to drop her and Aidan's personal items off at her mom's apartment that evening, as usual. He always texted them from his car and asked them to meet him out front. But last week, he'd helped Aidan carry his science project to Kim's apartment. Her mom was surprised by Jeff's presence, but her parents had been civil and polite. Hannah had left them to unpack her suitcase in her tiny room when she heard them chuckling about something. Hannah realized she hadn't heard her parents laugh together since she was in eighth grade. What the hell was so funny now?

As she clicked her lock in place, her friends strolled up to her. "Are we going to work on our psychology project?" Marta asked.

"Sure," Hannah said. "I'm going to my mom's, so you can come over if you want. She'll be at work till late."

"Your mom's like Sheryl Sandberg now," Caitlin joked. "She's, like, *leaning in* all over the place."

"Yeah, except she's writing websites, not running Facebook."

"Too bad."

"I'll say it's too bad," Hannah said, hoisting her heavy load onto her back. "Then I'd have a driver instead of having to run to catch the stupid bus."

"The loser cruiser," Marta quipped, and Hannah rolled her eyes.

"I'll bring snacks," Caitlin said. "When should we come over?"

"Whenever," Hannah said, her lack of enthusiasm evident. Her friends would assume her indifference was due to their homework project, but it was the thought of munching Doritos, discussing hot celebrities, and gossiping about which teacher was sleeping with which, that Hannah was really dreading. She should have been grateful that Marta and Caitlin had taken her back after everything that had happened. She *was* grateful. When things had gone off the rails with Hannah's popular crew, she'd wanted nothing more than the familiar comfort of her old clique. But now, months later, the reality of their friendship was just so . . . mundane. Caitlin and Marta were nice; they were kind; they were good people. . . . Maybe that was the problem?

She had to muster some exuberance. "How's four thirty?" Hannah asked. "I'll heat up some delicious frozen taquitos."

"Yum!" Caitlin said sincerely, as Hannah walked off.

THE BUS RIDE from school to her mom's wasn't long, but it was still pretty gross. Before they'd moved, Hannah was able to walk to and from school. Now, she had to rely on transit to get to both her parents' homes. She stared out the window, taking in the gritty urbanity of the Haight, so different from the sunny sleepiness of Potrero Hill. She kind of liked the new neighborhood; it had edge, it had personality . . . it suited her: not the Hannah she *was* but the Hannah she'd become. Sure, she missed their old house, but a new family lived there now: a husband, a wife, and two cute, blond daughters. Were they as perfect as they looked from the outside? Or were they, like Hannah's family before them, just putting on a show?

The bus stopped a block and a half from her mom's apartment. It wasn't far, but it was all uphill. With her burden of books, she trudged toward home. Ahead, she saw a man crouching near a shopping cart loaded with the leftovers of a life. He was fortyish, dirty, his hair matted, but he was smiling as she approached.

"Hey, Hannah."

"Hey, Pete."

"Wanna buy some crack?"

"I'm good, thanks."

As she continued past him, he said, "Study hard, girl! Stay in school!"

"I will. . . ." A few months ago, Hannah could not have imagined being on a first-name basis with a homeless drug dealer. Her parents had always kept her sheltered from the rough side of her city. But things were different now. This was her new reality: two apartments, transit, friendly relations with drug addicts. . . . The fallout from the party had fucked up her life royally. But still, Hannah's life wasn't the most changed.

Ronni had recovered . . . well, she had *lived*; recovery was up for debate. Some people said she'd lost her voice completely. Others said she could talk but her larynx was so severely damaged that she croaked and wheezed like an old lady who'd smoked for forty years. Some said she had PTSD and had to be homeschooled, but no one knew for sure. As soon as Ronni had been sent home from the hospital, Lisa had whisked her away to New York State. Lisa had a sister there. And with three million dollars in the bank, the Monroes could set up a nice little home.

Hannah had searched for Ronni on social media. Not surprisingly, she hadn't found her. If it were Hannah who had been driven to attempt suicide because of cyberbullying, Kim would have moved her into some Amish community with no technology. At the very least, Kim would have made sure she stayed off Facebook, Snapchat, Instagram. . . . Lisa would be just as vigilant with Ronni.

The Haight was full of colorful, intricate Victorian and Edwardian houses, but Kim's building was squat, nondescript, constructed sometime in the eighties. Hannah let herself into the musty lobby and climbed the carpeted stairs, her mind still fixed on her former friend. If Hannah was in Ronni's shoes, she'd change her name and live as an entirely new person. . . . Mia Harper from Seattle. Mia's voice was raspy because she'd been a singer in a screamer band and she'd lost her eye when their tour bus crashed. Everyone would buy the story—why would they not?—and Ronni would be accepted, even admired at her new high school.

Of course, it was entirely possible that Lisa and Ronni had become millionaire recluses, hiding out in an isolated mansion, emerging only once a month to pick up supplies. Maybe they could be happy that way, the two of them against the world. Like that documentary she'd watched with her mom about that weird mother and daughter: Big and Little Edie. They were batshit crazy, but they were basically fine.

Hannah wanted Ronni to be okay, in fact, she *needed* her to be okay. Because she still cared about Ronni, still felt bad about what had happened to her at the party. . . . But it was more than that. If Ronni wasn't okay, it meant Lauren Ross had won. It meant that Lauren had destroyed her best friend, had driven her to attempt suicide, had stolen her guy. . . . It meant Lauren was still on top, and the thought made Hannah's chest fill with rage and loathing.

She reached door 202 and let herself into the quiet apartment. Aidan wasn't home yet—he remained devoted to his soccer career despite the disruption to his domestic life—and her mom was still at work. It was sort of ironic how her mom had resented her dad's long hours at the office, and now Kim worked just as hard. Her mom's new job title was user-experience architect. When Aidan heard it, he'd remarked, "You haven't worked in years. You can't just start designing buildings." Hannah had laughed at him (she didn't know what a user-experience architect was, either, but she *did* know it had nothing to do with construction). Their mom had explained her responsibilities: writing and designing websites and applications with the end user in mind. Something like that anyway. It sounded super boring to Hannah, but her mom seemed to love it. Kim was tired (every time they sat down to watch TV or a movie, she promptly fell asleep), and she wasn't quite as polished as she used to be (Hannah had seen her covering her gray roots with mascara on more than one occasion), but her mom seemed happy. She seemed *fulfilled*. It wasn't fair. . . .

Hannah dropped her bag off in her room and walked through the cluttered living room to the kitchen. The furniture in the apartment was cobbled together: modern pieces from their old house mixed with thrift-shop finds. Somehow, it worked. It was *eclectic*. Kim still had a knack for decor. In contrast, her dad's apartment was sparse, almost barren. He had lots of space and a great view of the Presidio, but the apartment lacked personality. Jeff compensated for this with a huge flat-screen TV and a great sound system. Both abodes were adequate and comfortable; her parents were trying . . . but they didn't feel like home, not yet. Hannah was sure they never would.

Hannah looked in the fridge: packaged gyoza, packaged tortellini, a jar of spaghetti sauce, and a lemon. It was a far cry from the homemade, healthy snacks her mom used to prepare for her kids every day. Hannah grabbed the open box of taquitos from the freezer. Had her mom even read the ingredients? Calculated the nutritional content? The sodium level was off the charts! But Hannah put them on a pan and stuck them in the oven. Salt was pretty low on her list of things to worry about.

When her parents had announced their "separation," Hannah had been angry. After all the shit she'd been through, she couldn't believe her mom and dad were selling the house, splitting up, and making her and Aidan ferry between them like some misaddressed parcel. Hannah had blamed Ronni then. If not for her friend's selfish act, Hannah would be living in her beautiful house, in her spacious room, with both her parents. But the Sanderses wanted to give Lisa her money, and selling the house was the only way. Hannah had hated them all then—Lisa and Ronni, Kim and Jeff. . . . But it was a waste of energy. Hannah needed to save all her hate for Lauren. And she needed to focus on rebuilding her life.

The plan had come to her almost a month ago but she was still gathering the courage to implement it. Hannah knew it was wrong—she still had a conscience, still had a moral compass—but her parents had done the right thing and look what it had cost them? Fucking everything. If they'd been trying to teach her a lesson, it had worked: nice guys definitely finished last. And she had two whole years left at Hillcrest. She could wade through them in a state of fugue, wallowing in ennui and mediocrity. Or, she could try to salvage some of what she had had . . . what she had *almost* had. She took a fortifying breath, picked up her phone, and tapped the messenger icon. She typed:

Lauren was at Hillcrest again today

She hit send and waited. The tiny icon indicated that the message had been received and read, but there was no response. Hannah's heart was pounding in her throat. This strategy could backfire, it could solidify her outsider status, turn her into an object of laughter and derision. But she couldn't give up, not yet. Because as badly as things had turned out, Hannah couldn't forget the feeling of being popular: the admiration, the respect, the sense of power. . . . It was so much better than being invisible. She sent another message.

I can't believe she dares to show her face there after what she did

After a few seconds, it came. . . .

???

A feeling of relief flooded through Hannah. She had hooked her. Sarah Foster was dangling on her line, and she would not let the popular girl get away. Hannah knew exactly how to reel her in, because the two had much in common: they had both been in, they had both been out . . . and they both despised Lauren fucking Ross. Hannah tapped the tiny keyboard.

I haven't told anyone this but . . .

At my party, Lauren pushed Ronni into that glass table

No one saw it but I did

Hannah waited until she knew that Sarah had read the messages and then she typed again. It was just one more line, four little words, but Hannah knew Sarah Foster would not be able to resist.

We could destroy her

Nothing. Maybe Sarah thought Hannah was lying. Maybe she thought it was just some desperate attempt to get back on the A-list. Maybe she considered Hannah grasping, needy, and pathetic. And then it came . . .

Wanna get a smoothie? Bruno's in 20?

She had done it. Hannah had opened the door a crack and now she could slip inside. She would worm her way into Sarah Foster's inner circle, become her second-in-command, the Ronni to her Lauren, and together, they would crush that bitch.

C u there

A small but triumphant smile on her lips, Hannah flicked off the oven and walked out of the apartment.

acknowledgments

Huge thanks to Karen Kosztolnyik, Jennifer Bergstrom, Molly Gregory, and everyone at Scout Press. To my team, Joe Veltre, Matt Bass, and Bob Hohman. To Yvonne Prinz and Justin Young, my San Francisco insiders. To Andrea Thorpe and Nikos Harris, for advice on the legal process. To Tanya Shklanka, for understanding what this means to me. To John, Tegan, and Ethan . . . you guys are everything.

G GALLERY READERS GROUP GUIDE

the party

Robyn Harding

introduction

The Sanders family seems to have it all: Kim and her husband, Jeff, live with their two perfect children in a large house in a posh San Francisco neighborhood. But a sweet sixteen party for their daughter, Hannah, goes terribly wrong, upending their lives and the lives of those around them and exposing harsh truths about who they are as a family and as individuals. As readers shadow the characters through the aftermath of a gruesome accident, the façade of perfection falls away, revealing relationships strained by secrets, mistakes, and indiscretions. A lawsuit brings matters to a boil as neighbors, friends, and family members turn against each other. In this story of the unraveling of one well-to-do family is a much more expansive tale about how our desire for status and acceptance can wreak havoc in our lives and the ways that we judge one another while forgetting to first take a look at ourselves. *The Party* reveals the complicated matter of what it means to be human while cautioning us that it is what is inside of us—and not how people perceive us—that truly matters most.

topics and questions for discussion

1. Consider the organization of the story. Whose points of view are represented in the novel? Did any one point of view seem to overshadow the rest? Why do you think the author made the decision to structure the book in this way? How did this structure influence your overall interpretation of the events in the book and your assessment of the characters?

2. How well would you say the characters in the book know each other? What are some of the secrets kept by the characters and why do they keep these secrets? Do they ever reveal or confess their secrets to the other characters? If so, what motivates them to do so and how are their secrets received?

3. What is "the incident" that Kim refers to in reference to her relationship with her husband, Jeff? How does Kim respond

to "the incident" and do you agree with her reaction? How does "the incident" compare to Kim's own indiscretions?

4. Evaluate the theme of judgment in the novel. Who judges one another and what seems to influence them in forming their judgments? As a reader, how did you judge the various characters and what caused you to do so? Did any of your judgments change by the book's conclusion?

5. What seems to drive the characters' moral choices? Do the characters seem to share any overlapping motivations? If so, what do they seem to be most motivated by? What might this suggest about human nature?

6. How do the characters respond to their own wrongdoing? Are they able to acknowledge and own up to their own mistakes? Do they seem contrite? Does the book offer any examples of reconciliation, redemption, or peacemaking as the result of a character owning up to their mistake(s)? Discuss.

7. What does the novel suggest about appearances? Where do we find examples of things that are not what they seem? What causes the characters in the novel—or readers—to succumb to these misinterpretations?

8. How does Kim react to the tragedy that takes place at her daughter's sweet sixteen party? She is accused by some of the other characters of caring only about herself and her reputation. What causes them to believe this? Do you agree

with their assessment of Kim's response or do you believe that she is misunderstood? Discuss.

9. Consider the motif of tragedy in the book. In addition to the central tragedy of the book, what other "minor" tragedies are exposed? What causes them? Do you believe that any of them could have been avoided? Explain.

10. What are Lisa's reasons for suing the Sanders family even after they are found clear of any wrongdoing by the investigators? Do you agree with her decision? Why or why not? What impact does the lawsuit have on those it involves?

11. At the story's conclusion, how has Hannah changed or otherwise remained the same? Does she seem to have learned anything from the ordeal?

12. Revisit the conclusion of the book. What happens to the Sanders family and to Ronni and Lisa? Were you surprised by the ending of the novel? Why or why not?

enhance your book club

1. Consider an event that shaped the course of your own life or someone you know. Did the event unite or divide those it involved? How has your perspective of this event changed over time? Has anything positive ultimately come from this event? Discuss.

2. Use the novel as a starting place to consider the issue of bullying/cyberbullying among adolescents. What does the novel reveal about the culture around bullying?

   Visit stopbullying.gov to learn more, gather resources, and begin a discussion about ways you can help to prevent and/or stop bullying in your own community.

3. Compare *The Party* to other domestic or family dramas such as Jonathan Franzen's *The Corrections* or Herman Koch's *The Dinner*. Discuss what the books have in common, including any shared themes.

4. Visit the author's website at www.robynharding.com to learn more about her and her other works, including *The Journal of Mortifying Moments*, *Chronicles of a Midlife Crisis*, and *The Secret Desires of a Soccer Mom*.

a conversation with robyn harding

How did you get the idea to write *The Party*? Were you inspired by any particular real-life situation or would you say that you were more dependent upon your own imagination?

As a mother of two teenage children, the use of substances is a real and relevant issue to me. I talked to a lot of parents about how they were handling their kids' relationship with drugs and alcohol and I found vastly differing opinions. Some parents were zero tolerance, but many took a "they're going to drink anyway, I'd rather they do it under my roof" approach. This made me imagine the worst-case scenario of kids partying at home, and how parents would really deal with that fallout. I also thought it would be interesting to have this happen to *strict* parents, who would see their daughter's behavior as a betrayal.

Is there a particular character in the book that you are most sympathetic toward? If so, why?

All of these characters are very flawed individuals, but I feel sympathy for each of them at different stages in the story. While Kim Sanders is probably the least likable, ironically I feel the most sympathy for her. Initially, her character has lost touch with what's important in life, and what true happiness means. Sometimes, it takes a life-altering event to wake a person up to what really matters. But by then, it can be too late.

Why did you choose to tell the story from various points of view rather than a single point of view?

I always find it fascinating how people perceive situations differently, particularly conflict. I felt that a horrific situation like the one in the book would be infinitely more interesting if we were privy to multiple perspectives.

As you were writing, who did you envision as the prime audience for this book? It seems the book contains lessons that could be useful to several age groups.

I wrote this book for an adult audience, but I think teenagers will enjoy and relate to it, too. While most of the story takes place in the parents' world, the teen storyline is prominent and pivotal. My daughter is sixteen and she's a smart, sophisticated reader. While she still reads some YA novels, she enjoys a lot of adult fiction.

Were there any events in your own life or adolescence that you feel largely influenced the course of your life or the lives of those around you?

My dad died suddenly of a brain aneurysm when I was ten years old. Everything changed after that. When you experience a tragedy, you realize your whole life can be altered in a moment. I sometimes wonder who I would have become if he had lived, and if I would have made different choices with his guidance. My whole family was shaped by that loss.

How do you think people can best put a stop to bullying and cyberbullying?

As parents, we worry so much about our children getting good grades, making the team, or getting into a good college. But sometimes we neglect to emphasize being a kind and caring human being. And I think parents should monitor their kids on social media. It can feel like an invasion of their privacy, but the teenage brain is not fully developed. Kids post things online they consider benign but that could be hurtful or damaging to someone else. If children know there is even a chance their parents are checking up on them, they may reconsider posting something critical or cruel.

If you could go back in time and give your adolescent self one message, what would it be?

A perm is not a good idea. And also, that one day, you will feel comfortable in your own skin.

Who are some contemporary storytellers you find most inspiring or compelling today and why?

I just read Bill Clegg's novel *Did You Ever Have a Family*. I was afraid it would be too sad for me, but it was beautiful, so real and moving and smart. Liane Moriarty is amazing. Her writing is insightful and intelligent but still so accessible. I feel the same way about David Nicholls and Nick Hornby. And I am a huge Kate Atkinson fan. I don't normally read a lot of mysteries, but I love her Jackson Brodie series. She inspires me with her little touches of humor in even the darkest tales.

You have written several other works. How does this story relate to your previous work? Do you feel it's very different from your previous books or would you say there is a common thread among your works?

Before this book, I'd considered myself a humor/comedy writer. My first novels were humorous women's fiction (or "chick lit" to use a controversial term). I also wrote the screenplay for an indie dramedy titled *The Steps,* about a stepfamily meeting for the first time. It's very funny, but it does deal with some heavy themes (alcoholism, family secrets, parental neglect). Tonally, *The Party* is much darker than anything I've written, but I have always tried to create relatable characters and deal in real-life scenarios. To me, real people and this messy world we live in are more fascinating than a dystopian future or a fantasyland.

How did writing *The Party* change the way that you write? Was there anything that surprised you in the course of writing the book?

I took a lot more time with this book. I was very thoughtful with it. At times, it was tough going. I didn't want to sit down at my computer and deal with this tragedy, to drag these characters through this turmoil and strife. But I knew this was a book that I would want to read and eventually, I got into! I enjoyed the twists and turns, the lies, betrayals and drama. I was surprised to find that I won't plunge into a deep depression if I tell a dark and serious story. And there's still room for a sense of humor in dramatic writing.

Can you please tell us a bit about what you are currently working on?

I'm working on a novel inspired by Canada's most notorious female serial killer, who has served her time and is now a married mother of three, living in a new community. I'm exploring themes of retribution, redemption, and forgiveness. And I'm confronting some hard questions: Can people really change? Do they deserve a second chance? And can you ever outrun your past?

TURN THE PAGE FOR A SNEAK PREVIEW OF

HER PRETTY FACE

THE NEXT NOVEL FROM

Robyn Harding

COMING IN 2018 FROM SCOUT PRESS

THE ARIZONA GLOBE – FRIDAY, MARCH 1, 1996

Still no sign of missing teenage girl

Parents frantic one week after daughter's disappearance

PILAR HERNANDEZ

Phoenix

Courtney Carey, 15, left her parents' home in the Phoenix suburb of Tolleson on the evening of February 23 to meet friends, and has not been seen since. Carey's friends say she did not show up to meet them as arranged, which is out of character.

Police, family, and friends scoured the area but have found no sign of Carey. She is described as a white female, 5 foot 4, with brown hair and brown eyes. She was last seen wearing jeans, a red flannel shirt, and running shoes.

If you spot her or have any information regarding her whereabouts, please call police.

FRANCES
NOW

Frances Metcalfe was not the type of woman who enjoyed large parties, especially large parties where you had to dress up in a costume. Given the choice, she would have stayed home and pierced her own nipples with dull knitting needles, but fund-raisers for Forrester Academy were not optional. Despite the thirty-thousand-dollar tuition fee, the elite private school's coffers needed regular infusions of cash.

The night's theme was *The '80s!*

Like, totally come as your favorite '80s pop star!

Frances had taken the invitation literally and dressed as Cyndi Lauper. She admired the performer's LGBTQ activism and Lauper's music had been the soundtrack to a more innocent time. But the full skirt and layers of belts, beads, and scarves may not have been the most flattering choice for Frances's curvaceous body type. With her bright red wig and colorful makeup, Frances felt as if she looked like a cross between a deranged clown and a heavyset bag lady.

She wandered self-consciously through the school gymnasium, taking in the neon streamers and hand-painted posters.

SO RAD!

GRODY TO THE MAX!

AWESOME!

The childish, handmade decorations, courtesy of Ms. Waddell's sixth-grade class, stood in stark contrast to the high-end catering; attractive servers in black and white circulated with trays of ceviche on porcelain spoons, seafood-stuffed mushroom caps, and wagyu beef sliders. Frances had vowed not to snack at the party. She had filled up on raw veggies before she left home as all the fitness magazines recommended. Despite their plethora of articles devoted to the psychology of overeating ("Feeding Emotional Pain," "Replacing Love with Food"), the magazines still recommended loading up on crudités to stave off the assault of caloric party fare. But eating at a party had nothing to do with hunger; it had everything to do with fear.

Maybe fear was too strong a word for the gnawing in Frances's stomach, the slight tremble to her hands, the prick of sweat at the nape of her neck. It was low- to mid-level social anxiety; she'd suffered from it for years. When one had secrets, when one's past was something to be hidden and guarded, mingling and making idle chitchat became daunting. The extra twenty-two pounds Frances carried on her 5'5" frame, and the meager check she'd just deposited in the decorated donation box (it would undoubtedly prompt snickers from the fund-raising committee, several of whom were married to Microsoft multi-millionaires), did nothing to boost her confidence.

But the apprehension Frances felt tonight could not be blamed on her past, her weight, or her unfortunate ensemble. What she felt tonight was real and present. The parents at Forrester Academy did not accept her, and their hostility was palpable. Meandering through the crowd, watching backs turn on cue, Frances hadn't felt so blatantly ostracized since high school. She plucked a second glass of wine from the tray of a passing waiter and stuffed a truffle arancini into her mouth.

She'd had high hopes when her son, Marcus, was accepted into Forrester, one of greater Seattle's elite private schools. Marcus was entering middle school; he was more mature now, and calmer. The diagnosis he'd received at the beginning of his academic career—ADHD combined with oppositional defiance disorder—was beginning to feel less overwhelming. The behavior-modification therapies Frances had religiously employed over the past few years seemed to be working, and cutting sugar and gluten from her son's diet had made him almost docile. Frances knew Marcus would thrive in the modern glass and beam building, would blossom in the more structured, attentive environment of private education. The new school was to be a fresh start for Frances, too.

The Forrester mothers didn't know that Frances lived in a modest, split-level ranch dwarfed by mansions in tony Clyde Hill, a residential area in northwest Bellevue. They didn't know that her husband, Jason, had bought their '80s designed, cheaply constructed abode from a paternal aunt for roughly a fifth of its current value. They were unaware that the Metcalfes' Subaru Outback and Volkswagen Jetta were leases, that Jason's salary would not have covered their son's tuition if not for the help of a second mortgage on their run-down house, a house full of clutter that Frances seemed powerless to control. They were starting school with a clean slate. It would be a new chapter for their family.

It lasted three weeks.

It was the incident with Abbey Dumas that destroyed them—both Marcus and Frances. Abbey had teased and taunted Marcus until he had lashed out in a repugnant but rather creative way.

During recess, Marcus had found his tormentor's water bottle and he had peed in it. It wasn't that big a deal. Abbey was fine, basically. (She'd had no more than a sip before she ran screaming to the teacher.) It was the *disturbing nature* of the incident that the school community couldn't forgive. Disturbing: like the actions of a sixth grader could forecast a future spent torturing cats, peeping under bathroom stalls, keeping a locked basement full of sex slaves. Frances had promptly booked her son a standing appointment with a child psychologist, but Abbey's parents had called for Marcus's expulsion. Forrester Academy stood by him, though. They didn't just *give up* on their students. The school community was stuck with them.

The chocolate fountain loomed ahead of her, an oasis in the desert full of faux Madonnas and Adam Ants. Frances knew she shouldn't indulge, but dipping fruit in molten chocolate would give her something to *do*, keep her hands busy, and make her look occupied. She'd already exhausted the silent-auction tables, writing down bids for spa packages and food baskets, while desperately hoping that she didn't *win* any of them. Jason had disappeared, swallowed by the crowd of parents, all of them made indistinguishable by their mullet wigs and neon garb. She made a beeline for the glistening brown geyser.

She could have chosen a piece of fruit—minimized the caloric damage—but the platter of sponge cake looked so moist and inviting that she stabbed the largest piece with a long, wood-handled fork and dunked it into the sweet flow. She had just stuffed the sodden confection into her mouth when she sensed a presence at her elbow.

"Hi, Frances." There was a notable lack of warmth in the woman's voice, but at least her tone wasn't overtly antagonistic. Frances turned toward Allison Moss, so taut, toned, and trim in head-to-toe spandex. *Physical* era Olivia Newton-John. Great.

Frances mumbled through a mouthful of cake, "Hi, Allison."

"You're . . . Boy George?" Allison guessed.

Frances frantically tried to swallow, but the sponge cake and chocolate had formed a thick paste that seemed determined to stick to the back of her throat.

"Cymdi Lumper," she managed.

"The decorations are adorable, aren't they? I love that the kids made them themselves."

"So cute." It came out an unappetizing glug.

Allison forked a strawberry and put it in her mouth, forgoing the chocolate entirely. "How's Marcus?" she asked. "Enjoying school?"

Was there a hint of derision in her voice? A touch of cruel curiosity? Or was Allison genuinely interested in Marcus's well-being? The Abbey Dumas incident had occurred almost a month ago now. Perhaps people were starting to forget? Move on? "He's doing okay," Frances said. "Settling in, I think."

"Starting at a new school can be tough." Allison smiled, and Frances felt warmed. Allison understood. Being the new kid was hard, and that's why Marcus had done what he did. Abbey had picked on him and he'd overreacted. It was stupid. And gross. But he was just a boy. . . .

"How's—?" She couldn't remember Allison's daughter's name. Lila? Lola? Leila? The girl was Marcus's age, but they were in different classes.

"Marcus is so big," Allison continued. Apparently, she didn't want to shift conversation to her own offspring. "He obviously gets his height from his dad."

"Yeah. Jason's side of the family is really tall."

"It's nice to see him here. We don't have the pleasure very often."

Somehow, Frances's husband, Jason, was not the outcast that she and their son were. Jason was tall, dark, and handsome (all but his height inherited from his beautiful Mexican mother). "He could get away with murder with that smile," one of the infatuated Forrester mothers had once noted. Jason had also distanced himself from his difficult offspring and ineffective wife through work. His tech job kept him at the office until eight every night, and until midnight a few times a month. Obviously, the sole breadwinner, working to put food on the table for his family, could not be blamed for his son's behavioral issues. That fell squarely on the shoulders of stay-at-home mom Frances.

Her gaze followed Allison's across the room. It took a moment to recognize her clean-cut spouse in the fedora he'd donned for the fund-raiser, but she knew his confident stance in his pleated trousers, his strong broad back in the cherry satin blazer. (He was dressed as John Taylor from Duran Duran.) Jason was talking intently to a petite Asian woman with a lion's mane of synthetic hair, and a very short leather skirt. Tina Turner, obviously. She was laughing at something he said, her head thrown back, her hand lightly resting on his shiny red forearm. She was attracted to him; it was obvious even from this distance.

"He seems to be enjoying himself," Allison said, and there it was, subtle, but there: that condescending, mocking edge that Frances had come to expect from the Forrester mothers. Allison had veered from the usual narrative, though. Normally, Frances felt judged by these other parents as a poor mother, but Allison had taken a new tack and condemned her as an inadequate wife. It was effective. While Frances had developed something of a protective shell against criticisms of her parenting (albeit a shell as fragile as a robin's egg), she was completely vulnerable to assaults on her marriage. She knew that people, especially women, were surprised to learn she and Jason were a couple. He was gregarious, attractive, and fit. She was quiet, dull, and chubby. "Such a pretty face . . ." No crueler words had ever been uttered.

Allison was still watching the exchange between Frances's husband and his flirtatious admirer. "Isn't May adorable? And those legs! Her husband moved to Hong Kong to run Expedia's Asian office, and she decided to stay. Divorce is hard, but May's handled it so well."

The adorable May was now clinking her wineglass to Jason's. What were they toasting? Their mutual superiority to the people they had chosen to marry? Frances knew she was projecting her insecurities onto Jason. Her husband routinely assured her that he loved her, that he still found her sexy, that he had no regrets. . . . But it was evident—to Allison, to Frances, to everyone—that he could do much better. A bitter-tasting lump was clogging her throat as she watched her husband chuckle at May's comment.

"May will find someone better." Allison turned to Frances and smiled. "But not Jason, obviously. He's married to you." And then, as she reached for another piece of fruit, she murmured, "Too bad."

Had Allison really just said that? Was she that cruel? Frances wasn't sure she could trust her own ears. Her brain was spinning, lucid thought replaced by pure emotion: hurt, jealousy, anger. Time seemed to pause as she looked down at her diminutive companion, so poised and perfect and pleased with herself. In that suspended moment, Frances thought how good it would feel to kill her.

She could beat Allison to death with the chocolate fountain. The contraption probably weighed less than twenty pounds, and, once unplugged from its power socket, could be easily hoisted and swung like a club. It was an incredibly messy choice of weapon, but there would be a delicious irony in murdering toned, svelte Allison Moss with such a caloric and sugary vessel. Frances could almost hear the metal base cracking against Allison's bird-like skull, see the blood spurting, mixing with the melted chocolate to form a savory-sweet noxious puddle. How many blows would it take to ensure Allison was dead? Three? Four at the most? For once, Frances's heft would come in handy.

Alternatively, Frances could choke out the petite PTA mom with her bare hands. She could clutch Allison's sinewy neck between her chubby mitts and squeeze. Frances would enjoy hearing her croak and wheeze and struggle for breath; thrill as the cruel light drained from her eyes, as the boyish body slackened and then crumpled into a heap on the gymnasium floor. This was a definitively less messy option, but it would take a lot longer. There was a high probability that someone from Allison's crowd would tackle Frances before the job was done.

Frances knew she wasn't psychotic. It was a fantasy, a harmless coping mechanism. That was her self-diagnosis, anyway. She could never tell a therapist about these violent thoughts, at least not one who knew about her past. But given the treatment she'd received at the hands of the Forrester community, was it any wonder her mind went to these dark places? She wouldn't really kill Allison Moss—especially not in her son's school, and definitely not in front of its entire parent population. The scandal would be legendary. She could see the headlines:

Middle-School Parent Pariah Snaps, Murders Cool Mom at School Fund-Raiser

With the slightest shake of her head, Frances dislodged the homicidal whimsy. She gave Allison a tight smile and turned away, reaching for another piece of sponge cake.

"Hi, Allison." The voice was forced, frosty, familiar.

Frances halted her fork in midair. She turned to see Leigh Randolph's tall, willowy frame looming over Allison Moss, and her heart soared. Her friend—her only friend in the school community—wore a white button-down shirt knotted under her breasts to reveal a flat, tanned stomach; faded men's Levi's; and heavy black boots. Leigh's caramel-colored hair had been back-combed and sprayed into a sexy bouffant. The effect was that of a '80s supermodel (and not a homeless clown, like Frances).

"Leigh. Hi," Allison said, suddenly deferential. "You look great."

"Thanks." Leigh gave Allison's spandex ensemble an obvious once-over. "Wow. . . . You're really confident to wear an outfit like that at our age."

Allison's smile stayed in place, but insecurity flickered in her eyes. "I work out a lot."

"Still . . . gravity."

The tiny woman folded her arms across her breasts and changed the subject. "How's Charles enjoying sixth grade?"

"So far, so good. And Lulu?"

"Lila."

"Right."

"She's great. Really blossoming."

Leigh gazed around the gym. "With all the money we're paying, they couldn't have hired a professional decorator?"

Frances saw Allison flinch, like her precious Lila had painted the rad posters herself . . . which she probably had. The wisp of a woman set her strawberry fork on the table. "I should get away from this chocolatey temptation. Nice to see you, Leigh." With a slight wave to Frances, she walked away from the two of them.

"That was awesome," Frances gushed. Leigh's biting comments were far more rewarding than actual murder.

"Why, thank you, Cyndi Lauper."

Frances smiled. "I didn't think you'd come. You said you hate these things."

Leigh picked up a fondue fork. "I couldn't let you face these stuck-up bitches alone. And besides, Robert said Charles would be expelled if we didn't show up."

"He's probably right." Frances looked over to see Leigh's husband, Robert, a fit fifty-something, talking to Jason. Robert Randolph was tall and dignified, almost attractive except for a slight overbite that gave him a mildly cartoonish affect. The older man's costume consisted of a gray blazer with pronounced shoulder pads over a white T-shirt and a pair of black jeans. (David Bowie, maybe? Or David Byrne?) He'd been a lawyer in a past iteration (clearly a successful one to nab a hot, younger wife like Leigh); dressing up was obviously not part of his lexicon. Jason and Robert were talking, laughing, the adorable May suddenly neglected. Frances watched as May casually wandered off.

"I'm so glad you're here." Frances turned back to Leigh. "I was about to drink this entire chocolate fountain out of sheer boredom."

Leigh stabbed some cake and doused it in chocolate. How could she eat like that and still stay so slim? "Daisy agreed to babysit her brother tonight, but only if he was asleep before I left."

"That doesn't sound like such a bad gig. Charles is so sweet."

"Daisy hates him."

"No, she doesn't. She's just fourteen."

"I'm not so sure," Leigh said, through a two hundred calorie mouthful of cake and chocolate. "He drank all the orange juice this morning. I thought Daisy was going to stab him with her butter knife."

Frances laughed and realized she was enjoying herself. It was all due to Leigh's presence. The two women shared a sense of humor and a disdain for Forrester's snobby, cliquey, yummy-mummies. With statuesque, self-assured Leigh in her corner, Frances felt more confident, less vulnerable to attack. Their friendship was still in its adolescence, but Leigh had already earned Frances's devotion.

Leigh set her fondue fork down. "Where do I get some wine? Daisy's charging me twelve bucks an hour. I've got to make the most of this night."

"I'll show you to the bar," Frances said. Together, they picked their way through the crowd.